SHAMROCK
Patrick and Brigid in Ireland

BERN CALLAHAN

 FriesenPress

One Printers Way
Altona, MB R0G 0B0
Canada

www.friesenpress.com

ISBN
978-1-03-912928-3 (Hardcover)
978-1-03-912927-6 (Paperback)
978-1-03-912929-0 (eBook)

1. FICTION, HISTORICAL, MEDIEVAL

Distributed to the trade by The Ingram Book Company

For my Irish grandparents,
Brian and Anna, Patrick and Anne.
And for my personal Brigid

TABLE OF CONTENTS

PART 1

KIDNAPPED

1. Taken

Early March 402 AD

Now I am the old man known as Patrick, the name I was given when I was ordained a bishop. On that day of the pirates, I was called Maewyn, my birth name. The Irish just called me what I had become: slave.

They came from the sea. They were raiders and pirates. They rose from the waters silently, like mist. Suddenly, they were among us. They were terror. I saw round shields marked with swirling circles and triple spirals. I saw Nevio, my lifelong companion and slave, unmoving on the ground, a gaping wound in his chest. In death, his left hand held the stump of his right arm. I was filled with shame.

The last thing I saw before they took me was the rough burlap that was thrown over my head. It smelled of fish and sea and blood. Then I felt a sudden dull ache. Then darkness.

How much later I awoke, I do not know. I was laying on my side. I could feel the rough rope tightly binding my hands and feet. Burlap still covered my face. My head ached like it never had before. I could tell that I was in some sort of small boat by the feel of the wooden planks beneath me and by the smells of fish and tar and resin.

I heard their rough speech. Their words were dark to me, except those sounds repeated when someone began speaking. *Oengus. Ruarch. Lugaed.* And one that was repeated several times at the end of speaking, softer and with what sounded like respect, *Aitre*. From their repetition and answer, I gleaned these sounds were names. I began to repeat them to myself in my head. Oengus, Ruarch, Lugaed, Aitre. Oengus, Ruarch, Lugaed, Aitre. I vowed to find out, at least before they killed me, who Aitre was.

Shame bit at me sharper than the sting of the ropes that bound me. My heart ached more from shame than my head ached with dull pain.

My father, Calpurnius, was a Curiales, part of our local Roman government in Britain. He had inherited this role from his father who had also been a Christian priest. This civic role held a great burden. My father and others like him were responsible for collecting taxes. There was never enough money to do what was seen as needed by the Roman governor or the local magistrates. Roads required maintenance. More aqueducts were needed by our growing populace. Building new courts and civic monuments was being contemplated. And, of course, there was always the tax paid to the empire in Rome.

For those who paid when taxes were levied, too much money was asked from them. My father and all the other tax collectors were caught in the middle. When sufficient taxes weren't collected, the tax collectors themselves were expected— in fact, demanded—by the Empire to make up the difference.

My father was an angry, fearful, and tight-fisted man. Generosity had dried up in his heart. Left behind was the compulsion to hoard as much wealth as possible against future imperial demands. I feared him. And I hated him.

That hate stung me, even as I lay against the bulkhead of the Irish raiders' boat. Its sting provoked the grit around which my resolve to survive grew. I lay on the floorboards, awake yet feigning sleep. Passive yet listening, searching for any clue that would keep me alive while surrounded by pirates.

"*Oengus, luchtaigh seo isteach sa bhád.*"

My heart raced and I felt my hands shaking. Laying in the boat, I curled up as tiny as I could. The words offered only confusion to my ears. With my head covered in burlap, in the darkness, I could only assume that Oengus had been told to load the boat as, one after another, thumps resounded from things being thrown in the boat, around and on top of me.

"*Ta, Aitre,*" was all I heard grunted in reply.

Another set of baffling sounds was uttered in a commanding voice, followed once more by "Ta, Aitre." I was kicked in the stomach. I gasped for air and curled up even more as the ropes round my wrists and ankles were checked.

Again came the voice of command. Together, two voices answered, "Ta, Aitre." I felt and heard the movement of the boat along the sand and rock and then out into the waves. Up and down over small swells, rocking forward with the pull of oars, then resting between pulls. Forward, short rest, forward, up over a swell, and then down and forward into the next trough. Roman Britain faded away.

There was an afternoon and a sunset, a night and a dawning, and then three more full days of sailing before we made shore on the sands of the harbor at Loch Garman. Those four days forever changed me, like the heat of a fire changes wax. I had been a Roman youth at the cliff's edge of full manhood. Slight of build, I looked much younger than my 16 years. That saved me, for all the other captives were boys and girls younger than 12. I learned later that the raiders' custom had been to kill all young men over 14. They proved too difficult as captives to make worthwhile slaves.

During those four days, I realized that if I kept my Roman ways, my captors would kill me. My head was still covered with rough cloth, and I could see nothing. But I heard the music that the oars made with the sea, rhythms made by strong men pulling against the waves. Then I heard a shouted command, followed by the oars being pulled into the boat. I felt the thump that the ship's mast made when raised and dropped into the step. Then the sounds of ropes being pulled, and a sharp crack as the sail snapped open and filled with air. I took comfort from the sweetness of the ocean air and the cool winds. I allowed the tang of the salt air and sea spray to distract me from the fetid darkness within my burlap cell. I felt the heat of the first day leave and the coolness of evening coming on. Time passed and we sailed into the night.

A pirate roughly jerked the sack from my head. Allowed to sit up, I observed only open sea. Familiar stars filled the late winter sky. I knew that night was almost through its passage towards dawn. I saw two other captives: a boy and a young girl.

We were finally untied around midday. The boy seated next to me was named Marcus. He told me that he lived near my family's farm. Marcus's first act was to slap the captor who had cut his bonds. A thunder cloud darkened the captor's face. Then I saw the glint of a knife. Blood ran down the boy's tunic. He threw Marcus overboard without a word. The captor turned with his knife to glower at me. He cut the cords fastening my wrists. Trembling, I willed my arms to stay fixed at my sides. And so, the wax of Rome and Britain melted and was poured into a Hibernian mold. Less than two days before, I had awoken a citizen youth poised to take my place as the eldest son of the local tax collector. Now I was no one, a prisoner, not even a hostage, solely a prize of dubious worth from a coastal raid. I was a slave.

My wrists and ankles were raw and bleeding. I reached with my left hand to try and soothe the burning in my right wrist and remembered Nevio. We had been boys together. We played ball. We were very young and chased after rabbits on my father's farm. When we got older, we went to the woods and played at hunting, chasing the deer. I told Nevio everything. I unburdened my worries and hurts to his patient, listening ears. Yes, he had been my slave, and now I was a slave too. But I had planned on freeing Nevio as soon as I put aside the red toga of childhood, assumed the white toga of manhood, and was enrolled as a citizen. The day for those ceremonies had been just weeks away when the pirates came.

Father took Nevio's hand. My father's power in the home was absolute. Women, children, and slaves were his possessions. And slaves, most of all, had no legal rights. Father judged Nevio guilty of the intolerable crime of stealing from his master. Punishment was instantly decreed as the loss of his right hand.

Nevio and I had been relaxing on the porch of the main house. The main house was my home and also Father's treasury. Most of the buildings on our farm—the slave homes, workshops, and barn—were of the pre-Roman style. They were round, made of wattle and thatch, with conical roofs. But the main building was L-shaped and had a wonderful, shady porch along one side. There Nevio and I sat and watched Father storm towards us. He was furious, with spittle forming and foaming at the corners of his mouth as he yelled, "Someone has taken it!" Over and over, he raged, "Someone has taken it! Someone has taken it!"

Father drew near. Nevio and I stood. Nevio's mistake was not that he looked down in the face of Father's anger. It happened when he reflexively reached with his right hand to cover the small purse tied at his side with a cord.

"What do you have there?" Father demanded.

With fear in his eyes, Nevio emptied his small purse: a tiny charm for good luck, a bit of colored thread, a tiny wood carving of two friends I had given him, and the ring. It was small and gold and held an almost perfect amethyst set in a delicate filigree.

Father's face darkened even further. He seized Nevio by the throat and dragged him to the barn. I followed, stunned, afraid and silent. In the barn, he tied Nevio to the center post. Father ordered me to go and light a small torch from the fire kept burning outside the kitchen. Nevio just kept repeating, "Mercy, master, mercy." When I returned with the burning torch, Father had rolled a large, sawn round of wood in front of Nevio. Only Nevio's right arm was free of the ropes. The round of wood resting on its flat end was tall enough to come up to Nevio's waist.

I watched Father as he took a very sharp hand axe from among the tools in the barn. Holding the axe by his side, "Put your hand to the wood," he ordered Nevio. The axe rose. With mute compliance, Nevio put his palm to the block. "No, further," Father ordered. "Grab the far edge with your fingers." As soon as Nevio obeyed, the axe fell. With his left hand, father grabbed the torch from me and burned the bleeding stump of Nevio's arm. Nevio screamed, eyes wide with pain, then collapsed. "He's your slave," Father said to me. "But I took the hand that took what's mine. Burn the hand and tend to your slave." And with that father walked back to the main house. I held Nevio and cried.

But in that Irish raider's boat, as I held my right wrist in my left hand, I cried not a single tear. I knew that the raiders were even harsher than Father and equally without mercy. Marcus' body flung over the side was testament enough. So, I cinched up my resolve. I would survive. One day, I would return to my home. I would have my own vengeance on father. I would erase my shame.

There were nine of us spread amongst this boat and the two others. I found myself a seat just ahead of the mast, which I hoped was out of the way. The other captive, a girl around seven years old with the look of terror on her face, sagged down next to me and remained silent. During our whole time in the boat, I never heard her speak. I never heard her name and do not know, to this day, what became of her. But for those days on the boat, she held near to me as if I was her rock of safety in a storm-lashed sea.

One raider held the steering board at the boat's stern. Another two raiders held the ropes that kept the square sail trim and full of wind. The fourth and fifth raiders stood near the front of the boat, silently watching, their hands lightly resting on the short, heavy swords at their sides. A sixth raider, younger than the rest, approached where the girl and I sat. His face was serious but not dark with

7

violence. He sat down near me and reached out to offer a small water skin. He appeared unconcerned whether I took the skin or not. The gesture was cursory. This was the first moment of human contact I had with them.

I took the water and drank eagerly. It was warm and brackish. It was a gift from heaven. As the liquid washed my tongue and soothed my throat, I began to regain my sense of dignity. I was a young man. Even in my shame and terror, I remembered that I had good heart.

I had no way to ask for what I wanted. I looked at the girl slumped next to me and then to the pirate whose water skin I held. I nodded my head twice towards the girl and then lifted the skin while raising my eyebrows to make a question.

He nodded once and grunted "*Ta,*" the word I took to mean yes. I offered the girl the water, but she sat inert beside me. I lifted the skin to her lips, but they didn't open. I moistened my fingertips with some water and as softly as my hurt hands allowed, rubbed some on her lips. I sensed the pirate watching in the stillness just behind me. The girl's lips parted ever so slightly, but her mouth didn't open. I tried once more to get her to drink but failed. Then I turned and offered the skin back to the pirate. His green eyes had softened even as his face remained set and serious. He took the skin and returned to the front of the boat to talk with the two men with swords. I noted that, toward the rear of the craft, the seventh pirate was sleeping.

2. Loch Garman

We made landfall late in the afternoon of the fourth day. The sails were lowered in the boat. The other two craft followed just behind. Six of the pirates in our boat took seats at the rowing benches. One of the men with swords took hold of the steer board. I didn't know it then, but we had sighted Loch Garman, with its bit of a village. This was the pirates' home. The sea was mostly calm, and our boat was piloted between a spit of sand to our left and a forested headland to the right.

"Row, you devils!" cried out the man with the sword.

"Ta," they cried out.

Their voices were strange to me. They weren't in harmony. Their "ta," was not called out in unison like I'd heard our soldiers answer a command. Yet there was a curiously pleasing balance to it. It was a sound like different, strongly colored threads woven into a pleasing pattern.

"Row," came the command again.

"Ta, Aitre," flowed the response.

And then we were around the headland and in the sheltered waters of a tidal bay. A long, curving, narrow white-sand beach lay to our right. A small hill thick with trees rose above the sands. A mile ahead of us, where the bay narrowed, a finger of land almost touched the far shore, and a river opened to the sea. Aitre called a rhythm and the six pirates rowed towards where the river greeted the sea. The other boats followed.

Once the boats had rowed through that narrow opening, I saw a small village with its thatched roof huts, stouter barns, and work buildings. Uphill in a clearing, slightly above the gathering of huts, stood a fierce-looking palisade. Its timbers were heavy tree trunks stripped of bark, joined together, standing on end, and dug into the earth. Their sharpened ends pointed to the blue sky. A muscular gate framed the palisade's only opening. I saw two men with spears standing on its parapet. My first vision of Ireland was of that pirates' camp, armed, guarded, and ready to greet its sons and husbands returned from their raid.

Our ship was drawn up beside a short dock and tied off. One of the other boats moored alongside us and tied off to our craft. The third boat was tied to the second. Aitre jumped from the boat to the dock while the six pirates stepped their oars. He turned and laughed, looking at the six of them, us captives, the loot gathered in the craft's hull, and the other boats.

Aitre barked an order, then turned away.

The sharp smells of salt air mingled with the sweetness of river water, the competing bites of resin and pine tar woven with the unexpected laughter of children and the reek of fish. And then there were the dogs that ran out from the palisade and from the huts. Barking, jumping, greeting their masters. Then, their heads lowered, growling, hackles raised, appraising us captives.

A small trove of silver plates and gold jewelry and some captured weapons, including one legionary's shield, were piled onto the dock. As captives, we were the principal prize, prodded onto the dock to be joined by seven more from the other two boats. We stood, boys and girls and me, untied but corralled by snarling dogs. The women who had come down from the village glared at us. Small children pinched and prodded us.

One of the younger captured boys among us began to moan, and a women struck him on the side of his head with a short board. His moaning stopped. I noted that all the other prisoners slumped their shoulders collectively and looked down. I desperately held onto my sense of dignity. I was Roman, about to receive the toga of full manhood. I would inherit my family's farm and my father's imperial office. I looked down in submission but stood up straight. The woman with the board poked me hard in the chest and laughed. I staggered but kept looking down silently and then stood straight again. She laughed again, then spoke.

"This one will fetch a good price. Feed him well."

"Ta, Mor," said one of the older boys in the crowd.

Then she walked away and left us corralled by her dogs to wait on Aitre's pleasure.

Now I knew the woman's name, Mor. She was Aitre's woman and had power in this place. Why were names like Mor's important to me? My survival depended on learning names and relationships and words. Father had kept slaves at home.

So had most of the landholders who lived near us. Intelligent slaves were given more responsibility and were more useful. Dumb slaves, including those who didn't understand our language, were limited to tasks that were foul, base, or difficult. I didn't envision a future of hauling shit, digging in the fields, or pulling an oar on a slave galley. So, I lit the fire of curiosity within and learned every word, name, and phrase that I could.

I also knew that masters grow to feel close to their slaves. I had felt like Nevio was an extension of me. When Father took Nevio's hand, it felt like he had taken mine. When the pirates hacked Nevio to death, part of me died. This closeness is part of a slave's secret protection and his power over his owner. Gaining that power begins with knowing your owner's name. The power grows when you can anticipate the owner's needs or wishes and fulfill them.

Two young boys from the village approached carrying a pail. The way they strained told me it was too heavy for them. I used the only word I knew, "Ta," to gain their attention. I knew it wasn't the right word, but it worked to stop them and make them look at me. I gestured first to the pail, then to myself, making a motion that signaled that I would carry it. The two of them stumbled over to me and put the pail at my feet. I pointed at the pail and raised my eyebrows to ask its name.

"*Derb,*" one of the two said.

I smiled just a little and picked up the pail. "*Ta, derb,*" I said softly and motioned to ask what I should do with it.

"*Li'ach,*" said the second boy, pointing at the ladle which I now saw rested inside.

"*Li'ach cacht,*" added the first boy while gesturing around the circle of captives.

The other eight still slumped in a group. Their heads were bowed, but their eyes greedily followed the pail. I went to the youngest, a girl who looked to be no more than five years old. She was so much shorter than me that I had to squat to be able to see her eye to eye. I held out the pail with its ladle and water.

"Drink," I softly encouraged. "Drink, little one. There's no telling when we will get more and it's important to stay strong. Drink."

With hesitation, she picked up the rough wooden ladle and looked doubtfully at the water. Her first sip was tentative, like a bird. Then she eagerly finished the ladle and looked at me.

"Yes," I said.

She took another ladle. This time she drank a little more slowly. A small dribble of water coursed down her chin. There was a flash of a smile, then her eyes clouded once more with fear, and she looked down. I took the pail around the circle, then finally had two ladles of water for myself. At that moment, the future spoke to me. I saw lives of deprivation, beatings, and hard labor. I saw broken hearts and broken minds. Fear and shame threatened to stifle my spirit's flame. That flame was guttering in my companions. Only a slight breeze of dignity, hope, and courage fed my flame. I silently asked the fates, my god, and all other gods to keep that breeze blowing, to keep the flame alive within my heart.

I soon learned that all of us captives were *"cacht,"* slaves. We were to be sold onward to a slave trader. A small village, like this one, did not need many slaves. The women and children filled the tasks of farming and keeping house. Like all the others, the ship I had been taken in was crewed by the men of the village. They were fiercely proud of their freedom. I was just a war prize captured on a raid and brought home to be sold. As Aitre's prize, the copper or silver coin that I fetched would buy a knife or a pot or a bit of cloth for Mor.

We slaves were kept in a small, round, thatched hut. A three-foot-high arched opening allowed entry. A fusty animal hide that looked like dog skin covered the door. The hut smelled of pigs. Our shelter was the winter home for the village's livestock. There were slop buckets for us to use as needed. We were fed a thin gruel in the morning and a fish broth at night. Each of us was shackled to another slave. This alone would have kept us from running, as if there were anywhere to flee. Even more than our shackles, a village boy armed with a stout cudgel stood guard just beyond the opening. One of the boys had poked his head out of the hut and was rewarded with a bash on the back before he could look around. We were penned and fed. We were allowed outside the hut for an hour each day to stand and move around. Then we were herded back into our shelter and guarded once more.

On the fifth day in the village, the sounds of early morning changed. Beyond the sounds of children running and calling to each other, beyond the sound of morning's chores and the village mothers calling to their charges, beyond the sound of men waking up and tending to their boats, their nets, their weapons, a new sound gathered. Two men's voices and a woman's voice drew close. They were laughing then serious, then laughing once more. I recognized the grunting tones as Aitre's. There was Mor's harsh, higher pitch. I didn't recognize the third voice.

We slaves grew still inside the hut. The people belonging to the three voices stopped just outside the shelter's opening and then continued to talk. The various village sounds merged until a clotted murmur and shuffle served as the bass note to the conversation of the three voices.

The door skin was pulled back and the cudgel boy leaned into our hut. His grunted command and gesture could only mean "Come out." So we did.

I blinked as I stepped from the darkness of the hut into the unexpected brightness of that early-March morning. Keeping my head down, looking around as best I could, I saw what appeared to be the entire village gathered in a half circle around us. Our shackles were struck. Then we were herded by our guard into a circle within the gathering. Even the village dogs sat at the fringes with what felt like anticipation. Aitre, Mor, and the stranger stood at the center. The stranger wore leather boots and leather leggings. A heavy, coarse tunic, belted with leather, hung to his knees. A short club-handled whip hung from his belt. His face was strong, bright with curiosity, and he had the look of a warrior. He assayed each of us captives with a glance and moved on. I feared him as soon as I saw him.

The circle hushed as Aitre gestured and began speaking. "Ultan, these are our captives. They'll make fine slaves. Let's hear what you will offer for them."

Mor signaled with one hand and cudgel boy pushed me forward into the circle. At home, when trading livestock or wines or crafts or anything, Father held his best goods back and hoped for the offered price to rise. This was my first lesson in Irish slaving, where the strongest was offered first hoping that prices would be set high. Aitre stood silent, while Mor spoke. "This one has spirit. He'll make a fine slave for whatever task is chosen for him. He may even prove to have courage, mettle, but he has a good slave's sense to keep his gaze down. What will you offer for him?"

That March morning, I learned who Aitre was. He was the village headman, the raider captain who sold me into slavery. His cool silence gathered a higher price than posturing and shouting would have. Mor spoke with the voice of authority while Aitre held command standing in silence. There was power and balance and recognition between them. I was loaded onto a slave ship and sailed north.

3. On Slemmish Mountain

Late April, 404 AD

The hills were cold at night, and I was chilled to the bone. I had been traded from Aitre's village and sold three times before I came to roost as a field slave. When Muirchil purchased me for three sheep and a dull knife, I had already been in Ireland for two years. I had grown and stood almost as tall and just as broad-shouldered as Muirchil. My eyes were clear, my wits were sharp, and I knew more than 200 Irish words. My heart was breaking.

The nights with the sheep on the hills were beyond lonely. I had stars and clouds and rain for company, no one else. My fate was to keep the sheep from wandering into danger, from falling into a crevice in the rock, or getting "lost" into another shepherd's flock. I had a shepherd's crook, a dog, and a thin cloak to cover me during the day and to shelter under at night.

That April was the first time I saw her. She was coming up Slemmish Mountain. Her long red hair was uncombed, hanging almost to her waist. A simple white shift, belted high just beneath her breasts, draped her. The air around her shone in the early morning light. She took confident steps, pausing to look down. Then she collected something from the grasses and put it into the pouch that hung at her side. As she rose up the hill and came closer to where I herded sheep, I saw the flash of an ankle, the outline of her leg against her shift as she stooped to gather whatever she was gathering, the bend of her neck, and the slim, strong grace of her. I was already enchanted before I saw her face. When she drew near enough to see clearly, I was captured once again.

Red hair framed a fine, oval face. Her lips were both full and full of mirth. A small mole high on her left cheek drew my eye's attention and then allowed me to see her face fully again. I couldn't quite decide what color her eyes were—hazel, green, gray, chestnut—they appeared to shift in changing light. They were green when she looked directly at me. Hazel when she looked downward.

Chestnut when a cloud overhead darkened the light. And they flashed gray when she spoke to me in an Irish so rapid I couldn't unravel it. The beautiful conversation between the sadness and wisdom behind those eyes and the mirth of her smile held me quick as if I'd been chained to a boulder.

"You'd be Muirchil's slave," she said. Struck mute, I nodded. She continued, "You must have a name other than 'slave.'"

"Maewyn," I stammered.

"Well, Maewyn, slave, I'm called Brigid." Smiling, she added, "You've been watching me more than your sheep this past hour. You might as well help gather these flowers. They're speedwell and stitchwort and make an excellent healing draught. Let me show you what each flower looks like."

My Irish was limited. I knew enough to understand my master and know what he expected of me as a shepherd and enough for basic communication. But my poor 200 words weren't near enough to comprehend Brigid. Her voice quenched a thirst I hadn't known I had. I yearned for her to speak more but had no idea what to say. I spoke anyway.

"You're Dubtach's daughter?" I asked.

"Dubtach fathered me," she answered. "But I am Beorca's daughter, and she was Brigid's daughter. A line of Brigids stretches into the night behind me. I carry their name."

I know that my face betrayed my confusion. I just managed to make sense of her Irish but couldn't comprehend a lineage of Brigids stretching back in time.

Smiling, Brigid spoke to my bewilderment, "There'll be time enough later to learn more about that. For now, let's begin with learning more Irish. Tell me the words you know."

I began: "sheep, grass, dog, man, woman, hill, dirt, sky, night, sun, cloud, blue, white," and pointing at her hair, "red."

She smiled and blushed with pride. "And what of that?" she asked, pointing at small, unremarkable brown and white birds nesting in grasses sheltered by a nearby rock.

As she asked, one bird flew away, chirruping and calling while the other covered the nest with its brown and white body and almost disappeared into the grasses. I remembered what we called these birds at home, but that knowledge was of no use to me here.

"I do not know," I answered.

"They are called skylarks," Brigid offered.

"Skylarks," I repeated the word after her. "Skylarks."

Brigid's tutoring me in Irish began this way. That day I learned 10 new names for things. I learned how to say "friend" and "tomorrow." I learned how deep my loneliness had become during my two years of isolation herding sheep. I learned how broken-hearted I was. I also learned hope. Brigid was a spark of fire in the bleakness of my life as a slave. Later, when she returned down the mountain and I was left alone with the sheep once more, I was filled with the sweetness of longing and felt alive for the first time in two years.

I was never religious as a boy. Father was a deacon of the Christian Church. He treated that responsibility similarly to his role as tax collector. Both were inherited. His father had been a tax collector and a priest. Religion was a civic thing and part of the everyday. You plowed the fields, tended the livestock, fetched water, and gave service to the empire and its gods. Father told me his family once had worshiped the old gods, particularly Lugh and Mogons. That changed when the empire became Christian in his grandfather's time. "Everyone," he said, "prayed to the new god, honored its priesthood, and left the old ways and older gods behind."

Yet my mother kept a small shrine in the kitchen. There she offered the first, small pour of wine each day. There was a religious truce between her and father. In their own way they each honored the gods and demanded very little of me.

Night after night, I was with the sheep on Slemmish. I began to speak aloud to myself to remember the language of home, to practice my Irish words, to fend off the loneliness. I spoke to the dog that shared shepherding duties with me. He appeared to listen. I spoke to the sheep. They largely ignored me but listened to the dog. I spoke to the night sky and the stars and the gathering light at dawn.

I first heard the voice within my thoughts on that mountain. Whose voice was it? I don't really know. It didn't feel like my voice. Perhaps it was. The words seemed to come from a place not quite separate but not here. On Slemmish, that voice became one of my principal comforts. Long periods of silence grew between my words as I learned to listen. The voice was firm, demanding. *Stay strong*, it ordered. *Remember, you were free before they took you from your home.* Over and over again, *Nevio's death is your fault. Your father took his hand because of you. Without you, Nevio would still be alive.*

Every few days, Brigid climbed Slemmish. While she visited, the voice inside was calmer, sometimes even still. Days and weeks passed. Spring easily flowed by.

I wasn't the only shepherd on Slemmish that spring. Cathal, the youngest son of Flan, was also on the mountain with his father's herd. Flan was the local clan chieftain, the *ri-tuath*. I never met Flan directly but did see him once in the village. He was grand, large, and fearsome. I didn't know Cathal's age, but he was two hands shorter than me, wiry, and dark-haired. That first time we met on the mountain, he scattered the sheep I was herding. His dogs chased my ewes, barking and nipping, worrying them.

Cathal laughed, "You're a bit of an eejit and a scut all rolled together, aren't you?" His nut-brown eyes had the look of twisted mirth, like someone who enjoys another's pain. I did my best to ignore him as he continued, "Slave, fetch me some water." I used my shepherd's staff to push away one of his dogs as it nipped at my tunic. "Leave my dog alone, slave," he ordered, ignoring its behavior. "It's worth far more than you."

I shook with anger, frustration, and humiliation. It would take me more than half a day to gather and calm the herd. Only harsh punishment could follow any argument with Cathal. He spoke truly. As a slave, I wore almost no value next to his as the chieftain's son.

Just then I heard Brigid's laughing voice. She had climbed Slemmish, unseen by either Cathal or me. "Let go with acting the maggot and being a gombeen," she called with a smile and came to stand next to me. "Leave Maewyn be and tend your own flock. That's why Flan sent you up here, isn't it?" Her eyes flashed green. Her red hair flamed in the morning sun as she tilted her head slightly to the right and smiled. "Away with you now," she laughed once more. "I've got business of my own with this slave."

"And what would that be?" Cathal snapped back.

"My master, the druid Amergin, would speak with him. I've come to get him ready."

With that, Cathal stepped back and called his dogs. Druids held a rank at least as high as his father, the chieftain. They held the words of mystery and power and were to be feared. And they kept the clan's stories. Cathal didn't wish to be remembered as mean or stubborn in those tales. So, he left, muttering to his dogs but without a look back over his shoulders.

"'Gombeen?'" I asked. "'Acting the maggot?'"

"It just means a fool acting the fool's part," Brigid said. "Two more Irish expressions for your list of words."

"You were so brave," I said. "I couldn't find my words. I was afraid to fight back," I admitted and looked down. "Muirchil would flay me alive if I struck Flan's son."

"That might be so," Brigid answered. "Your courage showed itself in standing your ground while holding your tongue. That's not a talent many have."

"Does Amergin really wish to see me?" I asked.

"There's a tale to tell," Brigid replied and sat down. "First, let me tell you a story," she said and turned her green eyes to look deeply into mine.

"My mother, Beorca, was bondswoman to a chieftain to the west of Slemmish. His name was Dubtach, and he decided to cast my mother aside. Dubtach wished for a bed slave, not another mouth to feed. So Beorca was sold to Amergin. She gave birth to me in Amergin's home. He raised me and trained me. I am the druid's daughter. Yet, as the daughter of a slave, I am also a slave, just like you." Brigid paused to let me consider what she had said.

"I have status and no status," she continued. "This world is full of contradiction. Finding the balance between truths is my journey. Amergin pointed at this when he gave me the birth name, Brigid."

I had calmed down enough after the encounter with Cathal to smile. I raised my eyebrows and invited her to continue.

"Brigid is the name of the triple goddess. All three are named Brigid. They nurture the crafts of smithing, healing, and poetry."

I know my look betrayed confusion. No Irishman or Irishwoman had spoken to me of their beliefs before. Three goddesses all with one name echoed the Christians' three-part god. Brigid took my silence as an invitation to continue.

"I see one goddess holding a blacksmith's tongs and a sword. The second Brigid holds a pair of snakes. That's the one I'm named after, the goddess of healing. The third holds a wand and crescent moon." I held my silence. "It's a good name that Amergin gave me. He's taught me many secrets, especially herb craft." She stopped there and waited for me to speak.

One of the quickest ways to cement friendship is to share a story. It was my turn in our friendship exchange to reveal my vulnerability. I began, "On the day that the sea raiders took me, I betrayed my closest companion. His name was Nevio, and he was my slave. I sometimes think that my being a slave now is punishment for what I did to him."

Without saying a word, Brigid reached out and placed her warm, strong, gentle hand on my arm. She wore a different smile. I felt she was listening to my heart. So, I told my tale of Father hatcheting off Nevio's right hand, of Nevio's death, and my being taken. "I am to blame," I said dully. "The voice of God tells me so each night and calls me to penance."

Brigid asked me what I meant by penance. When I explained, her eyes held a sheen of sadness.

"I think your God is harsher than our goddesses and gods," she said. "We may suffer because of our choices, but our gods don't demand we stay in shame. They like courage and daring and laugh at our follies."

"But my God talks to me in the night," I stated.

"Ah, the voices of the gods; that's a topic for Amergin," Brigid laughed. Then she prepared me for his visit.

4. Amergin

April 31, 404 AD

They came up the mountain in stages. It was just after mid-morning when I first saw them. Brigid with her red hair and another figure stood near the foot of Slemmish. The sheep bleated, my dog barked, and I continued with the tasks of the day. I left the sheep grazing happily near the top of the mountain, safely in the dog's care, and took my water skins downhill to a spring. I told myself, *I'll have water on hand when they get here.* But my curiosity took me downhill to get a better look at who was walking so slowly uphill with Brigid.

An hour had gone by, and they seemed to be almost exactly where I first saw them. They would stop and the second figure would point at the ground. Brigid bent to look, occasionally gathering something into a basket she held at her side. They came on in slow procession as if time didn't matter.

I returned to the sheep with my water. My camp was near the crest of the mountain. It seemed small and untidy. It had a small ring of stones for a cooking fire, one place where I cushioned the rocks with my bedroll for a seat, and a diminutive cook pot that I used to prepare my evening meals. I only had a tiny gathering of wood for the fire, my now-full water skins, and some oats and dried apples for a porridge. I had almost no possessions beyond the bedroll and what I wore: a tunic, sandals, a small knife on a belt at my side, and my shepherd's crook. At that moment, my loneliness and poverty felt crushing.

I turned to look downhill again and saw that Brigid and her companion were now more than halfway up Slemmish. I could see that he was an angular, old man. Tall, lean, spare. The voice in my head was full of warning. *Be careful,* it whispered. *Is it Amergin? You're not ready to receive visitors. You're only a slave.* I looked around at my poor camp. *Remember, you are a Roman,* the voice commanded. I decided to go and meet Brigid and the old man on their way.

Downhill, I saw that the old man leaned lightly on Brigid's arm whenever they reached a steeper part of the path. She laughed at what he said and smiled at him. Her basket was full of grasses and roots, parsley, sage, garlic bulbs and flowers, deep-blue gentians, and cranesbill, both purple and white. They looked up the path as I drew near. The old man's beard was almost completely white. His eyes were deep gray, like ocean waves on a cloudy day. He wore a face that seemed probing and amused at the same time.

"Maewyn, this is Amergin," Brigid said. The voice in my head grew suddenly still.

I bowed slightly and said, "I've looked forward to meeting you." I offered him my arm to support his next step. Amergin transferred his grip from where it rested lightly on Brigid's arm to mine. His hands were strong, firm, certain, and full of power.

We climbed in silence. At the camp, the first words he spoke were, "You've cleaned this fire circle this morning." I nodded yes. "That's good. Shows respect for the element of fire."

I smiled, not knowing how to reply to his observation, then gestured for him to take the camp's only seat. "My camp is humble," I said, "but I'm very glad to welcome you here. Please make yourself comfortable."

"This old man thanks you for your kindness," Amergin answered as he took the seat. I offered him some fresh water in the only cup I possessed. "It's been many years since I climbed Slemmish. I wouldn't have done so without Brigid's help, and yours of course." I nodded in understanding. My trust that a listening silence would encourage Amergin to say more was rewarded. He began, "Your care for the fire circle inspires me to talk about the three elements: *nooivruh*, sky; *gooyar*, flow; *cahlass*, stone. Fire is the face of heaven. It makes present the element of sky. To show respect for the fire is to respect the sky." He paused and allowed me to take this in. "These three—sky, flow, stone—are always in movement, the balance between them like a dance." Again, he paused to allow me to consider what he meant.

"The Irish and we druids celebrate this dance. We are born into it. We join it as children playing alongside the dance, as grown women and men dancing, and as an old man like me pondering the wisdom the dance brings." He took a small sip from the cup of water beside him. "We Irish are fascinated by threes." Confusion clouded my face. "Three elements, three goddesses, and now the three of us here," Amergin laughed. "It's a perfect day to tell you this tale."

This was how Amergin began teaching me the old ways of Ireland. That first night, he spoke mostly of the dance of the elements. He revealed how sky was honored in the fire and how it expressed the world of the gods, how water was honored at a well or spring and expressed the world of the ancestors, and how stone was honored at significant trees and expressed the world we could see. This world that we could see, the Midworld, was only one of three worlds. The Overworld and the Underworld were equally true.

I took as much in as possible and then asked a question. I knew that Roman Christians preached their God had three faces but was still just one God. I asked, "Are the three elements and the three goddesses like the Christian God of my father? He is one god with three faces."

Amergin considered this question for a long while. Then he turned to Brigid, and they had a short, fast-paced exchange in Irish that I couldn't follow. At the end of their conversation, Brigid got up and left the circle. She began to gather more firewood and tinder. As soon as she had left, Amergin turned to me with deep kindness in his eyes. "I asked Brigid to tell me what she could about your Christian God. She told me some of what you had shared with her, that he had a humble birth and then became a famous teacher. He was killed and then came back to life. If you follow his commands, you will be reborn in the Otherworld with him after you leave Midworld. Is this so?"

What Amergin had said was close enough to what I had heard from Father to merit a nod and a "Yes."

"Brigid also tells me that your god speaks to you here on Slemmish. Is that also true?"

"Yes." I nodded again and looked directly at Amergin. His eyes were deep pools of understanding, he smiled and nodded slightly, and expressed both compassion and wonder.

"It is a gift to hear the voice of the gods," he said. "I studied many years to begin to be able to hear that voice. What does your god say to you?"

We spoke of many things that night. Brigid returned to the circle with armloads of wood and a gathering of fresh tinder for the night's fire. She sat between

Amergin and me. Sometimes, she rested her hand on my arm as I spoke. She helped me find words in Irish when my words stumbled. Sometimes she gently touched Amergin and encouraged him to say more. I told them both how the voice in the night spoke to me, encouraging me to be strong and remember my home. They looked pleased. Then I shared how the voice reminded me of my shame, of how I was to blame for Nevio's maiming and death, how I was worth nothing as a slave. Amergin's face expressed great sadness while his eyes deepened in compassion. Brigid lay her soft, warm hand on my right arm when I was finished speaking and looked at me with concern.

Then Amergin said, "It may be that more than one voice speaks to you in the night. One sounds compassionate, brave, and strong, the voice of courage and steadfastness of spirit. Another voice sounds wounded, jealous, and somewhat afraid. The voices may sound the same because you hear them both with your ears. But they may not be just one voice." He paused and allowed me time to take in what he said.

"Thank you for sharing your story of the voices with us," Amergin said. "Now, I bring a third voice to you, the voice of my druid ancestors." And with that he directed the flow of our conversation to the festival of the spring fire that he had climbed the mountain to celebrate with Brigid and me. "Tonight, stone and water and sky are alive with new life. The ground is soft. Trees bud and the grasses grow green. It is the time to sow new seeds and begin new life."

While he spoke, Brigid began placing tinder, kindling, and wood for a fire among the circle of stones. She also set a very small arrangement of tinder and kindling just outside the circle. Amergin continued telling how generation after generation of druids celebrated the spring fire. They climbed to the tops of mountains or hills and lit two fires. One smaller fire celebrated winter's letting go. A second grand fire celebrated the ascendance of new life.

"The grand fire is lit just after the setting of the sun," Amergin said. "The light of the grand fire calls to the sun's fire. Return, return. Grow, grow. Warm us with the light of new life."

Through the afternoon we talked about fire, about the coming of spring and about Slemmish. Brigid pointed to her basket and said, "I gathered herbs and roots to add to what you have already. It will make a fine pottage as we wait for the sunset."

She pulled a small loaf of brown bread from the bottom of her basket. "Something more for a celebration," she said. I hadn't tasted bread in months. Bread was a luxury only rarely enjoyed in winter when the sheep were down the hill and I labored on Muirchil's farm.

When the soup was ready and the bread was cut, the three of us enjoyed a simple feast together.

Soon after sunset, Amergin rose from his seat. His old man's weakness was gone, replaced now by a strange power. Bending low to the smaller gathering of tinder and kindling, he sparked a fire from a flint stone and a small bit of steel. Then, turning to the larger pile of tinder, kindling, and wood, he began to chant, "Return, return, grow, grow," and sparked that fire. "Warm us with the light of new life." A look of pleasure and peace suffused his face.

An alloy of emotions began to be mixed that night. Trust, joy, and anger blended. These were bound and made one by the fires of fear and grief and passion. I trusted Brigid. She brought the pleasure of friendship and new discoveries. I looked forward to seeing her walking up the mountain and was always sad when she left. I was overjoyed that she had spent almost an entire day and brought her father with her. Amergin's presence was a mixture of kindness and strength. I felt like he was truly interested in what I experienced.

5. Hand-fasting

The crushing solitariness of my days alone was cracked that day by the joys of friendship. Brigid and Amergin brought companionship, conversation, the delight of exploring new thoughts, and the unadulterated human comfort of sharing a meal together. They both touched me. Brigid's hand on my arm imparted affection, warmth, concern, shared pleasure. When Amergin leaned on me to climb Slemmish, his touch conveyed trust, appreciation, and blessing.

My anger was never far beneath the surface. Indeed, like a half-trained dog, anger has followed me as a constant familiar ever since. I was angry at Muirchil for keeping me up on Slemmish cold, alone, poor, and away. I was angry at Aitre and the Irish pirates for kidnapping me and selling me into slavery. I was angry at Father for his anger and for taking Nevio's hand. But most of all, and secretly, I was angry at myself for failing to stand up for Nevio, for being taken captive with almost no fight, for being a slave.

I felt challenged by Amergin. Perhaps that challenge was the spark that ignited my own tinder of fear. I wasn't ready to completely open to his wisdom. I was afraid that, if I let go of my anger and my Roman sense of me, I'd simply disappear. I felt like I might die. That terrified me. So, I held onto that sliver of fear and the fire of anger joined joy and trust into an alloy imbued with shame.

Brigid allowed the smaller fire outside the circle of stones to burn itself out while she tended the larger fire within. Amergin sang songs in Irish and told stories of the goddess and a strange being he called the Green Man. As the darkness grew towards midnight, Amergin asked Brigid if I was her chosen for a hand-fasting ceremony that night. She nodded her assent, and a sweet grin graced her face. Then Amergin turned to me and said, "Hand-fasting celebrates a union of friends in body and spirit for a year and a day." Taking a short length of red string from Brigid's basket where it lay nearby, he continued, "If you choose, your hands are tied together with a red string to mirror that coming together. You untie the red string to express that your friendship and union are a choice, not a prison." He paused and I considered what he had said. "Maewyn, do you choose Brigid for hand-fasting tonight?"

I was confused. My body said yes. My heart cried yes. My mind stuttered. Brigid saw that blend of body-heart-mind and leaned towards me. "You are free to say yes or no," she said. "We will be heart friends all the same and I will come and visit you still." Then she leaned back and smiled at me. For the first time, I noted the desire in her eyes as I felt eager desire stirring in me.

"Yes," I said to Amergin. "I choose Brigid for hand-fasting this night."

And so, it was accomplished. Amergin tied our hands together with the red string. He clasped both his hands around our now joined hands. Gently, he raised and lowered our hands three times, repeating, "May this hand-fasting bring joy and peace. May this hand-fasting bring joy and peace. May this hand-fasting bring joy and peace."

Shortly after, when Brigid and I had untied the string, Amergin told us he was tired and asked, "Is it acceptable for an old man to fall asleep by your fire?"

"Of course," we repeated together, a note of need in our shared voices. I arranged my sleeping roll for him while Brigid built and banked the fire to ward off the night's chill. As we left Amergin by the fire, my dog curled up beside him.

The moon shone half full that night. In the pale light, Brigid took my hand and led me away with no hesitancy. With sure feet, she walked away from the circle towards a soft fold in the ground. It was a short distance from the fire glow but covered in shadow. Our fold in the ground was carpeted with the softness of new grass and late-April wildflowers. A perfume in the air blended with the tang of the camp smoke.

"You knew this fold was here," I laughed.

"I choose you, Maewyn," she replied and then put her finger to my lips. I thrilled at her intimate touch. "Enough words," she continued. "Let our bodies speak for us now." And with that, she began to loosen the belt that banded her simple shift. Her hands reached for me and untied the rope that cinctured my tunic. I felt my hands begin to have a mind of their own. I stroked her face with my right hand.

"So beautiful," I said in Irish.

"Shhh," she replied and leaned her face towards mine. Our lips brushed together with a softness like the coming of dew. We embraced and her body enfolded itself to mine. Delight built steadily within. Joined lips parted and our tongues danced together. It was like being consumed and consuming all at once.

She raised her shift over her head, dropping it to the ground. The twin fullness of her breasts revealed, I took the soft red areola of her left breast between my lips. My tongue plied the tantalizing erectness of her nipple while Brigid's hands found manhood stirring beneath my tunic. She leaned her head back from my kissing her and grinned as she stroked me. Taking the hem of my tunic in her hands, she unclothed me.

Joined, we stood in the moonlight like that for some time, grasping and absorbing each other in youth and beauty and passion. Then Brigid lay down in the hollow of grasses and flowers and invited me to join her. And when our joining was complete, I felt as if there was only one heart shared between us.

6. Still a Slave

Brigid lay in my arms when morning came. Her face at rest was the first thing I saw when I opened my eyes. Night's shadow had barely left the east and I felt like the clear, open sky. Then the sheep bleated. I was still a slave. My role and task were to care for them. They would need water, to be safely led to the spring downhill. My crook, the dog, and I would get them there and back.

Brigid stirred and opened her eyes as I pulled my tunic over my head. "Maewyn?" she asked.

"Yes," I answered. "It's morning and I must tend the flock."

"So soon?" she said, and a look of sadness spread across her eyes.

There were no words for what I felt then. I longed to not feel the slave. I longed to stay with her. I longed to welcome the morning in her arms. Yet I was still a slave in my heart and could not break my chains. Brigid saw all this and more.

"If he's not already up, I'll see to Amergin's needs when he wakes," she said. "If we start downhill before you return, we'll see you along the path."

Now, as I look back from an old man's viewpoint, I wonder. How would things have been if more than sixty years ago I had chosen to stay with Brigid that morning. Eventually, the sheep would have found the water on their own. We would have made love once more and then stirred the embers from the night's fire to warm breakfast. I would have shared that meal with Brigid and Amergin. Our hand-fasting would have taken a path towards a life together. Perhaps Amergin would have purchased my freedom. I would have learned from him the secrets of the druids and taken a druid's place in Irish society with Brigid as my equal and heart companion. We would have children and they would have children and the current of life would have flowed through us eagerly.

All of this is just wondering. I didn't have the courage to break my chains that morning. I didn't yet know that the real chains of slavery bind the heart and mind much more than they bind hand and foot. I still believed that freedom was granted from someone else.

So, I remained a slave. Our hand-fasting took the path of Brigid's frequent visits. We made love and forged a friendship of the heart. I still see that sadness in her eyes when I contemplate that morning. I now recognize that the sadness that filled her was for the chains that constrained my heart.

I saw them as they came down the mountain. I was headed back up Slemmish with the sheep as they passed. Brigid's and my hand touched. The spark of desire flowed bright between us. Amergin said, "I won't make this journey many more times." And, "Brigid will share with you what I have taught her." Then they were gone. I was alone once more with sheep, dog, mountain, and the voice in my head.

7. Striking the Shackles of Bondage

Early May, 408 AD

Four springs and four summers passed. Brigid frequented my camp on Slemmish. We made love. With her tutoring, I learned to speak Irish like I had been born in Ireland. She taught me the way of the druids and shared with me the tales of Ireland, stories of Finn MacCool, the Children of Lir, Deidre of the Sorrows, and the warrior legend of Cuhullin. I shared with her the stories of Rome and the tale of the Christ. She nodded through most of that tale's telling and told me that she thought his betrayal by a friend and his death were very sad. Mostly, she wanted to know where he went after he emerged from the world of the dead.

Brigid was horrified that, unlike Ireland, so few women held any real power in Roman society. At home, women weren't warriors or poets, were never chief of clan. She told me that she loved her freedom as much as anything. She'd die a slow and ugly death in a society where women were constricted only to servitude, mothering, and home.

I felt free when Brigid shared my camp, even if I was still a slave. In the days and nights between her visits, I endured the drudgery of herding sheep during the day and strained to hear the voice in the night. I was three persons in one body: lover, enslaved herder, and the listener in the night.

Brigid had climbed Slemmish just as the sun was setting. No words were spoken. Her eyes smoldered with desire. Heat and eagerness surged within me. We clashed together like waves falling upon rocks. Tongues danced and nuzzled, we tasted each other, our hands stroked, petted, clutched, and squeezed. Then she was all around me and I inside of her. Brigid was on top of me as I sank myself, again and again, within her. I remember her red hair hanging down and swinging around my face as we moved together. I remember her musky scent and the salty taste of her sweat. I remember the green lights in her eyes. Most of all, I remember her growl as she climaxed, primal ecstasy, animal hunger, and delight and human freedom all in one wordless sound. She looked down at me, continuing to meet my thrust as a look of pleasure lit her face. I crested soon after. Spasm after spasm coursed through my body as I was carried on a wave of fierce pleasure out beyond myself.

Afterward, Brigid lit the campfire while I settled the sheep for the night. We drifted into companionable sleep by that banked warmth. When we woke the next morning, I ceased being a slave.

I awoke to the dog growling. She stood by the sheep, head down, hackles raised, menace rumbling from her throat. The sheep bawled and mewed and mixed confusedly in a clump. The noises roused Brigid from her sleep. "What is it, Maewyn?" she asked.

"I don't know," I answered, "but I'll find out." I quickly pulled my tunic over my head and belted on my sandals. I grasped my shepherd's staff and felt the energy of fear coursing through me.

During my six summers on Slemmish, I could count on three fingers the times that something other than the dimness of sheep had threatened the herd. They wandered from where they could easily find water, they wandered towards drop-offs, and they followed a wandering leader anywhere. That morning the herd was huddled together. The lambs at the fringes of the flock cried and mewled and struggled to find a more protected place at the center. Each of them looked outward and downhill, away from the campfire where Brigid and I now stood.

At the far edge of that mountaintop field where our camp lay, two dogs abruptly appeared. Snarling and with bared teeth, they charged. My dog continued to stand her ground in front of the sheep. I placed myself in the path of the two approaching hounds, took firm hold of my staff, and set my feet firmly. The first hound flew past me and fell upon my dog like a wave crashing against a rock. They tumbled away in a whirl of teeth, growls, and yelps. There was no time to go to my dog's aid. The second hound charged directly at me; fangs bared as it leaped for my throat. I didn't think. There wasn't any strategy to it. As I dodged the animal's leaping jaws, I struck its head with the heavy end of my staff. The hound fell at my feet, stunned but still dangerous. As it tried to rise again to strike at my legs, I hit it a second and a third time. The second time I struck that dog was necessary. That strike stopped its attack and rendered it still. The third time was for anger. I broke the hound's right-front leg.

I turned to where my dog still rolled and bit and was being bitten by the first hound. As I stepped towards my dog, a voice that I recognized called out, "Arawn, away from there!" The first hound rolled off my dog and sped to the voice. I turned round to see Cathal striding towards me.

"Slave," he roared, "you've killed my dog!"

"Your animal attacked me and the other was attacking my flock!" I yelled. "And it's not dead."

"You didn't need to break Balor's leg," Cathal growled and stepped close to me.

Brigid had silently stepped close in beside me. "Your dogs attacked Maewyn and this herd," she said in a muted voice. "He was only defending his master's herd."

"Shut your gob, you druid slut," Cathal snarled as he drew back his hand to strike her.

I felt my hands move. I saw the staff hit Cathal on the side of his head. He fell to the ground like a sack of grain and lay motionless yet groaning. Brigid's touch stilled my arms as I lifted my staff to strike a second time. "Maewyn, what have you done?" she asked.

"He's still alive. At least there's that," I said.

"You've struck the chieftain's son," she breathed out in a whisper of fear. "You're a slave. They'll kill you for this."

I looked at her face filled with fear and worry. I had no words. My fear, mixed with anger at Cathal for setting his hounds on the flock, flared up when I struck down his dog. But something deeper seethed when he moved to strike Brigid. Although we hadn't hand-fasted that spring, she was my woman, my heart-mate, my lover. All the frustration and humiliation of being captured by Aitre's raiders and sold into slavery bubbled up as Cathal stepped into my camp. His move to strike Brigid was the spark needed to ignite my anger into action. With that blow of my shepherd's staff, I had struck Cathal, struck Aitre, struck Muirchil, struck my humiliation. I had struck the shackles of bondage that held me a slave.

"If they'll kill me for being a slave," I said, "then I best not be a slave any longer."

Cathal began to stir at our feet. I kicked him in the ribs and Brigid frowned at me.

"You need to leave," she said.

"Leave this place?" I asked.

"Leave Ireland," she answered flatly, "as soon as possible." Looking at Cathal, Brigid's face brimmed with regret. "It's good you didn't kill him," she said. "It will take some time for him to recover enough to make his way down the mountain. That gives us some time for you to escape. If you're not gone from here by midday, Flan's men will find you and kill you." I nodded, still at a loss for words. "Let's be gone," she said and strode quickly downhill.

The dog followed me 100 steps down hill. Brigid turned to it and commanded, "Go, guard the sheep." It stopped, looked at her, then me.

"Go," I echoed. "Guard." As the dog bounded uphill, I asked Brigid, "What about the sheep? I can't just leave."

"You must leave," she answered. "By midday, Flan will hear word of his son being struck by a slave. Soon after that Muirchil will find out that his slave struck the clan chief's son and deserted his flock. Both will hurt him. Flan will demand an honor price for Muirchil's slave striking his son and each ewe and lamb lost will cost. They will both come looking for you. In the village, on the mountain— you'll have nowhere to hide."

Whether it was with the remains of my anger or with a new fear, I do not know. My right arm was shaking, and I was almost breathless even though we hastened downhill. "What will I do?" I asked.

"We will go to Amergin and ask his help," Brigid replied.

So, I fled to the Druid's home for refuge, for help, and for guidance. My thoughts spun. *Would Amergin pay the honor price? Would he know the words to calm Flan's and Muirchil's wrath? Would I be allowed to stay with him?*

8. Amergin's Hut

I recognized Amergin's *brugh* immediately. It had an air around it that spoke of power and energy at rest. A cleared area spanned the distance of 10 paces from the cottage's circular lime-washed walls. A collection of feathers, shells, and wood chimes hung from tree branches at the edge of the clearing. A copper-colored wolfhound sat at attention at the hut's pelt covered door opening. Unmoving, its eyes followed Brigid and me as we approached. The hound cried once with a deep-throated "woof" and then remained still.

"Amergin will know I'm here," Brigid said. "That's Fermac, his hound. And that cry is how he lets Amergin know it's me that approaches."

A thin column of smoke escaped upwards from the center hole of the cottage's conical roof and the scent of meat broth wafted past the door opening. It smelled of hare and carrot and wild garlic. My mouth watered and I turned to Brigid with a question in my eyes.

"It is good," she said. "He knows you're with me. That broth is for you. He told me you looked too thin and that he'd make you a meat broth if you ever came to his home."

"Maidin mhaith, Amergin," Brigid called out as she pushed the pelts aside and stepped through the door. I followed her into the cottage's round interior. The inside walls were hazel wood wickerwork, neat and trim. A small fire circle held the center of the beaten earth floor.

A stew pot suspended over the fire simmered with the broth. There was almost no ornamentation within the cottage. A single sleeping pallet rested against the wall opposite the door. Shelves held a collection of musical instruments. There were two small horns, some rattles. Amergin sat upright near the fire, his eyes closed, a painted hand drum resting in his lap.

"Good morning!" Brigid called out.

I saw his eyes open as if he were surfacing from a dream and far away. Amergin looked at her first, then to me, then laid his drum aside. "It is good you made it down the mountain safely," he said. "Already Flan worries about his son and Cathal struggles down Slemmish after you." Amergin's eyes shone with fierce intensity. "Tell me what happened," he breathed. I noticed the bloodied knife at his side and the cut on his left forearm. Glancing at the cut and then back to me he said, "Blood calls for blood, a small enchantment's price to pay for your safety. Tell me what happened at the top of Slemmish."

I told the tale of waking to my dog's alarm, of seeing Cathal's two dogs racing across the field toward the flock, of how Arawn had fallen upon my dog and how Balor had leaped for my throat. I told how I had struck Balor senseless with my staff and then confessed that I had broken Balor's foreleg in anger. Amergin sighed at my telling of this detail. "There is no blame for you in this," he said. "A dog that will leap at a man's throat is an animal gone wild. It would have been better if you could have withheld your staff from the third blow." He paused, looked me directly in the eyes and allowed a moment of recognition between us. "All things are in balance. Your heart flared out with violence. With your first strike of the staff, you struck open the bonds of slavery that held you. That third blow will cost you dearly. That blow will drive you far away from Brigid and here."

"Amergin—" I began with a sob in my throat.

He held up his right hand. "Do not waste energy on what cannot be," he warned. Lowering his hand, he continued, "You must flee from here at once. Brigid and I will help you. You must make for Latharna on the coast and from there find a ship and get away."

A great sadness filled me. Six years ago, I had lost home and freedom. Now I was to lose home again, even if it was a slave's home. More, I would lose Brigid. I knew she would stay in the village to care for and protect Amergin.

"If you stay, you die," Amergin said. Turning to Brigid, he added, "He'll need clothes, coin, and something to convince a ship captain to take a stranger onboard."

"You have two cloaks," Brigid replied. "The older green and red one is in patches." She continued, "Slaves are only allowed to wear a single color, like Maewyn's brown tunic. Two colors suggests that he is at least a freeman."

Amergin nodded and Brigid stepped toward the wall behind me. I turned to watch and saw a medium size chest, covered in skins, which I hadn't noticed before. Brigid lay aside the skins and opened the box's lid. The deliberateness of her actions struck me. Neither slow nor hurried, she moved with purpose and speed. Her arms reached deep into the chest and retrieved a man's traveling cloak of deep greens and soft reds. She handed it to me. "Wear this," she urged. "You're a freeman now, no longer anyone's slave."

I felt the cloak's rough spun warmth in its thick fibers. It was like a dream. I was in the fantastical yet singularly real home of a druid, gifted with a garment that symbolized freedom, yet soon to flee for my life. My mind wouldn't organize my words and I know that my face cycled quickly over and over through delight, shock, fear, sadness, bewilderment, and joy.

Amergin's voice cut through my reverie. "He'll need some coins to pay the ship captain."

Brigid dug deep within the chest once more and fetched a bag the size of her two hands held together. The clink of metal within was distinct as she handed the bag to Amergin.

"The villagers offer appreciation when they come to me for advice or to ask for a spell or a curse," he said, smiling. Dipping his hand into the bag, he pulled out a small circlet of gold that tapered at both ends like a cloak fastener. "Sometimes they offer ring money. Sometimes they bring a chicken or a hare. Once, a man brought me that cloak you are now wearing." Both questions and gratitude played across my face. "Take this," he continued, and handed me seven circlets of gold in various weights. "You will need it for your journey and for the ship captain."

A sudden stillness settled between the three of us. Amergin's voice broke that silence like an iron hammer falling upon an anvil. "Ship captains will be reluctant to take you onboard. You are a stranger and strangers bring ill fortune." He paused and removed a small amulet hanging on a thong around his neck and hidden by his tunic. Amergin closed his eyes and held the amulet between both hands. He raised his cupped palms to his lips and softly blew three times. Opening his eyes, he extended his right hand and offered the amulet to me. "This carries an image of the Moringa," he said.

My eyes were focused on the amulet. "The side facing you represents the triple goddesses of Ireland: Eriu, Fodla, and Banba. Each of the three are Ireland, the same and different. Eriu is married to the King of the Sea yet has an affair with the god of the sun. Fodla is the queen of mystery and mistress of the fay and hidden ones. Banba is goddess of the earth we trod and plough, where we are born and return." I nodded to signify that I understood, but in truth I had only begun to hear the story of Ireland's goddesses. "The other side is of the Moringa." I turned the amulet over in my hand. "She represents how the three goddesses are one, like a great river with three branches." My brow furrowed as my eyes took in the images on the amulet and my ears received Amergin's words. "You will know a friendly ship if it carries a mark of the Moringa on its bow. Look for the triple spirals within a circle and show this to the captain of the boat. He will let you on. If the first does not, seek another.

"I had hoped one day to teach you our ways," he declared, "but that is not to be. One day you will return, and Brigid will teach you. I will have long gone to where our ancestors dwell." Brigid nodded, her eyes brimming with tears. "There is one lesson we have time for," Amergin continued. Then he told me of the *Duile*. "It shows itself in our encounter with the land, the sea, the sky. Not solid, it is what we call the core of who each one is. You feel it in the effect that events have upon you. The gods themselves, the Moringa, and all the rest can be felt as Duile, especially at lakes, on mountain tops, and in certain haunted places." Amergin looked directly into my eyes. "Yours is a journey of the Duile, your personal Duile, and that of this place. You will change and you will return. And your return will change all of us. Guard the Duile well." With that, Amergin fell silent.

9. Latharna

Brigid tugged at my tunic and urged me to stand. "The time is now," she said, "to flee for your life. Don't stop until you reach the port at Latharna. It's to the east and a little south." Then her arms were all around me and our mouths joined. I tasted her tongue on mine, felt the fineness of her hair with my fingertips, pressed my hips to hers. Sadness brimmed up, filled my heart. "I will hold you in my heart until you return," she pledged. Stepping back, her green eyes flashed amber, then gray, then returned to green. "Be gone," she said and held the door skins back for me to leave.

It took a day and a night of walking and another full day to reach Latharna on the coast. That first afternoon, the sounds of Flan's men searching for me sped my steps. I did not stop for a meal that evening but kept walking, putting distance between me and them. I walked through the night. Beyond the sound my own feet made, I heard only the whirring call of the grasshopper warbler, the nightjars' rush of wings as it hunted moths, and the call of the fern owls.

Dawn found me 10 miles away from Amergin's hut, traveling through rough country. I continued walking as the day gathered light. I coursed through woods and crossed hills until, in midafternoon of the second day, I found the open fields that marked the grazing land around a village. I followed those fields past herders' huts till I crested a final hill to see the thatched roofs of Latharna and glimpsed the sea beyond. I paused then for the night, not wanting to enter the village at twilight as a stranger. I made no campfire. I walked just far enough back into the woods at the top of the hill to become unseen from below. There, I found an old oak against which I could rest my back. I had no belongings to lay down, only the green and red cloak, the coins in the bag, and Amergin's amulet. I'd even left my shepherd's staff behind in my haste to escape.

I sat awake, listening to the sounds of night gather, listening to the hoot, caw, whir, crack, snap, and padded footfall of the forest. I also heard three voices in my head. The voice from the top of Slemmish had followed me. *I'm with you as you return home to Britain*, it whispered. And the voices of Brigid and Amergin in chorus, *You are a freeman, no longer a slave.* My second dawn of freedom came, then full morning. I rose from where I had been resting on the oak and made my way to Latharna.

I drew some stares as I entered the village. A solitary wanderer, a stranger, roaming any village will. Some children shadowed my steps as I walked towards the water. I smiled once and then paid them no further heed. I had seen my Irish masters be kind to their children but not indulge them or offer them an excess of attention. One older woman stared pointedly as I walked past her hut. I made direct eye contact with her and nodded, not breaking my stride. I called out, "May the gods bless your day." She muttered something and turned her back to me.

Then I was at the seaside with its fishing gear and tackle and sailors and boats. There were three craft drawn up along that strand. One boat was too small to make the ocean journey from Ireland to Britain. It was barely large enough for the three fishers who labored at the nets strung next to her. The second craft was large enough and seven sailors sweated on it preparing her for the sea. That ship had a sea dragon painted on its bow. The third craft was as large, if not larger than the second, and had the circle holding three intertwined spirals.

As I drew near, a burly sailor who seemed to command the ship barked, "We want no strangers here." "You look as if you are ready to sail," I countered. "I have money for passage and can help row."

"Strangers bring ill fortune," the hulking voice stated.

I took Amergin's amulet from where it hung around my neck and held it out for the thick-set man to see. "A friend told me to show this to the ship's captain," I said. The sailor stepped closer and peered at the amulet. "This friend told me that your boat with its painted triple spirals within a circle would afford me passage."

The sailor took one step back and looked directly at me for a long time. "You're too young to be a druid," he stated flatly. "Your cloak says you're simply a freeman. But the amulet says you have an old one's blessing on your request." He stopped frowning for the first time. "I'm called Ronan," he grunted, "and I own this ship. We sail with the tide in one-half hours' time. Are you ready?"

"I'm ready now," I answered.

"Then load that bail into the boat. I'll take your coin and you'll help us row."

That morning I left Ireland with the outflowing tide.

PART 2

HOMECOMING

ECCLESIAE MILITANTIS

10. Homecoming

Late September 408 AD

The journey home was long. A two-day sail landed Ronan's ship at a fishing village on the Scottish side of the Irish sea. Ronan had kin there, so he beached his craft and said farewell after I helped unload his cargo. The village was called Dunaverty and was part of the same kingdom as Slemmish and Amergin's village. The Kingdom of Dal Riata gathered the varied under-kings, the chieftains of Northern Ireland, and Western Scotland into a whole. The villagers at Dunaverty spoke Irish and paid homage to the older gods. Amergin's cloak, ring money, and druid's amulet served me well. A welcoming farmer offered me a spot to lay down in his barn. He fed me in return for a day's work bringing in the harvest. I cannot remember that farmer's name. I do remember that I spent two days on that farm and got used to the idea of being a freeman, not running for my life but simply working and being alive.

My journey took me inland from Dunaverty to Tarber, then Dunadd then Dun Breatain, the fortress of Roman rule in Britain's northernmost province, Valentian. It was there that I heard Latin spoken for the first time in six years. I stopped where I could find labor, food, and a barn or stable to sleep in. Days spent laboring on the harvest were satisfying. I gained strength and vitality as I walked and worked and was fed well. Farmers seemed glad for the strength of my arms, for my willing exertion. At night, worn out by the toils of the day, I slept soundly and heard no voices.

I hoarded my remaining ring money, not knowing when I would need the gold. From Dun Breatain, I worked my way south and west, to the coast and steadily towards Inver Ayr, a fishing village at the confluence of the River Ayr and the Irish Sea. From there, my journey south took me into the Roman-Britain province of Brigantes. I spent seven days at one farm there, sleeping in the barn, being fed, and helping harvest the wheat. At the end of that stay, the farmer pointed me towards the seaport of Meols.

Along the way, I learned that the empire had withdrawn her last legion from Britain. No one was sure of the future in Brigantes. Would the legions return? Was Britain on her own? If there was no emperor, who governed? The Roman civil governor, the Dux Brigantes, now called himself a king. What there was of a small army owed allegiance to him. The Britain I remembered being torn from was like a tattered cloth unraveling from both center and fringe. The farmers didn't want to talk about the governor or the king. Their taxes remained the same no matter whom they paid. They were happy for my willing hands and strong back and told me in Irish or Latin that they "kept their heads low and spoke no ill" of their overlords. Then I would be urged to "stop gathering the wind and get back to work."

It was too dangerous to continue overland through Wales, so I joined a crew sailing south at Meols. I pulled an oar when the winds failed, loaded and unloaded cargo, helped with the tackle, trim and gear of the ship, and generally made myself useful. The days under sail were the best. The winds of the gods or of God pushed me ever closer toward home. Most nights, we sheltered close to shore to avoid Irish and Welsh pirates. Those nights the voices in my head clamored once again, an argument between the voice of Amergin and the night voice from Slemmish.

You deserved to be captured and taken away, spoke the voice of Slemmish. *You were punished for Nevio.*

Amergin's voice countered, *You are a freeman. Your journey is the journey of the Duile.*

They contended with each other in my head from night fall until first light, only growing silent when the ship's captain called us to wake and man the oars or raise the sails. We sailed west, with a cargo of leather goods and spear heads, to the old Roman fortress at the mouth of the River Seiont. There we exchanged one cargo for another, taking copper ore south to Moridunum with its stone fort and Roman amphitheater. I was close enough to my home to begin to smell it on the sea breeze.

Britannia Prima was less than a day's sail across the Sabrina estuary to Ilfracombe. My father's farm lay on the cliff's edge along the estuary's shore. Thanking my ship's captain for including me in his crew, I left him on the beaches near Ilfracombe. I walked past the cliffs where I had been taken captive and saw my home standing among well-tended fields. The barns and slave huts gathered around the L-shaped main house. I could see the porch where Nevio and I had sat before Father took his hand.

I backed away from the edge of the fields, just into the shadow of the oaks at their edge. I didn't recognize anyone. I didn't see either my father or Conchessa, my mother. None of my three brothers were in sight. But for the first time, I really saw the slaves laboring in the fields. Their backs were bent with the hard work of cutting grain. They gathered and bundled it into sheaves, then moved on to cut, gather, and bundle again. I watched for a long hour before I noticed a man with a short whip walking among the slaves, pointing and gesturing with a bitter energy. He stormed and ordered. They bent and cut. I decided to leave my blind among the oaks and walk across the fields to home.

The man with the whip noticed me when several of the slaves looked up in my direction. He shouted something and they quickly dropped their eyes and returned to cutting and gathering. I was close enough now to hear the sighing of their scythes as they cut through the air before biting into the stalks of wheat. Then the whisk as metal sheared the stalks from roots. Then the whickering sound of the stalks being gathered into a pile. I was close enough to see and smell the sweat pouring off the slaves. I was more than close enough to hear what the man with the whip shouted.

"You there, stranger," he challenged. "What business do you have here?" There was no space for me to answer before he shouted at the worker closest to me, "You, slave, eyes on your work. Work faster." I heard the slash of the whip before his use of it registered. The short thongs of leather reached out to flail the slave's back. His hand drew back for a second strike, and I stepped into the space between him and the slave.

"What's your name?" I demanded.

"I have no need to tell a stranger my name," he answered as his wrist began to lead his whip arm forward once more.

I was taller, broader, and much more muscled than the man with the whip. I remembered Nevio. I remembered striking Cathal and Cathal's dog. I felt anger rise within and my hand stopped his wrist before the whip could strike. "I am no stranger to the house of Calpurnius," I began. "I am . . . ."

11. Mother

Her voice cut my words short. "Marcus, who is that in the fields with you?" Her voice gnawed across the space. I looked closer at the man whose wrist I held. He appeared to have 20 years behind him. He wore a clean work tunic and proper sandals. His beard showed careful care that no slave or overseer could afford. Marcus was my brother's name.

"Brother?" I asked.

"You're not my brother," he snarled.

I pushed past him and strode towards the porch, calling behind me, "Use that whip again and I'll turn it on you." His steps sounded quick after me.

"Who are you?" he demanded again.

"Your brother." Marcus wouldn't accept my answer. We reached the porch, almost running together.

I checked my steps just at the foot of the stairs and paused to draw several deep breaths. I heard Marcus come to a stop. I felt more than saw or heard his hand on the whip. He didn't know that I had been whipped many times before. I wasn't afraid of the whip or of him. The trick to being whipped is to know that you will be whipped. I relaxed the muscles of my back and neck and let my awareness take in the possibility of sudden pain, the bite of the leather strips, and the burning left behind when the whip was pulled back. By then I also knew slave masters. I knew that relaxing before the whip strikes sends a clear message. Relaxing either intimidates them, "this one is not to be whipped," or it infuriates them to stroke the whip even harder. I had no idea whether Marcus would be intimidated or infuriated. My attention was focused on the woman standing beyond the top of the steps at the porch's edge.

Conchessa had become a stout woman. She looked taller standing there on the porch, but in truth her head barely came up to my shoulders. I remembered all the details of her face even though the shadow of the porch's roof obscured her expression. Her mouth was set into a thin-lipped scowl. Her nose, which should have appeared aquiline, looked more hawklike. Her hands were set on her hips in both challenge and defense. Most telling were the deep brown eyes fixed on me filled with questions and pain. She was the mother I remembered.

"Who are you?" she demanded, "and what do you want?"

"I'm Maewyn," I answered and looked directly at her eyes searching for recognition, for welcoming, for any acknowledgment.

"Maewyn's dead," she said with zero emotion. "You can't be him."

"Where is Calpurnius, my father?" I challenged.

"Also dead, soon after the raid that took Maewyn."

A throbbing pain blossomed at the back of my head, and I fell. Marcus struck me with the butt end of the whip and knocked me to the ground. I heard Concessa's voice order, "Take this stranger to the barn, in the back where no one else sees him. We'll deal with him there." Then I passed out.

The sounds of the farm's cow being led into the barn for the night prodded me back awake. I struggled to sit up and lean against a wall. My wrists and ankles were bound tight with rough rope. Smells of hay and dung and dry wood and animals filled my nose. The light was dim, only slightly slattering through the cracks between the barn boards. I could see the barn door, a square of bright green and blue framed in shadow. The small bag with the ring money no longer hung at my belt. I felt the weight of Amergin's amulet still pressed against my chest. At least they hadn't taken that.

For hours, I replayed the scene of my homecoming through my mind's eye as I sat and waited. Why hadn't I recognized Marcus? Why was he enraged just at the sight of me? Why didn't Conchessa welcome me home? What could I say to convince them that I was Maewyn, their son and brother who had been taken by Irish raiders? Was this still my home? The bright green and blue at the barn door gradually changed into moonlight and dark.

Four shadows appeared at the door, and I was no longer alone with my questions. Conchessa and Marcus and two other younger men advanced through the barn to stand over me. The two new faces so strongly resembled Marcus that I took them to be Gnaeus and Lucius, my youngest brothers. The youngest of them, Lucius, whispered just loud enough for me to hear, "Is it really Maewyn?"

Mother fixed him a hard look and croaked, "Be silent!"

Gnaeus pitched in, "Maewyn or not, let's free his feet so he can stand. I want to look him in the eyes and know."

Conchessa grunted and nodded assent.

Before Gnaeus could bend to unfasten the ropes at my ankles, Marcus kicked me in the legs. "Let him be," he said. "You can see him just where he is. He's dangerous, no standing."

And so, I sat, surrounded by the half circle made in the barn by mother and my three brothers. I remembered that day in Aitre's village where I was surrounded by his raiders and Mor, the village women and children, and the slaver, Ultan. I looked up in silence and waited for mother or one of my brothers to speak.

Lucius broke the silence. "You claim to be Maewyn." He held himself with forced gravitas.

"Yes," I answered looking at him directly. I kept my face calm, neutral, neither frowning nor smiling.

"How do we know you're telling the truth?" Lucius asked.

"Anyone could claim to be Maewyn," Gnaeus added. "He's the right age but he looks nothing like how I remember him."

"I was only 16 then," I replied. "Six years of hard work and being a slave among the Irish has changed me."

"Ah, a slave," Marcus sneered, "that explains why you stopped me from whipping the field slave." Marcus' eyes held both anger and fear, and something else I remembered from Calpurnius' eyes, greed.

"What happened to Father?" I asked. "Why isn't he here?"

"When the last legion left Britain," Conchessa spoke for the first time since entering the barn, "the villagers turned on us. They said Calpurnius had taken too much in taxes. They came in the dark of the moon late one night to take it back." Looks of remembered dread and alarm crossed all their faces. "We had to fight to keep the farm, the house, this barn and the other buildings, and the slaves. Calpurnius died that night, defending this place." She paused and looked at each of the three sons standing with her. Then she looked at me with anger in her eyes. "My oldest son, Calpurnius' heir, was taken by Irish pirates and killed. I was left with only three boys to defend this place. The oldest," she paused to place her hand on Marcus' arm, "had only 14 years. He took Maewyn's place as heir and head of this household."

"But I am Maewyn," I declared.

"Maewyn is dead," Marcus answered. I saw a small sneer cross his lips. "I hold and protect this farm for mother and this family." Tension stilled the air and I saw Marcus hesitate. "By your own words, you are an escaped slave. You'll either be killed or sold back into slavery. Either way, you won't be a problem here much longer." Marcus turned and stalked away, out of the barn. Gnaeus, Lucius, and Conchessa looked at each other. I could smell their fear. Then one by one they followed Marcus out of the barn and beyond where I could see.

It was still dark when I saw a shadow cross the door's opening again. The night insects had stopped their whirring and chirring. The night birds had fallen silent. The sounds of morning were a long time away. It was dead quiet. As the walking shadow approached, I saw the glint of steel in its right hand. It was only when she knelt beside me that I determined the shadow was Conchessa.

"You may be Maewyn, you may not be," she whispered hoarsely. "I do not know." I began to speak, and she shushed me. "No words," she commanded, "or he'll come and kill you where you lay." I held my tongue as she cut at the ropes that held my feet. "The Romans left soon after the Irish took my son. When Calpurnius died, we had already grieved Maewyn. Marcus took his place. Now he has a wife and two sons of his own. His oldest boy is called Calpurnius. Marcus holds this place and protects us." Finished with the ropes at my ankles, she began to saw away the ropes that held my wrists. "You may be Maewyn, you may not. I lost a son once to slavers. In case you are Maewyn, I don't want to lose you that way again."

"Then let me stay," I pleaded.

"There's no place for you here."

"Then where should I go?"

"If you're Maewyn, you know how to read and write," Conchessa replied. "Go to the priest in the next village. He'll take you in. If you're not Maewyn, go anyway. I don't want a killing here."

There was one other crack in the hardness that encased Conchessa. "Either way, you'll need this," she said as she threw a small purse on the ground. I heard the jangle of the ring money as it landed beside me. She turned and walked out through the barn door and into the darkness without a backward glance.

It was the last time I ever saw her.

12. The Wooden Road

I fled the barn soon after Conchessa left. I walked through the bitter end of night, into the gathering gray of dawn. My return home had borne grief, not rest. Cast out and fleeing once more, my steps first took me to the next village. I arrived just after sunrise. There was a very simple church there. A small thatched-roof hut with white plastered walls stood beside the church. I rapped three times on the hut's entrance post and then stepped back. The priest of the place opened his door scowling. "What do you want?" he grudgingly demanded. I answered with a very short version of my story, that I had been raised nearby, taken by Irish slavers, and had escaped only to find that there was no place for me when I returned home.

"You are the oldest son of Calpurnius, the tax collector?" he asked when I was finished.

"Yes," I answered looking at him directly. He was a fat man, the first truly fat man I had seen in a long while. His smallish black eyes were narrowly set within a round and layered face. His eyes darted to and fro. I saw his fear there.

"There's no place for Calpurnius' son here," he declared and began to push his door shut. I lay my left hand upon the door and held it open. My right hand clenched, unclenched, and clenched again.

"My mother told me that since I can read, there'd be a place for me here."

"There is no place," the priest repeated. "Three men of this village died on the same night that your father died. Widows and kin here still remember your father's greed and blame him for those deaths."

"But I can read and write.".

"Since the Legions left, there's no law here other than force." He tried to push the door closed once more. Much bigger than him, and taller and muscled where his fat folded, I held the door fast.

He looked up at me with desperation. "Please go," he pleaded. "Go to Calleva. It's a large town, much larger than this poor village." The priest paused.

"There's even a monastery there, a stone house with at least six brothers. Surely they will take in someone like you who can already read and write." The priest took several frightened breaths. I considered what he said. "It's three or four days' walk from here for a strong man like you," he added. I released my hold on his door and it slammed shut. My last glimpse of him was his surprised look as that door sped closed.

My path away from the village took me along the coastal hills that lined the Sabrina estuary and past Mynyd, a larger village surrounded by palisades. I skirted that place, still stinging from my rejections at home and my native village. Soon after, I came upon the wood road. A path of logs and boards was placed across the road, one log after another, on and on, only a little wider than a cart. It ran inland toward the east. It had been laid down so long ago that no one remembered a time when it wasn't there. Even before the Romans arrived, the road carried carts, fish, and pelts from the coast to Calleva and trade goods to the ocean.

My journey from Mynyd to Calleva took just under three days. At the end of the first day's walk along the old road, I found a small, well-used campsite. From the look of the place, many travelers had slept there. A fire ring lay at the center of a half-moon of foot-hardened ground. There was cold charcoal in the circle and signs of a recent visit in the wood pile nearby. Beyond the clearing's crescent, trees gathered and deepened into an old forest. I set up my camp 10 paces into those woods and went to sleep without a fire. I was traveling alone in dangerous times, and even though there were only four ring coins left in my purse they were still worth something. Before the Legions left, I would have made a fire and felt safe there, under the protection of Roman law. But that night in the woods I felt alone, unprotected, and afraid.

On the second day, I passed an abandoned village. The track cut near to the course of the River Brue and along lowlands for most of my morning's walk. Near noon, I saw the foundation posts for seven or more houses and the ruins of a dock along the river. That place felt very old and haunted. I hastened my steps to put distance between me and it.

I crested a slight rise near noon of the third day and saw Calleva. I had never seen a place so large. Looking across cleared fields, I saw farms with barns and other buildings spreading toward the settlement. Calleva had fortified stone walls and large stone gates. From that slight rise I could see that beyond the walls there were at least 100 buildings. More were square with stone walls and wooden roofs than were conical with thatched roofs. People and carts were going in and out of the stone gates. A hundred thatched huts sheltered just outside the walls. Calleva must be home to at least 1,000 people, more than I had ever experienced. My village was small, perhaps 50 people. Aitre's village in Ireland was home to perhaps 75. Near Slemmish, Flan was chieftain of a village of 70. I was in awe.

13. Aed

Two guards in leather armor with metal helmets and short Roman swords at their sides stood beside Calleva's heavy wooden gates. They held iron headed spears. I must have looked like any other traveler or peasant coming to Calleva in search of someone or in search of labor. My two-colored tunic marked me as a freeman. I had a small purse at my waist. Most important, I carried no weapons. Those guards didn't challenge me. They looked at me, dismissed me as a non-threat, and continued to be bored with their duties. And then I was within Calleva's walls.

I asked the first kindly looking face for directions to the monastery. An old woman carried a jar of water back from the wells. "Grandmother," I called to her, "can I help you with that?"

She turned and looked at me with bright eyes. "I can carry my own."

"Can you tell me where the monastery is?"

"Find the market in the old agora and you'll find it." She turned and looked towards the center of Calleva, then walked away. I followed the direction of her look, towards the market, the old agora, and the monastery of Saint George.

My steps should have led me straight to the agora, but they didn't. Farmers and merchants were walking towards it. The widest streets led there. I was a little afraid of what kind of reception I would receive at the monastery, so I wanted to see the city before knocking on its door. Calleva's houses were mostly made of field stone, joined together to form solid, two-story walls. The doors of the houses were unguarded. Children ran in and out. Women carried water. Men gathered at street corners or occasionally sat near the entrance of their homes working, a carpenter here, a stone cutter there. Calleva was a city alive, at work, and at peace. The only lonely looking building I passed was the city barracks. It appeared as if it could hold a century of troops. As I walked by, I peered inside the barrack gate. A soldier called out, "You there, boy! I haven't seen your face before. You must be new here. You look like a strong lad."

I immediately stepped back, out of the barrack's gate. He was as tall as me and was the only soldier I saw wearing the lorica squamata scaled armor of the Legion. It covered his chest and back.

"No need to run away," the soldier continued as a warm smile spread across his face. "I'm called Aed, and I'm captain of the guard here."

I stopped backing away. His warm tone and amiable manner calmed the alarms in my head. Aed walked towards me, maintaining that smile, and stopped a little more than an arm's length away. He reached out his hand in greeting. I looked down uncertainly at his outstretched hand. Then I looked in his eyes. They were calm and showed no menace. As my hand met his to return the greeting, Aed said, "It's good to be wary with strangers. But you're welcome here. We are always looking for new recruits, especially one with the good sense to be alert and cautious." He paused, "What brings a young man, a stranger like you, to Calleva?"

The possibility of becoming a soldier had an unexpectedly strong pull for me. I would have a role, a place to sleep, would be fed and paid. And I would be needed. But I couldn't tell Aed my story of capture and escape from slavery, fearing he might understand only that I was an escaped slave and take me captive again or force me to become a soldier. "A strong looking lad like you," Aed said, this time with a touch more urgency in his voice, "would be welcome here. There's 20 of us left in the guard and more are needed." He lowered his brow to gaze at me with deliberate intensity, still warm but focused. I wanted to talk with Aed, to find out more about Calleva and the guard, and why the Legion had left. Still, I hadn't yet lost my fear of armed men and their ability to hold me captive.

I stammered a reply, "I . . . I'm looking for the temple." In my fear and haste to answer, I used the old word, templum, instead of the newer words for church or monastery. Disappointment crossed Aed's face. He tilted his head to one side and gave me an evaluative look. Then he pointed down a smaller street. "That way," he said. "Come back when you're done with the priest," he called after me as I walked away.

14. Names Are Not So Important

Aed had pointed me towards the old, round temple of Calleva. I knew it was not the building I sought when I saw the painted circle on its whitewashed walls and the triple spiral laid out in stones beside the temple's portico. Those signs stopped me. I remembered the kindness of Amergin. I brushed the tips of my right fingers against his amulet where it still lay beneath my tunic. I stepped across the portico's threshold into the half-light within. My eyes adjusted to the temple shadows, and I noticed an old man. Dressed simply in an unadorned, long white tunic, he sat quietly on one of the two stools beside the door. He was silent but his eyes rose to meet mine when I gazed at him. They were deep pools of concentration and unspoken power. They held a fierce but sad kindness. He simply nodded at me and waited for me to speak.

"My name is Maewyn—

"Names are not so important here." The old man cut me off before I could say more.

I started again. "I escaped from slavery to return—"

From where it rested on his leg, he raised his right hand slightly, waved it back and forth, and said, "You will not find your past here."

I looked that old man sincerely in the eyes. They were questioning, probing, alive, intensely present. Remembering the amulet around my neck, I removed it and held it out to show him. A smile crossed his face. "What do you seek?" he asked.

"My journey is of the Duile," I answered. The old man gestured for me to have a seat on the stool beside him. I sat. Holding out the amulet, I began, "Amergin of the Dal Riata gave me this and set me on this journey." He nodded his gray and balding head. I told my tale, up to and including being recruited by Aed.

"Aed is a good man and an honest soldier," he answered. "Aed stayed here after the Legions left. Most soldiers didn't. They returned to their farms or became brigands and terrorized the roads. Aed stayed. He's the closest thing we have to a governor in this place that used to be a regional capital of Britannia Prima. Aed is like the squib of a candle still burning bright as night runs towards dawn. Soon, it will be a new day and the light of Rome will be replaced by another." The old man fell into silence.

When I could endure the silence no further, I blurted, "My mother sent me to the monks." A heartrending look sped across that old face and disappeared like a stone dropped into still lake waters. Calm restored itself to the old one's eyes. "For safety?" he asked.

"Yes," I replied. "She said they would take me in because I can already read and write."

"Ahh," the old man sighed. "They do place great importance on reading and writing. A new dawn replaces yesterday's light. Remembered knowledge is replaced by writing." He waited a bit, then added, "They'll accept you if you don't share with them that your journey is of the Duile."

"How?" I asked simply.

"Keep the Duile well-protected within the fastness of your heart. And keep that amulet to yourself. The new way is not friendly to the triple goddess."

"And if they find the amulet?"

"It is only an amulet," the old man leaned toward me and whispered. Then he smiled like the sun and sat straight up on his stool. "Keep the Duile in your heart. That's what is important. Everything else is adornment."

I rose to go and looked around. Within the darkness I could see one tall standing stone at the center of the temple's circle. The stone was rough, carved with symbols, and surrounded by a circular trench. I knew intuitively that offerings were poured over the stone and flowed into that trench. On that October day, autumn flowers and some apples lay at the base of the stone.

Turning to the old man, I said, "One more question," and paused. "Who are you?"

"Names are not so important now," the old man said, looking directly at me. "We are all called Amergin." Then he returned to stillness, sitting and looking towards the center of the temple.

I stepped back across the portico, out from magic and into the everyday streets of Calleva. I saw the bulk of the new church between and behind the stone homes across the street.

15. The Church Militant

Everything about the church building was at right angles. Its long walls were rectangles of stone. Three flat, rectangular stone steps led up to a deep-brown wooden door. A cross-shaped door knocker was fixed there. A square roof hung from the walls above the door to protect a traveler from rain or snow. Above the door, beneath the roof, carved in square letters into the stone read the slogan, "Ecclesiae Militantis." Those strange words, "Church Militant," startled me. I needed a place to sleep for the night, a place of refuge and safety. So, I struck that door knocker twice against the solid wood and waited.

Minutes passed. I wondered if I should strike the door again. I didn't. More minutes went by. I was just about to knock on the door again when I heard the rasping sounds of a latch being raised. I stepped back to the bottom stair and straightened my shoulders and tunic as best I could. The door slowly swung inward. Initially, I only saw the monk's cowl that hid his face. His hood topped a thin, angular body in old, gray robes. I noticed the sinewy arm and hand that at once held the door open yet was also ready to drive the door shut in an instant.

"Young man," a confident voice sounded from beneath the hood, "why do you knock at this door?" He placed a strong, sandalled foot against the base of the door to hold it open and with both hands pushed back the ashen-colored cowl to reveal a capable-looking face. His jaw was square and firm, his expression friendly, but not overly so. He had the bluest eyes I had ever met. They showed intelligence, questioning, resolve, and compassion with an undercurrent of ferocity. Most of all, I noted that his head was shaved, top and sides, except for a ringlet of hair at the crown.

I had never met a monk before. There had been Christian priests in my village for as long as I could remember, but no monks. The village priests had always been heavyset, jowly, and the opposite of captivating. Their only distinctive signs had been a small wooden cross hung on a leather thong around their necks and that they didn't do any visible work. My mouth stood agape at the shock of seeing this monk. "What do you seek here?" he asked again.

I couldn't find the words. Most of all, I sought a place to sleep for the night and a meal. But those seemed unworthy as an answer. My painful dumbness seemed to stretch forever, but he later told me that I was silenced for only slightly longer than a minute.

"I can read and write and was told that I could be of use in a place such as this," I began. "I seek a place of safety to stay for the night."

The monk looked at me, slowly, carefully, from head to toe and back again. "You can read and write?"

"Yes."

"There may be work for you here. You are welcome to spend the night. If you wish to stay longer, you may tarry three days." He paused. "After that, the brothers will decide whether you can remain with us." He held out his hand in greeting. As I grasped it, he added, "Welcome to the Monastery of Saint George. I am called Brother Durstan and I am the prior here." And with that, I entered the monastery.

16. Black and White Stones

On the third day, after the midday meal, Brother Durstan and the five other monks gathered in the long rectangle of the monastery's common room on benches around a large plank table. Durstan sat in a chair at the far end of the table. Until I came to St. George's, I had never seen a chair. They were rare, signs of authority usually only seen in the law court or at a governor's house. Brothers Cnywg, Faelan, Ninian, Mochan, and Elisedd, all older men, the youngest at least 35 years of age, lined the benches. The six brothers sat with hoods pushed back, probing eyes directed at me. I stood at the foot of the table.

"Maewyn," Brother Durstan began, "we finished work early today so we can consider together, as is our custom, whether to allow you to remain with us beyond sunset." He looked at each of the additional five brothers and continued. "You have shared with me some of your tale. It is time to share that story with the brothers so they can decide whether to accept you here or to ask you to leave. Each of the brothers has an equal vote and I, as prior, have two votes. But our custom is that you must be accepted by each of us in order to stay. If anyone votes 'no,' you must leave. The votes will be cast using black and white stones after you have told us your tale and answered the brothers' questions." He paused to look directly at me. "Do you understand?"

"Yes," I answered.

"You may begin."

My immediate safety and well-being depended on being accepted by the brothers. I could not return to my village. Going beyond Calleva on my own was perilous. I had no other place or refuge in Calleva other than the military barracks. That choice offered a life of hardship and danger. The civilizing influence of Rome had almost completely waned. At St. George's, I heard the rumors that the Goths had reached Northern Italy and the empire was almost prostrate before them. Here in Britain, the Roman peace was in tatters. Even though I craved adventure like most young men, I knew that life carrying a spear would be uncertain and violent. My best hope for safety was acceptance as a brother.

I told my tale. I included how I was raised as the eldest son of a tax collector and had learned to read and write while still young. I declared how I had been ready to take the white toga of full citizenship when I was captured by the Irish raiders. I disclosed my privations while herding sheep on Slemmish. I told how I had learned Irish while a slave and that a voice told me to flee. I shared how I escaped across the Irish Sea to the Kingdom of Dal Riata in the north. I spoke of my journey south through Dal Riata and the old Roman provinces of Britain until my homecoming. With visible sadness, I revealed that my mother and family had rejected me. In a moment of unexpected mercy, I reported that Conchessa had set me free before my brother could kill me. She sent me in search of a monastery. "So, I am a Christian," I finished. "My father was a deacon as well as a tax collector. My grandfather was a priest. I have no other place to go and ask that you accept me as a brother and give me refuge."

Brother Mochan broke the brief silence that followed my words. "If we do not accept you, what then?"

"I will return to the barracks and find a place among the soldiers," I answered.

"Are you ready to be a soldier for Christ?" Elisedd asked.

I looked directly at Elisedd and answered firmly, "Yes." Then I looked at each of the other five brothers, ending with my eyes meeting the eyes of Brother Durstan. "Yes," I repeated.

"Brothers, are you ready to cast your vote?" Durstan asked. There were nods around the benches. "A white stone signifies yes. A black stone means Maewyn must leave."

Two small jars were passed along the benches. Each brother selected a stone from one jar and placed it in the other.

I could not see which stones were selected as the jars were passed from Elisedd to Mochan to Cnywg, Ninian, Faelan, and then Durstan. Durstan looked at me and then tipped the jar with the ballot stones over so all could see.

Seven white stones lay on the table.

17. Monk

"Maewyn, you are welcome to abide with us," Brother Durstan said. "In three days, you will take tonsure. We will cut your hair and you will receive the white robe of a monk in training." I nodded understanding. "In three months, if all goes well, you will receive the cowl of a full brother."

Again, I nodded. "Use these three days wisely to pray and prepare for life as a brother." The other monks all rose from the table and clasped my arm in friendship. They told me how glad they were I had joined them. Tears moistened my eyes. This was the first true welcome I received since I fled Ireland.

Three months later I took the gray robe and hood of a full monk. The ceremony was on the feast of the Epiphany, January 6th, at the end of the Christmas celebrations. That day celebrates the full dawning of the light of Jesus' birth, the gift giving of the three kings to the infant Jesus, and at the same time the baptism of Jesus years later in the River Jordan. Just after the Epiphany Mass had begun, I was called forward from among the brothers. The prior's chair was placed in front of the altar. Days before, I had been trained in the ceremony. Brother Durstan took his seat as prior. I lay on the floor in my white robes, before his chair and spread my arms out to form a cross with my own body. "Maewyn Succat," Durstan chanted, "what do you seek?"

"I seek full brotherhood." I had been trained to answer this way.

"Are you ready to accept and keep the full rule of Blessed George, martyr and patron of this place?" he intoned.

"I am," I responded from my place at his feet.

"Are you ready to accept and keep the full rule of Blessed George, martyr and patron of this place?" he repeated.

"I am." I responded a second time, my voice full of conviction.

"Are you ready to accept and keep the full rule of Blessed George, martyr and patron of this place?" he repeated.

"I am," I responded the third time, calling out strongly.

"Do you accept the humble poverty of our life here?" he chanted.

"Yes," I called out.

Brother Durstan added, "Do you commit yourself to a life of chastity and of obedience to your prior and monastic authority?"

I answered once more, "Yes."

"Brothers," Brother Durstan intoned three times, "do you accept Maewyn as a full brother in this monastery?"

"We do," rang out their clear answer.

Then Brother Durstan and each of the brothers approached and offered me the kiss of friendship and brotherhood. After that, Brother Cnywg, the youngest among them, brought me gray robes to replace the white ones of a novice. When newly dressed in my gray robe and hood, Brother Durstan pronounced, "You are now Brother Maewyn."

Days as a monk at St. George's had a soothing rhythm and stateliness to them. We woke in the dark of the night to gather for first prayers. For the next three hours, we contemplated in silence. Dawn saw us gather again for the second of six prayer services sprinkled throughout the day. A simple meal of bread and water was followed by manual labor or work in the scriptorium copying books.

A short gathering for prayer punctuated the morning midway between breakfast and noon. We prayed together a fourth time at midday. Lunch was the main meal, usually a broth of whatever vegetables could be found, bread, and maybe cheese. After the midday meal, our schedule allowed an hour of individual time, in silence, followed by a return to work. Three days a week, I copied books. Three days a week I dug, planted, pruned, and weeded in the monastery farm plot just outside the walls of Calleva. Those were my favorite days.

In the late afternoon, we gathered once more to praise God before eating a simple supper, most often a bowl of grain porridge and a cup of ale brewed in the monastery. The guiding book of rules for St. George's allowed one cup of ale per monk per day. Each cup was blessed with a quote from our rule, "A cheerful monk rejoices in his labors in God's garden." The hours after sunset also allowed for personal contemplation and quiet. Non-work conversation with each other was only allowed during the two hours between supper and our final prayer service of the day. The monks of St. George's were quiet, cheerful, and generally solitary men. They didn't share much during the talking hours. Unless there was some surprising event within the city, they preferred to keep to themselves and rest.

I saw Calleva while walking to and from the monastery farm plot. My gray robe rendered me seemingly invisible. Calleva's citizens looked right past me. They hardly ever spoke to me or my companions. They looked down as we approached. Some made the sign of the cross. Some made a sign of the older religion. Some called out for prayers as we passed. Occasionally, someone called out a curse. Mostly the citizens left us to ourselves. From within this cocoon, I traced the gradual decline of civility within the city.

The citizens' clothing didn't change. Men continued to wear their simple tunics or leggings and work shirts. Calleva's women wore dresses, tunics, aprons. The rhythms of the city remained unchanged. The sounds of the cocks crowing and dogs barking greeted each morning as we monks gathered for the dawn service. On the days I walked to the monastery garden, I saw the same men sitting and working by their doors or collected in conversation at the corners. The same mothers chased children in and out of the city's doors. Calleva's soldiers still guarded the city gates, although I judged there to be fewer of them.

When I first began walking beyond the city walls, I never saw Captain Aed on guard, never saw the same guards twice in one week. Six months later, I saw Captain Aed standing guard every other time I walked to the garden plot. I often recognized the same soldiers at the gate. The change I noticed most was how fear crept into Calleva. The atmosphere of peace faded like morning mist, supplanted by a harsh, guarded coldness like winter sunlight. Calleva's citizens looked down more than up. People hastened here and there. Conversations at street corners seemed quicker, more pointed. There were fewer children in the street.

One night, I broke the silence between supper and the closing prayer service of the day to speak of these changes with Brother Durstan. "Do the changes you notice trouble you?" he asked.

"I want to understand them."

Durstan told me a tale of the Legion's leaving Calleva. "Emperor Honorius came to the throne 15 years ago as a child of 10. Since then, the empire has been torn by rebellion and invasion." I nodded. "A short time after you were taken by the Irish, the emperor withdrew the Legion from Britain's northern wall. Since that time, the north has been under the protection of local governors who are in fact little more than warlords." I bowed my head again. "Three years past, an army of tens of thousands, perhaps even 100,000 barbarians, crossed the frozen River Rhine in the depth of winter, north of Roman Gaul, and overwhelmed the Legions there. The emperor withdrew the remaining Legion in Britain to reinforce Rome against the onslaught. Constantine, the last Legion general here in Britain, entrusted Calleva to Aed as captain of the Roman auxiliary. He had 100 soldiers at his command." I nodded again, somewhat impatiently as I knew this part already. "Now, fewer than 10 soldiers remain," Durstan whispered. "Calleva is unguarded and there have been reports of Saxon raids on the ports at Anderida, London, and Regnum, closer than three days' walk from here." Brother Durstan fell silent for a short while. Then he continued, "The people are afraid of the Saxons."

"And you," I asked, "are you afraid?"

"We live simply here," Brother Durstan said, "and I trust in God. He will protect us." A hushed stillness gathered between us. "And when the Saxons come, I will throw open the doors and invite them into God's house. I will freely offer them whatever they choose to take. Our lives are more precious to God than silver or gold. I will pray that God holds us safe." He looked into my eyes. "Brother Maewyn, what are you afraid of?"

"I have been taken captive once already by raiders and endured slavery."

Brother Durstan considered my words and nodded. "Yes, you are young and strong. The rest of us here are older men, no threat to any Saxon raiders. But they might kill you out of fear or sell you back into slavery. We will find a way to safety for you."

18. Dreams and Voices

The next months were full of the routines of the monastery, praying with the brothers, copying manuscripts, and working. While awake, my nights were full of the voice of Slemmish, and while asleep, dreams of Brigid and Amergin. One dream of Brigid coming to me in great fear occurred night after night, three times. She appeared clasping her ripped tunic before her breasts. The garment was stained with blood and dirt and torn all around her. Her long red hair hung in disarray. Her green eyes brimmed with fear and tears. "Maewyn, help me," she pleaded. Then Brigid reached her arms across the space of dreams for me. Before I could hold her, I awoke. My heart raced. My whole body was tensed, ready to strike, my thoughts fierce and full of violence. And I was aroused.

After the evening meal, on the fourth night, I sought out Brother Durstan. "Brother," I began, "I need to talk." I told him of my dream and of the violence and passion within my heart. "Does this mean that I am not capable of holding my vow of chastity?" I asked. Tenderness filled his eyes and an understanding smile spread across his face.

"No, brother," he replied. "It means you're a man." Brother Durstan inhaled long and deep, then began his story. "I was married before I came to this place. Most of us brothers were. We are men, like all men. We feel passion. We have hearts and bodies like all other men. Our passions, hearts, and bodies are among the gifts we bring to the monastery." He paused to let this sink in.

"I was not much older than you are now," he said. "The Legion still held Calleva. Since I could read and write, I had a place at the governor's court as a clerk. I had a family, a wife and young son. Their names were Helen and Lucius. A fever took Lucius one spring when he was not yet five years old. Helen's heart broke and she stopped eating, talking, or sleeping. One morning, I found her. In her sorrow, she had taken her life. She was hanging from a tree. I buried her beside Lucius and grieved her. In many ways, she took my life also.

Months later, I sold my small plot of land to the former prior of St. George's, Brother Martin. He noticed the grief in my eyes and offered to listen. We became friends. At first, Martin listened to my story without expectation, without wanting anything from me. He just listened to my heart. In return, when I could, I spoke on the monastery's behalf before the governor, talking about my friendship with Martin and what a good man he was. Over the next few seasons, grief turned to acceptance. When I asked to be accepted here as a brother, Martin said yes."

Brother Durstan paused as if remembering unspoken details from his story. "That was more than 10 years ago. Martin has passed. The Romans have left Britain. And I dream of Helen at least once a week." He turned to me with sadness in his eyes. "I see her as she was, beautiful and full of life. I see Lucius young and playing. My dreams are a blessing from God."

"From God?" I asked with surprise.

"Who else would send such kindness to fill my nights?" he answered. "It is no fault to see those you love in your dreams and no break in your monastic vows to desire them. We are monks, yet still men." He waited for me to take in his words. "When you awaken in the morning and ready yourself for our first prayers together, that is the time to recommit yourself to your vows. Let God and his angels care for the night. We monks care for the days."

During the winter months, our monastic farm slept under a blanket of snow. The harvest was in storage, farming equipment mended and put away. New seeds lay waiting for spring. With less work outside the walls, my work focused almost exclusively on copying a Bible in the scriptorium. It was late March, and I was copying the story of Moses from the Book of Exodus. I formed the letters, *"Dixit Deus ad Mosen ego sum qui sum."* Those are my words, I heard the voice of Slemmish sounding in my ears. *God said to Moses, I am who am. That voice is mine.*

My hand shook. The feathered quill in my fingers shook along with it. I looked down at what I had copied. There was no blotch of ink to mar the precious velum.

I looked around the scriptorium. Six other heads bent over their work. Six quills painted the letters of six other chapters onto six other pages. No one else had heard the voice. I placed my quill back on its rest and held my page as if to examine my work.

Who are you? I demanded in my thoughts.

I am who spoke to Moses, answered the voice of Slemmish.

How do I know you are not the voice of a demon? I demanded.

I know your inner most thoughts. I know your heart, the voice responded.

I took a sharp breath inward and noticed Brother Mochan look up to gaze at me. I shrugged, offered a slight smile, and gazed back down at my page. Mochan's head returned to his work.

I know you struck Cathal, the voice continued. *I know your dreams of Brigid. I know you hate your brother Marcus. And I know you still hold Amergin's amulet,* the voice proclaimed. *I am who I am.*

I felt my heart race then as much as it had raced after my dreams at night. The voice that spoke to me on Slemmish, the voice that had followed me here to St. George's, was the voice that spoke to Moses from the Burning Bush. The voice that spoke to me on Slemmish was the voice of the God of Heaven.

I don't remember, but the brothers told me that I had passed out and fell to the floor. Two of them carried me to my monk's cell. When I returned to consciousness, all of them were standing near my bed or by the cell's door.

"It was lucky," Brother Elisedd said, "that you had put your quill down just before falling."

"You must have felt the weakness coming," Brother Mochan offered, "and saved the page from being destroyed." Concern occupied Brother Durstan's face while he shooed the others from the room. Then he took a seat at the foot of my cot. "They will talk about this for months or more," he said. "They will watch you in the scriptorium to see that you are all right. They will mean well, but . . ." his voice trailed off. Looking at me, he continued, "Your face has gone pale, there's a sheen of sweat on your brow even though the day is cold, and your eyes are wider than an owl's at midnight. What happened?"

I told him the story of hearing the voice on Slemmish and how that voice chastised me and reminded me of my faults. I shared that the voice had followed me here from Ireland and that it had spoken today in the scriptorium.

"Is it truly the voice of God?" I asked.

"Yes, Maewyn," the prior answered with pride. "Few hear the Father's voice so clearly. He has judged your faults of anger, passion, and pride but still holds you close to Him. It is a hard blessing to carry. You may be scourged, then lifted up.

For the present, I will keep this between us, lest the brothers become jealous. It seems that God has plans for you."

Durstan paused. "For the remainder of the day, rest here. I will have the evening meal brought to your cell." He stood to leave, then turned and stopped at the cell's door. "I heard news today that Saxon ships have been seen off the coast near Regnum." Silence filled the gap before his next words, "I know now that our Heavenly Father plans more for you. We must act soon to get you to safety."

19. Touched by God

During the days that followed, the brothers treated me with growing deference, sometimes with awe in their eyes. I had been touched by God, an experience both desired and feared. Within, I heard both the voices of Slemmish and of Amergin. With one exception, I felt the same as I had before the voice spoke to me in the scriptorium. The voice of Slemmish became more forceful. I believed in it more. I had a name for that voice, God. The voice of Amergin began to wane. When I thought of Amergin, I felt grateful, honored. But when I heard the voice of Slemmish, I felt awe. Steadily, within my heart, the balance between the old ways of the triple goddess and the new religion of the Christ tipped towards the new. I had become a believer.

I greeted my monastic duties with increased enthusiasm. I was often the first to take a seat in chapel for chanted prayers. I brought my passion to copying the remainder of the book of Exodus. The work took almost two months of careful hand lettering. When I finished my copy of Exodus, Brother Durstan directed me to start copying the first book of Samuel. In that story, the child Samuel awakens three times to hear a voice calling to him at night. He thinks that the voice belongs to Eli, his guardian. But Eli hasn't called him and twice tells him to go back to sleep. The third time, Eli recognizes the voice must be that of God and tells young Samuel how to answer the voice if it calls again. I understood that Brother Durstan ordered me to copy this text because the story was so like mine.

I grew even more certain that the voice within was the voice of God. I took to heart how Eli commanded Samuel to return to sleep and if he heard the voice once more to answer, "Speak Lord, your servant is listening."

Three months after I had fainted in the scriptorium, at the conclusion of the evening meal, Brother Durstan signaled for me to stay behind. The other five brothers left the dining hall, all wearing puzzled looks, wondering that the prior had selected me out. The looks on brothers Mochan and Ninian's faces suggested the question of what had I done to be disciplined? That night was just two weeks after I had begun my work on the book of Samuel.

"Brother Maewyn," he said, "I have news."

"Yes, Prior," I answered.

"Five Saxon ships landed at Regnum last week. Fifty warriors with their women and children entered the town. They intend to stay."

I listened for more. "A barrel-maker from Regnum came to the monastery door this afternoon, begging for food and asking for a place to stay. Before he went to sleep in the barn, he told me the story."

"Was there bloodshed at Regnum?" I asked. "Were there soldiers there? Did the citizens fight back?"

"Yes," Brother Durstan answered. "There was blood spilled." He paused to consider his next words. "There were no trained soldiers left in Regnum when the ships arrived. Several of the young men used whatever weapons they could find to resist. They had a few swords left behind by the Romans, scythes, pitchforks, small farming knives. They were no match for the Saxon warriors." He stopped to allow me to take in his words. "Twenty young men of Regnum and one Saxon warrior died. When the killing had stopped and the Saxons owned Regnum, they lined up the men in the town square. Seven young men were killed to avenge the warrior's death. The youngest of them, only 17 years old, was nailed to the door of Regnum's church like an X and allowed to bleed to death as a warning that any further resistance would be met with horrible violence."

I know my face turned white at the news. I felt the blood leave my hands and feet and draw towards my heart. My thoughts began to shut down in fear. Brother Durstan saw and shook me.

"This is what we have feared," he said. "Shake yourself to throw off fear and rouse your courage. Tonight, we prepare for your journey. Tomorrow, or the next day at the latest, you must leave Calleva and seek safety."

"But I am a monk now, no threat to the warriors. I won't resist," I pleaded. "Do I need to go? Will the Saxons kill all of us monks?"

"I do not know the answers to your questions," Brother Durstan replied. He looked at me with sadness and pride in his eyes. A visible tension had built in his arms and hands. Brother Durstan shook with energy as he added, "But I am certain that God has bigger plans for you than death at the hands of the Saxon invaders. It is my task to get you to safety, so God's plan comes true."

I couldn't argue with him. Brother Durstan, the book of Exodus, and the book of Samuel had convinced me that God had spoken to me in the night. I had answered the voice of Slemmish, and said, "Speak Lord, your servant is listening." That voice commanded that next I become a priest. I had already told Brother Durstan of God's plan for me, and he agreed. I was to be sent to another monastery of St. George in London.

"In Roman times, London was once the grandest city of the north," Brother Durstan said. "It was once home to more than sixty thousand souls." Uncertainty crossed his face. "Now that the Romans are gone, thousands have left. Soon it will be less than half of what it once was."

My thoughts were spinning. "How will I get to London?"

"You will walk, of course." With a sly smile, he retrieved an almost six-foot walking staff from a corner of the dining hall. I hadn't noticed the staff before. Now I saw that one end had been freshly sawn. "You are now a pilgrim monk on your way to the shrine of Blessed George in London."

"This staff . . ." I said, taking it in my hands and looking at the sawn-off head, "this staff was your prior's staff." Brother Durstan nodded.

"You've cut off the shepherd's crook at its head," I blurted.

"Maewyn, the sheep are worth more than the staff. I had hoped that one day, when I was gone, you might take my place as prior. But it seems that God has other plans for you." His blue eyes looked directly into mine. "When you are gone, I will trust in the Great Shepherd to protect us."

I spent the rest of that evening waiting for morning. My mind and heart were full. When Mother had rejected me and Marcus sought to kill me, the brothers at St. George's had become my family. Leaving the monastery meant losing my family again.

Although I was a monk, my heart and body still yearned for Brigid. I held her in my dreams, and we made love in the darkness of the night. During the days, a flower blooming reminded me of her. Copying the Scriptures, I'd come across a fantastic story or odd phrase and wonder, *What would she think of that?* Now I was getting ready to go even further away from her. Our hand-fasting passed before

I had fled Ireland. In my heart, I wondered, even hoped, that one day I would return to her. Village priests had wives. Could that be Brigid's and my future? But the Saxons were nearby, and Brother Durstan was ordering me to flee even further away from her. Sadness and fear battled in my heart.

Three hours before dawn, I joined the brothers to chant the first prayers of the day. After the service, Brother Durstan informed them he was sending me to London on a pilgrimage and mission. In turn, they each clasped my arm, and with a nod or a look wished me good fortune. None of my brothers broke silence.

Before the dawn service, I stood just inside the same door where I had entered St. George's nine months before. Brother Durstan stood with me. "Take this letter," he said, handing me a folded sheet of velum sealed with wax. "Do not stop your pilgrimage at London."

I nodded, understanding.

"Find a ship and go to Gaul. Perhaps the light of Rome still shines in that province." He stopped to consider his next words, then continued. "I have heard of an abbot in Auxerre in Gaul, Germanus. He is dedicated to Saint George. Go to him and show him this letter."

Brother Durstan looked at me with the fire of command in his eyes. "Do not lose the letter. Do not open it or show it to anyone until you reach Abbot Germanus. Show it only to the abbot. He will know what to do." Then he fell silent.

We embraced and I left. I turned back once to see him, leaning against that door's post. Then, directing my steps towards London, I walked away.

PART 3

ROME

20. A Welcomed Stranger

Mid-afternoon, Easter 418 AD

I kept the letter from Brother Durstan to Abbot Germanus. It was 10 years old now. Though the letters on the velum had faded, I could still read the words. They began, "To Abbot Germanus, my brother, from Durstan, prior at St. George's at Calleva in Britannia Prima."

My journey from Calleva to London had been only a few days' walk. The farmers I met on the road looked at my monk's robes and treated me as a pilgrim, an object of curiosity. They were satisfied when I told them I was on my way to St. George's monastery in London. The journey from London took me across the British Sea to Gaul, to where the empire and Roman ways still held sway.

I rested against a pillar and enjoyed the mid-afternoon sun and shadows in the abbey cloister. A series of open arches along each of the cloister's four walls looked out upon the courtyard. Underneath the arches, I felt at peace. The busyness of the abbey, with its more than 100 monks, scriptorium, kitchens, and gardens, faded here to a contemplative stillness. Here is where I came during the day to listen for the voice.

After the greeting to Abbot Germanus, the letter in my hand continued, "If this letter reaches you still sealed, the brother carrying my words is Maewyn Succat of a small village in Britannia Prima. He was captured by Irish pirates and enslaved for six years. He escaped slavery and made his way to our monastery, where he received tonsure and became one of us. I believe he has been chosen by the Almighty for great things. He is of humble birth, like Samuel and David. And like them, he hears the voice of God. That voice commanded him to flee Ireland and helped him find his way to us. That voice now commands him to seek ordination as a priest. I hope that voice will call Brother Maewyn back to Britain when he has been fully trained."

The page was warm and worn smooth by my handling. The letters, originally deep black, had faded to a pleasing old brown-gray. All that remained of Durstan's wax seal was the stain of the wax on the outer skin of the velum. I folded the letter half-closed and looked once more towards the shadow and light in the cloister courtyard.

Folding it once more, I returned the letter to the purse that hung from my belt. The letter, the amulet from Amergin, and one remaining ring coin were all the bag held, my dearest and only private possessions.

I had been summoned to appear before Abbot Germanus in the scriptorium an hour before sunset. The command had been given to me directly by Father Aulus, the brother in charge of monastic discipline. It was sealed with the mark of Prior Charles.

To celebrate the Easter festival, no work was done in the monastery that day. The monks of Auxerre were given a day of rest after the demanding rituals and ceremonies of the week leading to Easter. They were not tending the fields, cleaning, repairing, or building the monastery. No monks labored copying the Bible and other texts. The scriptorium would be empty. I had served as a monk at Auxerre for 10 years. I heard the voice urging me to take ordination as a priest. One week ago, on Palm Sunday, I formally supplicated Abbot Germanus to be ordained. This summons was my answer.

At the far end of a very large scriptorium, between where the master's podium stood and the copying desks began, Abbot Germanus sat on a tall, straight-backed chair with arms. Above Abbot Germanus' head, I could see the motto of Auxerre carved in wood, "Work and Pray." Prior Charles and Father Aulus sat on simple stools, one to the right and the other to the left of Abbot Germanus' chair. A summons to see the abbot was unusual. I had never heard of anyone being summoned to appear before an abbot, prior, and monastic disciplinarian unless they were to be punished, perhaps even expelled. I was afraid, so I paused at the door of the scriptorium and allowed myself time to raise my courage, time to take in each detail of the room.

The smells of velum, ink, and candles filled the place. A wan spring, late-afternoon light filtered through the room's high windows. Sixty-four copying desks with their high benches stood in 16 rows of four. Spare quills, ready for the next stroke of a letter, rested on several of the desks. An open space lay between where Abbot Germanus sat and the first copy stations began. There was neither stool nor bench for me to sit. I felt the rough texture of my gray robes and the weight of the monastic hood resting upon my back. Dust motes were visible in one stray beam of light above the master's podium. Somehow, taking that pause allowed me to find courage where before I had found only fear and confusion.

"We have considered your petition for ordination as a priest," Abbot Germanus began, "and there is a problem." He looked to Prior Charles, then to Father Aulus.

Father Aulus added, "Your conduct as a monk is exemplary and that is the problem."

Confused, I asked, "How is that a problem, Father?"

"Because no one really knows who you are," stated the Prior. "Your conduct shows no edges. You keep the silence. Your work in the scriptorium is excellent. You talk with the brothers when it is appropriate, but no one feels they really know you." He paused. "For almost 10 years, you have been a monk here, yet you hold back from letting us see your heart."

Father Aulus added, "The brothers say that you never talk about your past before becoming a monk, never about any feelings for women, or worldly ambition before you came here. You answer every question only with your love of our monastery, your desire to serve, and what the voice of God tells you."

"We would allow you to continue to hide behind the shield of perfection," Abbot Germanus said, "if you weren't seeking holy orders. But you have asked to become a priest and that means you must drop perfection and allow us to know you."

I looked down, my thoughts racing, energy coursing through my arms, legs, and hands. I wanted to flee the scriptorium yet felt as if my sandalled feet were fixed fast to the floor. My eyes narrowed; my breath became shallow. I began to lose awareness of the scriptorium except for the three men in front of me. I forced myself to take a long breath. Tears began to gather at the corners of my eyes.

"We know you came from St. George's in Britannia," said the Prior. "Before that you escaped slavery among the Irish. And even before that your father was the local tax collector." A long breath interrupted his words. "But beyond the skeleton of your story, no one here knows your heart. You don't talk of your family, of your past, of your fears and hopes."

I started, "But Prior—"

Abbot Germanus joined in, saying, "Brother Maewyn, please listen. I want to ordain you. But from the day you arrived from London until now, you remain a welcome stranger among us. You only talk of the voice of God and your desire for ordination, letting no one in."

Father Aulus continued, "We wonder if you suffer from arrogance, thinking us unworthy of your heart's thoughts? Or is there something that you are holding back, something you are deeply ashamed of which will disqualify you from Holy Orders? Perhaps you simply suffer from a stubborn pride."

Abbot Germanus finished, "Whatever it is that holds you back, we must know that before deciding whether or not to ordain you as a priest."

With that judgment, silence grew and deepened between us.

21. Maewyn's Confession

I was stunned. Long minutes passed and the late afternoon sunlight began to fade from the scriptorium. After a very long while, when there was more twilight than sun left in the room, I spoke, "My story, I am so ashamed."

The chapel bell tolled, calling the abbey to Easter vespers. Abbot Germanus looked to Father Aulus, then to the Prior.

"Prior Charles," the Abbot suggested, "will you go and lead Vespers? The brothers will be waiting. Father Aulus and I will hear Maewyn's story."

A look of concern crossed the Prior's eyes. "Come back after vespers is finished and join us here," Abbot Germanus continued. "Don't forget to tell the kitchen to put something aside from the evening meal for the four of us."

The Abbot nodded. Prior Charles rose silently to kneel before him, kissed his ring of authority, then left. Abbot Germanus and Father Aulus both looked at me to continue.

This short interruption allowed me time to decide to tell my whole tale. I hadn't told anyone the entire story. I had carried the burden of betrayal and shame for such a long time that they were part of me, like an old scar or like lost teeth, a part of me and a lack of me at the same time.

"I am so ashamed," I began once more.

Abbot Germanus sat slightly forward in his chair, a look of tender interest in his eyes. Father Aulus sat straight on his stool, his face composed, unreadable, listening.

"I was within two weeks of assuming the toga of a full citizen," I began, "within two weeks of my sixteenth birthday and being recognized as a man. Camilla owned my heart."

Abbot Germanus raised one eyebrow at the mention of a girl. Father Aulus's face became, if anything, even more unreadable.

"Camilla had beautiful hazel eyes and the face of a goddess. She was lithe and graceful. We had known each other since childhood. She was the daughter of the local Roman magistrate." I hadn't spoken of her aloud in more than 16 years.

When I was 16, as an almost-man, my attention was fixed on Camilla. I pushed away everything that didn't have to do with her as much as possible. She became the sun of my world, and I would do anything for her.

"Camilla told me she would marry me when the toga ceremonies were past, when I was a man and could establish my own house." I held my next words, weighing them for truth, before speaking. Those words would either reveal the core of my shame, what I had told no one all these years, or they would continue to hold back.

"I stole an amethyst ring from Calpurnius, my father," I said. "And, when he found out, I allowed him to blame Nevio, my slave." I took a few long, silent breaths. "I was afraid and thought Father would just punish Nevio. I thought he would beat him, not cut off his hand. When the axe fell, it was as if it fell on my hand, not Nevio's."

"Was your father's anger so terrible?" Father Aulus asked.

"Yes," I answered truthfully. "He was always afraid that there wouldn't be enough for the taxes. His fear turned to an unquenchable greed. The ring I stole was equal in value to one farmer's taxes for a year, worth perhaps as much as one cow."

Father Aulus asked, "Do you diminish your sin of stealing?"

"No, father," I answered. "I'm only trying to offer a context. Father had more than 50 such rings and had collected more than three years' taxes ahead." I took another breath. "He could not abide letting go of any of it. His anger at the ring's theft was terrifying."

"Why did you take that ring?" Abbot Germanus asked.

"For Camilla," I answered. "The ring was to be my gift to her, sealing our pledge. I asked Father for something to give her. His answer was that any woman worth attention brought a dowry into the house. She didn't take wealth away."

"Your father must have known then that you took the ring," Abbot Germanus declared.

"I've thought on this for 16 years," I answered. "Yes, he knew." I paused. "He knew that I took the ring, and he took Nevio's hand anyway."

Both Abbot Germanus and Father Aulus shook their heads.

"Father knew I was afraid of him. He had beaten me many times before. He also never let go of anything. I was his son, his possession. If he could take my dignity and honor, then even when I assumed the toga, I would still be a boy in my heart. I would still belong to him. So, he took Nevio's hand before I could regain my courage and own the act."

"How did your slave come to have the ring?" Father Aulus asked.

"Just before Father stormed towards the house in search of the ring, I was showing it to Nevio. He was more than my slave. He had been my companion since childhood and was the closest thing to a friend I had. We were inseparable. I told him everything, shared everything. When I told him that Camilla had said, yes, that she'd be my wife, Nevio had only a smile. When I showed him the ring, he immediately became afraid and told me that I must put it back. Nevio knew Father's greed and wrath as well as I did. He had just told me that he'd put the ring back when we saw Father. He must have slipped it into the pouch on his belt as Father came to the house."

"Why didn't you just tell your father it was you who took the ring?" Father Aulus asked.

"It all happened too fast," I replied. "I was scared, too scared to say it was me. Then Father hacked off Nevio's hand. After that it was too late. Nevio's hand, my worth as a man, and the ring had all been taken back by Father."

"What happened afterward?" Abbot Germanus asked.

"Father cauterized the stub of Nevio's arm, and I bound up his wound," I said. "That was shortly before noon. I held Nevio in my arms for a long time and we cried. Sometime before sunset, we left the barn and walked to the cliffs nearby that overlooked the Sabrina estuary. I told Nevio how ashamed I was that Father had taken his hand, not mine. Nevio was my slave, not Father's. I told him that when I took the toga and became a man, I would free him. Nevio's eyes went wide just as I promised freedom. My back was turned towards the cliffs. I was looking at him. His eyes went wide in fear, not surprise at being promised freedom. The Irish had climbed the cliff behind us as we talked. Nevio, with his one good arm, stepped forward to put himself between me and the raiders. They cut him down and threw a sack over my head to take me captive. But it didn't matter. By the time that sack was over my head, I had already become a slave in my heart. My dignity was gone."

A deep quiet grew between the three of us there in the scriptorium. After a long while, Prior Charles rejoined us. "Brother, cook has put something aside in the kitchens," the prior said, taking his seat once more upon a stool.

Abbot Germanus nodded, then replied, "Brother Maewyn has been telling us the tale of his loss of honor, how he let his slave shoulder the blame and lose a hand for his theft of a valuable ring from his father, the tax collector."

On hearing this, Prior Charles' face became very disturbed. His mouth set in its own anger, and he looked intensely at me and then at the abbot. "A thieving spirit; that's difficult to live with in a monastery," he said. "But a dishonorable spirit, that's impossible." Prior Charles looked at me with zero mercy in his eyes.

"It has grown late," Abbot Germanus said. "Maewyn, I am relieved that you are at last telling us your true story." The Abbot looked at Prior Charles and Father Aulus, then continued. "For now, I must say 'no' to your request for ordination. In a week's time, two hours before vespers, we will meet with you again in my private chambers to hear the rest of your tale."

I looked up. My heart was unburdened at having confessed the theft of the ring and my part in Nevio's death. I wasn't being expelled from the abbey immediately. The voice still clamored in my head, *You must be ordained*. But the voice of Slemmish now competed with the voice of Abbot Germanus.

"Thursday coming, at our weekly public confession of sins and faults, you will take your place in front of the entire monastery and confess to your theft and shame," Father Aulus ordered. "Then the brothers will see you for who you truly are,"

Prior Charles added, "A sinner like all of us, not the perfect monk who only hears the voice of God."

"Yes, Prior," I replied almost in a whisper. Then I knelt before Abbot Germanus to kiss his abbot's ring. Before I could rise again, he placed a gentle hand on my shoulder. Then he slapped me very lightly on the right cheek, a slap so soft it was almost a caress. "Our sufferings make us strong," he said. "We are as gold in the Almighty Refiner's fire." An enigma of a smile crossed his face then faded. I bowed to the prior and the head of discipline and left the Scriptorium.

22. Chapter of Faults

Four days later, Easter Thursday, after the monks had chanted the dawn service, I left my seat among the brothers and walked to the middle of the chapel till I stood in front of the prior and Abbot Germanus. Then I kneeled. Once on my knees, I spread my arms in the shape of the cross and intoned, "Father, brothers, please forgive me for I have sinned."

I had done this many times over my 10 years as a monk at Auxerre. Those previous times, I had confessed the minor faults of falling asleep during the service, gossip, anger at another brother. These are the everyday sins of monks. During the long chanting services, each of us sometimes fell asleep, especially during the pre-dawn and late-night services. We all gossiped. Becoming irritated with each other is natural. Confessing these faults, I let no one see me beyond an ordinary monk with ordinary, even boring sins. That day was different.

"I am a thief," I chanted. Not one monk said a word, but I could feel the sudden, collective intake of breath. Thieves are difficult to live with when you have no real personal possessions, like a monk, and share everything in common. Thieves are a great threat to the tranquility of the monastery.

"And I have no honor." I felt every eye on me as I held my own gaze fixed on the body of Jesus on his cross high above the chapel altar. "I stole a ring from my father and allowed my slave, Nevio, to be blamed for that theft. When my father found the ring, I allowed him to think that Nevio had taken it. He cut off the slave's hand in punishment. That same day Nevio was murdered by the Irish pirates who enslaved me, unable to defend himself with one hand. I lost my honor when I allowed another to bear the punishment for my action. Each day since, I have hidden this story. I have continued to live without honor."

Silence filled the chapel. I heard no other steps approaching from the benches, heard no other brother moving to confess his faults. I was alone, exposed, waiting for the judgment of Auxerre.

After a very long while, Prior Charles spoke. "Brother Maewyn," he began, "you have confessed the grievous sin of stealing. Theft threatens the peace of this monastery."

He looked at Abbot Germanus, then at the ranks of monks seated to his left and right. "As penance, you will remain here in this chapel kneeling with your arms held out in prayer until you are released."

The sounds of held breath being let go softly echoed through the space. Prior Charles stood and chanted, "In the name of the Father, the Son, and the Holy Ghost, this chapter of faults is closed, amen."

I looked down to my knees, to the slate flagstones on which I knelt in shame and shock. The brothers rose from their seats, shuffling their feet. I felt when the Abbot left the chapter and heard the brothers begin to leave their places among the benches. No one came to speak to me. No one offered a kind word or encouragement. I was alone in my punishment. Then, when I thought everyone had left the chapel, the voice of Father Aulus spoke from behind.

"Brother Maewyn, you will stay where you are, kneeling until I come to release you. You will keep holding your arms out in prayer, just as you are doing now. I have left Brother Quintus, our youngest novice, with an hourglass to keep time. When the sands run out, Quintus will signal you to stand for five minutes. Then he will signal again for you to resume kneeling. You will obey or you will leave the monastery. Do you understand?"

"Yes, Father Aulus."

I spent that long first day kneeling and standing on the slates of the chapel. By midafternoon, my knees bled, and my arms ached. It took all my willpower to remain in place. Prayer was replaced by the test of endurance. The brothers chanted the noon service and I kneeled. Mass was chanted and I kneeled. The evening service was chanted and I kneeled. After vespers when the brothers had left, Prior Charles returned with our monastery's infirmarian.

"Brother Martin," Prior Charles said, "this monk is to spend the night in the infirmary. Please clean and bind the wounds at his knees. Make sure he has something simple to eat. He is to return to kneeling in the morning when we return for prayer."

I spent all day Friday and again all day Saturday kneeling in the chapel. On Friday night, the infirmarian again cared for my wounds, cleansed my cuts, bound my knees, and brought simple food. I began to thank the prior and Abbot for the very public nature of my penance. My confession of theft had cut the ties of trust that bound me to the monastic community. Confessing my lost honor leveled any sense of specialness or privilege which my years in the community conferred. Yet, my public endurance of the trial won some respect from the brothers. On Thursday, they came and went without a pause, passing me without the slightest suggestion of sympathy. By Friday afternoon, I felt several of them pause as they approached. They stopped just short of passing where I knelt. I could feel them wishing me strength and endurance. By Saturday, their pauses became regular. Whispers of compassion and support floated past me as one brother or another walked to his place among the benches. On Sunday morning, the infirmarian brought word from Prior Charles that I was not to return to the chapel until I was sent for.

Just before Mass, Brother Quintus knocked on the infirmary door. "Brother Maewyn is to come with me," Quintus said. I followed him to the chapel door where he stopped. From the front of the chapel, from beside where Abbot Germanus sat in his abbot's chair, Prior Charles intoned, "Brothers, Maewyn Succat has confessed his sins against this community and done public penance. Do you accept him back into the community of brothers?" A chorus of voices, perhaps even a majority of the brothers, answered, "Yes!"

"If there are any among us who wish to cast Maewyn out from this community of brothers," the prior chanted, "let those brothers stand and say so."

Silence settled among the benches. Those brothers who had remained silent when asked to accept me back held their silence and remained seated. Looking towards me, the prior spoke in a loud, clear voice. "Brother Maewyn, you may enter."

I took my seat among the brothers. We chanted the hymns and prayers for the Mass. I was absolved and absorbed into monastic life once more like a stone dropped into a lake is covered by the waters, leaving individual ripples that fast fade as the lake returns to its ordinary calm or storm.

23. Holding Back

Two hours before vespers on that same Sunday, I was summoned to appear once more before Abbot Germanus, Prior Charles, and Father Aulus. When I entered the small study connected to Abbot Germanus' private rooms, I noticed a smaller version of his abbot's chair and three stools. Prior Charles and Father Aulus sat once more to the right and left of Abbot Germanus. But this time, in front of them, there was a stool for me.

Abbot Germanus had a glint in his eyes. He styled himself in the fashion of old Rome, viewed the monastery as the army of God, and liked toughness in his monks.

Father Aulus wore an expression of grudging respect.

Prior Charles looked sour.

"Last Sunday, you told us the story of your theft and of how you lost your honor," Abbot Germanus began. "Your story was cut short, before you were taken to Ireland. Is there more you have to tell us?"

Those three long days on my knees, with arms spread wide, I had contemplated my answer to this question. Would I tell Abbot Germanus of my nights on Slemmish, of my hand-fasting with Brigid, of being helped by the druid Amergin. I had decided to tell most of it.

"Yes, Father Abbot," I answered.

I told the tale of the journey into slavery. I told how Aitre had captured me and sold me to Ultan, who in turn sold me onwards until I became Muirchil's slave, tending sheep on Slemmish mountain. I spoke once more of beginning to hear a voice in the night, a voice that reminded me of my sins and called me to penance.

Abbot Germanus nodded at this.

I revealed my love for Brigid, and how her father had helped me escape. I told of our hand-fasting.

"A pagan ceremony?" Prior Charles asked, disturbed.

Abbot Germanus raised his hand to still Prior Charles. "A pagan ceremony among slaves in a pagan place." Before he became a monk, the Abbot had studied in Rome and practiced law there in the tribunal of the prefect. Prior Charles began to speak, but Abbot Germanus' look silenced him. He wanted my full story, not the opinion of the prior.

I confessed that I had longed to return to Brigid when I fled the Saxons in Britain. I thought of leaving the monastery of Saint George and returning to Ireland, where I might, as a simple priest, live with her as my wife.

Abbot Germanus leaned forward, inclined his head toward me and asked, "Do you still carry passion for this pagan in your heart?"

"Yes, Father Abbot," I answered. "I still long for her."

Abbot Germanus smiled and sat back. "It is good that you admit this," he said. "You are but a man. All monks are but men. We must learn to hold the fires of passion, to bank them and turn them towards God." Then looking at the prior, he continued, "This fire is only dangerous when it goes out or is denied." Looking at me directly with his penetrating, deep-brown eyes, Abbot Germanus asked, "What of this woman's father, the druid? Did you pray with him to his gods?"

"We did not pray to his gods," I answered. "His name was Amergin, and he told me he was sad that he wouldn't have time to teach me the old ways—"

"This is too much," Prior Charles interjected angrily before the Abbot could silence him. "He brings the ways of pagans into our monastery."

"He had no time to teach me," I answered. "He gave me only an old cloak, a few ring coins, and directions where to flee." This is where I had decided to hold back. I didn't admit that Amergin had told me of the Moringa, the triple god-desses, and of the Duile. I knew if I admitted those things, then Abbot Germanus would have no other choice than to ask me to leave his monastery. I would be spoiled, soiled by pagan teachings, and unworthy of staying. I wanted to stay. The voice of Slemmish still demanded that I seek ordination. I chose to hold back, and on that choice the remainder of my life has hinged.

A battle was being fought in my heart. I believed in the Christ. I believed in the stories of the Old Testament and New Testament. I loved life in the mon-astery. It was simple, beautiful, disciplined. I had a place there. Now that I had admitted my secret shame about my role in Nevio's death, I had the possibility of finding honor and dignity again. It felt like the last chains of slavery were being struck from my wrists. Yet, I still loved Brigid. I loved Ireland with her freedom and fierceness and the wild beauty of the place. I loved that Ireland had its own sense of honor, valuing steadfastness, integrity, and strength of heart. That night, I could have taken either side, that of the church or that of pagan Ireland.

Abbot Germanus, Prior Charles, and Father Aulus looked at me intensely, waiting for more. I had confessed all I was going to confess. While I had spoken, I kept my eyes directed to the floor. In part, I still held the fear that I would be expelled. In part, while I looked down, I could imagine the scenes I spoke of. Also, my passion for Brigid was private, intimate, personal, not something I was used to speaking of. When I was finished speaking, I looked up. My eyes met the deep brown of Abbot Germanus' and held them. I opened the windows to my heart and allowed the Abbot to look in for as long as he wished. Then I looked directly but without challenge at Father Aulus, then into the flint gray eyes of the prior. I returned my gaze downwards, this time not focused on the floor at my feet. I looked toward the feet of Abbot Germanus and waited for one of them to speak.

I felt Abbot Germanus looking, waiting, weighing my story. One moment it felt like he would ask Prior Charles and Father Aulus for their thoughts, but that moment passed.

Finally, he spoke, "Brother Maewyn, you may stay with us here at Auxerre. Before I can consider your request to be ordained, we must become familiar with your heart."

Abbot Germanus paused, then continued. "I need a secretary to assist me, to write messages from the monastery to Rome, to organize the scrolls and messages I receive. You will now take that task—"

Father Aulus interrupted, "But Father Abbot, if Maewyn is to stay here he will be needed in the scriptorium for copying texts."

"Brother Aulus," Prior Charles spoke, reminding the disciplinarian of his monastic rank, "there is wisdom in the Abbot's decision. This way, our Abbot will see daily whether Brother Maewyn is worthy of remaining a monk here at Auxerre. Our Abbot will discern whether the voice Maewyn hears is the voice of pride or the voice of God." He waited a short moment, then added, "We can always train another quill for the scriptorium but how many of us claim to hear the voice of the Almighty?"

Father Aulus relented, nodding his assent. And so, I became secretary to Abbot Germanus, Bishop and Abbot of the monastery at Auxerre.

24. Called to Rome

October, 422 AD

Abbot Germanus didn't speak of his past. I knew some details of his story from reading his correspondence and writing letters for him. Other details I gleaned from how he was received at monasteries and churches. He was born into a propertied and noble family in Roman Gaul. Gaul had been part of the empire since before the first Caesar. After receiving the best Roman education Gaul could offer, young Germanus journeyed to Rome. Almost a decade before I had been captured by the Irish raiders, Germanus was practicing law and impressing senators in the imperial capital. His marriage to Eustacia elevated his status even further.

I once asked him about her when I was alone with him in his private study. "What was she like? Did you have any children with her? What happened to her when you became a bishop and abbot at Auxerre?"

Anger flashed across his eyes at my questions. They were impertinent, not something an ordinary monk, even his secretary, would ask. I felt every muscle in my back, neck, torso, and arms tense at his look. It was like preparing to be whipped. Then his eyes softened and filled with tenderness. My body relaxed and I looked at the Abbot as if for the first time. A man stood in front of me, a man with a grand heart and a sharpened mind.

"Since I compelled you to tell me the tale of your Brigid," he said, "I'll answer your questions about Eustacia." He took a few, long, silent breaths, then continued, "But I will only tell you this tale once, only on the condition that you never repeat it to another monk. Do you agree?"

"Yes, Reverend Abbot," I answered.

"In this tale, I am simply Germanus of Gaul," he began. He told of returning from Rome to his family's properties near the city of Auxerre. His service in Rome had earned him an appointment as governor of the area around the city. While he practiced law and governed, he also earned the enmity of the then Bishop of Auxerre. Abbot Germanus had seen how Rome, now officially Christian, allowed the old ways of honoring the gods to fade slowly in place. No one was punished for making an offering to Jupiter or having a statue of Mars. Pagan festivals and ways were slowly absorbed into the new way. They were baptized and became part of the new religion. "This is the way Rome has always conquered," Abbot Germanus told me. "The new absorbs the strength of the old and grows even stronger.

"So as Governor at Auxerre, I took offerings from the hunt to the sacred tree of the Gauls outside the city. I placed the choicest, best cuts of meat at the base of the tree and left a small offering of wine or mead. The citizens of Auxerre, with roots in both the Frankish tribes and Rome, loved me for honoring the old ways, even as we all went to the Christian church to worship together. However, the Bishop of Auxerre in those days, Bishop Amator, both hated me and respected me for that very thing. He once said to me, 'Our God is a jealous God, He hates your offerings to the pagan idols and will punish you for them.'

"I governed at Auxerre for three years," Abbot Germanus said. "In the second year, Eustacia conceived. Eustacia was beautiful, fascinating, alluring. To look at her was to desire her. Her eyes were amethyst, her face the face of the goddess, Diana. She could read and write, which was very unusual then. We spent days together talking of poetry and philosophy. At night, our bodies spoke the language of love. She died with our first child still in her womb. I try not to remember the days of blood, of her crying out in pain from our bed, of the women carrying pots of steaming water and clean white cloths to her, then coming out of the room with pots of bloodied water and rags. They told me later that our son—yes, the child would have been a boy—became stuck while being born. Only his tiny right foot emerged from Eustacia before she bled to death."

My heart was pierced by the sadness of Abbot Germanus' story and by the look of complete desolation that settled on his face. "After her death, of course I continued to govern and, to the best of my ability, honor the old and new ways at Auxerre." Abbot Germanus lapsed into a long stillness before continuing. Gradually, as sorrow left his eyes and face, tranquility took its place.

"Amator ensnared me one Sunday after Mass. He asked that I remain behind when the ceremony was finished. When the doors were closed, I was surrounded by his monks. He told me that he was very ill, soon to die, and needed a successor. He begged me to take robes as a monk and told his followers that God had told him that I'd be the next Bishop of Auxerre." Germanus paused and smiled at me.

"You heard the voice of God on Slemmish," he said, "I heard the voice of Amator."

He finished his story rather abruptly as another monk rapped on the door to the study and interrupted. "That is how I was called to be bishop and abbot. That is all there is to say."

My heart was touched by Abbot Germanus' tale. He once loved a woman, just as I now did. She still filled his thoughts with tenderness, desire, and sadness. Fortune had turned joy to sorrow for him just as it had for me. He had lost Eustacia and their unborn son. I had been captured by pirates and lost family and home. The old ways had a place of honor in his tale, just as they still had a place in my heart. We were both strong Christians who remembered the strength of the old ways. He had lost a wife and a son. I had lost a lover and a father.

I was walking south, with Abbot Germanus and a party of monks, to Rome and to the Pope. Germanus, as abbot, rode a pony. Our baggage of hand-painted copies of the Bible, cooking pots, and tents fit on the backs of three mules. Seven monks accompanied the Abbot for his safety and to assist him when he reached Rome.

Some nights, we found a place to sleep in a church or monastery along the way. Most nights, we slept under the cover of the stars. Fortune and the lingering effect of Roman law favored us. We encountered no bandits along the road. Our party rose each day, hours before dawn, to chant the first service, cook a simple meal, and load the mules. Two weeks of steady walking south by east brought us to the fortified Roman city of Turin. The monastery there allowed us to stay for almost a week. Abbot Germanus was offered a room in the monastery. The remainder of us slept under the arches of the monastery cloister at night.

Imperial Roman roads still afforded the best route of travel between Gaul and Rome. Waves of barbarian tribes had crashed against and over the sea wall of Rome's legions to flood the empire. Twelve years previous, only two years after I first arrived at Auxerre, the horde of the Visigoth chieftain, Alaric, had breached the walls of Rome and sacked the city. For safety, a weakened emperor moved the capital north from the Eternal City to Milan. Just four years ago, Emperor Honorius granted the invaders the rights of kings in southwestern Gaul. Now that same emperor lay dying at Milan, and Abbot Germanus had a critical mission to see the Bishop of Rome.

Abbot Germanus told us, as we left Turin and headed for the capital, "The soul of Christ's church is in danger. First, God withdrew his support from the emperor. Now a pernicious and seductive voice spreads its poison in the ears of the faithful. We go onward to Rome, to rouse the Pope to defend Christ's body."

Our party reached Rome five weeks after leaving Auxerre. Leaving Milan and heading south, we stayed in monasteries or churches along the ancient road. Placenza, Parma, Modena, Florence, Orvieto, Viterbo, these were just a few of the places where our party halted for the night. In each monastery Abbot Germanus was welcomed as an honored abbot and famous citizen of the empire. The welcome for our party steadily improved, moving inside from under the arches to sleeping on the benches in monastic dining halls, to being offered individual sleeping cells in the monasteries of Orvieto and Viterbo.

It was at Viterbo that we heard that Pope Boniface had died, and that Celestine of Milan had been elected to replace him. As secretary to Abbot Germanus, I was very familiar with the name of Celestine of Milan, who was now Bishop of Rome.

On our way to Rome, other abbots deferred to Abbot Germanus, seeking his opinion about teachings of the faith. More than once, the Abbot of a monastery along the way between Auxerre and Milan gave up their personal room to host the great Abbot Germanus. He had gravitas and dignity. So, I was prepared for the reception we received when we arrived at Rome.

We crested a hill just after dawn, walking along the old Roman highway, the Via Flaminia, and saw the Aurelian walls of the city.

"Those walls are 11 feet thick and 26 feet high," Abbot Germanus said to our party. "There are guard towers and forts built every 100 feet along them. And behind the walls shelter almost 800,000 souls."

That number itself was incredible. It was the largest city in the world. More people were behind the walls of Rome than lived in all of Britain.

"When Alaric left the city, he took with him 5,000 pounds of gold, 30,000 pounds of silver, and most of the city's slaves. But he let the citizens of Rome keep their lives and didn't burn the city to the ground."

Abbot Germanus smiled the smile of a man returning to a place of the memories of his youth as his pony carried him across the Flavian Gate into the city. The rest of us were silenced by the size of the place.

I was in awe of Rome. Building after building crowded her streets and rose to the skies, most three stories tall, some four or even five stories high. Not a thatched roof nor wattle-daubed wall was in sight. The walls were marble and brick and worked stone. The roofs were tile and wood. The citizens of Rome were everywhere, thick as ants on a hill, carrying burdens in and out of buildings, mothers chasing children and children running away, the sounds of hammer on wood or stone sounding from within. Twelve years after being sacked by the Goths, Rome's heart beat strong with life. I fell in love with the city.

Our journey took us across Rome's vibrant breadth from its northern most gate to the Caelian Hill in the southwest. We halted at the entrance to the plaza of the Lateran Palace, the home of the Bishop of Rome. My mouth gaped open as I looked across the large public square. To one side lay the palace of the Bishop of Rome, now the principal citizen of the city since the emperor had fled north. Across the plaza lay the impressively grand Basilica of Saint John, built on the former grounds of the barracks of the imperial calvary. And in the middle of the plaza, like a finger pointing to God, the Lateran obelisk rose 150 feet into the sky.

Abbot Germanus said, "Dedicated by a pharaoh to their god of the sun, it was brought from Egypt by the son of Constantine to honor his father's conversion to the Son of God."

I couldn't make any sense of the picture writing on the obelisk but could read the Latin at its base, "For Constantine who gained victory through the cross, baptized into the glory of that cross by Silvester, Bishop of Rome."

Abbot Germanus laughed as he saw me parsing the meaning of the Latin inscription.

"Actually, that's a lie," he said. "Constantine was baptized by Eusebius, Bishop of Nicomedia. But Eusebius was a heretic. Silvester re-baptized the emperor on his death bed." After a short breath, he added, "The bishops of Rome have a gift for writing history in their favor."

Abbot Germanus dismounted near the obelisk and handed the reigns to one of the monks. Gathering our party together he told us, "The Holy Father summoned us here. The priests and monks of St. John's Basilica are expecting us. I will take Maewyn with me and let them know at the Lateran palace that we have arrived. The rest of you, find the brother in charge of hospitality at St. John's. Let him know we are here, that we all will need rooms, and that this pony needs to be stabled and fed."

Heads nodded all around, welcoming the promise of a room in a monastery after more than five weeks on the road.

"How long will we be here?" one of the brothers asked.

"As long as the Holy Father needs us," Abbot Germanus answered, then turned around and walked towards the palace.

The suddenness of his turning caught me by surprise. We were in Rome now. Abbot Germanus commanded our squad of monks. He expected to be obeyed as much as he expected himself to obey the summons of the Pope. He was a general reporting to his emperor, except that emperor had been succeeded by the Bishop of Rome. He expected me to follow him without questions and equally for the other monks to find rooms and a place for the pony without question. You give an order; it is carried out. Receive an order; you carry it out.

25. Grandeur

I caught up with Abbot Germanus at the entrance to the palace. A pair of massive doors covered in bronze, each taller than the height of two men, stood framed within carved-stone pillars. The doors themselves were adorned. They were carved into squares holding rosettes of flowers. Each flower was wider than the spread of my hand. Above the door was a crest of crossed keys carved in stone with a legend underneath. We hastened so quickly through the opening that I didn't have time to read it. The palace was grander than any building I had ever been in. The floors were marble-colored tiles. I saw the chi-rho anagram for the first two letters of Christ's name inlaid within the marble. Further on, we passed a mosaic memorializing the story of Constantine's vision, a cross appearing in the sky with the words floating above and around it: "With this sign you will conquer." And that was just a small part of the floor.

Stately grand columns lined the hall holding a decorated roof at least 35 feet above the floor. The palace's pagan decoration had been erased. The ceiling panels were painted with sacred symbols, the chi-rho, the cross, the papal keys, chalices, and angels. Empty niches for statues stood in between grand columns. Statues of the gods and emperors had been removed. Only three statues remained: Blessed Constantine who had brought the empire to Christ; Saint Helena, his mother, who uncovered the true cross and brought that relic to Rome; and Pope Saint Sylvester memorialized on the obelisk in the palazzo.

I was a simple monk then. I had grown up on a farm where a square building with a porch stood out as a sign of Rome's civilizing influence. The monastery of St. George paled in size to the grandeur of Auxerre with its scriptorium for more than 60 monks and its chapel that could hold more than 100. Auxerre's chapel rose to the height of 30 feet and was more than 100 feet long. Three of Auxerre's chapels would have fit in the space I crossed as we entered the palace. This was just the first of three floors. My awe alternated with wonderment and shock. I hastened to follow Abbot Germanus who, unfazed, seemed to take everything in stride.

He headed across the floor towards a clutch of priests and soldiers busy in conversation. Three paces from this group, Abbot Germanus paused and waited to be recognized. One of the priests glanced up to take in who was waiting, then quickly returned his gaze to the documents he held in his hand. He looked up again suddenly as recognition crossed his eyes. "Germanus, is it truly you?"

"Regulus," Abbot Germanus said and held out his arms in greeting. "Old friend." Their embrace and kiss of peace announced bonds of remembered camaraderie.

"We were students together here in Rome," Abbot Germanus said looking at me. "We practiced law together. When I left Rome with Eustacia, Regulus had just taken tonsure and become a member of the clergy."

Abbot Germanus looked back at his old comrade. "You have done well, Regulus," the Abbot declared. "The chain of office around your neck is that of the archdeacon of Rome and chamberlain to the Holy Father, no?"

"Yes," Regulus said, now holding his friend at arm's length. "You are here, so you received the letter I sent for Pope Boniface summoning you?" Abbot Germanus nodded. "And who is this young monk with you?" the chamberlain asked.

"My secretary, Brother Maewyn," Abbot Germanus answered, adding, "I'd like Pope Celestine to meet him. He's a worthy candidate for the mission that the Holy Father has in mind."

Regulus turned a longer, evaluative eye toward me. His head tilted slightly to the right as he asked, "Germanus, are you sure? So much rests on our choices now."

Abbot Germanus placed a brotherly hand on Regulus' arm and leaned in softly to say, "Yes, I am sure. You know I've chosen well in the past. I am sure." The chamberlain and the Abbot both looked at me. Then Abbot Germanus said, "Now let's talk about what is so troubling that His Holiness sent for me."

I followed, acknowledged but unspoken to, just listening.

Regulus began, "Belvedere[1] was made a bishop and sent by Boniface to convert Ireland. His work bore little fruit, a few small churches, fewer than 100 converts. News of Belvedere's death reached Rome shortly before Boniface died."

---

1   The actual missionary was Bishop Paladius. I renamed him to avoid confusion with Pelagius.

The chamberlain looked over his shoulder to make sure his next words were not overheard. "However, Pelagius' poisonous words have met thousands of willing ears in Gaul, Britain, and beyond."

I couldn't contain my curiosity. "Why do people listen to his words and what makes them so dangerous?"

"Brother Maewyn goes directly to the heart of the problem, doesn't he?" said Germanus, covering my breach of etiquette. As a monk secretary, I was expected to listen and remember, not to speak or ask questions.

"Indeed, he does," smiled Regulus. "He reminds me of a young lawyer of Rome I once knew."

Considering his next words carefully, the chamberlain continued., "Pelagius teaches men that they already have everything they need to reach heaven. They don't need God's church. That is the essence of his poison and the danger in his words."

I nodded understanding even while my eyes furrowed with questions.

"The questions are," Regulus continued, "why and how much do we need God's grace and where does that grace come from?

"Pelagius preaches that men are created good with the possibility of heaven and hell already within each heart. All each of us needs do is choose."

A pause allowed me to take in the theological point.

"The grace of Christ merely empowers us to choose what is already here, so the church and bishops and Rome are not needed. It is the perfect teaching for an empire that is falling apart."

Abbot Germanus added, "If we can each choose from our heart what is good, then each man will call his choice good no matter what he chooses. There will be no law. Piety will be replaced by barbarism. The faithful need to be convinced that they require God's grace to be saved and even more that they need God's church to find that grace."

"That's the legal mind I remember!" Regulus exclaimed. "This is precisely why Boniface summoned you. You will know the arguments to make against Pelagius to win back his followers. Come, let me escort you to the papal audience hall."

Regulus turned and led the way towards a set of stairs. Abbot Germanus followed him, and I followed Germanus. The stairs seemed quite ordinary, except for the two monks and a nun climbing them very slowly on their knees. As we passed them, I heard each of them praying on their step before scaling the next one. Abbot Germanus paused at the top of the stairs and waited.

"These are the sacred stairs that Christ climbed when he was summoned to see Pilate and was condemned to death on the cross," Abbot Germanus said. "Constantine's mother, Helena, brought them back from the province of Palestine almost 100 years ago."

"Yes, yes," Regulus joined in. He had come back from hurrying to the papal chambers to see what was causing the delay. "The stairs remind us of Christ's death and that we all climb to judgment." Then, with an exasperated look he said, "And if we don't wish to be judged as laggards, we'll hurry to the Pope's council chamber. This way," he pointed down the hall and shepherded us towards another grand set of double doors.

Soldiers guarded the doors. They wore the kit of the Legions, thigh-length skirts of leather adorned with insignias of their rank, breast plates of polished bronze, and helmets with crests of horsehair dyed alternately red and purple. Each of the soldiers stood with the gladius sword at his side and held a long spear. Their crossed spears barred entry. Both legionaries looked grim.

Regulus whispered something to one of them. He raised his spear and said simply, "They are allowed to pass."

I looked at the second guard, still standing with his spear barring the door, and grinned. My eyes met his. He appeared to be a few years younger than me. I could have been him, on duty with Aed at Calleva. My grin was one of recognition between two young men. His dark-brown eyes met mine as he raised his spear, and a slight smile crossed his face.

"I've never seen one of them smile," Regulus said to Abbot Germanus while looking at me with renewed attention.

The audience hall was as large as the chapel at Auxerre, 30 feet long with a ceiling at least 20 feet high. A slight figure robed in deep scarlet sat on a chair at the hall's far end. Around and in front of him clustered priests and monks. A brace of legionaries stood behind the scarlet robe's chair. To the side, a table stood cluttered with parchments and maps. The scarlet figure looked up as we entered. The room dropped into hushed stillness.

"Chamberlain," the scarlet figure cawed. "Who have you brought with you?"

"Abbot Germanus of Auxerre has answered the summons, Your Holiness," Regulus answered. "He has just arrived in Rome. This," he said pointing at me, "is his secretary and assistant, Maewyn Succat, from Britannia Prima and also a monk of Auxerre."

Regulus bowed a deep bow and Abbot Germanus echoed his bow. My grin faded as I felt the weight of all the eyes of the room upon me. I bowed deeply and held the bow until I was certain that both Regulus and Abbot Germanus had stood straight. As I raised my head, I saw Abbot Germanus move to kneel at the foot of the scarlet robe's chair and kiss the ring on his right hand.

"Holiness, your servants are here," I heard him say as Regulus motioned for me to also kneel and kiss the papal ring.

"Your Holiness," I whispered and kissed the ring.

Celestine motioned for both of us to rise from where we knelt. "You must be weary from your travels," he said. "Your robes carry the dust of many roads." Then he turned to Regulus and gestured to the maps and parchments, saying, "Today's conversations focus on grain shipments to the city. Rome is a dangerous mistress when she is hungry." Looking once more at Abbot Germanus and me, he said, "Allow our brothers time to refresh themselves. Then bring them to the ceremonies in the chapel at sunset."

Regulus motioned for Abbot Germanus and me to back away from the papal throne. Celestine returned his focus to the discussion of grain shipments. We left the audience hall and were shown to our rooms.

I had a meal of bread, cheese, and dark-purple grapes, a fruit I had never tasted before. I beat the dust from my robes as best I could. I rested on the cot assigned to me. A dry room inside, with a large window to allow in fresh air and the early-afternoon light, a simple stool, and a basin of water—these were luxuries after the long walk to Rome.

26. Bell, Book, and Candle

Brother Fabian of Auxerre knocked at the door to my cell. "Maewyn," he said somewhat out of breath. "The Abbot waits for you outside, near the obelisk." A few hastened breaths in and out sped from Fabian. "He sent me to run and tell you that it is almost sunset. You are both expected at the palace."

Looks of surprise, excitement, and question darted across Fabian's face. As I rested, I didn't recognize the passage of the hours. I had simply collapsed, overawed by the power of Rome. Almost before Fabian was done delivering his message, I rushed from the cell to meet Abbot Germanus.

When I reached the obelisk, Abbot Germanus simply turned and walked quickly towards the palace. I fell into step behind him. We met Regulus near the entryway. He led us, once more, up the sacred stairs to the Pope's chapel. We were ushered inside this shrine to Saint Lawrence the Martyr. We waited in the gathering twilight silence for Celestine and the ceremony.

My eyes, ears, nose, and hands were full of the majesty of the place. The ceiling was painted gold. A mosaic of Christ, the ruler of all, sitting in judgment on the world adorned the space over the altar. In front of and to the right of the main altar sat a marble throne chair with crossed keys on its back. The floors were inlaid with designs of the crossed keys, the alpha and omega, the Christian fish symbol, and the red crown of martyrdom. We sat on cool marble benches along the side of the chapel. The aroma of frankincense and sandalwood incense filled the space. On one wall, twice as large as life, was a gilded wood painting of the death of Saint Lawrence.

I knew from Regulus, before we entered the chapel, that Lawrence had been one of the seven deacons of Rome killed on the orders of the Emperor Valerian. Nearly 200 years before, he was killed by being grilled over an open fire. In addition to the crime of being a Christian, Lawrence had refused to hand over the riches of the church when the emperor demanded them.

Three loud knocks of a staff pounding against the doors behind the altar startled me from my consideration of Lawrence. A long pause was followed by three more repeated knocks. An even longer pause ended with a third set of knocks. Then the doors were pushed open by legionaries in full armor, swords drawn. A younger monk swinging a censor led a procession of 12 deacons and priests. Each held a candle, half as tall as a man and thicker than my fist. Each of the 12 candles, with thick brass rings, cradled flames at their heads. Two bishops wearing miters followed the candles. One held a large book bound with heavy, blood-red leather and studded with jewels. The second carried a large bell on a cushion in front of him. The bell was square, fashioned from bronze, with a hand grip adorned with a gold cross.

Last, at the head of the procession came Celestine. Starched-white robes showed under night-black vestments. He wore the stole of a priest. The short band around his shoulders, signifying his rank as an archbishop, and his great cape were all in the deepest black, studded with gems and adorned with the chi-rho symbol in gold. On his head he wore a pure white miter of a bishop with a single black stripe down its center. His eyes were terrible.

The procession halted in mid-chapel with Celestine standing in front of his throne. The bishop with the bronze bell stood just to the pope's left. The bishop with the jeweled book opened the tome and stood slightly to Celestine's right.

"In the name of God, the all-powerful, Judge of All, and of blessed Peter, chief of all apostles, with the strength of the power given Peter and all his heirs to bind or loose in heaven or hell, we cut Pelagius of Britain away from the body of Christ. We cast him out from the city of God and from the company of all believers. We exclude him from the nurturing kindness of holy mother church and declare him excommunicate and anathema."

Celestine reached to his left and vigorously rang the bronze bell. Returning the bell to its cushion, he continued, "We publicly declare Pelagius condemned to hell, and all those who follow his teachings condemned along with him until the day that he repents his poisonous errors and publicly prostates in penance before the bishop of Rome. Until that day, Pelagius is a non-person, outside the laws of God and man, damned and doomed."

Celestine nodded towards the bishop on his right to close the jeweled book. As the book slammed shut, Celestine declared, "Judgment is issued on Pelagius of Britain, heretic and enemy of God."

The 12 priests and deacons holding their candles chanted together, "So be it, so be it," and dashed their candles to the ground.

The bishop holding the jeweled book declared, "The bell has been rung, the book has been closed, the light of Pelagius dashed out in the eyes of God. Let the word go out."

Then the young monk holding the censor led the procession of priests, deacons, bishops, and Pope back to where they entered the chapel. Two legionaries, still holding their swords drawn at attention, pulled the great wooden doors shut. The procession disappeared. All that remained was the scent of authority and 12 extinguished candles strewn across the marble tiles.

27. God's Silence

The young monk who led the procession with the censor re-emerged just a few breaths after the doors closed. He walked directly to where we sat and whispered something to Regulus. Then he left.

Regulus turned to look first at Abbot Germanus, then at me. "The three of us are summoned to meet the Pope in the vestry—now."

Abbot Germanus and Regulus both quickly rose from their seats. Two steps from where we sat, Regulus turned and looked to me.

I was still sitting.

"What is it?" he demanded. "A summons for now means immediately."

Abbot Germanus reached out a hand to soften Regulus' ire. "He's seeing the power of Rome," the Abbot said, "the full power of the Roman church for his first time. You and I might forget, but it is shocking."

I looked at Abbot Germanus. His deep brown eyes were full of understanding. He had the glimpse of a smile and his head tilted ever so slightly towards me, as if he were calling me to join him. "Brother Maewyn, look down at your feet and take a long, deep breath."

When I accomplished that breath, he continued, "Gather your wits and come with us."

I rose from the bench. The Abbot turned and walked with the chamberlain towards the vestry door. I hastened to join them.

After the grandeur of the Papal chapel, the vestry appeared normal to me. Its high ceilings were covered with carved wood panels. The floor showed a simple diamond inlay. The cabinets that worked their way around three sides of the room were of excellent quality, well-made, solid, strong, yet undecorated. Celestine stood in his scarlet robes. The cape and white miter he wore for the excommunication ceremony were arranged on top of the cabinet behind him. He looked up as we entered.

Regulus and Abbot Germanus immediately went to Celestine, kneeled on one knee before him, and kissed his ring. I followed their example. The three of us stood and waited for the Pope to speak. Celestine held his words while there were still other clergymen in the room. A single nod with a grave look on his face was all that he communicated.

The brass censor was cleaned of its burned coals and hung in its place. The jeweled book was returned to the Pope's private library. Two other miters rested upon the cabinets along with the bishops' vestments. Celestine remained silently standing.

When the four of us were alone in the room, he closed his eyes for a long while and rocked on his feet, gently to and fro. I looked at Regulus. Then Abbot Germanus gave the slightest of gestures, one I knew well from Auxerre. "Wait!" it commanded. "Keep your place."

Celestine's eyes fluttered briefly, then opened. He looked up, looked directly at each of us, first at Abbot Germanus, then Regulus, then finally at me. "Just now, I was listening for the voice of God," he began. Three heads nodded, eager to hear what the vicar and regent of Christ would say next.

"I felt God's silence," Celestine said. "The authority to bind or loose has been placed in my hands. Along with that authority is the responsibility for Christ's Church."

Again, three heads acknowledged.

"You witnessed the ceremony. Pelagius is now cut off from the love of God."

Once more, three heads bowed, indicating understanding.

"I need your help to carry out that sentence." Celestine looked straight into my eyes as Abbot Germanus and Regulus nodded.

"If God wills, I will live another 10 years," Celestine said. "However, the chair of Peter seems to speed men to their graves," he added with a wry smile. "Germanus, if I live another decade, you could sit next on the chair of Peter."

Shock reverberated among us. "You have the skill, you're a citizen of the empire, educated here in Rome, a lawyer, a rhetorician, former governor of a province, an abbot." He paused. "The choice, of course, will be up to the seven papal electors. I will be gone to my reward, and they will rule until the next Peter is chosen. But with my support, I am confident they would choose well."

I never saw Abbot Germanus at a loss for words until that moment. His jaw dropped slightly, and he looked to his left and right as if searching for anything to say. "You would have to leave Auxerre," Celestine added.

Finally finding his words, Abbot Germanus said, "I am God's servant, Your Holiness. Whatever He commands through you, I will do." I saw him look Celestine directly in the eyes, then look down humbly and wait for the command.

"Excellent," pronounced Celestine as he turned round and placed his right hand upon the jeweled black and gold robes on the cabinet behind him. Then, as if speaking to the robes, he added, "Before you come back to Rome, I have a mission for you." Abbot Germanus' head rose quickly to attention. "The bell has been rung. The judgment of Pelagius must be carried to where it will have its greatest effect."

"The heretic has many followers in Southern Gaul," Regulus interjected.

I wondered later if the drama I witnessed was planned, if Celestine had coached Regulus when to suggest Southern Gaul for Germanus' mission. Southern Gaul was still nominally within the Empire and an easy journey from Auxerre. I watched as Abbot Germanus imagined a pilgrimage from Rome to Paris, Chartres, Orleans, Lyon, and beyond.

"Pelagius lives and spreads his poison in Britain," Celestine said as he turned back to look at Germanus. "I need someone to take the word to the Church in Britain, someone to cauterize the poison where it lives, where it is strongest."

If this was a court of law, I would think that Abbot Germanus had been cleverly trapped by Celestine into agreeing to go beyond the Empire, to leave his beloved Auxerre for the wattle and daub of Britain. But that would mean that the encounter was orchestrated, staged, maybe even rehearsed, and not the voice of Peter repeating the command of God.

"I will go wherever Your Holiness bids," Abbot Germanus said.

"And you, Maewyn Succat of Britannia Prima, will you follow your Abbot?" Celestine said now looking at me.

"I am God's servant," I answered, echoing Abbot Germanus but alert for any hidden meanings.

"Brother Maewyn has requested ordination as a priest," Abbot Germanus asserted. "I brought him with me to Rome to recommend him to Your Holiness.

He is a good monk, full hearted in his devotion to Christ, obedient, smart, and occasionally even funny."

Celestine's head turned at this last remark. "Obedient, smart, devoted we hear recommended constantly. Funny is unusual." He looked directly at me and asked, "How is funny useful to God's Church?"

I raised my gaze and looked openly into his deep gray eyes. They were like a gathering storm over ocean waves. "God freed me from slavery in Ireland to make me his servant."

Celestine replied, "Wit is rare in the councils of God's church. It opens the heart to receive the deeper meaning of God's word." He bent his head towards me with a smile that bordered between warmth and chill, "Maewyn Succat, are you an obedient servant or willful?"

I remembered the brief discussion of Pelagius with Regulus and Abbot Germanus and I answered, "Your Holiness, I count upon the grace of God and strength of His Church to tame my willfulness. I aspire to obedience but am merely a man." Then looking at those stormy gray eyes directly, I added, "like all others," and bowed my head.

For the first time I heard Celestine laugh. "Germanus, you have tamed a tiger. He's much too dangerous to leave in Rome. Perhaps his tiger's wit will win converts among the Celts. He should accompany you to Britain and then continue onwards to Ireland."

Regulus leaned in and whispered something in Celestine's ear. "Yes, yes," he said and looked at Regulus. "Rome's previous missionary to Ireland, Belvedere, has died. Word of his death arrived in August, and we haven't had the time to appoint the next apostle to Ireland." Without asking if I was willing, ready, or able, Celestine pronounced, "Maewyn Succat, you will carry the word of God to Ireland as our missionary and as our Bishop."

28. Patrick

I raised my head to look at Celestine, then Abbot Germanus, then back at the Pope. I felt my eyes widen. My heart suddenly tightened against the jolt of Celestine's words like when it tightened against the shock of that burlap thrown over my head by Irish pirates. My muscles tightened as if I was about to be whipped. I was to be carried to Ireland once again without any choice of my own. Jolted from my silence by Celestine's pronouncement, I stammered, "I am Your Holiness' humble servant."

Celestine held out his ringed right hand. I genuflected and kissed the papal ring. As I rose, he said, "Maewyn is not a proper name for you as you carry our words to Ireland."

I waited, held by the command of this scarlet robed master of Rome. "You carry the richness of God's word, from this moment onward you are called Patrick." Celestine stepped forward and offered me the kiss of brotherhood. "Patrick of Ireland."

The next two weeks were a blur of ceremony, conference, and change. My monastic companions on the trip from Auxerre to Rome were Fabian, Gaius, Crispus, Blaise, Silas, and Otho. We knew each other with an easy familiarity that comes from tasks shared over many years. Silas and Blaise were younger than me as monks, having entered the monastery less than 10 years ago. But we were all brothers. We prayed together several times each day. At Auxerre, most of them labored in the scriptorium where I was still allowed to work occasionally. On the road, we made camp together, gathered firewood together, carried water together. Blaise, the youngest among us, kidded me one night on the road as we prepared our camp. We were cutting some wood with two hand axes when he said with a grin, "I see now, the hands of a secretary do still know how to swing the blade."

I laughed back to him, saying, "Be careful. These old hands know how to keep all their fingers. You might become secretary one day if you keep all of yours."

It seemed like nothing at the time, only the banter of two friends, two brothers at work. When I returned from the palace with Abbot Germanus, all the casual ribbing and small talk was supplanted with a respectful distance. Silas met us at the door to the Monastery of St. John's. He bowed to Abbot Germanus and sustained that bow as he told me, "Brother Maewyn, the brother in charge of hospitality has asked me to show you to new rooms."

I turned, startled and full of questions. Monks love order and regularity. Our lives are built upon the stately repetition of ancient ceremonies and feasts, upon careful observance of traditions and calendars and rites. Change is most often unwelcome, met with suspicion.

"Brother hospitaller has already had your things moved to your new quarters," Silas added. I saw a slight smile cross Abbot Germanus' eyes.

"His Holiness has given brother Maewyn the name 'Patrick,'" Abbot Germanus told Silas. "He is now to be addressed with that name."

Then the Abbot turned to me. "Words fly in Rome and gossip flies swiftest of all. It seems that news of the Pope's choice of you for bishop reached here before we did."

I know he saw my confusion. "When we left just before sunset, you were simply one of the brothers. You return as the bishop elect for Ireland. Many things begin to change around you. It will be best if you can change with the changes."

"Your quarters are this way, Brother Patrick," Silas said pointing down the same corridor that led to Abbot Germanus' rooms and those rooms of the prior of St. John's.

I followed him, hesitant, fearful, holding the Abbot's advice about accepting change in my heart. My new quarters were the same, yet different from before. Like the other room, this one contained a cot, a stool, and a basin of water. But they were more nobly made. This room had two windows rather than just one and was almost half again larger than the first. Underneath the second window, the room also had a bench for kneeling and praying. And a small, simple wooden table stood available for texts or parchments. I found the flat emptiness of the tabletop sadder than expected. I was used to only seeing tables in the scriptorium or official rooms. Abbot Germanus had a table in his rooms at Auxerre that was always full of papers and texts. The wide-open quality of the vacant tabletop spoke volumes to me. Much was about to be demanded.

Three hours before dawn the next morning, I made my way to St. John's chapel for the first prayers of the day. As I approached the benches where we monks sat and chanted, I saw that my usual place between Otho and Fabian was gone. We sat in order of seniority. I had become a monk after Otho and just before Fabian. I walked to my place and gestured for the two of them to make space. Keeping silence, they grinned and vigorously shook their heads, "No."

Then Otho signaled by wagging his right thumb to an open space, the most senior space to the far right. My eyebrows knit in question as I looked at him. I shrugged my shoulders, pantomimed with raised, open palms the question, "What's happening?" Otho simply repeated the gesture, his grin settling into a smile. He wagged his thumb again and reinforced the expression with a nod to the right. The only open spot on that bench lay between Abbot Germanus and Silas, the most senior monk. Neither reacted as I took my seat between them. Suddenly, Silas began to tap his feet against the stone floor. One after another, Silas, Otho, Fabian, Crispus, Gaius, and Blaise joined in the rhythmic tapping. My heart was full. This was an ancient, wordless sign among silent brothers of full acceptance and support. They were cheering my election as bishop.

The ceremonies progressively left me dazzled and fascinated. I lay on the floor with my arms outstretched to form a cross as Abbot Germanus and the monks called upon all the saints to help me. I kneeled before Germanus as he placed his hands on my head and called down the Holy Ghost to empower me. Finally, he anointed my hands with sacred oil and bound them with fine, unused white linen.

"Now that you are a priest, is the voice you hear satisfied?" Abbot Germanus asked afterwards in the vestry of the chapel at St. John's.

I nodded, "Yes." The voice of Slemmish was indeed stilled within my thoughts. I felt a quiet joy.

"It is all good," the Abbot added. "Prepare yourself for the rest of today. Tomorrow, you become a bishop."

On November 25, the feast of Saint Catherine of Alexandria, I was consecrated Bishop of Ireland. I remember the saint's day because Celestine mentioned her in the words he addressed to me before the ceremony. "Catherine offered up her life," he said, "refusing even the offer of marriage to the Emperor Maxentius, preferring the Gospels above all worldly glory. You must do the same." On orders from the emperor, Catherine was beheaded 117 years before I became a Bishop. On Catherine's day, Celestine held the book of the Gospels above my head and commanded me to be true to that book above all else. He anointed my head and invested me with the miter, ring, and shepherd's staff of a bishop. As the priests and monks of the Lateran chanted hymns to end the ceremony, I was shocked to hear the voice of Slemmish begin speaking again. *You are my shepherd now,* the voice said. *Mine.*

PART 4

IRELAND

29. Pride and Discomfort

April 423 AD

Salt spray and the roar of the surf at the front of an early spring storm roused me from my reverie. I stood on an ocean cliff, not far from the Roman settlement of Deva and looked out from Britain across the Irish Sea. Four and a half months had passed since our party left Rome. I was a different man, called by a different name, but gazing across the same sea I had twice already crossed.

Our journey from Rome to Auxerre had a bittersweet quality. Before we left Rome, Abbot Germanus procured a second pony and demanded that I ride alongside him. My elevation to bishop had happened so quickly. I was challenged to adapt.

Previously, I had shared all the work with the brothers. Now they saw to all the details of breaking camp in the morning, preparing our ponies for the day's journey, and setting camp back up at night. They cut wood, carried water, cooked the food. I was expected to bide by Abbot Germanus' side while these labors were accomplished. Once or twice on our long walk back to Auxerre, I stepped in to carry firewood or build a shelter for the evening's rest.

The first time I slipped back from bishop to humble brother, Abbot Germanus found me with an armload of wood. "Patrick," he said with gentleness in his voice, "we have things to discuss. Allow the brothers to gather wood for the fire."

The second time was a rain-filled night. I had sat on a pony for a long, wet day. We halted at a clearing somewhere in the mountainous woods between Milan and Lyon. It was quite far from the nearest monastery or church. In fact, it had been two days since we had seen a town or farm of any size. I was impatient to be out of the rain and thought to myself, *we'd be dry sooner if we had six monks working and one bishop waiting instead of two bishops and only five sets of hands to arrange cover and gather wood.*

I tethered my pony to a low-hanging branch and looked for where I could be helpful. I tried to help Otho and Fabian tie a tarp between trees for a shelter. They both shook their heads when I asked one of them to pass me the rope. Fabian asked me, "Does Bishop Patrick think we are not equal to the task? Or would you take our monk's work from us and leave us with nothing to do?"

I was stunned. I told myself that I was only trying to help. But in truth, I was merely impatient, irritable, and wet. I returned to where I had tied my pony to the tree.

Abbot Germanus had tied his pony alongside mine. "This is a good place for the horses to rest," he said when I returned. I could tell from his expression that he knew I had gone to help the brothers. I loved him at that moment for not saying anything about it. "Let's talk about how long we will stay at Auxerre," he began, "and how we will carry out Celestine's mission."

Pride and discomfort struggled within my heart for supremacy. I could hardly believe how quickly my status had changed. The homeless man who had fled his family and found a happy refuge in the life of a simple monk was replaced by a bishop, a man of status and power, a man with a personal mission from the Bishop of Rome. Instead of being a servant, the monks now acted like servants towards me. Before, where I had six brotherly comrades and an abbot as leader; now I had five men looking to me for leadership. My only brother was Abbot Germanus. At that moment in the woods, I found the pride of status lonely.

When we finally reached Auxerre, Abbot Germanus suggested that we rest for a month before going onwards to Britain and Ireland. Our rest would allow him time to set the affairs of the monastery in order. My few possessions were moved from my cell to the guest rooms for a visiting bishop. Abbot Germanus informed me that I would be allowed to take two monks from Auxerre as companions for my journey. They would be under my command, see to my daily needs, and help me as I saw fit. Those days at Auxerre were filled with contemplation, long hours deciding which brothers would be most helpful among the Irish, and long conversations with Abbot Germanus.

30. Inventing Saints and Heretics

One late afternoon, as vespers approached, I asked Abbot Germanus, "How did Pelagius' teaching come to be so accepted in Britain?"

We were alone in his study. He sat in his abbot's chair. A smaller, open-backed chair had been brought into the room for me. The study's table, piled with parchments and texts, stood between our chairs.

Abbot Germanus looked at me with his evaluative eyes and waited to reply. I could tell he was thinking, searching his memory for details, deciding what answer would best illumine my question.

After what felt like five minutes he spoke. "Pelagius was not always considered a heretic," he began. "The issue at stake is whether the faithful need the guidance of God's church or not." Abbot Germanus waited for his words to have their effect.

I nodded understanding, so he continued.

He leaned forward and searched among the parchments. He unrolled one scroll, searched it quickly, then rolled it back up again. When he reached the sixth parchment, he paused after he scanned the document. Abbot Germanus nodded to himself, then without word handed the document to me pointing toward these words: "From the beginning, God made man free, made him to possess his own power of choice for good or evil just as he made man to possess a soul."

When I finished reading, I looked at Abbot Germanus. "These are the words of?" I asked.

"Continue reading," was all Abbot Germanus said.

"All men are of the same nature," the parchment read, "able to hold to and choose what is good." I am no theologian and so was confused by the words.

"They are the words of Irenaeus of Lyon," Germanus said. "He was bishop of that city during the reign of Emperor Marcus Aurelius, more than 200 years ago. His writings are considered a strong foundation for our Church."

The Abbot paused, "and Irenaeus agrees with Pelagius."

"How can one be declared a heretic by one bishop and counted as a pillar of the church by another?" I asked.

"It grows even more complex," Abbot Germanus continued. "Clement of Alexandria," he handed me another parchment, "who is equally considered a pillar of our teachings and who died before Irenaeus, wrote that we are saved by our voluntary choices."

"But that view is exactly what Celestine condemned as heresy."

Abbot Germanus added, "An ecumenical council of bishops met at Lyon, where Irenaeus is buried and agreed with Pelagius."

"Pelagius is not a heretic?"

"Pelagius is a heretic," the Abbot answered, "Celestine has declared him so."

"But what about the council at Lyon?" I challenged.

"Pope Innocent, who was Bishop of Rome when the council met at Lyon, did not attend."

Abbot Germanus allowed me to consider the lawyerly point he was making. "Popes can overrule ecumenical councils, especially Councils they don't attend. Celestine is Innocent's successor on the chair of Peter. If he declares Pelagius a heretic, then he is one."

"Why share this with me?" I demanded.

"Because I agree with the council fathers at Lyon," Abbot Germanus admitted. "And because I'm charged with the mission of eliminating teachings from Britain. My mind agrees with Irenaeus but my obedience belongs to Celestine. You might find the same tug of war within yourself. It's important to know, before you are put to the test, which side you will choose."

Abbot Germanus waited again for his words to sink in, to have their impact. "I have chosen Celestine," he said.

"Bishops are commanded to protect the Gospel," I argued, remembering the words of my consecration.

"Protecting the church is protecting the Gospel," Germanus replied. "If the faithful forget their need for the Church, the Gospels will fade away. That is the true danger in Pelagius' words."

A strained silence settled between us.

The importance of Abbot Germanus' words was underscored after we reached London. We arrived one rainy Tuesday and were welcomed warmly by Bishop Brannok of London. He invited the Abbot to preach at the Church of All Hallows, near the river, on the following Sunday. All Hallows was then London's cathedral. Brannok sent out word that an important visitor, an emissary from Rome and from the Pope would speak on Rome helping Londoners stave off invasions and threats.

When the time came for Abbot Germanus to speak, All Hallows was packed. The crowd spilled outside onto the streets near the river. They wanted to hear how Rome would save London from marauding Saxons and hear how the Empire would rescue its stranded British citizens. The throng grew serious and silent as Abbot Germanus mounted the steps to the pulpit.

"Brothers and sisters in Christ," he began, "I come among you armed not with the spears and swords of Rome but with the sword of faith and the armor of the truth."

The crowd restlessly stirred.

"I bring word of our Holy Father in Rome's judgment on Bishop Pelagius."

Hushed whispers could be heard gathering within the church. As Abbot Germanus' words were repeated to those gathered outside, shouts of "No!" and "Pelagius is a good man!" could be heard.

"He is condemned as a heretic and cut off from the body of Christ," Abbot Germanus continued. Several of the assembled faithful turned their backs and made their way out of the church. The whispers within the crowd grew into a turmoil of many voices speaking all at once within a large open space.

"This condemnation of Pelagius is this the only news you bring from Rome?" shouted one voice above all the others.

"This is the word of the Holy Father," Abbot Germanus roared.

I could hear anger gathering on the steps beyond the church, gathering like distant thunder as this answer was repeated.

"Pelagius teaches that we must stand on our own, choose our own goodness," a woman's voice cried out.

"Heresy," Abbot Germanus answered. "We each need holy church and God's grace to be saved."

"That won't save us from the Saxons," a man to the left of the pulpit clamored. It was right then that the first stone broke the scraped horn panes of All Hallows' great window. More stones followed and anger gathered fast, like an inflowing tide among the congregation. Bishop Brannok hurried from his seat and said something to Germanus.

The Abbot left the pulpit and signaled me to follow him. Then he and Brannok walked quickly from the sanctuary. I smelled the smoke as I hurried towards the vestry. The crowd outside had filled a cart with straw and old wood, placed it against the wooden walls of All Hallows and set the cart aflame.

The congregation within the church instantly transfigured into a mob. They surged forward and overwhelmed the five monks and priests that remained in the sanctuary protecting the church's treasure. The gold altar cross, the silver cup, and plate used at Mass, the brass candle sticks, the great tapestry behind the altar; they all disappeared as a great wave from the crowd surged forward. When the wave was gone, so were all the treasures and the five clergymen with them. The mob carried the monks and priests outside and beat them with stones and sticks.

All Hallows caught fire and burned to the ground that Sunday. Two monks and a priest lay dead on the street when the crowd finally had spent itself in fear and fury. Brannok, Abbot Germanus, and I retreated across the old Roman bridge to the far side of the river and the safety of the bishop's home

In the safety of Brannok's study, I witnessed Abbot Germanus invent a saint. "It is so sad," he began, "that I didn't have the chance to tell the crowd of my dream last night."

"They almost killed us," Brannok declared. "How is a dream important?"

"The dream would have convinced them," the Abbot declared. Then Abbot Germanus spun a tale of a young, Roman centurion serving in Britain who was martyred for defending the Church.

"During the reign of Emperor Gaius Quintus Decius almost 200 years ago, word went out that every citizen was required to offer sacrifice to Caesar as a god." This much, I later gleaned from parchments in Brannok's library, was historically accurate.

"The first Christian priests had reached Britain and the light of the church was welcomed on these shores," Abbot Germanus continued. "Alban, a centurion stationed with the Legions at London, welcomed those priests into his home. When the Roman governor found out, he ordered them to be seized and put to death."

The Abbot paused and looked at both Brannok and me. "This is the dream I had last night. The spirit of Blessed Alban appeared to me and spoke. He told me his tale, how the governor's soldiers seized him when they couldn't find the priests. The governor later had him executed in their stead when Alban wouldn't reveal their hiding place."

I looked at Brannok with questions in my eyes. Had he ever heard this tale before?

"This is the true story of Saint Alban, Britain's first martyr and soldier of Christ," Abbot Germanus said.

"Amen," echoed Brannok.

"This is the dream I will share with the faithful of Britain, the dream of how they and they alone can defend Christ's church from evil and death," Abbot Germanus added. "This is what I will preach to the people, against Pelagius."

That was almost a month ago. Abbot Germanus went north, closer to where Pelagius lives and preaches. I heard that he is well-received wherever he tells the story of a brave British soldier standing up against a corrupt and evil empire. Saint Alban has become the scourge of Pelagius.

31. Dunbur and Death

A mosaic of memory filled my mind's eye as I stood on the cliffs near Deva. Abbot Germanus' advice on choosing sides, remembrance of the journey from Rome to Auxerre to London and now Deva on the west coast of Britain, recollections from being consecrated a bishop, awareness of the grandeur and reach of Roman power, the riot at All Hallows, and the stirrings of my heart all filled me as I looked out to sea. I felt more than heard brothers Blaise and Otho join me in my watch on the cliffs.

"When do we take ship for Ireland," Blaise asked.

"When the storms calm and the sea allows," I answered.

The storm lasted nine days. Waves and wind beat against the rocks. No ship that wanted to return to land sailed. I waited and prayed and thought of Brigid. Otho and Blaise took care of my daily needs. Mornings, we joined each other for prayer in the hours before dawn. I celebrated Mass in Deva's tiny church. After prayer, they brought food and water to my room. They largely left me alone until midday. At noon Otho would return with news from the beach. Was any captain willing to sail that day? When did they think the storms would end? "When the gods of the sea grow tired," was the repeated answer.

The mention of gods other than the Christ brought the smile of memory to my heart along with worry. Brigid emerged from remembrance to occupy my thoughts. In my mind's eye, she was still young, slim with a young woman's hips and ample breasts. When I thought of her, when I remembered our hand-fasting, I desired her. Her smell, her hair, her hazel eyes, her arbor, her altar of pleasure. I was now a bishop. She was still a pagan. Even so, I longed for her. Brigid's body kept her youth in my imagination, but her face grew in age and wisdom. I imagined both sorrow and joy in her eyes and lines of wisdom beginning to show on her.

Then Blaise or Otho would interrupt my thoughts.

"Is there anything we should do while we wait?" Otho asked.

"Do you need anything?" Blaise added.

"Pray for strength," I replied.

On the tenth day after the storms began, shortly after sunrise, we took ship. Two days later, our small party jumped from the boat into the waves lapping at the shore near the beach at Dunbur. We came as shepherds to pagan, wild, untamed Ireland. Very soon we would need to become warriors.

Our ship's captain didn't beach the boat or linger beyond the time needed for the three of us to transfer our baggage to the shore. Otho and Blaise wouldn't allow me to shoulder anything beyond my shepherd's staff.

"You carry the faith to Ireland," Otho said. "Allow us to carry the baggage." And so, two monks, a bishop, two rather large packs containing relics, cooking pots, and camping gear, as well as a spare robe for each of us, and a tarp were transferred ashore.

I had a bishop's ring on my finger and a small bag of coins at my belt. A second, slightly larger bag of coins was secreted in one of the packs with our spare robes.

"Why land here?" Blaise asked once the packs had been fetched above Dunbur strand's high-water line. "The captain told me you asked to be left here, alone on the shore, when there's a perfectly good fishing village less than a half day's sail to the north?"

I liked Blaise for his curiosity, for his youth, and energy, for asking the captain about where we were to land, and especially because sometimes he treated me like a brother rather than his bishop.

"Two reasons," I answered. "The Irish already know we're here."

Blaise and Otho looked at each other with the suggestion of fear crossing their eyes. "Fishers from that village saw us while we were still on the Irish Sea. When I saw their boats, I asked the captain to sail south to the nearest place to put ashore on a wild beach."

Questions played across Blaise's face. Doubt clouded Otho's eyes. "I came to Ireland once before as a slave." I paused to allow this to penetrate. "This time, I wanted to land on these shores as a freeman."

The purse hanging on my belt held 12 solid, heavy gold ring coins. They were more than enough to pay my ransom price. "I intend to go north to Slemmish to see my old master Muirchil and pay my ransom," I stated. "I am a freeman and the emissary of the Bishop of Rome. No chieftain or king will keep me in the chains of slavery."

"Where did you get the gold?" Blaise blurted.

Smiling at his completely practical and totally impertinent question, I replied, "I added a gift from Bishop Brannok of London to the gold given for our mission by Celestine in Rome."

I turned to see what Otho made of this pronouncement. His deep-blue eyes widened. Otho was pointing across the beach to the low hills that rose beyond the dunes. "Five men on horses." We watched them approach. Then he added, "Carrying spears."

I estimated that we had about 15 minutes before the horsemen would reach us. I directed Otho and Blaise to move the packs from the beach to a small, rocky promontory that overlooked it.

"The second reason to land here," I said, "was to greet the Irish on my own terms." My companions looked baffled. "The Irish place a great value on honor, on how they appear to each other. The public visage of a chieftain, noble, or warrior is very important. I've returned to Ireland as a chieftain, and you are soldiers of Christ. I did not want to be taken by villagers and presented as a captive."

I stood on that rocky overlook and directed my eyes towards the approaching warriors. I held my crozier as if it were a spear and continued to reassure myself as much as Blaise and Otho, saying, "The voice of God spoke to me on Slemmish. Celestine of Rome, the voice of God on Earth, commissioned us as apostles to Ireland. We stand here with God as our shield and His word as our sword."

The five riders drew to a halt a short distance from our low, rocky stand. Even though they were mounted, I stood just above their eye level. Their horses were brown. The five warriors were all bearded with wild manes of hair and ferociously wide eyes. Each held a spear. Swords or clubs hung from each saddle. Four of them wore tri-colored rough-spun garments. The horseman in the center wore a cloak with four colors. He was their chieftain.

"May God bless your day," I called out locking eyes with him.

He spat on the ground in front of him. "Who are you?"

"I am called Patrick," I answered. "A chieftain sent as a messenger by the King of Gods and the Pope of Rome." The eyes of the warriors didn't waiver or show any recognition of what I had said. "Who are you?" I asked.

"He is the *ri*, Dichu," answered the warrior to the left of the chieftain. "And you are on his land."

"What is yours is now mine," Dichu pronounced, and the five horses stirred. "If you wish to end this day alive, you will hand over those packs and that purse I see on your belt."

I didn't move or take my eyes from Dichu's eyes. Those eyes were a deep green, like an angry, cold sea. I felt Blaise and Otho prepare to run. "I come as the messenger of the King of Gods," I repeated. "I bring a powerful *draíocht*, the special magic of Rome." I knew this word from my lessons with Brigid. With "draíocht" I declared myself equal to the druids, holding the special lore, art, and magic of Rome.

"He's a Roman druid come to conquer our gods," declared the rider to the left of Dichu.

Before I could react, the rider on Dichu's right lowered his spear and thrust it at my heart. Just as the spear moved, Otho stepped in front of me. He stood there, nailed on the point of that Irish spear, and locked his eyes on the green eyes of Dichu. It took Otho a long time to fall. "God is our shield," were his last words as he stumbled and pulled the spear from that warrior's hands.

I looked down at Otho with great sadness and an even greater pride. I would echo his steadfastness and courage even if I also met a martyr's death on those rocks. Turning cold eyes towards Dichu, I stated, "Each one you cut down, my draíocht will replace with a hundred. That is the power of Rome."

Dichu's horse stepped back two paces. "You have cut down my brother, and if you cut me down a thousand will come to replace me."

The chieftain looked at the warrior on his right whose spear now lay beside Otho's body.

"You have broken the law of hospitality and killed my brother. His honor price is very great. How will you pay?"

"What is the price of his face?" asked the warrior to Dichu's left.

Taking my eyes off Dichu for the first time, I looked at him. He strongly resembled Dichu, like a younger brother or a son.

"Otho's honor price is to be replaced by one of your blood, one of equal strength and courage given to my service until I release him. Also, the worth of 15 cattle."

A look of shock crossed Dichu's face. The younger man to his left moved to thrust his spear at me and Blaise moved to shield me from the blow. Dichu reached out his left hand and stopped the younger warrior before he could strike. Not releasing the young man's arm, Dichu spoke, "This is Niall, my youngest brother. He is now yours." He released the young warrior's arm. "You are welcome in my hall this night where I would hear about this draíocht of the King of Gods. We'll settle the rest of the honor price afterwards." Turning to his younger brother he added, "Niall, remain here and guide our guests to our village."

Dichu turned his horse and rode away with three warriors, leaving Niall speechless and sitting on his horse.

"Patrick will ride," I heard Blaise say to Niall. "We will walk, and you will help carry the packs."

"First, we must bury our brother, Otho," I said.

We dug a grave for him in the sand by the rocks. We piled stones on the grave to mark where he rested, and I placed his brother's cross under a rock above his head.

32. In Dichu's Hall

The sun had set by the time we entered Dichu's hall.

I had been in Rome. Dichu's village was small, holding maybe 50 souls. The buildings were as I remembered: low, circular, whitewashed wattle and daub walls on the outside, with thatched conical roofs. Dichu's hall was similar, only with much higher walls and large enough to welcome 20 warriors. Two men stood guard at the hall's door, with feet braced, sullen faced. They stood with clubs at their sides. Between them a dark brown, tanned cow hide covered the opening.

I sat on my horse and looked at them for five long breaths. I stared each of them directly in the eye, not looking away until I knew that the guard knew I had taken his measure. I had taken the first steps towards establishing my honor, my face value, when I demanded the honor price for Otho's death. As a stranger to this village and as an unknown in Ireland, every move I made would either confirm and add to my face value or take away from it. With no warriors and only Blaise as a monastic companion, face value was our only protection.

"Find a stable for this horse," I said to Niall, looking away from the door guards for the first time. "Then join me in the hall."

"Niall," called out one of the sullen guards, "who is this stranger to give you orders?"

"He is called Patrick," Niall replied, "and is a Roman druid." The guards looked at one another with both fear and questions. Their hands gripped the clubs at their sides. "Dichu gave me to him as an honor-hostage when we killed his brother on the beach. He also invited this Roman to dine with him tonight." Confusion replaced fear in the guards' eyes and their hands relaxed somewhat on their clubs. "He is our guest and subject to the law of hospitality. Now stop your gawking and allow the man into Dichu's hall. I've got work to do," Niall finished.

I allowed a small smile to soften my face as I caught Niall's eye. An echoing smile crossed his face as he led the horse past me, "It was wrong for Cronon to kill your brother," he said. "It was rash. He gave away his courage and lost his head." These were the first words Niall had spoken to me since the beach. Looking at me, he continued, "I am your honor-hostage to command as you wish. I will join you in the hall when I am finished with this horse."

Turning to the hall's door, I faced the guards. Neither one stepped out of the way or moved to open the door covering. Blaise stepped in front of me as I neared the door and pushed aside the guard to my right. The guard grunted and lifted his right hand to strike at Blaise. I met the guard's gaze and asked with ferocity in my voice, "Is this how Dichu welcomes guests to his hall?" The guard's hand paused where he had pulled it back, just below his own right ear. "Is this how Dichu keeps the law of hospitality?"

The hand dropped to the guard's side as he barked, "You and your gods are not welcome here." Then Blaise and I went through the door and into Dichu's dimly lit hall.

I took two steps towards the center of the structure and paused to look around. The hall appeared to span 10 paces from its entrance to the far wall. Dim light filtered through the smoke opening in the thatch above. The floor was hard beaten earth. A small fire burned at the hearth stones in the hall's center, only three paces in front of me. There were two other openings in the wall. Each one was half the size of the door. Their hide coverings had been partly pulled back to allow in fresh air.

Dichu sat on a wide bench directly across from the hall's opening. One of the warriors from the beach stood behind him, still armed with a sword. Two torches fixed to the wall behind the warrior gave their light to the room. I had passed two more torches as I stepped into the hall, but they remained unlit. The hall was rich in the stink of grease and sweat, ale, and smoke.

As my eyes adjusted to the dimness, I noticed three more seated warriors. Two sat on the ground along the wall to my left. One sat on a stool to my right. I figured that along with the two guards at the door and the warrior behind Dichu, they represented the full complement of warriors he could gather on short notice. If I included Niall, that meant Dichu commanded seven men. He was a small village chieftain. But his warriors outnumbered mine seven to zero. I had only honor and face and the aura of Rome. I decided to begin with humor.

Four women were also in the hall. A middle-aged mother dressed in a linen tunic dyed with four colors sat to Dichu's left on the bench. Two others, younger, with long, dark hair hanging past the middle of their backs, wearing rougher cloth tunics of three colors, sat on the earth with the warriors to my left. A fourth, a servant, a girl in a simple dark-colored rough tunic, perhaps a slave, stirred coals at the fire pit.

"Thank you for arranging a warm welcome at your hall's door," I offered with a laugh. I heard two of the women snicker at my remark. Dichu, somewhat shocked, glared at me across the fire. "Are you not going to ask me to sit with you?" I continued. Just then, I heard the door covering behind me pulled back and fall into place again. Niall entered and stood beside me. I offered Dichu a smile. "My honor-hostage has joined us."

Dichu grunted grudging acceptance and gestured at a place for us to sit on the floor. Blaise began to move there but I stood fast.

"Do you welcome the draíocht by placing it on the earth?" I asked.

Niall gestured for the warrior on the stool to my right to get up. Looking at Dichu he grumbled, "You placed me in his service as hostage." Niall took the stool and placed it alongside Dichu's bench.

"You have no right of hospitality here," Dichu began, "other than by my command. You are a non-person, a stranger thrown up upon our shores. There is no honor price for one who belongs to no clan."

I returned a calm face for Dichu's grunts. "I am a druid of the *druadh*," I replied. "As such I belong to every clan and no clan."

Dichu answered with silence.

"My honor price is the worth of my draíocht. To know that price, you must listen to my tale."

"He will bind you with his words," cried the warrior now displaced from the stool.

"I am not afraid of his words," Dichu stated. "We will hear his tale and then decide."

In the dimness of Dichu's hall, as the apostle to Ireland, I told the story of the Christ for the first time. I told of how the King of the Gods had sent his only son as a warrior to help men and how those men had killed him. I told how this warrior was stronger than death and had returned alive from the land of the dead after three days. "And thus, if you wish to hold a draíocht that is stronger than death," I said as I finished my tale, "you must follow this warrior's commands."

"If this tale is true," the warrior whose stool I sat upon said, "this is powerful magic."

"If this is true," said one of the warriors seated beside him, "why didn't this Christ bring Patrick's brother back from the dead when Cronon killed him on the beach?" All heads turned to me, waiting for an answer.

"Only one great heart has so completely followed this way as to come back to life since the Christ," I said.

"Who was he?" Dichu asked.

"She was his mother," I answered and saw shock on their faces. Looking around, I noted that the women sat forward. "Only she was brave enough to come back from the land of the dead." I saw a smile on the girl slave at the fire.

"And where does this mother live?" Dichu demanded.

"After he woke her from the sleep of death, the Christ took his mother up into the skies to reign as queen with him until time ends," I answered.

"She rules in the sky with Taranu, the thunderer?" the woman at Dichu's side asked.

Before I could answer, Dichu hushed her and asked his own question. "If this warrior can bring those who follow him with bravery back from the land of the dead, why didn't he bring your brother back? Nothing can be braver than to take a death blow meant for another."

Again, I felt every eye in the room turn towards me. "Some warriors must sleep the sleep of the dead until the end of time," I answered. "Then the Christ will return and awaken them to live once more." I saw several heads nodding.

"How will this new Taranu find his warriors?" Dichu probed.

"I placed his sign on Otho's grave. He will find him."

"What is this sign?" Cronon asked.

I learned soon after that the woman by Dichu's side was named Sabd. She was his wife, and her words broke the string of questions and answers.

"Our guest has told us a tale and given us much to consider," Sabd began. Then, looking at Dichu, she asked, "Isn't it time to offer him food and drink before asking him for more?" Dichu nodded. Sabd clapped her hands and nodded to the serving girl. Then, looking at me, she continued, "we will hear more when Lia-dan returns with food and drink. Till then, tell us of your journey across the sea to our sands."

The meal was simple yet hearty. While I spoke, the village women had been preparing a small feast. The men kept their swords and clubs at hand. This night would end with either a meal or my death. Fate had not yet decided.

Food was brought in, a hearty fish and vegetable stew, warm bread, and an acrid, barnyard-like smelling cheese. I ate it all, knowing that to refuse anything was to risk forfeiting the right to hospitality. Death was delayed, at least for now.

"What price does this warrior Christ ask for the draíocht that is stronger than death?" Dichu asked, wiping his mouth and signaling the end of the meal.

"He asks only three things," I answered, remembering the Irish reverence for that number.

"He asks that you acknowledge him as the son of the King of Gods," I began. Several heads nodded that this was reasonable. "He asks that you have any wrongdoing you have done washed away in his name." Doubtful looks replaced nods. "And he asks that you pledge your honor to be his warrior when he calls."

"He wants to be our chieftain, our ri?" Niall asked.

"He is already the high chieftain, the ard-Rí of the sky," I replied. "He honors this village with his invitation to join him."

"How do we know you speak for him? How do we know he is even real?" Niall pressed.

Niall teetered on the edge of belief and doubt. I rose from my seat. Niall stood also, taking a warrior's stance less than an arm's length in front of me. I grabbed the sword that he wore at his side. "I release my claim on you as honor-hostage," I declared to him. Handing him his own sword, hilt first, I softly said, "Accept my words as true or kill me and find out for yourself."

I saw Blaise trembling with fear as the blade waivered in Niall's hand. The serving girl backed away to the far side of the fire. I could feel, taste, and smell the anger and fear in the room.

"This one has the courage and heart of a true druid," Niall finally said, returning his sword to its scabbard. "Why release me as hostage?"

I believe to this day that just then I had God's help. Christ and the Father God and the Moringa clashed in the heavens while I stood in Dichu's hall. "The Christ has all the riches of heaven," I answered. "He does not need you as an honor-hostage." Just at that moment a clap of thunder resounded. "And as his messenger to Ireland, neither do I." A log smoking over the coals broke and a shower of sparks rose towards the smoke hole. The hall fell silent. "Now, do you wish to hear the way of this Christ, or not?" I demanded.

I ended that night still alive. After all the talking was done and the last ale had been served, Blaise and I slept on straw pallets near the fire. The next morning, I awoke to find a cup of fresh water, bread, and more stale cheese beside me. Later that day, I baptized my first three Irish converts: Dichu, Sabd, and Niall.

33. Easpag

For three nights, Blaise and I were given a place to sleep in Dichu's hall. He welcomed us into his clan and pledged that my honor price should be half of his chieftain's price of 20 cattle. Blaise, as my brother servant, was given an honor price of half of mine. Otho's honor price was set at five cows. Cronon was made to pledge payment of Otho's face price before the end of the year.

Dichu, Sabd, Blaise, and I were breakfasting together in the hall when I told them of my capture by Aitre's pirates. "You were a slave?" Dichu asked in horror that he had given such a classless person a status half as high as his own.

"I was a captive," I answered. "I followed the captive's way and did the captive's duty. I escaped back to my own village. Eventually I gained the title of a chieftain of Rome, a druid of the Romans, a bishop." I paused to allow that to sink in. "Indeed, a bishop is higher in status and greater in power than a druid. In Rome I am a druid who is also a ri. They call me Episcopus," I said, using the Latin word for bishop.

Dichu tried to wrap his tongue around the Latin word and failed. His best attempt yielded only the sound easpag. *"Easpag,"* he said pointing at me, "ri and druid." I smiled.

Each of the three nights I was offered Aiofe, a slave girl, as a sleeping companion. Aiofe looked willing and happy when she was brought to me the first night. I declined, telling my hosts, "I am promised to sleep with only one other." The three of them, Dichu, Sabd, and Aiofe, looked confused at my words. Why would a healthy man or woman refuse a willing and attractive sleeping companion?

"My promise gives power to my draíocht," I added and saw them relax. Disappointed, Aiofe returned to her sleeping place among some rags along the far wall.

On the second and third nights, Dichu again offered Aiofe to me as a sleeping companion. The second night, I repeated my tale that I would sleep only with the one to whom I was promised. The third night, recognizing that my refusal risked violating my host's hospitality, I thanked Dichu for the offer and asked Aiofe to join me.

A surprised Blaise grudgingly moved his sleeping mat to the far wall and allowed us space. I sat down and, spreading a pelt on the ground next to my pallet, pointed at a place for Aiofe to sit.

"I cannot take you into my bed tonight as my woman," I said, "but I can teach you some of the way of the Christ." Disappointment and curiosity played across her face.

"Would you like to hear?" I asked.

"Yes, druid easpag," she answered.

"Call me Patrick."

"Padraig," she replied.

"Close enough," I said and began the tale of the Christ once more. That night, I spoke for almost three hours without stop. At the end I told Aiofe, "In the eyes of the Christ, slaves and chieftains and chieftain's wives are equally children of the King of Gods. If you wish, and only if you wish, you are worthy to become a follower of this draíocht." Pleasure and excitement filled her eyes.

"Yes, Padraig, I wish it," she said.

"Return to your sleeping pallet," I told her. "In the morning I will tell Dichu that you are to be baptized and that he is to treat you better."

"Am I your woman now?" Aiofe asked.

With a sad smile I told her, "I too once served a master. You are beautiful and if my heart and magic were not pledged to another, you would be my woman tonight. But that heart and magic are pledged, and I cannot take you to my pallet."

Tears formed at the inside corners of Aiofe's eyes and tenderness tested my courage. "Hush now," I told her and kissed her tears. "You may not be my woman tonight but in the morning, you become a child of the King of Gods." Aiofe's shoulders heaved with silent sobs as she turned away. I spent the remainder of the night sitting on my pallet, wondering if I had chosen well.

Morning came. Dichu and Sabd had questions in their eyes when they awoke to find me sitting alone on my pallet and saw Aiofe asleep among her rags. "We spent half the night talking," I told them, "Then I sent the girl back to her place." The older couple nodded. "Aiofe is beautiful, and I would like . . ." I paused allowing them to wonder if I was asking for a gift that would bind me to Dichu. "I would like to baptize her, the same as I baptized you and Niall."

"But she is only a slave!" Sabd exclaimed.

"The power of the draíocht of the King of Gods is that it raises both chieftain and slave to be his children," I answered. "It is his way, and you have sworn to accept it."

"Will she still be my slave?" Sabd asked.

"Are you claiming her as your own?" Dichu demanded.

"Aiofe remains here and at your command," I replied. "But she will remain here as a child of the King of Gods, your sister in the draíocht of his Christ."

The stunned, doubt-filled looks on their faces were as plain as the day. I steered away from questions about how a sister-child of God could also be a slave, steered away to my plans to leave that same morning.

"This easpag seeks to journey far to the north," I told Dichu. "There is an old one of the druids there who helped me and taught me when I was a young man. He is called Amergin, and his daughter is named Brigid. She and I hand-fasted three times before I escaped back to my people and Rome."

Dichu and Sabd nodded, understanding.

"This Brigid is the one to whom you are promised?" Sabd asked.

Sabd had gray eyes. I looked deep into those pools and allowed all the passion, love, tenderness, and hope I felt when I remembered my time with Brigid to fill my own eyes. My answer to her question was wordless. In those days, especially in Britain, bishops still took wives. The custom of Episcopal marriage had fallen away in Rome and was a fading memory in most of what remained of the empire. I had heard it said in Rome that even simple priests were beginning to put away their wives and live without women. But in the Frankish and Germanic territories to the north and west, in Iberia to the south, and in Britain, bishops still took wives. Bishop Brannok of London had a wife. Germanus of Auxerre, as an abbot, did not. I had been released from my vows as a monk of Auxerre when I was consecrated bishop. All these thoughts played across the field of my mind as I looked into Sabd's eyes.

"Brigid holds my heart," I said to Sabd.

"If I'm not mistaken," Dichu laughed heartily and grabbed himself, "she holds more than your heart." Clapping me on the back, he asked, "Where do this Brigid and her druid father live?"

"In a small village, just to the east of Slemmish Mountain," I answered.

"I have heard of this place in tales," Dichu answered. "It lays many days' walk to the north."

Sabd completed his words. "We can help you on your way as far as the fishing village a day's walk north. It is a larger settlement, and they will know the way to this Slemmish."

"You landed with two companions but now have only one," Dichu pondered aloud. "We can send someone with you, if you wish."

Unacknowledged, Niall had listened from just beyond the circle of our conversation. "I would like to go with you, Easpag Patrick!" he exclaimed.

"You are not his hostage," Dichu protested.

"I would go with him as friend and brother," Niall said. "Of my own choice."

"Let it be thus," Sabd said and turned away from the talking.

With her words, it was decided. Niall left his village along with Blaise and I later that morning. We took two ponies and a mule along with us. Niall and I rode. Blaise walked, a smile on his face, as he led the mule who now carried our packs.

34. The Awen

That night, we camped in the woods. Blaise gathered kindling and water. Niall set up camp and started the fire. Together, they cooked a fine camping stew. I spent most of the evening explaining to Niall the way of monks and brothers as spiritual warriors. I saw the spark of heroism catch in his heart. From my time on Slemmish with Brigid, I knew many of the tales of Irish heroes. The Irish love heroes and aspire to gain their steadfastness of spirit, their loyalty, their strength of heart.

"The soldier of Christ," I told Niall, "lives a life of courage. His heart is hard when he faces evil but full of love towards his brothers."

Niall smiled and looked pleased at this description.

"He has a great face price and is held as honored by all who know him."

Niall looked excited.

"Just like Blaise," I said as I finished. Niall's lips drew tight as if he were chewing on a question. But he held his words to himself as we each arranged a sleeping place near the fire.

The next morning, I awoke to the smells of broth already warming above the fire. Niall and Blaise were in deep conversation. Niall was teaching Blaise Irish. Their talking continued when we broke camp. Niall walked his pony and kept pace beside Blaise.

We halted when our path through the woods came to an opening. We stood on a slight rise and looked down across wide fields planted with grain, then a clearing, then a fishing village. It was mid-morning. The village was guarded on three sides by a palisade of sharpened tree trunks. Each stake was taller than a man and larger than my hands could reach around. A stout gate with wooden doors faced the path we were traveling. Above the gate, atop a fighting platform, stood a man with spear keeping watch. The wooden gates stood open. I could see at least 50 thatched roofs and a larger hall behind those walls. Beyond those, I saw seven fishing boats floating in a cove and a larger trading ship tied up along shore. Men carried bundles and packs from the trade ship to the shore. Fishers tended the gear in their boats. I could hear the barking of dogs and the shouting of children. The warrior keeping watch saw us and shouted a warning. Two more warriors joined the guard at the gate. Niall, Blaise, and I walked downhill.

"Who are you?" called the gate guard when we neared the palisaded walls.

"I am called Niall, of the clan O'Toole, descended from Tuathal and the Kings of Laigin. I am the brother of Dichu, chieftain of a village one day's walk south."

The guard grunted. Niall's was a worthy name with a substantial claim on face power. Recovering his voice, the guard growled, "The two with you are not clan O'Toole. Who are they?"

Niall turned to consider me and Blaise. He wore the smile of mischief on his face. This moment was like play for him. One of three possibilities lay open. He would talk our way into the village and then the rest was up to me. Or the guards would bar us from the village, and we would face the choice to continue walking north or return to Dichu. Or the guards would allow us entry into the village where we would later be beaten as intruders and strangers before being thrown out of the gates.

The game of the moment was to get inside the gates. Turning back to the guards, "This is Easpag Patrick, both druid and ri," Niall called out gesturing at me. "And this is his warrior brother, Blaise."

"If they be warriors, if he is a chieftain, then where are his weapons and his armor?" the guard challenged.

"I have no need for sword or armor." I said to the guard. Catching Niall's eye, I grinned. "My draíocht is both sword and armor for me."

I waited while the guard considered what I claimed. "Since I and my brother carry no weapon, allow us entry into the village. I have a tale to tell your chieftain."

"You two may enter because you carry no weapons," the guard replied. "But this Niall of the O'Toole is armed. What of him?"

"You are in charge of this gate," I answered the guard. Then I caught Niall's eye once more. His grin was gone, replaced by a question. I smiled at him. "The decision is yours, guard," I said and led my pony through the gate. "Join us at the chieftain's hall if they let you inside the gates," I called to Niall and laughed. I saw him hold back a laugh as he kept his face stern to argue with the guard.

The fishing village was notably larger than Dichu's. Once inside I saw new, wooden walled buildings scattered between older wattle and daub circular walls. The thatch on many roofs was new and the whitewash on the outer walls was fresh. Fishing kit and gear hung in front of many buildings. Nets were drying or being mended. Outside of one house we passed, two women worked on a new sail. They were sewing stiffened hemp stays into the sail to strengthen it.

As they sewed, I noticed the symbol painted on the front of the sail: three long red rays crowned by three circles of black, one circle atop each ray. I motioned for Blaise to halt as I approached the women and waited for one of them to look up from their stools. Their faces were deeply creased, and long white hair hung down to their shoulders. A scent of cloves hung faintly in the air around them and I noticed that everything within reach was tidy, well-kept, and clean. One of them was humming softly to herself as her gnarled hands moved a needle in and through the cloth. In and through. In and through. Finally, she looked up at me with eyes that appeared sightless, clouded with age. "What is it you want?" her voice croaked.

"Mother," I began as respectfully as possible, "I am a stranger here."

"That much even I can see," she laughed. "I know every footfall in this village, from our chieftain's heavy feet to the softest step of the newest walker. Your steps I have never heard before." She looked at me with fearless curiosity. "What is it you want?"

"Your ears are sharp," I acknowledged. I stepped closer to where the old woman sat and kneeled on the ground before her. "Even though I am a stranger," I said, "I too am some mother's son, some grandmother's grandson." I paused to allow her to consider my words. "I have come from beyond the sea with a tale for your chieftain." The old one nodded. "Years ago, before I crossed the sea, I herded sheep far to the north," I explained. "There I met a druid's daughter who taught me many of the symbols and signs of power." Again, I paused. The woman nodded once more for me to continue. "But I do not know the symbol painted on the sail you sew."

"To know the symbol, that is all you wish from me," the old woman cackled.

"That is all I ask," I answered and waited.

The old woman searched the sail with her hands. Her fingers ran the lengths of the painted rays and gently rested on the circles atop them. "This is the Awen," she answered as if that was enough.

"What does it mean?" I asked.

"A druid's daughter taught you and you do not know this symbol?" she asked with suspicion creeping into her voice.

"My training was interrupted." I saw a look of doubt on her face. "I had to flee," I explained. "I fought with the local chieftain's son over her. I struck him when he insulted her. Then I fled before his clan could kill me."

Comprehension replaced doubt on the old woman's face. Her companion, with equally sightless eyes, leaned forward and said, "Ask him if he's going back to her."

"He's right in front of me," the old woman laughed. "You just asked him yourself."

"I am. And what is the meaning of the Awen?"

"The Awen signifies the balance of male and female power in our world," the old woman stated flatly. "The ray on the right signifies male energy. The ray to the left signifies female energy. The center ray signifies their balance."

"And what do the circles mean?"

"The circles stand for individuals," the old woman said. "There are some who hold only male energy, like great warriors. Some hold female energy, like great grandmothers. There are some who hold the two great energies in balance like great kings and heroes."

"Why is it painted on your sail?"

"The balance of energies brings great fortune," she laughed. "It is a good symbol for a fishing boat to have."

"One last question, Mother, before I am gone."

"Yes."

"What is your name?"

"I am called Luigsech." She gently patted her companion's arm. "This is Fedlimid, my sister. What is your name?"

"I am called Patrick."

35. Outcasts

Two hours later, Niall met us at the chieftain's hall. "It took a mighty long time to argue my way in," he said as he joined us at a bench near the hall's door.

"How did you finally win entry?" I asked.

"The guard's mother is a cousin to my uncle's youngest daughter's husband," he answered as if that clarified everything.

"And?" I asked.

"Family connections are worth more than hundreds of swords," Niall laughed. "When the guard recognized that we were almost related, he relented and let me in, though with a strong warning."

"What was that?" I asked again.

"That I was to keep the peace." I grinned at Niall's words. "And that I was to make sure you did not disturb the peace either." With that Niall smiled back at me. "And that, Easpag Patrick, may take work," he laughed and sat down next to me.

We waited on that bench for another hour before the chieftain returned. The time allowed me to take the measure of the hall. It was oblong, like a Roman building. The hall spanned more than 20 steps and was at least 10 paces wide. A thatched roof rested on wooden beams at least 15 feet above my head. There were three fires burning in the hall. Fireplaces with stone chimneys stood at both ends, and a large fire circle held its place under the hall's smoke hole. The floor was beaten earth. Hunting trophies hung along one wall; shields hung on another. A large trestle table with a bench sat across from the entrance.

Maedoc, the village chieftain, entered his hall with four warriors and the sightless old woman leaning on his arm. He led her to a stool near the trestle table. Three servants followed them. He signaled for the servants to bring him and his warriors some food. Then Maedoc turned to look where we sat near the entrance. "Which one of you is the druid and ri called Patrick?" He asked.

I stood and stepped forward three paces from the bench. "I am Patrick," I stated, looking directly at Maedoc. I knew the Irish highly valued courage and boldness of purpose. They also had a finely tuned feel for social status. I had to hold firm to my status as easpag, ri, and druid. I wanted Maedoc to feel the strength of my heart without fearing that I had come to threaten his status.

"I have come with a tale for your hall," I added, "if the chieftain has ears to listen." I smiled and then subtly lowered my eyes to allow Maedoc to consider my words.

"Why should I listen to your tale?" he asked.

"I have come from a distant land, from far across the sea and beyond," I stated. "I landed near the village of chieftain Dichu and was welcomed into his hall. My companion," I said while pointing at him, "Niall of clan O'Toole, descended from the Kings of Laigin, can tell you this is so,"

Maedoc glowered at Niall. "Is this true?" he demanded.

Niall stood and replied, "Yes. I am Dichu's brother and what Patrick says is true." Niall knew enough to hold his tongue to those few words and allow the chieftain to fill in the rest with his imagination.

"Then I will hear this one's tale," Maedoc said, "after I've had some ale." He drank heartily from the ale horn offered by the servant standing behind him. When finished, he wiped the back of his fingers on his whiskers, smoothed his beard with a stroke of his hand, and said, "I'm listening now; get on with it."

I told the tale once more. This time I told how I had been nobly born in Britain, then captured in a raid to become a shepherd far to the north. There I studied with the druid Amergin and his daughter, Brigid. Then I returned to my own people to study the ways of their God. I told how my journey took me all the way to Rome.

Maedoc and the old woman turned and talked to each other when I named the eternal city. "My mother wishes to hear more about this Rome," the chieftain said.

I looked at Luigsech with astonishment, glad that I had greeted her respectfully.

"Ten thousand of your village would not fill a quarter of Rome," I said with the power of truth underneath my claim. "A thousand warriors guard Rome's palace, 10 times more stand watch upon her walls. The floors of the palace," I said looking down at the dirt and exaggerating, "are worked with silver. The palace walls are covered with gold." Luigsech's mouth hung slightly open in astonishment at the image, a tear glistened at the outside corner of her right eye.

"I told you, Maedoc," she throatily whispered, "that one would come." Turning her eyes in my direction she pointed, "Beware. This stranger holds great powers. He is the one who asked me this morning about the Awen." Falling back into silence, her hand shook and clung to the chieftain's arm.

I continued with my tale of crossing the seas once more, this time to land near Dichu's village. I saw Maedoc and Luigsech relax as my tale reached familiar shores. "I bring news of glad tidings from the King of Gods," I began once more. The chieftain and his mother listened while I told the Christ story. Sometimes they smiled as they recognized a theme, like heroism in the face of death. They looked frightened when I mentioned the Christ magic, a draíocht more powerful than death.

"What does this Christ want?" Maedoc demanded when I reached the end of my tale.

I was interrupted by a commotion at the hall's entrance.

"He wants to steal our gods and to kill our spirits," bellowed a voice from behind me. I turned and saw at the door a powerful man, standing a head taller than me, dressed in rags, and holding a stout staff. Small bones clanged and clinked on his cloak as he reached out his right hand to point at me.

"I knew Amergin of the North," the man thundered. "This is not his apprentice, nor his daughter's companion."

"What do you know of Brigid or Amergin?" I demanded.

"Silence, fool," the bone man growled. "I am Vercingetorix, druid of this place and of the Laigin. I know you have come to silence our gods and steal our ways."

Turning to Maedoc, the old druid said, "Kill this man now. Have your soldiers take him outside and gut him, put his head on a stake by the harbor, and warn his gods that we will not welcome them. Do it now or lose everything," he warned.

"I am Niall of the Laigin," I heard a voice from behind join in. Niall came to stand beside me. "I am brother of chieftain Dichu, and these men are under my protection. We claim the right to hospitality under the old laws."

Maedoc and his mother turned to hear from the druid.

"This Niall has a claim on our hospitality," Vercingetorix roared, "but these strangers have no claim. Kill them and honor the O'Toole claim."

"Who is this Amergin of the North?" the chieftain asked.

Drawing up to his full height and rattling his bone cloak, Vercingetorix said, "He was a powerful master of the ways of the druid. He was ancient when he died." I turned in shock to look at the bone man. In my heart, I hoped, I expected Amergin to be alive. "He was killed by a chieftain of the Clan Ui Neill after he helped a slave escape."

"Why would they kill their druid over a slave?" Maedoc asked.

"Because that slave struck the chieftain's son," Vercingetorix answered. "The son and his chieftain father lost great face power when the slave escaped. Amergin adopted a slave's bastard daughter as his own when she was cast out by her owner. That daughter helped this slave escape, and the chieftain went to the druid looking for her." He paused and looked at me with hate in his eyes before he continued.

"The chieftain, Flan, went to the druid's hut. Amergin resisted, refusing to tell where either his daughter or the slave had gone. In his anger, Flan struck Amergin down and claimed his hut and cattle as his own to pay the honor price." A gnarled finger rose to point at me again from under the clanking cloak. "This one is responsible for the death of Amergin. He has returned with strange gods from the land of strangers to steal our ways. Kill him now!"

That finger continued to point at me as Maedoc turned to speak with his mother. I could hear their hushed whispers crossing back and forth. Finally, the chieftain turned to the bone-draped druid and me.

"It is not right to soil any claim on hospitality with spilled blood." He turned to his warriors and commanded, "Seize them!"

One warrior quickly moved to pin my arms behind me. A second did the same with Blaise. A warrior stood on either side of Niall, restraining his arms at his side.

"I will not spill your blood in my village or hall," the chieftain said. "Nor will I have your head on a stake in my harbor, lest visitors gossip that Maedoc of the Laigin knows not the ways of hospitality."

I breathed out a sigh of relief. I saw tension still shaking in Niall's arms and fear in Blaise's eyes.

"You are banished from this village. The trader ship leaves in an hour, on the tide. Take them to the ship and make sure they stay aboard until it sails." Then turning to look with dark, angry eyes at me, Maedoc said, "You have brought discord into my hall and threaten the ways of our gods. The death of Amergin of the North falls at your feet. If you step foot in my village, if you leave the boat before it sails, or if you ever return, I will kill you myself. Now begone."

The soldiers frog-marched us with our baggage to the trader's boat. They kept our two ponies. "Maedoc commands you to take these three aboard and see that they don't return to our village," one of the soldiers said.

"And who pays for their passage?" the captain of the boat asked.

"I can pay for our passage," I answered and stepped aboard an Irish boat once again.

"Who are you that Maedoc spits you out and demands I carry you away in my boat?" the captain asked.

"I am called Patrick. I brought a tale of new magic to Maedoc's hall, a tale not to his liking."

"He is an easpag," Niall hastened to add, "both a ri and a druid come from far away."

The captain spat over the side of his craft. "That's nothing special. I'm the gift of the gods to womankind." He laughed and held out his hand for payment.

"Who do I pay for passage?" I asked.

"I am called Cadhla Fionn," he answered.

I looked confused and turned to Niall for an explanation. "Cadhla means 'handsome.'"

"Well then Cadhla," I laughed as I placed a substantial ring coin in his palm, "my brothers and I are happy for the refuge of your ship. Where do we sail?"

36. On Cadhla's Ship

There were eight of us on that ship: the captain, four crew, and the three of us. A quick discussion with the captain established that his plans were to head north to the larger settlement at Baile Ath Cliath. "Ath Cliath holds almost 4,000 souls," he told me, "and sits at the mouth of the river that divides the kingdoms of Laigin and Brega." Looking over his shoulder towards Maedoc's village he added, "It's a town that knows how to welcome strangers."

A day's sail took us to Ath Cliath. The ship's hold was full, heavy with salted fish, bales of wool, 15 baskets of copper ore, and more than 50 iron ingots. Even after we cleared the cove, the crew remained busy at the ship's oars. The winds did not stir, and we were pulled through the waters at the speed of the dipping and flashing of four great oars.

"You've taken to the sea with me," the captain said to Niall, Blaise, and me. "You'll pull on the oars too if the wind doesn't come up."

Niall looked young and strong and could easily handle a great oar. I had pulled oars many years ago on my wandering course from Ireland back to Britain. I knew that I still looked like I was ready for my turn at the rowing bench. The captain looked askance at Blaise. He was slight of frame and looked as if a stiff wind would bowl him over. "This one won't make much headway with the oars," he laughed and poked Blaise on the shoulder.

"Your eyes must be dim," I retorted. "My brother is far stronger than what you see." As the ship inched north, Blaise and Niall found places to lay our baggage down amidship. They sat nearby, out of the way of the oarsmen. I stood in the rear of the ship, near the tiller where Cadhla worked as steersman.

"Why did Maedoc expel you from his village?" the captain asked again. "This time I want to hear the whole tale."

I spoke mostly of the confrontation with Vercingetorix and how his words had turned Maedoc and Luigsech against me. At the mention of Vercingetorix's name, Cadhla spat over the side of the ship once more and made a warding-off gesture with his left hand. "That old bastard," he said. "He must have thought you came to poach deer in his park."

My look conveyed my lack of understanding of the captain's words.

"He must have thought you'd come to steal his place," Cadhla continued. "Ach, he's one of the druids, but he's also the meanest old man I've ever met. He'd as soon squish you like a bug if he feels threatened."

"How would I, with only my two companions, be a threat here?" I asked.

"We have a long day's sail in front of us," Cadhla answered. "My boys are more than capable to pull the oars until wind comes." Then lifting his nose to scent the air, "And it will come, soon. I'll trade you a tale of Vercingetorix for the tale you came to tell Maedoc."

"That's a deal," I said.

Cadhla switched hands to hold the tiller in his left, then spat on his right hand and held it out for me to shake. I smiled, spat in my own hand. I looked into Cadhla's eyes as I took his hand. Those eyes were strong and clear.

"Not two years ago, a stranger like you arrived at Maedoc's fishing village," he began. "He called himself Belvedere and came with a few companions, just like you. He wore the symbol of the *ailm*, same as you," and he pointed to the small metal cross I wore on a chain around my neck.

I held the bottom of the cross away from my chest with my thumb and forefinger and asked, "What does this mean to you?"

"The ailm symbolizes strong energy that survives through the challenges of winter. It is the symbol of the fir, one of the sacred trees, with its resilience, strength, endurance." I listened to what the captain was telling me. "Vercingetorix saw the stranger's ailm as a challenge."

"How is the fir symbol a challenge?" I asked.

"After this Belvedere arrived in the village, he convinced a few of the town slaves that his power was greater than the power of Maedoc's druid. Those slaves told a tale of a powerful wizard who was nailed to a tree and killed but came back to life to vanquish his enemies. Those slaves began to claim that the wizard and his druid, Belvedere, held the only true power." The captain allowed time to consider his tale.

"For attacking the old gods and the power of the druids, Maedoc declared the stranger a non-person, outside the protection of the laws. Vercingetorix and some soldiers dragged Belvedere to the harbor and tried to drown him. Some fishers and ship masters intervened and stopped the drowning, warning the soldiers and the druid that the sea gods would be angered at this killing. Belvedere sailed away soon after. I heard from another captain that he died across the water among the Romans in Britain."

"And what of the slaves who believed in him?" I asked.

"Returned to their masters," is all Cadhla could tell. "Vercingetorix saw you, a stranger claiming to be ri and druid, saw your ailm, and decided you were just like this Belvedere. He decided to squish you before you infested his home."

I nodded, holding the cross symbol in my fingers and contemplated Cadhla's words.

"When I was a boy," I began, "I was the oldest son of a Roman official in Britain." Cadhla nodded at this turn in my tale. "I was captured by raiders from the south," I said pointing behind me along Ireland's coast, "and sold into slavery." The captain's dark eyebrows furrowed, and his eyes narrowed. "I escaped and returned to my home where I studied and became an easpag."

"When I was near Slemmish in the north, a druid and his daughter befriended me." Cadhla tilted his head to look at me with a question forming on his face. "The druid was called Amergin, and his daughter is Brigid," I stated. "Do you know of them?"

Cadhla looked down at his hand on the tiller and then out to sea for a long while. When he broke his silence he said, "So, you're the one."

"Which one?" I asked.

"You're the one who Amergin helped escape," the captain answered.

"Yes, he helped me," I admitted. "He gave me an old cloak, a staff, some ring money, and pointed where I could find a ship to take me away from Flan's wrath."

"Ship captains talk and pass tales," Cadhla said. "They tell the tale of Flan's wrath and the fall of Amergin."

I know sadness crossed my face and made a home in my eyes. "After you fled, Flan found Amergin alone in his hut. Four warriors came with him, and his son limped behind."

I nodded.

"Cathal wasn't worth Flan's spit, but he was his son and you struck him with your staff," the captain continued. "They came looking for vengeance."

"But I wasn't there!" I cried. "Why take out their fury on the old man?"

"Cathal told Flan that you were in love with the druid's slave daughter." He waited for me to absorb this detail. "When Flan reached Amergin's hut, there were three bowls, still wet with the dregs of broth, sitting by the fire. Flan demanded to know where you were. Amergin just remained silent. Unsatisfied, Flan shouted at the old man that he must know where his daughter was. The druid remained like a stone in the face of the chieftain's anger." Cadhla knew how to tell a tale. He waited for me to imagine the scene, the shouting within Amergin's small hut now crowded with six angry men, the smoldering cook fire, the empty bowls.

"The ship captains say that Flan struck Amergin a mighty blow to the side of his head before the chieftain even recognized he had made a fist. The druid was already ancient. He toppled over like a felled tree next to his fire and was dead before his head touched the ground." Cadhla paused again.

"In a fury, the six men tore through the druid's things and took everything of value or use. Then they set fire to the hut to cover their crime."

"What of Brigid?" I asked.

"She hadn't fled far," the captain answered. "When the druid's hut was engulfed in flame, they heard her keening in the woods nearby, overcome with grief at her father's death and the loss of her lover."

"What happened to her?" I demanded.

"They raped her," Cadhla said and turned his now sad eyes to meet mine. "First Flan, then Cathal, then his four warriors. They left her in the mud with no father, no home, no honor, no place."

Tears streamed down both my cheeks. My hands shook with anger.

"That was many, many years ago," the captain said. "Brigid appealed to the local king to restore her honor and avenge her druid father. Not wishing to punish a chieftain over a slave, that king told her she was a non-person and had no honor to restore."

A long silence settled between that detail and Cadhla's next words. "The ship captains say this Brigid still lives in the north, that she has a dark and terrible beauty, and she waits for her lover's return."

"You look worried," I said to Cadhla.

"It is also told that the druids met in council soon after Amergin's death," the captain continued. "Their council judged Amergin's death a terrible crime. They decreed that in giving you his cloak, Amergin had transferred his power to you. In giving you his money, he symbolically gave you the wealth of Ireland." Cadhla's words struck me like hammer blows.

"The druid council feared you. They prophesied that you would return one day in wrath, either to wreck Ireland or lead her to a new light."

The captain looked at me directly. "Vercingetorix had more than enough reason to fear you. But, if you are this Brigid's lover returned, I am willing to help you on your journey to her."

With that, our ship rowed slowly north. Silence gathered between us.

37. Black Pond

The first thing I noticed about Ath Cliath was the ships' masts gathered along the southern bank of the harbor. There were more than 50 masts. The settlement had as many ships tied at anchor as London. "Why is this place called Ath Cliath?" I asked Cadhla.

He pointed to the bank on the far side of the harbor and said, "When the tide is high, like it is now, the river empties into the harbor and grows more than 150 paces wide. There is no place to ford the river until you reach a narrows upstream." The captain paused. My face displayed lack of understanding. "Even though this is a fishing village and port, it's necessary to be able to reach the city by land. Upstream, the local chieftain maintains a ford at the narrows."

"Ath Cliath is the name for the ford?" I asked.

"Yes, Ath Cliath, ford of the hurdles," he answered.

Our boat pulled slowly alongside two other merchant ships on the muddy banks of the river. The crew stepped their oars. The stone anchor was dropped. The sailors readied the boat to be unloaded. Niall and Blaise rose from their places amidship, gathered our baggage, and joined me in the stern near the steering board.

Cadhla turned to me and asked, "What now, Easpag Patrick?"

I looked to the docks and the busy paths leading to the wood walled city on a slight hill just beyond the river. "Now I'll seek an audience with the chieftain of Ath Cliath," I said.

"Last you talked with a chieftain didn't turn out so well," laughed Cadhla. "Why seek out the chieftain, when in Ath Cliath there might still be followers of your Christ left from the visit of the stranger before you? Some of his followers were sold north after Maedoc's troubles."

"We might find a welcome with Belvedere's converts," offered Blaise.

"One of Belvedere's follies was to begin by converting the slaves. I don't look to repeat that mistake."

Blaise looked confused. Niall's eyes considered the point.

"The chieftain, the king holds power," I continued. "If we convert the chieftain of a place his followers will join us. If we threaten the chieftain of a place, no matter how many low born we convert, that chieftain will force us to leave. Beginning here by preaching to the slaves is like throwing good seed on untilled ground." I allowed the captain and my companions to consider my words. "I'll begin by seeking men of power."

Niall smiled at this strategy.

"The local druids who hold spiritual power here are likely to oppose us," I added. "Our Christ is the son of a jealous God. That God doesn't tolerate other gods. The druids will sense that and fight us."

Niall and Blaise nodded. Concern showed on their faces.

"They will try to stop us, imprison us, perhaps even kill us."

Blaise turned pale as he remembered Otho's death just a few days before.

"We must be stronger than them, wiser than them, craftier than them."

I surprised the captain with my next words. "Cadhla, you are chieftain of this boat. You are chieftain, even if only over the four men on your crew. What do you make of my tale of the Christ and his draíocht?"

"It is a tale of powerful magic, Easpag," the captain said, using my ecclesial title.

"You have a rare opportunity, before even the chieftain of this place hears my words. Will you freely choose to be joined to this magic or to let it pass by?" I asked.

The captain tensed at my question. "What would I need to do to know part of this magic?"

"It is simple," I answered, "not difficult." I saw Cadhla relax.

"Only three things are asked of you. First, you must acknowledge this Christ as the son of the King of Gods." I paused and waited for a sign that Cadhla agreed. When he nodded yes, I continued, "Water is poured over your head in this Christ's name to wash away anything that keeps you away from his draíocht." The captain nodded once more. "And you must pledge your honor to follow his way and help me, when I ask, as his Easpag here in Ireland."

Cadhla considered this last request for a significant time. I allowed silence to deepen between us as I stared across the boats and docks to the town walls.

At last, he laughed heartily and clasped me on the back. "Easpag, you are a bit of a pirate as well as ri and druid. Yes, I'll freely choose this Christ draíocht. Let's get it done. Then we'll get this boat unloaded."

This is how I made my fourth convert to the Gospel in Ireland. Cadhla was baptized in his boat with water from the river Liffey. He commanded his four crew to join him, and they did. I now had a flock of a chieftain and a chieftain's woman, a warrior, a slave girl, a ship captain, and his four crew. I jumped from the boat to the dock. Niall and Blaise followed.

As the boat was being unloaded, Blaise asked me, "you said begin with the chieftain. But you began your mission here with Cadhla. Why?"

Niall joined in on the question. "Yes, why, Easpag? A ship captain commands, yes. But a captain of four is much lower than the local chieftain. Why?"

"Because he was ready," I answered. "We spoke through the day while you two slept with the baggage. He listened, he was ready, and he can help us."

With the boat unloaded, Cadhla joined us on the dock. "I need to know the name of the chieftain of this place," I said, "and whatever else you can tell me about him."

"He is called Alphin, son of Eochaid," Cadhla began. I learned that the port had a second name. "It is also called Dyflinn after the black pool of water that forms where a second river joins this one on the far side of the walls. Between the walls rise more than 500 roofs. Dyflinn's chieftain's great hall and the roofs of his home lay behind a second wall within the walls. Their fortress overlooks the black pool on the far side of the town."

"What does this Alphin, son of Eochaid, need?" I asked. "What does he desire?"

"He has more than any man can want," answered Cadhla. His face grew slack as he considered with his mind's eye the great wealth and power of this chieftain. "He has three wives, many sons, and commands more than 100 warriors. The land for more than four days' journey surrounding the town pays tribute and brings its produce to him. Ships come and go and each one pays a tithe to Alphin that fattens his treasury. What more can a man want?"

"Honor and battle glory," spoke Niall.

"To be important more than feared," I added.

Cadhla, Niall, and Blaise all looked at me. I explained no further.

We made our way from the docks through Dyflinn's gates. They were wide, thrown open like arms holding a basket waiting to receive an offering. Four soldiers guarded the gate and asked travelers entering or leaving what their business was. When we reached the guard, Cadhla answered for our party.

"My ship has just landed," he winked. "My friends and I would like to explore the ale houses of Dyflinn." He leered at the soldiers conspiratorially. They looked bored and waved us past. We weren't carrying weapons. Cadhla had demanded that Niall leave his sword with our baggage. We weren't carrying trade goods and so had nothing to tax or rob. We simply looked to be three sailors and their captain off the boat to get drunk and whore in the port. Nothing new or extraordinary.

Once inside, Cadhla led us to an ale house deep within the port quarter of the settlement. It was filled with sailors, captains, and traders but no warriors.

"If you want to know what's going on in a settlement, find the ale house where the traders drink," he said. "If you're willing to pay for good information, someone will tell you."

"How do you know who to ask?"

"I don't," the captain answered. "I tell the tavern owner that I'm looking for information and that I can pay, then let him find the right person for me." Cadhla waited for questions we didn't know how to ask. His patience wore out and so he continued. "I buy a tankard of ale and pretend to drink. It's important to have your wits when someone approaches you."

I nodded this time for him to continue. "He'll ask how much you have. Don't answer. Don't show your coins." I nodded once more. "Tell him you'll pay what it's worth only after you've heard his information."

38. Dyflinn Ale House

Blaise appeared overwhelmed. He still had the air of Auxerre around him, an atmosphere of trust and letters, chants, and prayer. The stale smell of old ale and sweat, the sounds of curses and raucous laughter, the sway and thrill of the bar-maids were new to him. Watching Blaise that day was like looking at a man who had never swum thrown overboard at sea. He would either sink and be absorbed by the waters, or he would rise and swim. I was proud of my brother that day. He rose and swam. His eyes, wide open, took it in. Later that night, when we remembered what happened, he was able to tell the tale to its finest detail, with laughter and wisdom. That day, Blaise became my warrior monk.

"What do you want to know?" asked the old man who sat down on the bench next to me.

Three fingers were missing from his left hand. His right hand rested on the table. It was gnarled with scars and the marks of a life lived at sea. He wore a cloak of two colors, but I noted that the material was finely made. It was a heavy wool, not coarse spun. And its colors, red and green, were deeply set and true. The cloak communicated wealth without privilege or status. His eyes were alive with intelligence beneath their deep browns. A half-laughing smile crossed his face that suggested he could be either friendly or dangerous. Most of all, I noticed the triple spiral amulet he wore around his neck.

"Who asks me?" I replied.

"Names are not as important here as information," he answered, beginning to rise.

"Friend," I said, placing my hand on the table in front of us, "I am a stranger here and only seek information to help a wanderer become more welcome."

"Information such as . . .?" brown eyes asked.

"Word of what is new or troubling here," I said. "Something to help me when I meet the chieftain. Information about the local druids."

Brown eyes looked at me with suspicion, then laughed. "You're a fool," he said. "You're like that other stranger, the one who the druid tried to drown."

"Tell me," I said and touched my purse. His eyes eagerly darted to follow my hand. "Tell me something useful and I'll make it worth your while."

News began to flow out of the old man. Dyflinn had been under a cloud of sickness for the past three moons. A fever had taken Alphin's youngest wife and one of his sons. The fever had spread through the quarter of the city nearest Alphin's inner fort. One in three households there had been touched by death. To quell the sickness, Alphin summoned a druid who calls himself Diurmid. Diurmid cast bone oracles and decreed that the sickness would pass in two moon's time. One moon had already come and gone and the second was near finished. The sickness still spread. Diurmid had chanted, fasted, and prayed very loudly in the chieftain's compound. But there was no sign that the fever had passed. "Alphin fears for the lives of his youngest son and the boy's mother," brown eyes said. "Diurmid fears for his life if his power is shown to be weak."

With that, the old man sat back and looked at me with the question in his eyes: What is that information worth to you? I removed the smallest ring coin from my purse and cut a significant sliver of gold from its circle. He looked at me with raised eyebrows. I moved my knife to slice another sliver of gold when Cadhla reached across to stay my hand. "He'll return in two days' time and cut another sliver for you," the captain said, "if your information is true and if you keep silent about this." Brown eyes nodded. Our conversation finished; he left the table. I turned to look at Cadhla. When I turned once again to thank brown eyes for his information, he was gone from the ale house, disappeared. "In two days time you can pay him," the captain said. "Or we'll be dead."

39. Alphin's Hall

We found a room above the ale house for the night and allowed word to spread that three strangers had entered Dyflinn with Cadhla. A small exchange of coins guaranteed that word would spread of a ship's captain, a warrior from the south, and two strangers from away. We had one large room with neither cot nor fireplace. But it was dry and clean. When night fell, we lay on the bare wood floor, rolled our spare cloaks to make rests for our heads, and pulled our traveling cloaks around us for warmth.

Shortly after dawn, the door to our room resounded as a heavy fist pounded three times. "Awake in there, awake!" shouted a voice. A heavy boot kicked the door open, and five warriors strode inside, hands on their swords and ferocity on their faces.

Startled from sleep, we each hurried to stand up. "What is this?" I began to ask and Cadhla silenced me.

"The chieftain's guards," the captain said.

"Cadhla," one of the soldiers said, "you are known here. But these three are strangers, two are not even Irish." He paused to look at each of us with stern eyes. "Alphin orders us to bring you to his hall." Four of the soldiers moved to surround us while their leader's attention seized on me. "Who are you?" he demanded.

"I am called Patrick," I answered. "I am an easpag, a druid and ri from Rome."

The soldier's right hand left his sword to touch what I assumed must be an amulet beneath his tunic. "Bind them," he commanded. "We're taking them to Alphin's hall."

Alphin kept his home and his hall within a second palisade inside the wood walls of Dyflinn. The sharpened tree trunks of this inner wall were framed by three watch towers. Alert soldiers stood in those towers. More guards stood at the palisade's only gate. Heavy iron-reinforced oak doors stood closed as we approached Dyflinn's inner fortress. Courage and fear both hung in the air.

Alphin's soldiers might be wary and brave. Yet no amount of watchfulness would keep sickness outside.

Once inside the fortress, Alphin's hall was the grandest I had ever seen in Ireland. Its wooden walls rose almost 30 feet high and were crowned with fresh thatch. The outside walls were painted with druidic symbols, the triple spiral, the coiled knot, the Awen, and more. I noticed that the cross limbed symbol of the fir, the ailm, was missing. One newly painted splash of white covered what might have been the ailm's place. The hall lengthened more than 100 paces from end to end and spanned twenty paces across.

Inside, the hall was lonely. Darkness settled from the thatch to its beaten earth floor. Trophies of war and of the hunt hung forlorn along the walls. Nothing burned in the three fire circles that stood in the center of the hall. Small flames lit one fireplace at the far end. Beside that fireplace, on a chair sat Alphin. His head hung down; his gaze focused on the dirt at his feet. He appeared an exhausted and defeated warrior at the verge of despair. The soldiers marched us to within three paces of the chieftain and halted.

"You commanded we bring the strangers to you," the leader of the guard spoke. Alphin nodded. "This one is Cadhla, the trader," he said pointing at the ship's captain. "And these are the three strangers you heard of."

A voice from the shadows emerged, "They are like the other one," the voice croaked.

"Silence, Diurmid," the chieftain commanded.

"They are like the other one. He brought the fever with him. Because they are here, the fever cannot leave."

Alphin looked at the druid and then at us. "Speak," he commanded.

"When my hands are free my tongue will speak," I said.

"I could just have you killed," Alphin said.

"Yes, you could. But then you will never know."

"Unbind him," Alphin ordered his guard.

As the warrior cut my bonds, I said, "And free my companions."

Alphin nodded and the warriors freed Niall, Blaise, and Cadhla from their ties. "Now speak and tell me why you are here and why you spend your first day in Dyflinn asking questions about me."

"I have heard of Alphin's strength and wisdom." His eyes fixed on mine and probed for weakness or deceit. "And I have heard of his troubles. That a fever has taken your son and wife and threatens Dyflinn."

Alphin nodded. "Continue."

"I bring a draíocht with me that is stronger than death. A draíocht from the son of the King of Gods that should belong to a great chieftain like Alphin."

"Lies," croaked Diurmid. "Lies! The strangers brought the fever with them. They bring death, not magic. They scheme to take away our gods and leave us weak."

"Quiet!" thundered Alphin, half rising from his chair. "For two months you have chanted, fasted, and called on the old gods. Nothing has happened. Nothing!" The chieftain fell back into his chair. "It is time to hear someone else's words. Perhaps they can take this fever away."

"I make no false promises, unlike Diurmid," I said. "Fevers come and go from all great villages. In Rome and in London, when fever strikes and will not leave, their chieftains burn the homes where death has called."

"He will have you burn your own city," the druid accused. "Nothing will be left."

"Rome holds more than 100,000 houses," I answered. "London holds more than 10,000. If what I say didn't work, they would all be empty. But both are great cities, far larger than Dyflinn."

"Will this drive away the fever?" Alphin asked.

"I understand that your druid has said that the fever will be gone at the end of two months of his chanting and fasting. Is that so?" I asked.

"Yes," hissed Diurmid.

"And when are those two months up?"

"In two days time," Alphin answered.

"Then, in three days time, when the fever remains, do as I say," I commanded. "I will pray to my God. If the fever does not diminish within a week, you may do with us as you will."

Alphin looked at me, then at my companions, then finally at Diurmid. "It will be done, just as you say."

Diurmid began to voice his objection. "You have had your time. If in two days your promised deliverance isn't here, we will try the stranger's way."

The chieftain waved a hand to signal the end of our audience. My companions and I were taken to a large building in the compound that was home to Alphin's servants. We waited for two days while the fever continued to ravage Dyflinn. On the third day, Alphin called for me.

40. A Tale Worth More Than Gold

Many years later, I had heard what happened described as a miracle. I simply told Alphin to do what I knew had worked in Rome and London. The bodies of the dead were burned. Houses where death called were cleansed with lye then burned where possible. The belongings of the dead were burned along with their houses. The places where death hid became a visible enemy for Alphin's guard. They had something to combat, and a fighting spirit returned to his warriors. And I prayed. I called on the voice of Slemmish and on all the saints I could remember. Sometimes a miracle is just a matter of timing. Sometimes it is just luck. I don't pretend to understand what drove the fever away. But I do know that at the end of three days there were fewer citizens of Dyflinn who suffered from the fever than the day before.

"We are winning," I encouraged Alphin. "Keep fighting."

So, the chieftain and his warriors continued on the path I asked of them. At the end of a second week, the fever was almost gone. At the end of the third week, it was a memory.

One hundred houses were burned shells. Two hundred citizens of Dyflinn were dead. Diurmid's anger smoldered. And I stood ready before Dyflinn's chieftain's throne to tell him my tale.

Alphin's hall was different from the first time. It was full instead of empty. Eager fires burned in the fireplaces at both ends. The firepits down the center of the hall were lit and three fingers of smoke from those cooking fires rose to the smoke holes in the thatch above. More than 50 warriors were present that day. I noticed that only Alphin's immediate guard wore swords at their sides. The others had short daggers on their belts, having left their larger weapons for safe keeping at the hall's door.

But most of all, I noticed the women and children. Theirs was the spark of energy that lit the hall and made it come alive. Small ones darted in and around the servers with their platters of food and flasks of ale or mead. Even smaller children held to their mothers' skirts or sucked thumbs while sitting on laps. There were young men and young ladies in the hall dancing the timeless dance of hunt and chase; although who was the hunted and who the chased was often difficult to tell. The ladies of Alphin's stronghold were in that hall, too. Cloaks, dresses, and tunics displayed their owner's status. The wife of the chief of the guards wore a tunic spun of three colors adorned with a brooch of amethyst and copper. I saw the wife of an ordinary warrior in a dress of two colors chasing her toddling child through the melee.

Alphin had no need to display his rank with his colors. He wore a tunic of simple green. A toque of gold hung around his neck. Alphin's ladies sat next to him, also in simple green. On a chair to his right sat a noble-looking lady of equal years to the chieftain. She wore a chain of gold around her neck and a small gold brooch on her right shoulder.

"That is Alphin's first wife, Queen Mugain," Cadhla whispered from behind me. I bowed to the lady.

To Alphin's left on a small chair, also in a simple green shift but with a small child on her lap, sat a younger woman of startling beauty. Her auburn hair hung in waves almost to her lap, her blue eyes flashed in a face that stopped my thoughts. To look at her was to experience desire, joy, sorrow, and hope all at once. She was gazing at her child when I approached Alphin's throne chair. A guard whispered something to her from behind and she looked up from her child and straight into my eyes. A suggestion of a smile crossed her face, and she offered the slightest of nods. I bowed to her and to Alphin and then looked directly at the chieftain and said, "You summoned me, and I am here, ri Alphin, son of Eochaid and chieftain of Dyflinn."

The hall fell into silence. Behind me, I heard Cadhla whisper once more, "The lady to the right is called Aideen. Alphin's youngest son, Faelan, sits on her lap. The chieftain is bewitched by Aideen and loves Faelan dearer than any possession. It was Aideen's and Faelan's lives you saved."

Faelan took his eyes off his mother and looked to Alphin as silence gathered in the hall. He followed Alphin's gaze towards me. I saw the boy's tiny fist reach out in my direction. Then his fingers extended to grab the air between us as if he could pull me to himself. Aideen looked down at that tiny hand and gently pulled it back.

"Today we celebrate our victory over the fever," the chieftain declared into the silence.

"And we thank our visitor from strange lands for helping us," rang out Aideen's voice. The sound of her voice was like sweet chimes heard in a wood. Alphin's jaw hung open. His lady had interrupted him just as he was beginning his speech. I saw his anger flare to be replaced almost immediately by simmering consternation. As he started to speak to her, Aideen smiled, and the chieftain stopped before the first word left his throat.

"Today, we celebrate our victory over the fever," Alphin began again, "and we thank our visitor from strange lands for helping us."

He nodded towards one of his warriors who held a small chest. The warrior placed the chest in front of me. "Open it," invited Alphin.

I opened the chest and saw within a pile of silver and gold coins, chains, brooches, and rings with red and blue jewels. "The chest holds one year's tax," Alphin stated for the benefit of the hall. "I gift you with it and the thanks of Dyflinn and of its chieftain."

A buzz of whispers murmured through the hall all around me. Alphin's gift was enormous, a gift that a chieftain would offer in supplication to an overlord. A gift such as this would impoverish another settlement or another ri. But Dyflinn was rich and Alphin had many such chests in his treasury. Still, it was a noble offering.

I gently closed the lid on the chest and bowed to the chieftain. "I am honored by your gift and thank you," I said. "But I fear it is more than I deserve."

Alphin and his ladies smiled. Aideen leaned forward to hear what I would say next. Faelan reached out again with his tiny fingers to grab hold of the space between us. I smiled at the child and then met her eyes as I continued, "All I ask as gratitude for helping with the fever is a chance to tell my tale." I could feel Niall's alarm from where he stood behind and to my right hand. "You risk dishonoring the chieftain," he said as quietly as he could. "You are turning down a king's ransom."

I didn't care about the gold and the jewels then, and I don't care about them now even though some have accused me of being greedy. I cared about my mission from Celestine, the mission to bring the Gospel to Ireland. Pelagius might be the threat to that Gospel in Britain but here in Ireland, the Gospel was threatened by smallness of mind and heart, an unwillingness to listen, and the power of the druids.

Closing the lid on that chest and asking for the opportunity to be heard directly addressed each of those obstacles. I valued my tale more than gold, which inspired a greatness of heart and a curiosity. What could make a tale worth more than the treasure chest I had been offered. And my willingness to forego a reward for the telling of my tale untied the knot of fear from the druid's warning. The Irish are a courageous people with curious minds. They love a good tale. And I sought to tell the tale that would capture their hearts, minds, bodies, and souls.

"What is this tale?" rang out Aideen's voice once more.

"It is a tale of sorcery and dark magic," began Diurmid from his place, standing behind the throne chair.

Alphin abruptly raised his hand to silence the druid, then looked at Aideen. "Would you hear this Roman sorcerer's tale?" he asked her.

"Yes, my lord," she demurred. Faelan had turned in his mother's lap and his grasping fingers now caught the bottom of the sleeve on Alphin's tunic. The chieftain's free hand tenderly reached out to hold his son's tiny hand in his own. Looking into Aideen's eyes, he said, "My lady would hear your tale. Begin."

"More than 20 generations ago, in a land far, far away within the empire of Rome," I began, "the King of the Gods decided to send his only son to be born on earth." I could feel the hall begin to settle in to listen to my tale. "The child was born in very humble circumstances. He was the only son of an only daughter from a line of the youngest sons of youngest sons that stretched back to the kings at the dawn of time. That is to say, the forgotten blood of kings flowed through him even though he was born in a stable."

"How are you certain he was noble?" asked Aideen.

"When he was born, messengers from the God of the sky sang for joy in the night and strange kings from far away visited to offer gifts." Heads nodded. "And even more proof, the evil king of the land who had stolen his throne from the true king sent soldiers to kill him."

I saw a look of horror on Aideen's face. "They didn't find the child so in their wrath they slew more than 200 other newborns still at breast." I turned and looked around that hall and saw the right hands of several mothers clutching their hearts. "The child's parents fled that evil king and took the baby boy to hide in the city of the great King of Egypt."

I could feel relief flood the room. I continued my story of how that boy grew into an excellent manhood, full of courage and power. "He was filled with the spirit of the King of Gods," I told them. "The druids of his own people grew to fear how much power the young man had. They refused to recognize that he was the child of the King of the Gods." My tale continued with how the party of Caiaphas, the high priest, along with Herod, the Roman under king of the land, conspired to put the son of the King of the Gods to death. "So, they captured him, whipped and beat him, then nailed him to a tree."

Looks of dread and dismay filled the hall. "And when he wouldn't die, one of their soldiers," I said looking at the captain of the guard, "stabbed him in the side with his lance."

The captain held my eyes for a moment and then looked away. "They buried him in a stone tomb and thought that they had silenced the messenger of the King of Gods," I added. "They believed with the messenger silenced they need not listen to the message."

I allowed silence to gather around the end of my words. Heads began to turn and whisper to one another.

Dissatisfaction with my tale was rising like a tide in that hall. I knew that the Irish love tales of courage and heroism. But they like their tales to end well, with a heroic death that is the price of victory, or a death that stems defeat, or a hero rewarded by the gods. My tale hung on an ending of a defeated hero tortured to death and quickly buried.

"Is that your tale?" asked one of the serving women from her place behind the chieftain's ladies.

"Telling this tale is worth more to you than a chest of treasure?" asked Aideen.

"Bah!" spat out Diurmid. "A worthless horror."

"Three women who loved the messenger, his mother, his lover, and his heart friend, went to his tomb three days after he died. They went to honor his body and mourn," I began again. Heads rose to attention and silence fell once more in the hall. "The body was not there," I stated. "A sky messenger, called an angel, rested beside the tomb and told those three women that the son of the King of Gods had defeated death.

"'He lives,' the angel said." Looks of doubt emerged on both the men and women around me. "He rose from death and was seen by those women and by his friends many, many times."

"Where did he live after returning from the Kingdom of the Dead?" asked Aideen.

"He walked among his friends for almost two moons," I said. "Then he rose into the skies and returned to his father, the King of Gods."

Nods and smiles grew on the faces around me. This was a proper end for a tale. "Never to die again," I added. More smiles and murmurs of "Good story."

"But, before he went back to his father, he shared with his friends the secret of his draíocht that is stronger than death." An expectant silence flowed back into the hall. "And that is the draíocht I carry with me from Rome to this hall," I finished.

A few very young children whimpered, uncomfortable in the strange stillness of that moment. Aideen handed Faelan off to one of her maids and then turned to confer in whispers with Alphin. I stood in my place before the three chairs and looked straight ahead. I composed my gaze to express calm steadfastness and openness of heart. I reminded myself of the sweetness of the message in the Gospels, of the grandeur of Celestine in Rome, and of my friend and mentor, Abbot Germanus. I tried to be brave. It took the greatest courage to just stand and wait.

"Is this the magic you used to save Faelan and Dyflinn from the fever?" Aideen asked, turning her eyes back to measure me. I nodded my head once in assent. "If I follow your magic, will it keep Faelan from death?" she asked.

"Each of us dies, lady," I answered. "Even the son of the King of Gods tasted death. My draíocht will allow your son to rise to new life after death."

"What must I do to possess this magic?" she continued.

Alphin held up his hand to still the conversation. Turning to Aideen, he said loudly enough for all to hear, "You will continue to question this druid in private."

From behind the throne, Diurmid began to hiss his objection, "I will listen to your counsel when we are alone," he told him. "For now, this easpag has my gratitude. Keep the treasure," the chieftain said. "We will consider your tale."

41. Freezing the River of Words

My audience with Alphin was over. Warriors of the guard motioned for me to step back from my place before the chieftain's chair and return to my stranger's place at the rear of the assembly. Later, the captain of the guard summoned Blaise, Niall, Cadhla, and me to a private audience with Aideen. Along with her attendants, the chieftain's lady and Faelan were quietly baptized late that afternoon.

Spite simmered around Diurmid whenever I was in his presence during the days that followed Aideen's baptism. I entered Alphin's hall almost daily. Frequently, the druid stood slightly behind the chieftain and to his side, whispering. Diurmid's hard gray eyes would meet mine, then he would return to whispering to Alphin.

One afternoon, Aideen asked me to visit her, privately, in her sitting room. "Is the death draíocht the only magic you have?" she asked.

I looked at her. "Is this not enough, my lady?"

"It is more than enough. Even so, Diurmid pours poison daily into Alphin's ear. He tells him to fear you, that you've come to take his throne for the son of the King of the Gods. He tells him that this Christ is lonely in the sky and longs for a chair on earth to sit upon."

"Why Alphin's throne?" I asked with disbelief in my voice.

"'Rome grows old and feeble,' Diurmid tells the chieftain. That is why you are here. That is why the other stranger came before you and spread discord among the slaves." Aideen paused and looked directly into my eyes. I felt my heart weaken. To see her was to be enchanted. To desire her was to be ensnared. "Do you have any other magic?" she asked again.

"We know the magic of freezing the river of words," Blaise chimed in from behind.

Startled, I turned and looked at my young brother. What would possess him to offer such a response? What magic could turn words to ice?

"Writing," Blaise said softly to me and winked.

I understood immediately. "What are the twin sources of any druid's power?" I asked Aideen.

"They draw on the power of the old gods," she answered. "They have trained their Duile to draw on the Moringa and all the others."

"Yes," I agreed, "and what else?"

"They know the tales of power. They spend years learning and remembering the stories until they can draw on them at will."

"What if anyone could remember their stories of power?" I asked. "What if all their words were a well anyone could drop a bucket into?"

"Then the druids would lose their hold on chieftains and warriors." Aideen answered. "Do you have the magic to accomplish such a thing?"

"I do," I answered. "Tomorrow, call another druid, someone other than Diurmid, and ask him to tell you a short tale of one of the old gods, a tale of a warrior hero to combat the Christ." Aideen looked at me full of doubt. "I will sit here and listen with you, so you know that I am not interfering. Have Blaise sit and listen from a hidden place." Aideen nodded consent. "I will leave my brother here after the tale is finished and will not return until you call for me." Wondering how this would prove this new magic, her eyes turned serious.

"Blaise will need three objects to make this draíocht," I added.

"What are they?" Aideen asked with concern in her voice. She didn't want to risk Alphin's anger by asking for something precious or rare.

"He will need a quill, the feather of a goose will do," I said.

Doubt crossed the lady's eyes.

"Your servants will have to bring the quill. I will bring a pot of ink and velum."

"What is velum?" Aideen asked.

"It is the skin of a goat or cow," Blaise said. "It will have been bleached and stretched, then scraped clean so I can paint on in. Without it, we cannot work the magic."

The next day arrived and my arrangements were all in place. Just after the morning meal, I stood silently to the side of Aideen's chair as she requested her druid to tell a tale of magic to defend Ireland against the Christ. Blaise sat at a small table hidden on the far side of a door to the room's porch. A pot of ink, a sheet of velum, and three goose quills lay on the table.

"I sing the tale of the spear of Lugh, and Balor, one-eyed," began the druid. He told a tale from the dark mists of Ireland's memories, the tale of Lugh, the son of the King of the Sky, who helped the Gaels defeat Balor of the evil eye and claim Ireland from the Tuath de Danann. "And so, with his sling, Lugh hurled a stone that drove Balor's evil eye from his head."

Aideen smiled as the druid had finished his tale. "Thank you," she said.

"This Christ is like Balor of the Evil Eye," said the druid. "He can see only one place among the gods. But he can be driven out just as Lugh slew Balor." The druid scowled at me, then bowed and left the queen's chambers.

"And what of your magic," Aideen asked me when the druid had withdrawn.

"How long will you need?" I called out to Blaise.

"Till just before sunset," Blaise called back. I could hear the scratching of the quill. "And more than likely, two more goose feathers. It was a long tale."

"With my lady's permission, I will leave now," I said. "Blaise will remain here to work our magic. I will return shortly before sunset to prove how words can be frozen." I bowed to her and left her chambers.

As the day's light lengthened towards sunset, Aideen summoned me to her rooms. She sat in regal beauty, still and poised. I bowed to her then called with hope in my voice, "Blaise, are you ready?"

"Yes, Easpag Patrick," came his eager voice.

"Then begin," I commanded.

"I sing the tale of the spear of Lugh, and Balor, one-eyed," began Blaise, word for word matching the tale sung earlier by Aideen's druid. The words flowed out of Blaise until he reached the tale's end, "And so with his sling, Lugh hurled a stone that drove Balor's evil eye from his head." There was a slight pause. "I chose not to add the part at the end comparing the Christ to Balor," he said and fell silent.

I saw a look of shock on Aideen. "How did he do that? You might have known the tale from your time among us. But your younger brother is not one of us. He couldn't know the tale with all its details."

"Join us and bring the velum," I called to Blaise.

"This draíocht is called writing," I told Aideen. Pointing at the velum in Blaise's hands, I said, "Blaise holds the tale of Lugh of the Long Spear, the tale of Lugh and Balor, in his hands. Your druids are not the only ones who can own the stories."

Sly comprehension filled her eyes. "Alphin will be very interested in the power of this new draíocht," Aideen said. "You have showed great power and given me a gift that will convince the chieftain to allow me to continue to follow your Christ."

News of this new magic spread quickly through Alphin's hall and household. When Blaise accompanied me into the hall, he was treated with a deepening respect. He was more than my shadow. He could capture a tale and put it on parchment. Two afternoons after demonstrating the power of writing and reading, as we entered Alphin's hall, I turned to Blaise and said, "You'll have to teach them how to make ink."

Blaise blinked and shot back, "Why me? Why ink?"

"Because you'll teach them how to write," I said.

"Why can't one of the others?" Blaise began to object and then remembered that neither Cadhla nor Niall could write. "But I want to go with you," he pleaded.

"And if I had more monks, I would take you with me and leave another here," I answered. "But there are only the two of us who can read and write. When I leave here my journey will take me north into dangerous lands among Irish who already want me dead."

"Then I should be with you to help you," Blaise argued.

"You will stay here and strengthen the converts we gain before I leave."

"But Patrick—"

I held up my hand to silence him. "Am I your bishop? Are you my monk or an untamed vagabond?" I asked, my words turning hard and commanding.

"Your monk, Easpag Patrick," Blaise answered using my Irish title.

I softened my voice. "Blaise, you are my brother, dear friend, and companion on this adventure. When I leave, it will be just a temporary parting of our paths. I will return and we will be together again, share this journey again. But until then," I leaned forward to put a hand on his shoulder, "I need you to do this for me." I waited for him to take in what I'd said. "Will you do this for me?"

Blaise's eyes turned down towards his feet. I could see him struggling with his disappointment at being left behind and with his fear. As a monk, before we left for Rome, his world was the scriptorium. I was about to leave him surrounded by soldiers and druids and, maybe even most frightening of all, women. I saw Blaise win the struggle with himself and then his shoulders squared. He looked up and into my eyes. "Yes, Easpag," he said. "It will be done as you command."

"Thank you, brother," I said and saw affection replace his fear. "I'll have to ordain you a priest, of course, so you can lead a church here."

Shock joined affection on Blaise's face as I turned and continued into the hall.

42. The Tale of the Lost Son

"Easpag Patrick," Alphin called out when he saw me enter the hall, "approach!"

I hastened, along with Blaise, Niall, and Cadhla, towards the chieftain's chair at the end of the hall. "Rí Alphin," I said and offered a slight bow. From the corners of my eyes, I saw my companions mirror that bow. I glanced to see the Lady Aideen at the chieftain's side. Queen Mugain's chair sat empty and Dyflinn's principal druid was nowhere to be seen. "I am at your service," I said and waited.

"Aideen has shared with me the story of how your brother," he said pointing at Blaise, "worked strong magic when you visited her and her ladies in her sitting room." Alphin stared at Blaise as if he could not believe that such a gentle soul possessed power. "Is this true?"

"Yes, Rí Alphin," I answered, allowing a simple phrase to carry the weight of all the rumors that circled through Dyflinn.

"Show me here, now, in front of my guard so I can see that this is no dark magic," demanded the chieftain.

"Gladly, my Lord," I answered. "We need but one thing."

"Lady Aideen said that you needed three," the chieftain said.

"To freeze the river of words, that is true," I answered. "And we can freeze the river of a new tale, just as Blaise," I said and pointed, "froze the tale of Lugh and Balor. But," I paused and allowed Alphin to wonder what draíocht I would propose. "The river of the tale that contains all my power is frozen and kept in our rooms. Send a warrior with this ship captain," I pointed to Cadhla, "and have them return with it."

A look of suspicion stole across the chieftain. "What if he brings dark magic into my hall?"

"Then kill him," I replied, "and us too." Startled whispers spun all around me. "Send your guard with him to prevent him from bringing back anything dangerous. He will fetch a large leather object filled with many, many sheets of parchment. The leather cover is painted with an ailm, and the parchment has painted pictures that hold my story fast."

Alphin looked doubtful at my request. "Order your guards to have Cadhla open this object and show them that nothing dark happens. Station a guard outside our rooms, just in case. They will return and assure you that this draíocht is safe."

"Do it," Alphin ordered his guard.

Cadhla lead when the guard returned. He held the book, a copy of the Gospel of Luke, at arm's length in front of him like it was a venomous snake. He showed the unopened book to the chieftain and then, quickly as possible, handed it to Blaise. Blaise kissed the Gospel cover, then touched the top of his head with it. The guards stepped back wary of what magic was about to take place. Smiling his gentle smile, Blaise simply held the book at the level of his heart and waited for my command.

"If Rí Alphin allows it," I said, "my brother will unfreeze one of my favorite tales of power. It is called the Story of the Lost Son."

Alphin nodded his permission to me. In turn I nodded to Blaise and said, "You know the place in the book. Begin there."

Blaise opened the leather binding and found where the tale began. It was one of my favorite stories from the Gospels. I had been beaten by my father, rejected by my mother, and my brothers had wanted to murder me when I returned home. This tale of mercy was what I had hoped for but not found with Calpurnius or Conchessa. Blaise began in a very soft voice, "There was a man who had two sons."

I held up my hand and halted his reading. "This is one of the four Gospels of the Christ," I said to the chieftain. "It contains the way of his draíocht. It is a noble tale full of stories, adventure, heroism, and even treachery." The chieftain leaned forward, eager to hear more.

"Begin again," I said to Blaise, "but this time with power in your voice."

"There was a man who had two sons," Blaise read strongly. "The younger one said to his father, 'Father, give me my share of the estate.' So, he divided his property between them."

Alphin and several of his guards nodded understanding but looked troubled at this beginning.

"Not long after that," the words continued to flow from Blaise, "the younger son got together all he had, set off for a distant country, and there squandered his wealth in wild living." The tale continued through the younger son's decision to return and ask forgiveness of his father, his father's welcoming embrace, and the enraged older brother's jealous protests. "My son," the father said to the jealous son, "you are always with me, and everything I have is yours. But we must celebrate and be glad. This brother of yours was dead and is alive again. He was lost and is found."

There were tears on some of the faces in the hall, smiles on others. Alphin wore a look of profound thought. "Why unfreeze this tale?" the chieftain asked.

"Because you are a father who has lost a son to the fever," I reminded him. "I knew you would understand the power of the father's love for his son in this story. My Christ teaches that his Father, the King of the Gods, is like the father in this tale. You need only to seek him, and he will welcome you with mercy and celebration."

"Is that all?" Alphin asked.

"I also wanted to show that there was no dark magic in this Christ draíocht. It is good magic, and it holds power over the river of words." I waited for the chieftain to show he understood me.

"If you command, Blaise can open any page and read another story. The strength of many rivers of words are gathered in this book."

"Aideen told me that you promised you would share how to work this draíocht over words. Is that also true?"

"Yes, Rí Alphin," I answered. "This magic is called reading and writing, and I have asked my brother Blaise to teach it to whomever you decide."

"What do you ask for in return for this word draíocht?" Alphin said.

"It is my gift to you, Rí Alphin," I said. "Freely given in friendship. I ask nothing in return."

"Is this magic hard to learn?" asked Aideen.

"Yes, lady," answered Blaise before I could stop him.

"No, my lady," I said. Then, looking at Alphin, I added, "Choose someone who is noble, quick of wit, steady, and, most importantly, willing to learn something new. They'll learn fast enough."

"Bring my second son, Kevin, to the hall," commanded Alphin. "He'll master this magic for us."

"Kevin is Lady Etroma's child," Cadhla whispered from behind me. "Queen Mugain will not be happy at this command."

"Easpag Patrick," Alphin called out. "Thank you for this gift. My son will learn your ways." I nodded. "I have a gift for you," the chieftain said. I had not asked a price for the magic of writing but could not refuse a public gift from Dyflinn's chieftain. "I own a farm outside the walls. It has fertile lands and two buildings, a small house, and a great barn. Accept this land and be my friend."

I bowed my thanks and smiled at the chieftain. With this gift, I now had land to call my own in Ireland, was friend to two chieftains, and had an honor status.

Alphin signaled that our audience was completed, and we returned to a place at the back of his hall. "I'm sorry for saying it was hard to learn," Blaise apologized.

"There is no blame between us," I answered. "It turned out excellently. Teach the boy to read by learning to copy that Gospel you carry. He will fall in love with the stories, as each of us has. You will set up a scriptorium at my new farm to teach him. Soon enough, Kevin will be one of us."

43. News From the North

A week came and went. Niall, Cadhla, and I visited Alphin's hall each afternoon. Blaise taught letters to young Kevin. On the eighth day, as we were about to leave the hall, one of Aideen's servants gave me this message. "My lady has gone to her sitting room and asks to see you, now."

"We will come immediately," I answered.

"My lady asks that you come alone," the maid said and was gone before I could say anything more.

"Is this a trap?" asked Niall. He hastened on with, "Why would the chieftain's woman wish you to come alone except to ensnare you? Perhaps she will call out to her guards and accuse you of attacking her. We will all be killed."

"Aideen believes we saved her son and that we have freely given our draíocht to Alphin," I said. "She has no reason to trap me. I have no choice but to trust her."

When I reached her rooms, I was relieved to see that Aideen's two maids sat sewing in one corner and that a guard stood inside her open door. Alone meant without my companions but not without hers.

"Easpag Patrick," Aideen said as I entered the room. "Please sit and join me, I have a question to ask of you."

"Yes, lady," I answered and took my seat on a stool beside her chair.

"When you were a young man," she began, "and a captive in the north, did you love a woman called Brigid?"

Surprised, I nodded yes.

"And you were lovers, hand-fasting at least twice?" Aideen asked. I nodded again. "I have word of the lady Brigid," she continued. "Do you wish to hear where she is, what has become of her?"

I nodded, eager to hear her news. "Is this why my lady asked that I come without my companions?"

"Yes," Aideen answered. "I thought you might wish time to consider this beyond the others' hearing."

"Please tell me everything you know," I asked.

"It is finally my turn to offer a gift to you," Aideen began. She told me the tale of what happened to Brigid after Flan's soldiers raped her. She started, "You already know that Brigid went to the local king to appeal for justice. He rejected her claim. Brigid is the daughter of a slave and that slave's master. Under our law, Brigid is a slave herself."

Aideen could see the questions in my eyes. "Brigid was fostered with the druid Amergin, this you already know. What you may not know is that Amergin shared all his power with her. He gave you his old cloak. Amergin knew, before Flan came, that he was going to die. Just after you left, he gave his good cloak, a new staff, and an amulet of great power to Brigid. She was hiding these in the woods when Flan's soldiers heard her keening."

"Did the soldiers take these from her?" I asked.

"No, she hid them well before the soldiers took her," Aideen answered. "When the king refused her appeal, Brigid was furious. She is the daughter of Amergin. She fled first to Slemmish mountain because of her memories of you. Then she made her way to the fortress on the hill of Tara to appeal to the ard-Rí, the high king of all Ireland. She gained an audience with Niall of the Nine Hostages."

"Nine Hostages?" I asked.

"It is told that the ard-Rí held hostages from each of the five provinces of Ireland as well as one each from the Picts, the Brittons, the Saxons, and the Franks. But that is another tale. Brigid plead for the ard-Rí to restore her honor. He laughed at her and asked how many cattle she brought with her to purchase his support. Of course, Brigid had none.

"'Then you are still a slave,' the ard-Rí told her, 'and have no place here.' He banished her from Tara and allowed his guards to have their rough ways with her before she was cast outside the fortress's walls."

I considered Aideen's words. Almost all the beauty had left her face as she told Brigid's tale. It was replaced by a deep pool of sadness and a hard look that communicated more than many volumes. "I am also the daughter of a druid," Aideen continued. "I know the ways of enchantment. I know tales of power. But most of all, I cherish my honor. I was horrified when I heard how my sister druid Brigid was treated by Flan, the local king, and the ard-Rí. Brigid is a druidess, perhaps the strongest of us all. She holds Amergin's power and line. She deserved respect." Aideen's voice had turned from forest bell to steel. "Brigid made her way from Tara's hill to near the sea village where you took ship to Britain. She waits there for your return."

"Brigid knows that I am in Ireland?" I asked.

"I am told she has known since the day after you landed," Aideen answered. "She listens to the waves and the woods and hears many things." There was a slight pause in her words. "Amergin told her you would return and that the future hung in the balance. Ireland's future will be decided in the measure of what happens between you and her."

44. Unanswered Questions

Almost a month passed before I could leave Dyflinn. Alphin was loathe to see his new Christian druid leave. He wondered if more magic could be squeezed out of me. Aideen began to refer to me as "my Easpag." It is challenging to correct a queen. I wanted to reply that I was Ireland's and the Church's, but each time I considered the words, they rang hollow. I visited my new farm twice, the second time for more than a week. Blaise had set up the scriptorium better than I could imagine for the first of its kind in Ireland. There were four writing benches in the barn, a good sign. Blaise expected more students. Young Kevin progressed well. He was confidently making his first letters either with a pointed stick in sand or on a wooden board with charcoal. When they weren't practicing letters, Blaise was teaching him how to make ink and how to prepare a parchment.

I asked Alphin for calves' skins and, as they were to be used for teaching his son, he sent 10. I also asked a trader sailing to Britannia from Dyflinn's port to bring back as much parchment and velum as his craft would carry. Alphin commissioned the trade with a guarantee of payment and gave the captain ten heavy gold ring coins as surety. Maybe most importantly, I asked Alphin to protect Blaise and the new scriptorium. I was a bishop, and before that a monk. Blaise had zero experience defending himself against violence. And I was about to leave him, shepherd now to almost 30 converts and surrounded by Diurmid and other wolves. He needed help to keep himself and his flock safe.

The last day on my farm, I was happy when I took leave of Blaise. "We sail on the morning's tide," I told him. "Cadhla will sail Niall and me to the north, to Latharna."

"Latharna?" Blaise asked.

"It is the fishing village I took ship from when I fled from slavery and returned home," I told him. "It is near Slemmish, where I guarded sheep and near where my old master lives. I go to pay him my ransom and preach in the north."

Blaise's jaw dropped slightly open, his lips turned down, and his eyes widened. His face said, "What are you holding back from telling me?" My brother had worked alongside me for years at Auxerre and had walked the long road to Rome and back. He knew me well in a way that made it difficult to deceive him.

"Years ago," I began, "when I was a slave in the north, I loved a woman named Brigid." Blaise nodded. "Although we were slaves, and very young, we were husband and wife for more than two years." I allowed Blaise to consider what I had told him. He knew this much of my story already.

"I will look to find her near Latharna." I continued. "I have news that she lives still, in a sea cave along the cliffs beyond that harbor." Blaise nodded. "I owe her a debt. I would have died without her help," I finished.

"And will you love her?" Blaise asked shooting straight to the question most critical in his monk's mind.

"I do not know," I answered. "I do not know if I will be with Brigid as a man is with his wife. I do not know her heart or if she still desires me. She has been injured and done a grave injustice. I go to see her because I love her. Love of the heart is always worth honoring."

"But you are a bishop," Blaise said.

"Yes," I sighed. "And a man. And this is Ireland, not Rome or Auxerre." I saw Blaise's look of confusion. "Brother," I began again. "Peter the apostle had a wife. Saint Timothy writes that 'bishops should have only one wife.' Many priests and bishops have been married. The demand to remain celibate started less than 100 years ago, when the emperor legalized the Church. The demand turns all priests and bishops into monks."

Blaise nodded understanding. "I have ordained you a priest," I reminded him. "This is Ireland, not Rome. You have a choice." Again, a nod. "If you wish, you can marry."

A question crossed Blaise's eyes.

"I have no idea who," I told him. "And only one," I laughed. "Or you can remain single," I finished. "The choice is yours."

"And what of you, Easpag Patrick?" he asked again.

"I do not know how things stand between Brigid and me," I answered. "I know only that I have loved her for many years and must find her. Then we shall see."

Blaise was kind at that moment. He allowed my words to trail off into the sky, his unasked and unanswered questions following them. He granted me time to stare across the fields while absorbed in my memories until I came back to myself.

Finally, when I looked down at my feet and took a deep breath, I felt his strong, young hand on my shoulder. "Brother and Easpag," Blaise changed our conversation, "I will teach Kevin, and perhaps even more. This will be a place of letters as well as a farm when you return."

I turned to smile at Blaise. He was a loyal friend, an uncomplaining companion on our adventure, and he loved me as a brother. His smile of acceptance gave strength to my heart. I left the farm well-guided by Blaise and kept safe by four warriors from Alphin's personal guard. I would sail north in the morning.

44. On the Beach at Latharna

Latharna was much as I remembered it, a small fishing village tucked away in a cove on the Irish Sea. Four fishing boats were hauled up on the beach. Fishers and sailors tended nets and worked on hulls. A small collection of ropes and sails lay beyond the boat furthest down the sands. That boat looked as if she was being readied to be launched for her first sail. The planking was new and the hull completely clean. Five men climbed over and around the craft, all looking busy. It was already near noon. When Cadhla's ship approached, a skiff manned by two fishers rowed out from the beach to ask our intent.

"Ours is a poor, small village," cried out a voice from the boat. "Few traders call here." I could see the men searching Cadhla's ship with their eyes for signs of warriors or raiders.

"May peace be on your day," I answered from the stern, where I stood next to Cadhla. Both heads at the oars turned in my direction.

"We seek only fresh water and whatever trade your village can offer," called Cadhla. "We have but one warrior aboard, Niall, youngest brother of Dichu, chieftain of a village to the south of Dyflinn." Cadhla saw my raised eyebrows and quizzical look. "Details are calming," he said softly to me. "They reassure the prospect at the beginning of a trade."

"There are six others aboard, myself and four sailors, and my friend here," the captain called, clapping me on the shoulder.

"Who is he?" called out the voice from the boat.

"He is a teller of tales to shorten the long dark length of night," Cadhla called out. I smiled, amazed. It was completely true and didn't answer the rower's question.

"Drop anchor in the harbor," came the call from the rowboat as they began to turn their craft back towards the beach. "Come ashore in your own boat when you're ready."

Cadhla turned to me. "Are you sure this is the place?" he asked. "They're not too friendly."

"I'm sure," I answered. "I sailed from here on a trader's ship, much like this one. But it's a small village and they're afraid of raiders. Ten warriors would completely overwhelm them. They're wise to be on guard with newcomers."

"Aye," said the captain. "Then we must load our rowboat with something they'll desire and make friends."

"What would that be?" I asked.

"A gift cask of ale from the Chieftain of Dyflinn no less," Cadhla laughed. "That should win us some friends."

Afternoon and evening passed. Cadhla traded fishhooks and axe heads and a few copper bowls for the fresh water, salt fish, and supplies he needed. The village was indeed small. It had neither tavern nor hall. At nightfall we gathered with the village men around a fire above the shore. Cadhla's cask of ale was emptied to be followed by another from the village. At the hour when the constellation of the hunter rises, the voice of the village headman called for a story. "Sing us a song, teller of tales," he asked. I looked at Cadhla and Niall and they both nodded. It was time.

"Many, many years ago," I started, "in a country far across your sea and then another one and then an ocean of land, a great injustice was done." I had their attention. "The hard heart of that country's king ordered a man put to death. His crime, teaching that men should be friends to each other and hold themselves as children of the King of the Gods."

"How can fishers and simple folk like us be children of the King of Gods?" asked a voice from across the fire.

"That is the tale I have come to tell," I replied. The night was almost half gone when I reached the story of the Christ's return from the land of the dead.

"Your Christ became a revenant?" one disbelieving voice called out in horror.

"His enemy, the king, should have cut off his head and buried him facing downward with his head looking up from between his knees," whispered another voice. "That would have prevented this Christ from becoming a twice walker."

"The Christ was the only son of the King of the Gods," I answered. "His draíocht showed itself stronger than the power of death. He came back to life, fully alive, not as a walking ghost or revenant."

"If he was the only son of the King of the Gods, how can simple folk like us also be children of this King of the Gods?" asked another voice.

"When he returned from the land of the dead," I answered, "the Christ shared with his friends how to become children of the King of the Gods. He told them to share his draíocht with anyone who would hear his tale and follow his way."

"What does it take to follow this way?" a voice called out from one side of the circle.

"The Christ asks only three things," I began. More than five heads nodded when I had finished explaining baptism, the call to choose Christ over the old ways, and the need to follow my commands as easpag.

"I will consider your words," said the village headman at the end of the night. "Perhaps in the morning I will let you wash me in this Christ water." I offered him my best, non-threatening smile.

But in the morning no one came forward to be baptized. Several fishers were friendly and thanked me for the tale from the night before.

"Your Christ was a good man," one fisher told me. "But the old ways are cherished here. They are kept strong by our local druidess."

Surprised by his words, I looked intently into his eyes. "You should meet her," he offered. "She'll want to hear your tale of a draíocht stronger than death and of a man who returns from the dead but is not a twice-walker."

"She?" I asked, hopeful.

"She is called Brigid of the Sorrows and lives less than a day's walk south, along the cliffs," the man answered.

46. The Remembered and the Present

I went alone to seek Brigid. After fetching the amulet and the old red and green cloak that Amergin had gifted me, I left Niall and Cadhla on the ship. This reunion belonged to me alone.

South from Latharna, the land at the edge of the sea rose in small hills that gave way to larger ones. I simply walked in the direction that the fisher pointed. I walked without stopping for rest or to eat. Gradually, progressively, the sands along the shore were replaced by an escarpment, a bluff, then cliffs. I continued to walk, knowing that I would know her place when I got there.

I left early in the morning. As the shadows slanted towards sunset, I felt the air change. One moment I was walking above the cliffs, feeling the sea's salt spray on my face. The next moment was as if the mist and space had a personality, a presence.

I stopped after just a few more steps. I had found the place I was seeking. I let my thoughts drop away. It's not as if I ceased thinking. I simply stopped naming things in my head, answering my own "What if's," or following my thoughts to any conclusion. My mind came to rest, and I opened my heart and senses fully.

Fear, worry, desire, sadness, excitement, and hope were all mixed at that moment. I heard the cries of the gulls, the song of the sandpipers, the whisper of wind through the dune grasses. I felt the heat of the day leaving, the weight of Amergin's cloak around my shoulders, the weariness of my feet after a day's long walk. I gazed out beyond the cliff and across the waves and let my thoughts go free.

"It's not many who know how to do that anymore," I heard her voice.

She walked towards me along the cliff's edge. "Not many strangers bother coming to this place." She stopped when she was three paces away. "Maewyn," she breathed.

Silver threads graced the red hair that hung to the middle of her back. Those eyes I remembered flashed gray with intelligence, then green with mirth, settling into simmering hazel passion. The remembered mole on her left cheek broke my heart. This was Brigid, the same yet changed. The remembered and the present.

"Maewyn," she said once more and held out her arms.

Our embrace was the coming together of the long-separated hearts of two lovers from a different time; the embrace of the friends of youth, the embrace of sorrow and joys to be shared, the embrace of reunion. I held her and she me for a long, long time. Tears flowed from my eyes. I felt the warmth of her tears on her cheek against my own. We remained wordless until our hearts beat one steady beat of joy. Thrum, thrum, thrum, heart notes sounded.

Stepping back from our embrace to view me at arm's length, Brigid said, "There's more of you now than when you left me at Amergin's hut."

"You are more beautiful than I remember," I replied. "And, more than that, you wear strength and wisdom like a cloak and a crown." Brigid looked down and smiled. I allowed some space before my next words. "I am sorry for all your troubles," I began.

She held up her hand and pressed a gentle finger to my lips. "There will be time enough for memories later," she said. "Now is different."

Our lips met with an exploratory tenderness, like a first kiss. Softness and strength, passion, and salt. Brigid rested her hand above my heart. "I wondered how much you had changed," she said.

"What do you feel?" I asked, placing my hand atop hers.

"That underneath whoever you have become, Maewyn is still here," she answered. I felt her palm grow suddenly warm with energy. Then we kissed again, this time allowing passion free reign. I caressed the firmness of her breast as she moved to press her hips against me. My excitement rose to meet her.

"Here?" I asked her as if coming up for breath from deep underwater.

"Now," she answered, kissing me once again.

I unfastened the belt around my waist and took off my tunic. I stood as if born anew before her, exposing slavery's scars and my passion all at once. Laying my tunic on the ground for us to lie upon, I lowered myself down among the grasses. When I looked back up at Brigid, her hands hesitated to unfasten the brooch that fastened her cloak. The tenderness I felt in my eyes spoke for me. A slight nod and a hint of a smile were all the words I offered.

Slowly, claiming the right to reveal herself at her own pace, she unfastened the brooch. The plain cloak Brigid wore fell to the ground beside mine. She looked down towards her heart then, as if centering herself, and with grace she stepped out of her tunic and stood clothed only in beauty and power. Her hair hung down across one shoulder to cover her left breast. Her right nipple rose firm and pink from a creamy whiteness. Her hips were full, her thighs strong and graceful. Her arbor of love was covered with thick auburn curls.

I felt her strength as a woman inviting me even as I felt her deep sorrow from the place where it lay, put aside for the moment slightly beyond her cloak.

"You honor me," I offered. A knowing smile grew on Brigid's face. "May I honor the goddess within you?" I asked.

She nodded once. I rose to my knees. My hands paid homage to her cheeks, explored the crack between them. I stroked and kissed the inside of her thighs. Then, with one look upward, into her eyes, to be sure she was ready, I kissed her mound of love. Slowly, my tongue found where her own excitement rose to match mine. Her dew greeted my tongue. I tasted, caressed, stroked her, and felt her hand grasping then releasing the curls on my head. I paid homage at the altar of her love until I heard her small groan. Her fingers relaxed their grip, and I felt her shudder. Only then did I pull my attention back from her.

When our gazes met, a deep hazel flared within her eyes. A gentle pressure from her right hand, now on my shoulder, bade me to lay down. When I was ready, she joined me. With a practiced wisdom, Brigid lowered herself on top of my excitement. My eagerness met her joy. Her warmth and welcoming wetness were all around me. My hands found their place above her hips. She moved like waves on the ocean, sometimes with a gentle swell, sometimes like a great storm. As she moved above me and all around me, her hair hung down to frame her perfectly oval face. At last, when I thought there was no more pleasure to be found in me, Brigid threw back her head and stretched upward. My final wave crested and exhausted itself upon her beach. Then she looked down, deep into the pool of my eyes.

"Now we can talk," she laughed and lowered herself to rest beside me in the grasses.

47. The Hag and the Throne

Later, Brigid took me to her hut, above the cliffs, nestled among the trees at the edge of the woods.

"You don't live in a sea cave?" I asked

"No," she laughed. "I let the villagers think that and almost never bring them here. The sea cave is where I meditate. Often it's where I meet those who come to me seeking help or answers."

"And here?" I pressed.

"After what happened to Amergin, I'm very cautious," her voiced dropped away into almost a whisper.

Silence lingered between us for a while. Brigid busied herself stirring her cook fire and heating a pot of broth that had been left to simmer over its coals. Her hut was somehow small and spacious at the same time. Barely five paces across, each thing rested in what seemed to be its own special place. Two pegs hung near the door for our cloaks. A stout staff stood at the right-hand side of the door, ready when the door was opened, ready when Brigid left. A wood chest, with the goddess's triple spirals carved into its top, sat along one wall. Her bed lay along another. A small table with a candle in a carved wooden holder sat alongside the bed. Her cook things, pots, pans, an iron poker for the coals, and a set of tongs for the wood, all had places on the remaining wall space. Above the fire was a smoke hole in the thatched roof.

What made her hut remarkable was its painting inside and the lack of painting outside. Where normally Celts whitewashed the outside walls of their huts, Brigid had left her wattle and daub walls their natural browns and grays. As we approached from the grasses above the cliffs, it was invisible, until we were just two or three steps away. Then, only if you were looking, would you notice a disruption in the pattern of the trees and branches. Even more remarkable were the paintings inside the hut. Where customarily the walls were only brown, Brigid had painted them white and then woven a pattern of symbols and color.

The triple spiral repeated several times as well as the symbol of the awen, several knots, a set of five connected circles in a cross pattern, the single spiral, the ailm, and a bull. Near the door, on the other side, was painted a Sheela na gig, a grotesque figure of a woman, squatting and holding the lips of her vagina open. She was beautiful, powerful, enchanting, and somehow distorted all at once. I turned from right to left as I surveyed the room. The Sheela painting was the last in the series. My jaw dropped slightly open, my head tilted to the right, as if to ask a question. I looked to Brigid. She looked directly into my eyes, waiting.

"They are symbols of power, beauty, and life," I said.

Without taking her eyes off mine, she nodded once.

"They tell the story of life and the balance of the elements of sky and tree and sea." Brigid nodded again. "In them are balanced the three worlds, above the world, our human world, and the realm beneath our feet." A third nod invited me to continue. I put my right hand to my heart and looked down to gather myself. Then I raised my eyes to meet hers, gestured at the Sheela, and said, "And this is you, in both mystery and power."

The first rumor of a smile since we entered her hut graced Brigid's face.

"Your beauty and power are shrouded in mystery, just like this hut," I offered. "But they are there for anyone with eyes and a heart that is open."

"Yes, Maewyn," Brigid said. "Open eyes and heart are a good beginning. Yet they are only a beginning. To really see, you need to hold your heart open among the flow and change of life, to hold your heart open to what is greater than you."

"Is this," I gestured at the entire wall, "what Amergin gave you?"

"This and more," Brigid answered. "He had a humility around him that belied his greatness. He taught me that each of us only glimpses the vast sky of knowledge that lies beyond our small stories. As a man, he said he could only glimpse the power of the Moringa. But I, as a woman, would be able to enter more deeply into her power and glimpse even beyond her."

"And you have seen the Moringa?" I asked.

Brigid threw back her head and laughed. I blushed, thinking I had said something stupid or, worse, shamed myself. When she looked at me once more, I saw Brigid see my blush. "Maewyn," she began with tenderness, reaching out to touch my arm, "I laugh only because you go right to the essential point with your first question." She paused. "No one sees the Moringa. She is not a thing to be seen. But everyone experiences her. She is all around us. She is what it means to be alive. It is only because we look for her in all the wrong places that we don't see."

Confusion was evident on my face.

"Let's have something warm to eat first," Brigid said. "There's a broth warming on the coals, and I have some bread and cheese. After we've eaten and rested, I will tell you a story."

That night was the most magical night I remember. After we had eaten, Brigid warmed some mead above the coals. "It's honey wine," she said as she poured the warm liquid into a cup. "One of the villagers brought it in thanks for my helping cure a sick child."

"You are a healer?" I asked.

"I know some of the way of herbs and plants," Brigid offered, "but that is not my story. I only wanted to say that I live here with the gratitude of the villagers. Beyond the nuts and seeds and occasional wild apple I find, everything you see here was brought to me by the people of Latharna and beyond." I looked around at the cooking pots, the fire equipment, the sack of grain, the small container of salt.

"Everything?" I asked.

"All of it," she replied. "I brought with me nothing but my hands and knowledge, and Amergin's cloak and amulet." She waited for me to show understanding.

"When first I made my way here, after Tara, I did live in the cave by the sea. I intended to stay only long enough to gain strength for moving on. But a villager saw me and came to ask who I was."

I nodded understanding.

"When he learned I was a druidess, the heir of Amergin, he showed me great respect and immediately offered me his fire stone and the cloak he was wearing as a second cloak. He said, 'Amergin's cloak of power is too grand for wearing while gathering shells on the beach.' Then he left.

"Two days later, the first villager came asking for help. Her man had suffered from a terrible pain in the head for days. I told her to gather some mead wort. The villagers call the plant meadowsweet. I guided her in how to brew a tea and sent her home. Two days later, the woman returned with the pot that your broth was cooked in and a sack of grain as thanks. Her man's pain had gone, and she knew how to make a remedy if it returned. She was the first of a stream of visitors."

"Do they all come with pains?" I asked.

"Some do," Brigid replied. "Others come looking for guidance. They hear that I am Amergin's daughter, and they come seeking guidance or wisdom."

"And you teach them all?" I asked, surprised.

"I freely give each one a full measure of whatever I have," she replied. "To do so was Amergin's final instruction to me." Brigid allowed stillness to settle between us before saying more. "Are you ready now for the story I promised?" she asked.

"Yes," I replied eagerly.

"It is a tale of the Moringa.". The tale she told was that of the goddess Fodlha, mistress of mystery and of the hidden people. She is but one of the three forms that the Moringa wears when she walks among humans. Sometimes she appears in beauty and enchants men. Other times she wears the cloak of an old hag and appears in ugliness. "The true kings of Eire must be crowned by her before they become ard-Rí."

I saw a look of sadness cross Brigid's eyes.

"A long time ago, before the Romans were rumored in your Britain, nearer to the dawn of time, just before he was to be crowned ard Ri, Labraid Lorc, son of Ailill Aine, crossed the path of the goddess Fodlha wearing her hag's cloak." Brigid paused to allow me to form the image in my mind. "The young, power-ful, and soon to be king sees a very ugly woman. 'You are handsome and strong,' called out Fodlha, 'and I am a poor woman.' She held out her hand begging. Labraid's heart was touched, and he offered her a gold coin. 'You are generous and kind,' called out Fodlha, 'and I have not known the kindness of a man for a long, long time.' She pulled back the hood of her cloak to show a face ravaged by time, with three teeth, a squat nose, and scraggly gray hair. Labraid leaned down and kissed her gently on her forehead. 'You are virile and full of life,' Fodlha called out a third time, 'And I am lonely and alone.' She pulled her tunic up from her feet to above her waist, revealing herself to the soon to be king. Fodlha was the goddess who guarded the throne of the true ard-Rís of Ireland," said Brigid. "Only those who could see the goddess within everyone they encountered merited the throne. Labraid has passed her first two tests, that of generosity and kindness.

Her third test was the most difficult. Would he be able to see the goddess in a hag? Labraig indeed saw the goddess. He stirred his passion and moved to lay with her even though the hag repelled him. As soon as his passion touched the hag, she transformed into her beautiful form as the goddess, Fodlha. Labraig's passion spent, he asked her, 'Why did you appear in the form of a hag?' It was then that Fodlha told him that she guarded Ireland's throne and that he had proven worthy of sitting on the stone of Tara."

I considered Brigid's words for a long time before I asked my first question. "What does this tale have to do with you?" I asked.

"This is my tale," Brigid answered. "Leary sits now on the stone of Tara, the throne of the ard-Rí. But he is not worthy. He only sees worth in that which serves him. He has forgotten the Moringa even more than his father, Niall, who shamed me." The words seemed to have rushed out of her.

"After I fled Tara and Niall's soldiers, I wandered for two winter seasons. I let my hair grow wild and took on the appearance of Fodlha the hag for safety. In my wanderings, I sought one who would be worthy of the throne of Tara. My journey led me here, where I paused to rest. You already know the story of the kindness and generosity that the villagers have shown me." I nodded, yes.

"So, I tarried 13 winters here, watching and waiting for the third sign, that man who could see the goddess in the hag. Then you arrived."

"What do I have to do with your story of the goddess within the hag?" I asked.

"You are that man," Brigid answered.

"You are beautiful to me," I answered. "How could you ever seem a hag to me?"

"I have heard of your contest of cures with Diurmid at Dyflinn," Brigid answered. "You treated him and the teachings he holds as the hag, an ugly old thing to be cast aside to wither."

I was stunned. Diurmid had seemed like more of an obstacle than a man to me. I never considered what wisdom he held. It didn't occur to me to seek him out and attempt to bridge our rivalry. Diurmid was right, of course. I did want to supplant him at Alphin's hall. My mission was to supplant Diurmid and his brothers wherever they could be found in Ireland. I had been sent back to Ireland by Celestine, the voice of God on Earth, called back by the voice of Slemmish.

"Now you think you and your Christ are the only way," she answered. I nodded. "Yet you were moved to passion and honored me in your lovemaking." I nodded again. "You were able to see the goddess in me even though you serve a jealous voice." I nodded a third time. "That is how you saw the goddess within the hag," Brigid said. "You saw beyond your cherished voice to something else. It may be there is still room within your heart for something more."

"And the throne of Tara?" I asked almost incredulous.

"For you, I have something even more valuable," Brigid said. "I will give you the key to the heart of all Ireland."

48. Sophia

We made love again that night. A look in Brigid's eyes called me. I rose eagerly to meet her. This time was more like a sudden storm than waves on the beach. Our tunics shed, her bed too far, we clapped together like thunder. Lips, hips, my manhood, her arbor, like a flash of lightning. I tasted her. She tasted me. The ferocity of the storm's hunger crescendoed. And then it rained warmth. All over my body and in my heart was warm. My thoughts were calm. Inside Brigid's hut, the voice of Slemmish was silent.

It was morning when I awoke. Somehow, we had crawled into Brigid's bed. I held her in my arms, our two bodies barely fitting on her pallet. Slowly her breathing changed from sleep to that in-between state. Then her eyes opened, and I looked at her. A smile spread across my face and I saw its mirror on hers.

"Since that day on Slemmish when I struck Cathal," I said, "I have longed for this." Brigid tilted her head slightly and gave a look encouraging me to continue. "You risked everything to help me then," I said. "You lost everything." I paused. "When I heard that Flan killed Amergin and raped you, I blamed myself."

Consternation filled Brigid's eyes, followed by kindness. "Maewyn, what happened to me wasn't about you. Yes, your escape provided the excuse, but Amergin's death and my rape were about the violence and smallness in Flan, not about you. Don't make this about you. To do so cuts the connection between you and I and cuts you off from the aliveness of things. The way of blame is the way of the small heart."

"Don't you blame them?" I asked full of doubt. "Don't you hate them?"

"Hating them hurts only me," Brigid answered, "It is foolish, like eating poison and expecting an enemy to die." There was a hint of laughter in her eyes. "Anyway, doesn't your Christ teach you to turn the other cheek?" she asked.

Surprised beyond belief, I responded, "You know the teachings of the Christ."

"The ship that carried Belvedere away from Ireland was blown north by a storm to Latharna," Brigid said. "He was quite ill when the ship pulled into the harbor. The villagers sent for me saying that a stranger had been blown ashore and was sick to death. I went, worried that it might be you." She took a breath, then went on. "Vercingetorix had cursed him and poisoned him. It was only luck that blew him ashore near someone who could recognize the poison and mix the antidote."

I saw the drama in my mind's eye. Brigid appearing to Bishop Belvedere as a healer. The bishop sick, almost dead, grateful for her kindness, sharing what he could of the Christ story and our teachings.

"So, you have decided to turn the other cheek to those who hurt you," I asked, "to Leary who sits now on Tara's stone throne?"

"I choose not to follow the way of anger," Brigid answered. "All things are connected. When they are in balance, they are healthy. The chieftains, kings, and druids have lost sight of the connectedness of all. Their eyes only see the ways of power and greed. Belvedere was not the enemy. Vercingetorix's smallness of heart was his enemy. I seek to redress that smallness."

"But how?" I asked.

"Will you stay with me here for one week?" Brigid replied.

"Of course," I answered.

"We will each teach one another our way of power."

I nodded.

"I will teach you the things that Amergin asked me to teach you so long ago. You will teach me about your Christ way. Between us we will forge a third possibility beyond the violence of Vercingetorix and beyond jealousy."

Two days later, a man from the village came seeking Brigid's help with a cure. She spoke with him for an hour then mixed some herbs into a tea. "That will help your wife with her morning pain," I heard her tell him as she said goodbye. In return, she asked the villager to carry a message from me to Cadhla and Niall, that I was well and would return to Latharna at the end of seven days, and to please wait for me until then.

During those seven days together, Brigid told me that for at least three generations the druids of Ireland had been divided between the court druids and the wandering masters. The druids who held a place of honor in the halls of chieftains and kings gathered status to themselves. They were jealous of their power and influence. Whenever another druid appeared in their halls, they challenged them, using spells, trickery, and poison, as if there was room only for one window to wisdom. In that way, druids like Diurmid and Vercingetorix gained a reputation for miraculous power and strength. They had become the whispering voices behind the thrones of Ireland.

The wandering masters lived simply, like Amergin, like Brigid. They sought the accomplishment of true power. They studied the natural lore learning both cures and poisons. They contemplated the old stories for wisdom and gathered what power they could from the elemental forces of the land. She told me that she had seen one old druid call the rains. "He chanted and danced a shuffling dance," she said, "and the rains came before he stopped dancing." I was amazed and wouldn't have believed another if they had told me. But this was Brigid, and she had no reason to be untrue with me. "I saw another druidess," she continued, "summon the wind."

"And you, what power do you have?" I asked.

Brigid looked a bit askance at me. "That is usually not a question to be asked," she said. "But since we are lovers and students to each other, I will show you just this once." She took one deep breath in then held up her hand. The breeze gradually slowed then ceased. Birds singing in the woods gradually became quieter. The buzz of insects faded. A great stillness of heart grew all around her. Then the space filled with joy. It was as if everything became brighter while no colors changed. "This is the power that Amergin passed on to me as his gift," Brigid said. "It is the gift of stillness, of peace within the chaos, of recognizing the aliveness of all connected things."

Brigid dropped her hand to her lap and the world breathed out in sound once more. Bird song filled the woods, insects buzzed, the breeze flowed. This is Amergin's song, she told me, "I am the wind on the sea. I am the wave of the sea. I am the bull of seven battles. I am the eagle of the rock. I am the flash of the sun." She sang until her song ended, "I am the word of knowledge. Who can tell the ages of the moon? Who can tell the place where the sun rests?"

The glad space of open heartedness stretched between us. Words were not needed. I simply rested and recognized the strength and wisdom she had shared.

SHAMROCK

On the third morning, walking along the cliffs above her sea cave, Brigid asked me to tell her the Christ tale. I did. I told her the story of the birth of Jesus. She was pleased at the humble beginnings of the story. She nodded understanding when I shared some of Jesus's teaching stories, the parables. She understood completely the story of the widow's mite and the pearl of great value. Tears showed in her eyes when I shared the parable of the good Samaritan.

"This Samaritan was like a wandering druid," she said. "Unrecognized but powerful in his kindness." Brigid asked me to stop when I reached the story of the torture and death of the Christ at the hands of the Romans. "I must consider what you are saying before I hear more," was all she said. Then she quickly walked to her cave and disappeared. It was nightfall when I saw her next.

"We have no story like the one you are telling," Brigid began. "Our tales tell of heroes and gods and the doings of men. Your story tells of the killing of the divine. It horrified me so much I needed to center myself before hearing more. The killing of the divine is what I fear most for Ireland."

I told Brigid the story of the three women coming to Jesus's grave only to find it empty. "Had he already gone to the land of eternal spring?" she asked.

"No. His power was to be able to return from the land of the dead. He returned from there and shared his draíocht with his followers."

"And this is his Christ way?"

"It is."

Silence fell between us for a very long time. We spent the remainder of that night in silence as Brigid considered my tale. The next day and the day after that were spent in silence. Brigid smiled at me, prepared meals over her cooking coals, shared her bed with me. But she held silent as the Christ story searched for a place of resonance within her heart.

"Where is the Moringa in this Christ story?" were Brigid's first words when she next spoke.

"She is Mary the mother," I offered, "and Magdalene the lover, and Mary his friend."

"It is not enough," was Brigid's plain response before she returned to silence.

193

"This spirit that descends and is seen in the form of a dove at the end of the story, the one that carries the Christ draíocht to his friends and sets it aflame above their heads, what is this spirit called?" Brigid enquired.

I spoke the old Greek name for the spirit of God" "Hagia Sophia."

"This Sophia; is the name feminine or masculine?"

"Sophia is a feminine name."

"There is the Moringa," Brigid stated with strength in her voice. "Your tale falters until you recognize that the spirit is the mother." She looked at me expectantly. "It is the mother, the Moringa who brings life to all, unifies all, enflames all with wisdom. Without her, your story is merely one of heroic death. With her, your story takes you to a transformation beyond the smallness of heart."

Now it was my turn to turn silent. "I need to consider your words," I told Brigid.

Our sixth morning together dawned cool yet bright. Dew glistened in the sea grasses. A fresh breeze stirred the leaves in the wood. Gulls called to each other above the waves.

"The Christ way has found a home in Rome," I began. "Rome is in love with the male strength of arms and empire. The Christ tale in that city is one of the Father and son god. The wisdom of women plays little part in Rome's telling of the tale."

I allowed Brigid to consider my words.

"But this is Ireland. Here the Moringa is more important than the King of the Gods." Brigid nodded. "The Holy Spirit, Hagia Sophia, can be the breath of the Moringa, calling her daughters and sons to the Christ way."

"When you came to me, six days ago, in the grasses above my cave, you were wearing Amergin's old cloak?" Brigid asked. "Do you still carry the amulet he gave you?" I reached into the purse at my belt and withdrew the amulet with its triple spiral symbol.

"That is good. I will show you how to speak to the heart of Ireland." She withdrew her amulet from around her neck and under her tunic. Holding it out to me, I saw the same triple spiral on one side and the image of a shamrock on the other.

49. Are you a Freeman or a Slave?

I recognized the triple spiral symbol of the Moringa, the unseen but ever-present divine force that shows itself as Eriu, Fodlha, and Banba, the triple goddesses of Ireland. It symbolizes the balance of the elements, the divine within everything. "What is the meaning of the shamrock?" I asked Brigid.

"It is simple, profound, and full of power," she began. "Look around you when you walk in the grasses or are in a meadow. They are everywhere, taken for granted like the earth and sky. Being everywhere allows them to be overlooked. Noticed or unseen, they are still there. This is how it is with the Moringa."

I began to understand.

"Three leaves on one stem. Together they are one but can be considered individually." The power of the image began to speak to me. "Unless they are part of the whole, there is no shamrock. You might pick one leaf and still have a shamrock but pick all three apart and you just have leaves and stem. Just like the Moringa, you can consider one goddess or one element of power. But they are always part of the pattern of interconnected wholeness."

"How is this profound?"

"Being everywhere, expressing the interconnected wholeness of things, whether seen or unseen. They remind us that the Moringa cannot be found except in her expression in the world. And that the world is nothing else than the expression of the divine." She paused for a moment. "To know this truth opens the door to living in service to the mystery of the Moringa. Beyond that door are both power and compassion. But to step through, you must drop the cloak of a small mind, small heartedness."

"And how do I drop the cloak of my mind and heart?" I asked.

"My love," Brigid answered, "Maewyn, that is the journey of a lifetime."

We spent the long hours of the night talking about the meaning of the shamrock and the other symbols in Brigid's hut. In the quiet hours before dawn we made love once more. Then the seventh sun rose since I found Brigid along the cliffs. I had promised to return to Cadhla and Niall. "I must go," I told her.

A look of sadness and deep disappointment filled her face. "It is too soon to say goodbye again after losing you for so many years,"

"If I could stay, I would—"

Brigid held up her hand to hush me. "Do you mean that?"

"Yes."

"Then stay. There is no one holding you here or there.

"But I have promised my masters in Rome."

"Maewyn, are you a slave or are you a freeman?"

"I am a freeman."

"Then act as one," she said flatly.

"But I must keep my vow."

"Then keep it as a freeman keeps his promise," Brigid replied. "Keep the promise in your own way, not as a slave following the imagined demands of a faraway master. Don't just keep the words of your promise, figure out how to keep it as a way that expresses your heart."

I was shocked. No one had ever spoken to me like this before. Brother Durstan at Calleva told me to listen and to submit to the monastic order. Abbot Germanus had expected the obedience of a well-trained soldier. Celestine had assumed fealty and fidelity to his command. I had promised to obey him and all his successors. I had found safety in all that obedience. Brigid called on me now to find another way.

"Would you have me stay with you here?" I asked.

"For a while," she answered.

"I will go to Latharna and find my companions. I will send them south to Dyflinn where they can help my brother, Blaise." Brigid nodded. "The harvest will soon be ready, and they can help Blaise with the work." Brigid raised an eyebrow and gave me a look that asked why I was blathering on about details she didn't need to concern herself with. "And then I will return here. How long will you have me?"

"Let's start with one moon," she answered, "and decide then, more or not." She smiled. I nodded. It was done.

Niall and Cadhla accepted the news easily. Niall was anxious to return to his village, his family, and help prepare for winter. Cadhla was anxious to sail again. "An anchored ship profits no one," he told me. I made them both at least promise to take news to Blaise and help him with the harvest.

"When will we see you again?" Niall asked.

"Should we come back here?" Cadhla added.

"I will meet you at the farm near Dyflinn in five months," I told them. "Look for me on the first full moon of the year."

And then they were gone. I stood alone on my own in Ireland, as a freeman for the first time.

50. Shamrock

Those months with Brigid hold my sweetest memories. They are sweeter than those of when we were young and I herded sheep on Slemmish. We were both free. We chose that time together. The fall nights grew long with love and conversation. I emerged from that time transformed.

Brigid and I talked and exchanged stories of the Christ and the Moringa for more than two months. During those days, I built, with her help, a small, simple hut where I could be alone and think. "It's not good for two people to always be together with no way to be alone," she said. "There will come a time when you need this space." That hut was monastically simple, with just enough space to lay down and still hold a fire circle. Its inside walls were painted white in the same style as Brigid's hut. On the walls were painted three symbols, the shamrock, the ailm cross, and the three rays of the awen.

One long night stands out in my memory. I had withdrawn to my hut to pray and contemplate. Was I still Easpag Patrick or was I becoming a wandering druid, like Brigid? For many days the voice of Slemmish had grown more insistent in my thoughts. When I was alone, when I woke in the morning, when I sat silently alongside Brigid, as I fell asleep at night, the voice demanded, *You are mine. I set you free. I saved you from your mother and brothers when they would have killed you. I lead you to refuge at Calleva, sheltered you at Auxerre when they would have thrown you onto the streets. I made you a bishop. You are mine!*

I would shake my head to clear my thoughts only to have the voice demand, *Why are you not doing what I command? Why are you not converting the Irish to my way? Why do you keep company with this pagan witch? Why? Why? Why!*

During our two months together, I told Brigid my story of shame over Nevio's death, how I held myself accountable, how I saw myself as a coward when we first met on Slemmish. She listened with tender attentiveness and then assured me that she saw the grown man before her as courageous. "Old wounds heal," she said. "Sometimes scars remain in our memories."

Brigid asked me one night, "When you returned to your people, why did you choose to become a monk?" I told her the full truth of my fear when Marcus, my brother, conspired to kill me rather than accept my homecoming. When my mother cut my bonds and encouraged me to flee for my life, she had spared me and rejected me at the same time. The villagers hated my family and would have killed me if they found me. I had no other place to turn than the monastery.

Bonds of conflict and loss followed me to the only refuge I could find.

The orderly routine and rituals of the monastery embraced me like a mother's arms. I found a sense of purpose and identity within the monastery's walls. Almost 15 years had elapsed since I first passed through monastic doors. I had spent almost as much time as a monk as I had lived before the Irish pirates captured me. Monks had become my family.

"You journeyed to Rome and the ard-Rí of the Christ way made you a bishop?" she asked.

"Yes, and I pledged him loyalty and service for as long as I live," I answered. "I am bound by ties of duty and honor to carry out his command and bring the Christ way to Ireland."

"You have been bound all your life, in one way or another," Brigid said. "You must find your own way, or these chains will kill your spirit. You may live, but you will not be alive."

All these thoughts, the voice of Slemmish, Brigid's words, and my memories fought within me during the long hours of that night. I argued back and forth with myself. *I will become a wandering druid,* I told myself, *and put aside my duties as a bishop.* But that felt hollow and desperate. I could no more turn aside from whom I had become than I could turn back time.

I will forget the teachings of Amergin and the words of Brigid, I argued with myself. *I will be only a Christian.* But how could I forget the wisdom, good heartedness, courage, and kindness that Amergin and Brigid had shown me? I could not un-see what I had seen, un-know what I knew.

There must be a way, I told myself again and again. *There must be a way,* I encouraged myself when I wanted to give up and throw myself over the cliffs. *There must be a way.*

It was nearer to dawn, and I sat holding Amergin's amulet between the thumb and forefinger of my left hand. My eyes journeyed back and forth between the awen, symbol of the balance of masculine and feminine, and the ailm cross. One symbol pointed me at the Moringa and one pointed at the Christ. Each time I considered the symbols I came to rest on the shamrock. Amulet, awen, ailm, shamrock, amulet, awen, ailm, shamrock—over and over.

Brigid's words began to resonate once more in my mind: "Unless they are part of the whole, there is no shamrock. You can consider one goddess or one element of power, but they are always part of the pattern of interconnected wholeness. This world is nothing else than the expression of the divine."

Understanding blossomed in my mind all at once, as if I was transported from the depth of winter to the fullness of summer in the blink of an eye. Both the triple goddess and the voice expressed the divine. They were part of the pattern of the whole. The Christ story told of how divine life became human and trans-formed us. The goddess story told of how those divine energies played among us and called us to deeper knowledge. The unseen mother goddess, Hagia Sophia, and the mother of God. The Father and son god and the balance of energies. One stem with three leaves. I would serve the divine mystery that all these symbols spoke to but could not capture, the mystery beyond words.

I would carry out both Celestine's and Amergin's commands, to bring the Christ way to Ireland and to search for the Duile. At that moment, Celtic Christianity blossomed full blown in my mind with its shamrock emblem. After the dawn, after eating, I told Brigid my thoughts.

"But how can these two ways go together?" she asked. "Your voice from Slemmish is a jealous voice. Your god allows no others to remain."

"After all these many years," I told her, "I recognized one more important thing during the night."

"And what was that?"

"The voice in my head is mine," I said. "It may be that God speaks through the voice, but the voice is mine. Not every thought I hear is the voice of God. I can recognize when it is small hearted, even when it mimics the tone of the voice of God. I can choose to listen only for wisdom."

Brigid's face expressed her doubt. "And wisdom tells me that the old ways and the Christ way must speak to one another, or the old ways will be lost, and the Christ way will be twisted."

"Yes," she said.

"I am no longer anyone's slave," I said, "not even slave to the voice of Slemmish."

51. Matthew

One day, a villager from Latharna arrived carrying a gift for me. A tanned-leather hunter's pack was strapped to his back. When he reached our huts and announced himself, he called out, "I have a gift for Easpag Patrick from the chieftain of Dyflinn."

Brigid stared at me, both amused and with a question in her eyes. She hadn't grown used to my new name, Patrick. In private, she giggled at my title, easpag. "A new name and a title don't change you," she told me many times. "What you realized that night you spent arguing with your voice, that changes you."

The villager opened his pack and revealed a large object cradled inside. It was too heavy to carry in his hands on the long walk from the village. It looked too precious for putting down on a rock or log or earth when tired. The villager removed the object and unwrapped the cured skins that had covered and protected it during his trek. It was a large, wooden box. The sides of the box were white and on each side was a red ailm cross within a blue circle. The unpainted lid of the box was adorned with a roman cross with a circle carved at the junction of its four arms. I lifted the box's lid and smiled. Inside rested a book. Its simple tanned-leather cover was inscribed with the word "Matthew."

"What is it?" Brigid asked.

"It is the best of my Roman draíocht," I told her. "It is called a book." Opening the cover, I showed her the heavy parchment pages with their rows of marching letters. It was a beautiful work. The capitals of each chapter had been heavily ornamented and painted so that they appeared alive with vines and flowers and animals. Just inside the cover was a message on a small scrap of parchment, with the words: "I copied this with the help of Brother Blaise. It is the first book I have worked on. Blaise sends fond greetings, Kevin."

In my excitement at seeing the book, I forgot the villager was still standing there until he spoke. "I was told to repeat this message," he said. "The book was sent from Kevin to Alphin, Ri of Dyflinn. Ri Alphin sends it to Easpag Patrick with his thanks. He does not need books yet. He hopes it will be useful to you." The villager took a step back, showing a touch of fear at the magic he had carried. He waited for either Brigid or me to ask him to stay or send him away.

"Thank you, Angus," Brigid said. "No harm will come of this. You are under my protection here."

Angus touched the brim of the hat he was wearing, offered Brigid a smile, and left.

"Let us see what this Roman draíocht is," she said.

I scanned the first page and skipped over the list of the 42 generations between Abraham and Jesus. There would be time later to examine the family lineage of the Christ. I began reading, *"Christi autem generatio sic erat cum."*

Brigid held up her hand to stop me. "What does it mean? Is that Roman that you're speaking?

"The language is called Latin," I answered. "Yes, it is the language of Rome. And this book," I continued, picking it up and holding it in front of me, "holds one of the great stories of power from the Christ way. It was composed by Matthew," I pointed at the name on the cover page, "one of the heart friends of Jesus." Brigid's eyes showed understanding and a little fear. "By what magic does this thing hold a living story?" she asked.

"This draíocht is called writing," I replied. "It allows you, or anyone who can write and read, to catch the flow of the river of words that make a story. The words are painted with these symbols," I said, pointing to the letters on their parchment pages. "Then you can read the same story over and over. The power of the draíocht is such that the story remains true, never changing from one telling to another. And the story belongs to everyone who can read, not just to the druids or the bards."

"But what will the bards or druids do?" asked Brigid.

"Make new stories," I offered. "Tell the old stories truly. Share the power of both old and new stories with everyone."

Brigid's jaw hung slightly open, as if she was about to speak but the words caught in her throat before they could be voiced. Intelligence, questions, doubts, fears, wonder all played across her face and sparked in her eyes. Finally, she asked, looking where my finger rested, "What is this story?"

"This is how the Christ came to be born." I began to read. "Mary, his mother, was pledged to be married to Joseph. Before they were together as man and woman, Mary was found to be pregnant through the draíocht of Hagia Sophia. Joseph wanted to obey the law but did not want to disgrace Mary so he thought he would divorce her quietly."

"It is a good beginning for a story," Brigid said. "But it needs some more detail. How did the Moringa get Mary with child? Was it this King of the Gods who did it or someone else?"

"Those are very good questions," I replied. "The story continues, 'A spirit messenger of the King of the Gods appeared to Joseph in a dream.'" Over the course of an afternoon, an evening, and into the dark hours of the night, I read the Gospel of Matthew out loud for the first time in Ireland.

Brigid asked many questions at the start. "Who was this Moses that was mentioned in the story? What did they do with the leftovers after the feast of the loaves and fishes?"

I answered each question as best I could. Brigid's questions slowed in frequency as the afternoon turned toward twilight. We made a small fire for warmth and light outside between our two huts, and I continued to read. After hearing the story of Jesus walking on the water and calming a wild storm on Lake Galilee, Brigid listened without question. I could see she had settled into listening to a draíocht story. There would be time for her questions when I had read the last words of the tale.

"All authority in the skies and on earth has been given to me. Therefore, I command you, go teach everyone, baptizing them in the name of the Father, the Son, and" I translated the Latin words, "the holy breath."

"What is this holy breath?" was Brigid's first question.

"It is the Latin name for Hagia Sophia, what you call the Moringa," I replied. *"Spiritus sancti.* 'Spiritus' means breath or spirit, like the spirits that leave our bodies when we die."

Brigid nodded, understanding.

"'Sancti' means holy in the sense of more special or set apart from ordinary things. It is like the best of something, the best and first cut of meat for a feast, the light at dawn, the first flowers after the cold of winter."

Brigid paused and considered what I had told her for a long while. "I see where I can help you tell your story," she began. "This 'sancti' of yours misses an important point. It is not what is different that is special. Everything that lives breathes with this holy breath. Even the stones and the waves have it."

I looked at her, dumbstruck. No one I knew had the directness to simply question the assumptions of the Gospel.

"I will think on your Matthew tale," she said. "And when I know how the Moringa can converse with this Christ way, we will talk more." Brigid stood up and stepped back from our small campfire. She smiled warmly, communicating more than any book. "I love you," her eyes said. "And tonight, we will each sleep alone." Brigid turned and walked to her hut. "Good night, Patrick," she called, using my Latin name for the first time in many days. Then the leather door curtain closed behind her and I was alone.

I spent the remainder of that night outside by our campfire. I allowed my mind to grow wide and still as I looked at the stars. I remembered my commission, along with Abbot Germanus, to exterminate the teachings of Pelagius. But perhaps there was some truth in the heretic's teaching. Perhaps, with the Gospel and the Moringa, men did already have everything they needed to reach heaven. Perhaps, as Celestine's chamberlain had asked, the real question was why and how much do we need God's grace?

If that goodness was available to all, then it could no more be contained, controlled, or owned by Celestine in Rome, than the Moringa could be owned by Diurmid at Dyflinn. These thoughts roiled in my mind as the fire coals burned to embers. Regulus had said, "It is the perfect teaching for an empire that is falling apart." Perhaps remembering the Moringa while reading the Gospels was the perfect teaching for Ireland beyond the fraying fringe of Rome.

50. Night Raid

Diurmid abandoned Alphin's hall before I sailed north from Dyflinn to Latharna. He disappeared soon after I had shown Aideen the magic of letters. I feared that he lingered, unseen near Dyflinn, a threat to Blaise. That morning, I was to learn that he was more of a threat to Brigid and me than he was to my Christian brother. Diurmid had not yet learned to respect the power of written words. He felt that Blaise was no threat to him. However, I held the threat of the Christ way magic, and I could stop a fever. I threatened his power.

Three villagers hastened across the meadows that spread on top of the seaside cliffs. They carried only stout walking staffs, no packs, no gifts, no goods for trade. They hurried to our huts. I heard them approaching and came outside. Bypassing my small hut with covert gestures to ward off evil, the three men stood outside the entrance to Brigid's hut. The oldest of the three was preparing to call out for her, when she opened the door flap and said, "What is it? What has happened?"

The old man quickly skimmed off his hat, looked over his shoulder to where I stood, and then looked down at Brigid's feet. "They came quickly from the hills, and they took our children," he answered.

"Who came?" Brigid asked.

"Seven warriors from the chieftain of Ulaid came down from the hills outside the village with clubs and swords. Just as the sun was going down." He hurried his words as if he feared his breath would run out before his story finished. "We were all about the chores at the end of the day, bringing in nets, gathering the cows into the barn, making sure that our gear was stowed. Then the eight of them were all around us with no warning."

"You said seven warriors," I said from behind. Brigid gave me a look that silenced me.

"Yes, seven," she gently repeated.

"There were eight of them," one of the younger men said. Two of the villagers appeared to be brothers. The one that spoke had a large bandage on his head. "Yes, Colum," said his brother, "eight."

"He wasn't a warrior," said the old man. "He carried a tall staff but never used it like a weapon. But you could feel the threat in it." The other two nodded. "He wore a dark hood, so we never saw his face. He never spoke to us but did speak to the warriors, telling them to gather up the village's children. And so, they did. They went house to house and found the little ones there. They left the bairns who are still on the breast, but they took with them any child who could walk."

"Didn't you try to fight them?" I asked, unable to keep my silence.

"That we did," said the old man and looked at Colum. "This one nearly had his head bashed in with a club. The warriors killed Eoin, their father," he pointed at the two brothers, "Ita, their mother, and another mother, Ornat, when they fought back." He paused in the rush of his words to allow the news of their deaths a respectful space. Then he continued. "The warriors and the hooded man left with the children before dawn. The women of Latharna are preparing Eoin, Ita, and Ornat for burial. We rushed here to ask if you could help?"

"How can I help against warriors?" Brigid asked.

"The hooded one spoke to the warrior who killed Ita. That one told us that we had seven days for the false Roman druid who stays with you to leave. Only then will they return our children."

I saw Colum's brother dart a glance over his shoulder at me, then return his gaze to the ground at Brigid's feet. "You have been kind to us for many years, healing our sick, and tending our troubles," the old man said to Brigid. She nodded. "Can you help us now?" he pleaded.

Brigid looked at me, then at the three villagers and said, "You must be exhausted and famished, hurrying here from Latharna with this news. I will do what I can. First, let's get you something to eat and drink to restore your energy. We will all need it before this night is over."

Looks of relief and appreciation filled their faces. "While you are eating, I will talk with Patrick," she said. Fear and doubt flickered in their eyes. "Together, we will resolve how to get your wee ones back and get these warriors to leave Latharna in peace."

Brigid turned and re-entered her hut. I was left uncomfortably standing with the three villagers who dearly desired me gone from their land. In short order, Brigid returned with her cook pot and a loaf of merely day-old bread. Looking at the villagers, she ordered them, "Get a fire started for under this pot." Then, with a furtive smile towards me she said, "Patrick, fetch bowls for our friends." I did. The soup warmed over new coals in the fire ring between our huts. The villagers found logs and a rock to sit on as the tension of their tale left them and the soup warmed their bellies.

I joined Brigid in her hut while the villagers ate. Brigid busied herself, tending first to her cooking things, and then looking in the chest along the far wall. "What will we do?" I asked.

"You'll have to leave, of course," she answered without looking up.

"Leave?" I cried, my heart breaking. I had been with Brigid only two months. Three months remained before I had promised to return to Blaise near Dyflinn.

"Yes," she said. "The village children's lives hang in this balance. You must leave." She saw my heartbroken look. "If what the villagers told is true, then we have five or six more days," Brigid continued. "Our conversation between the druid way of the Moringa and the Christ way can deepen for at least three more days. We can plan how you can safely leave."

Till that moment, I hadn't thought of my safety. I felt only my sense of sudden loss at being torn away from her. "The hooded man," Brigid said, "he must be Diurmid or another druid he sent."

It made sense to me in a dark, twisted way. Diurmid retreated from Alphin's hall when he saw the power of written words. He knew he was defeated in the eyes of Aideen and diminished in the eyes of Rí Alphin. "Diurmid would have gone north from Dyflinn into the Kingdom of Mide," Brigid said. "It's most likely he went from Rí Alphin's hall to the seat of the ard-Rí at the hill of Tara. There he could pour poison into ard-Rí Leary's ear."

"But how would he know I was here?"

Brigid looked deeply into my eyes. "It is time, Maewyn," she said, then corrected herself. "Patrick, it is more than time for you to take hold of your own power. You hold the Christ draíocht. You received emblems of power from Amergin. These past months, I have been sharing the way of my powers with you." She allowed her words to sink in. "Think," she commanded. "What is the answer to your own question?"

"Tara is the seat of the ard-Rí" I began. Her nod encouraged me to continue. "The five major roads of Ireland converge there. From Tara, the ard-Rí's command goes out. News and rumors flow to Tara like the tide." I considered for a moment then added, "Tara is the center of the web and Diurmid now sits at the center receiving the news of each trembling strand."

"Yes, that is how he knew," confirmed Brigid.

"How do I fight him?"

"Look to the mirror of your own awareness for the answer," she commanded.

I allowed my mind to grow still. Doubts and thoughts and fears chased each other in my mind. But I didn't chase after them. I saw them speed by with my awareness and let them go. I kept returning to a feeling in my heart, a feeling of strength and presence. I didn't have a strategy at that moment, just heart.

"I must return south to Dyflinn," I finally said. Brigid said yes with her eyes. "To where I am safe." Again, she indicated agreement. "And I must let Diurmid and the warriors think they have frightened me away so they will release the children." Brigid smiled.

"Yes," she breathed almost in a whisper. "You will go to Latharna in five days and take a ship south from there. The roads between here and Dyflinn will not be safe with Diurmid sitting near the center of Tara's web." It was my turn to indicate yes. "We will send Colum and the other two back with word to Latharna to prepare a ship. The villagers will help since your leaving will return their children."

"I will miss you," I said.

"I'm coming with you," she replied.

53. The Second Road

Much later, after the battle of the fires, I learned that this is what happened. Diurmid had indeed gone from Dyflinn to Tara. As druid to the chieftain of the largest settlement in Ireland, Diurmid was second in rank among the court druids, second only to the ard-Rí's druid at Tara. Once he reached Tara, Diurmid spun a tale of how a stranger from far away had washed up on Ireland's shores to the south of Dyflinn. After enchanting the local under-chieftain, ri-Dichu, this Roman who styled himself as easpag, both druid and ri, made his way to Dyflinn.

This easpag had sent a fever ahead of him to weaken the town. When he arrived, he called off his demons and the fever withdrew. But he convinced Rí Alphin of Dyflinn that he had saved the city. It was also told that he had a magic that would freeze the words in your throat, painting them on a page and robbing you of the power of speech. The court druid of Tara was horrified.

"Didn't you resist this black magic?" asked Tara's druid.

"I did," answered Diurmid. "But I didn't yet know how powerful this easpag was. I should have asked for help from another druid to overcome him."

"Will you help me?" Tara's druid asked and sealed his fate.

"It will be my duty to help you," Diurmid answered and began to pour his poison into the court druid's ear. Soon, the court druid doubted his ability to handle Patrick on his own and presented Diurmid to ard-Rí Leary.

"A great king, such as you, should not have to worry over this," Diurmid told Leary. The ard-Rí showed his agreement. "This stranger is a threat to your kingdom." Diurmid added. "He must be stopped." The high king inclined his head to hear more of Diurmid's advice.

Leary knew that the throne of the ard-Rí was a three-legged stool, supported by his army, the bards, and the druids. His army enforced the peace and ensured that he received payment of annual rents and tithes from the subject chieftains. The bards made sure that the stories told of ard-Rí Leary praised his accomplishments in battle and his justice from the throne. The druids protected the loyalty of Ireland, assuring all that the ard-Rí was in harmony with the old ways and the Brehon law. If the court druid or another high druid questioned Leary's commitment to the old ways, then his captains, subject chieftains, and even the serfs would begin to doubt Leary's right to the throne of Tara.

"I've heard that this Patrick consorts and plots against you with a wandering druidess near the fishing village of Latharna. The village is undefended. Send your court druid with a small guard to force the villagers to banish Patrick."

"How will a small guard force the villagers?" Leary asked.

"Have your court druid seize the village children as hostages," Diurmid answered. "The villagers will rid themselves of the stranger."

"What then?" asked Leary. "This easpag will be abroad in Ireland to make trouble."

"Have your soldiers seize him on the road when he has left the village. Your court druid can kill him."

If Diurmid's stratagem had worked, I would be dead, and he could claim the victory. Maybe he would return to Dyflinn. Maybe he would supplant Leary's court druid because the plan had been his.

If the stratagem failed, Diurmid could blame the court druid and push him aside and so become Leary's new druid and advisor. Either way, Diurmid advanced.

I learned all this, much to my sadness, after the fires on Slane and Diurmid's death. I would have been dead alongside the road if Brigid had not convinced the villagers to provide a ship for safe passage back to Dyflinn. On the fourth day, after Colum, his brother, and the old man had brought word of the hostage-taking at Latharna, Brigid and I set off to the village. Where before the villagers had happily listened to my Christ tale and enjoyed draining a cask of Cadhla's ale with me, now I was greeted with downturned eyes and suspicious looks. I heard whispers as I passed. They said, "He is the one who brought this suffering," and "Why is our druidess with him?" Door flaps fell shut as I neared huts. The village men would not meet my gaze.

"They are just afraid for their children," Brigid assured me. We found the old man who had brought word of the kidnappings and he took us to the village headman. Brigid greeted him with a sad smile, "Owen."

"You came," the headman answered.

"Of course, we came," Brigid said, making a point of including me. "How could we not come to help save Latharna's children?"

Owen's head bobbed twice to show his agreement.

"We will need a ship."

The headman looked doubtful. "The soldiers and the hooded one asked us to banish this one," he said gesturing at me.

"And banish him you shall," answered Brigid. "Did they tell you which way he must leave the village?"

"No," answered the headman. "There is but one road that leads away from the coast and cliffs. They knew he must go that way."

"You know they will kill him as soon as he is beyond the village," Brigid continued.

"It is likely," the headman agreed.

"And you also know there is a second road away from the village," she said.

Doubt and questions crossed Owen's face. "Which way is that?" he asked.

"The sea way," Brigid answered. "We will need a boat." Owen began to object but Brigid powered on. "A small boat will do just fine. We will leave together. After the warriors have dealt with Patrick, they will come asking for me. You will have banished both Patrick and me from your village. The warriors will return your children. And you will have avoided being part of a murder."

Relief flooded the space between the headman and the druidess. Owen looked down at his feet. When he raised his eyes, they held tears.

"You have been kind to all of us, more than a friend," he said to Brigid. "When you return, you have a place here in our hearts." The two of them embraced. A small fishing boat with a crew of three was made ready to take us away from the village. We sailed on the tide at sunset. It was a long time before I saw Latharna once more.

54. The Time is Not Yet Right

It was a week before I finally reached my farmstead. Three days of sailing took us from Latharna to Dyflinn. I had been gone almost five months. It felt necessary to pay my respects to Rí Alphin. Brigid came with me. I noticed the differences as soon as I was there. A small, carved-wood cross hung over the main door to the hall. Inside, the chi-rho anagram for Christ was carved into the door pillar. There were more candles lit in the hall and generally the place felt fresher, lighter.

As soon as he saw me enter his hall, Alphin greeted me. "Easpag Patrick, welcome, welcome!" He rose from his chair. "I feared you had died in the north." Then turning to inspect Brigid, he said with a laugh, "Have you brought me a druidess to replace Diurmid? Or are you two . . .?" his voice trailed off.

"Rí Alphin," Brigid spoke up. "I am called Brigid, daughter of Amergin of the North." She offered the slightest of bows when she finished.

Alphin took a second look at her. "You're no court druid, are you?" he asked An almost inscrutable smile was her only answer.

"Ah, Easpag," Alphin said, clasping me on the shoulder. "You found a real druidess. I didn't know there were any like her left in Ireland."

"Yes, Lord Alphin," I answered. "We have known each other since we were very young. This is the one who helped me flee from Flan's wrath in the north, helped me find my way back to Britain—"

"Patrick is too modest," Brigid interrupted. "He and I both received power from Amergin. We are both his heirs and carry his teachings. I have studied the druid way since Amergin's death." She allowed silence to fill in the depth of her study and to tell what powers she had achieved. "Patrick has studied the Christ way. But this you already know." Alphin nodded. "These past months, we have been seeking how the Christ way may speak with the Moringa."

I looked at Brigid, shocked. She hadn't told me that she would say anything like this to the chieftain.

"What is this new way of the Christ and the Moringa?" Alphin asked.

"Easpag Patrick will share that with you soon, Rí Alphin," Brigid said. "The time is not yet right."

Alphin looked to me and then to Brigid. "Is this so?" he asked.

"It is, Rí Alphin," I answered, putting confidence into my voice. "I will come back to you very soon with word of this. We are on our way to the farm you gifted me and wished to pay homage at your hall before going there. Your hall will be the first in all of Ireland where this new way is taught."

Alphin looked satisfied but impatient with my explanation. He was about to say something more. Lady Aideen entered the hall with their son, Faelan, stopping his words before they were spoken.

Aideen looked shyly in my direction. Faelan held onto her hand with his tiny fingers. "I can see that my Christ druid has returned with a druidess," Aideen said. Then, with a warm smile, "This will be good."

Brigid and I bowed to Rí Alphin, then to Lady Aideen, and took our leave. "Why didn't you tell me you were going to say that?" I asked her as soon as we were alone.

"I didn't know," was her simple answer. "The words moved within me before I had time to reconsider them. They just felt right."

My look of consternation inspired her to say just this much more. "I could feel Diurmid's power lingering in the hall. Your life and your work hang here by a thread, Patrick. You need to add the power of the old ways to your Christ way if you're going to succeed."

I acknowledged the truth in her words.

"We must find this way, or you will leave me once again." I looked into the sadness of her eyes. "If we do not find it soon, I fear you will leave me for the land of the dead."

"I do not fear death." My reply was rash and not completely truthful.

"I do not want to be separated so soon," was Brigid's answer.

55. Together

Alphin sent two warriors with us for safety and two ponies laden with parchments and supplies for the scriptorium. Our party of four approached the farm at midday when the sun was high and warm. The grain had been harvested from the fields and brought into the barn for threshing. The krek-krek bird calls of corncrake sounded from the grasses and field stubble. As we walked past the small pond and the stream that fed it, I saw the distinct black and white plumage of lapwings and smelled the ripeness of several green apples that had fallen from the apple tree at the pond's edge.

As we drew nearer, I noticed a second new and smaller building just next to the barn. Seven men emerged from the barn and carried sacks into the smaller building. One of them must be Blaise.

The first one of the men to see me was not Blaise. I knew that as soon as he dropped his sack and ran for his spear near the door to the barn. He called to his companions, and we soon faced five spears and two confused others. One of the unarmed, confused men must be Blaise. "Hold back," I ordered my two guards. "They don't recognize us. They aren't expecting me."

It was late fall. We had been walking with our hoods drawn over our heads for warmth. I pulled back my hood and began to walk towards them and Brigid followed me. I turned to her and whispered, "I must do this alone."

"We are in this together," she whispered back, "or we are not in this at all." Her eyes held a steely firmness that entertained no argument. I would either agree or not. I felt the entire future of my work in Ireland tremble at that moment. Would I recognize, accept, and support the power and place of the Moringa and with her, Brigid, or I would follow the Roman-Christian custom of pushing the goddess and the old ways into the shadows? There was no time for deliberation. Just as it had when Father raised his axe to take Nevio's hand, I felt my heart quake. This time my courage stirred before the fatal moment passed. I nodded yes and smiled at her. "Together."

Turning back to the farmer warriors and Blaise, I called out. "Is this how you welcome your brother and easpag?"

"Patrick, is it really you?" Blaise cried out. He ran towards me, and we fell into a brotherly embrace. "We heard that you had been captured in the north. We heard you might be dead. We heard—" and his eyes caught sight of a wry smile on Brigid's face. "Who is this?" He stepped back, his voice growing defensive and cautious.

Brigid pulled back her hood to reveal her auburn beauty. Blaise blushed and then turned to look at me. "I am called Brigid," she said. "You must be Patrick's heroic brother, Blaise, about whom he talks so much." Blaise turned to look at her. "I am so glad to meet you," she said and bowed slightly.

I know she did it purposefully. In three short sentences, she went past his defenses and won his heart. Later, she said that she just spoke, once more from the heart. "I allowed graciousness to fill me," she told me. "He is your brother in the Christ way and your friend. I wanted him to be my friend, too." Her smile completely convinced me.

"Who are these warriors?" I asked, moving the greeting to what I hoped was more solid ground.

"They are the warriors that Rí Alphin sent to guard this place," Blaise began. "All five of them have become Christians. I am teaching three of them to write while two keep the guard."

"Rí Alphin sent four guards," I reminded Blaise.

"Yes, that is right," Blaise corrected himself. Then pointing at one of the young men with a spear, he said, "This is Segnat, the brother of Ronan, one of the guards." I gave him a look that told him to continue. "His name means 'hawk,' and he heard about the Christ way from his brother and wanted to join us."

"Why?" was Brigid's question from behind me.

"He told me he was tired of constant war, constant killing, and constant raiding. He wanted a different way to prove his honor." Then, startled at being questioned by a woman, Blaise shot back defensively, "Who are you to ask?"

The air bristled between them. Blaise was jealous for my attention and protective of his status at the farm. "She is my woman," I answered Blaise, "she will be our sister in the Christ way." His shocked look was eloquent. "We can all be of one heart, but our hearts must be bigger than before," I continued. "Is this not what Abbot Germanus taught us of the way of Christ?"

Blaise's face showed doubt and distress. "Is she your wife? Are you still a bishop?"

"We are man and woman," Brigid said.

"She is your sister," I added, "Like Magdalene, Mary, and Martha were sisters to the disciples. I am still your bishop. She is my woman. And we are still brothers. Is your heart big enough to hold that?"

"I will try, Patrick. I will try to make my heart bigger," Blaise replied.

I clapped him on the shoulders and embraced him roughly, as a brother. "That is all any of us can do," I said. "Let's see what you've accomplished in the scriptorium."

56. Striking First

January 424 AD

Blaise came up with the symbol. Druids carried staffs of authority. Staffs were often handed down from one master to the next. Bishops carried ornamented shepherd's staffs, the sign of their authority as shepherds of Christ's flock. It was Blaise's idea to put the shamrock, druid symbol of the interconnected oneness of life at the center of the shepherd's crook. Combine pagan and Christian into one new symbol.

Combine the triple life force of the mother goddess with a sign of the three-fold single god of the Christ way. The familiarity of the shamrock would open Irish hearts for hearing a new tale.

Niall arrived at the farm the day after Blaise had come up with his idea. Cadhla arrived the day after that. He brought news from England and beyond. Celestine was preparing to make Belvedere a saint. The influence of Rome had waned even further. It was now necessary to employ armed guards for his ship when he was in port. The coastal pirates had become so bold that now they simply sailed into the larger ports and took what they desired. "Leaving your ship unguarded," he told us, "is unwise." Cadhla also told us that the Germanic tribes, the Saxons, Angles, and Jutes, were migrating to Britain in larger numbers. London was becoming a Saxon town. Latin was heard less and less frequently, replaced by a new language he couldn't name.

Niall was full of his own stories. He told tales of his adventures sailing with Cadhla after they left me at Latharna, the storm with waves taller than Alphin's hall, the wind that howled like a ghost in the night, the sea maiden he had seen one night while standing watch. "She took off her skin as a seal and became a woman, right in front of me," he said. "She was beautiful, and her voice was sweet. But she smelled too much of the sea. I couldn't kiss her." He told the tale of fighting off two brigands while on the road on his way back to Dichu's village. He hinted at a tale of love between himself and a maiden.

It was good to have my companions together once more. Blaise and his students inked out letter after letter on new texts in the scriptorium. While I had been away at Latharna, Blaise, Kevin, and the others had produced two copies each of the books of Matthew, Mark, Luke, and John. With the new parchments from Alphin, they were working on a complete copy of the New Testament. When finished, it would be the first copy produced in Ireland. The five warriors welcomed Niall into their company. They trained with their weapons. Most days, Cadhla disappeared. He said he was working on something in the new barn and didn't want to be disturbed.

With help from the warriors, Brigid built a small hut away from the house and barn and scriptorium.

"It isn't good for you and me to be together all the time," she declared. "If that is what the gods had intended, that is what would have happened." Brigid's only concession to ornament on her hut were the paintings on the door hide. Facing out the hide was marked with the triple spiral. Facing in it was marked with the shamrock. The hut was just big enough to hold a central fire, a place to sleep, and a place to sit. When I visited her hut, which I did often, one of us would have to sit on the sleeping pallet while the other sat on a simple, three-legged stool.

The weather turned cold. In late December, the first frost arrived. Now, in early January, a cold, wet rain filled most afternoons, and a heavy frost lingered most mornings. I saw stars at night three times that January. All the other nights, wintry mist and clouds occupied the sky. It was a good time to be inside, to pray, and to plan for the spring.

"You cannot stay here and wait for Diurmid's next move," Brigid began one night. "He will kill you. He must kill you or lose his power."

I fell into silence at her words. I knew they were true. Diurmid would convince high-king Leary to send for me at Alphin's hall. If Alphin refused, he rebelled against the ard-Rí. If Alphin complied, I died. Of course, I could flee. On the run in Ireland, I would eventually be caught and handed over to the ard-Rí's men. Returning to Britain and then Europe was not a choice I was willing to consider. I grimaced at the thought. I had returned once from Ireland, an escaped slave full of disgrace. I would not return a second time, a failed missionary full of the shame of running away from martyrdom. If I were to die, I wanted my death to have dignity, to show courage, to mean something.

"We will not wait for Diurmid to come to us," I eventually said, looking over the glowing coals of Brigid's fire. "I will go to him. But when?" I asked.

The air between Brigid and me was heated by the intensity of the question as well as the coals. Her hut was almost dark. The small candle by her sleeping pallet had guttered out. The hut's only light was the red glow from the fire. As she moved to light another small candle, I saw the slyness of a smile slowly creep onto Brigid's face.

"I know when," she said and looked at me, still holding the candle to be lit. "Beltane," she continued and lit the candle. "When all the winter fires in Ireland have been extinguished and the ard-Rí lights the ceremonial fire."

"Why then?" I asked.

"Because the first fire is sacred, whoever lights the fire is king. You say your Christ is a king. Light a fire before Leary and claim Ireland for your king," she answered.

"They will never allow me to get near the fire," I objected. "They will take me captive and kill me long before we get near the king."

"Beltane is a sacred festival," Brigid explained. "The peace of the ard-Rí extends to all who come to the fire festival bringing homage from Ireland's chieftains. If you go as Alphin's druid, then you are guaranteed safe conduct to and from the festival." She paused and considered. "Not even Diurmid will break the truce. He would be ripped apart by the other druids and his body thrown to the dogs for breaking the peace of all Ireland."

"Then I must convince Alphin to send me as his druid," I agreed. "I will not run away or hide as an outlaw. I will not wait here to die. I will allow fear and shame to rule me no more."

We made love that night. It was fierce and tender and free all at once. I gave pleasure. I took pleasure. Our sweat and spit and juices mingled. As Brigid rose to meet and encompass my final thrust, I looked deep into her eyes. They were a dark, dark green. We peaked together in that hut within the winter's mist and cold. We peaked together and sparked the next Beltane's fire.

57. Irish Saints

By the end of January, Cadhla had finished work on his secret project. Very serious, he approached one morning and asked, "Will you allow me to follow you, to serve you?"

The request took me by surprise. Cadhla was one of the roughest of Ireland's sea captains and traders. His independence and lack of needing anyone's support seemed total. His work in the barn, separated from the rest of us at the farm, appeared to fill his need. He had a woman in Dyflinn port but no children. There were other women in other ports. He never shared details about any of them. "Will you take me?" he asked.

"Yes Cadhla, of course," I answered. Then looking into his lined face, "Why now?"

"Patrick," he began and then corrected, "Easpag Patrick, I've lived a hard life." Cadhla had a tale to tell but not the one I expected. "I've sailed on raids, like the one that captured you. More than one man has died at my hands. I've not always been honest as a trader."

I kept my attention on the ship captain and allowed space to offer his word an accepting port.

"My heart was broken, and my courage tested by a girl." The ship captain paused and wiped a tear gathering at the corner of his left eye. "Her name was Diedre. She was seven years old. She died in Dyflinn's fever the week before you came to Dyflinn port." A short silence fell between us as he remembered her. He looked down at his feet and continued. "Diedre was my only child. She was smart and funny and as beautiful as a summer sky. Then her wee body burned up with the fever and she was gone." Cadhla looked up at me, "Ever since you saved Dyflinn, I've wondered why you didn't come sooner. I've told myself that if I was a better man, I'd have been able to help Deidre. Her death is like a millstone around my neck. Its sorrow hangs on me."

"This is why you want to follow the Christ way?" I asked.

"You speak of a draíocht stronger than death," the captain answered. "I want to be touched by that magic. I will pray to your Christ god to share that magic with Deidre."

"You are already part of the Christ way," I reminded him. "You were baptized in your boat on the River Liffey."

"I know," he answered, "but it is not enough. I still feel the sorrow around my neck. I want to follow you, to be like Blaise."

To say I was startled does not even begin to tell how surprised I was. I looked at Cadhla for a long time. He was rough, lined, scarred by life. He was no longer young. A captain in his own heart, it would be difficult to train him to take orders. He was a discipline challenge knocking at the door. He was, like the Apostle Peter, perfect for the first one among the Irish to answer the call to serve the Christ way.

"Customarily, a gift is offered to secure acceptance into a monastery," I said.

"You will have half the revenue from my ship," Cadhla answered. "The other half will go to my woman in Dyflinn port. And one more thing." He hurried away to the barn and then back, carrying a long bundle wrapped in coarse cloth.

"What is it?" I asked.

"Your staff is such a poor thing," Cadhla said with apprehension. "I know you brought it with you from far away. But it does not speak with power," he hastened to add. "I thought you needed a new one."

I nodded.

"A staff that shows the combined power of the Christ way and the Moringa," I know that the lines at the outside corners of my eyes began a smile. "I've been carving this for you," he said and unwrapped a new shepherd's crook. On top of a stout staff as tall as my eyes, a shepherd's crook was carved and mounted. The crook turned in on itself and was carved to resemble the unfolded tip of a fern. At the center of the unfolded circle, held in a carved cross, was a medallion of the shamrock. The cross that held the shamrock itself was a wonder to see. Celtic knot patterns covered its four arms. At the base of the crook's cross was a small triple spiral. Another symbol was carved at the head of the cross, the awen. Cadhla had smoothed and polished the wood until it glowed.

"The staff is made of yew," Cadhla offered. "I carved the top from a piece of yew that I traded for on my last sailing."

"Why yew wood?" I asked.

"Yew trees live almost forever," Cadhla began. "They are favored by the druids and the wood is difficult to burn. It is a good wood for carving the symbol of a magic that is stronger than death."

Together, we entered the scriptorium with the new crozier. Blaise fell in love with the beauty of the staff the moment he saw it. He had been lonely on the farm as its only monk and was glad for a new brother. Later that night, in a small ceremony witnessed by Niall, Brigid, and Blaise, I accepted Cadhla as a monk. Instead of taking a saint's name as was the custom in Europe, he kept his Irish name, Brother Cadhla. I told him, "We are not looking back to Europe; we will make Irish saints now."

58. Mugain's Sorrow

After the full moon of January, before Imbolic, the time when the first snow drops appear, all 10 of us left the farm and traveled to Dyflinn. Segnat and Ronan and the other warriors, with Niall as their captain, served as our guard on the road. Blaise led a pony burdened with the sacred texts that had been copied over the long months. Brigid and I rode horses. Cadhla carried my shepherd's crook, although it was covered once again with rough cloth.

Dyflinn was still wet with mist and cloud, still cold with a lingering chill. It was the final day of January, the day before the druid festival of the growing light. Even though it was still winter, the days grew slightly longer, and the first little white flowers appeared along the paths in the wood and the lanes between Dyflinn's homes. We reached Alphin's hall at mid-morning. A strange guard stood at the door and barred our way. "What do you want?" he demanded.

"I am Rí Alphin's friend," I said. "I seek to speak with him."

"Ri-Alphin is not in his hall," the guard barked. "Queen Mugain sits in her chair." Then looking at Brigid, Blaise, and Cadhla holding the cloaked staff, he said, "She will not hear the likes of you today. She's told me to turn away all strangers."

"This is no stranger," Niall said. The guard at the door looked to his right and left as several more guards joined him to bar the door.

"He is from away," the door guardian said. "And you," he added looking at each of my companions, "keep company with him. He is no druid, and you are," he paused, "friends of this stranger."

The noise of a commotion of hoofs and horsemen interrupted us. While the guard had been denying us entry, Alphin and three mounted warriors had ridden up behind us.

"Easpag," he greeted me, "I've just returned from the hunt." He pointed at a brace of rabbits hanging from his saddle horn and a clutch of dead pheasants stuffed into a game bag. "Why are you here?"

"We came to share the combined magic of the Christ way and the Moringa," I answered.

Alphin looked at Brigid, and then to me. "Is this so?"

"Yes, Rí Alphin," we said together.

Looking around at my companions, the chieftain asked, "Your party grows larger. I sent four men to your farm, and you return with six?"

"Yes, Rí Alphin," I laughed. "It seems Irish soil agrees with the Christ way. Followers grow even in the winter."

Alphin laughed back at my answer. "But why are you standing out here?" Then looking at the guard, "Why are you barring their way?"

The guard looked down, "Orders from Queen Mugain."

Alphin sighed and looked at me. "Easpag," he said, "mark my words. One wife is a blessing. Two are a trial. Three . . ." The chieftain allowed his words to trail off, then dismounted and turned his attention back to the guard, "Open the door, fool. I'll deal with Mugain." Then to one of his companions, "Take the horses to the stables and the game to the kitchen. They'll know how I like rabbit stew. When you are finished, join me in the hall."

The guard unbarred the way to the door. Alphin indicated that he wished our party to enter the hall before him. Uncertain, I stepped into the twilight beyond the doors. Queen Mugain sat on her chair to the right of the chieftain's seat. Only two small torches behind her cast illumination into the hall. Beyond their circle of light, the hall huddled in gloom. Mugain looked up as I stepped from the shadows,

"I thought I told the guard to bar you from the door," she said, then called out, "Guard, guard," a strident note in her voice.

"The guards are with me," Alphin answered as he followed us into the circle of light. "More torches," he called. "Enough of gloom and winter's doubts."

Several servants scurried to light the torches along the wall and stir the coals of the hall's heating fires to flame. As the light grew, Alphin softly approached his first wife's chair. "Lady," he said, "Mugain, will you not relent?"

"Diurmid told me that this black magician," she pointed at me, "caused the fever. He sent it ahead of him to take our children." Mugain's tears flowed down her cheeks even as she raged. "The fever took our son, Finn, and your second wife,

Etroma." Stretching clawed fingers towards me, she cried, "Don't you remember? Don't you remember? How can you welcome him into our hall?"

At that moment, I saw a tenderness in Alphin that I hadn't seen before. "Mugain," he whispered. "I do remember, and I cry each night for Finn and Etroma." His tears matched hers. "But they died a week's time before Patrick entered our hall. How could their deaths be his fault?"

"Diurmid told me!" Mugain screeched and turned on the chieftain. "If we hadn't welcomed this stranger, our son wouldn't have died. He died because of you, because of this . . ." her words trailed off as her hand fell away from pointing at me.

Alphin took Queen Mugain in his arms and held her. "My heart," he said, "breaks with yours." Then he signaled Mugain's attendants. "My wife needs kindness and rest," he told them. "Help her to her rooms. I will visit her later."

None of us— Brigid, Blaise, Niall, Cadhla, or I—spoke a word as this tragedy played out before us. We held our gaze towards our feet while Alphin comforted Mugain. I didn't look up until the sounds of Mugain being led from the hall faded and I heard Alphin take his seat.

"Well, Easpag," Alphin started, "I meet you and you are barred from my hall. We enter to find my Lady consumed by sorrows. I hope you've brought something to brighten the darkness of winter."

"I have," I answered and indicated to Cadhla that he should stand beside me with the covered staff. "I've come with the symbol of the joining of the Moringa with the Christ way."

Interest flickered across Alphin's face.

"I hold this way on my own. I hold it by the strength of the Christ way that was handed to me in Rome. I hold it by the power that was gifted me by Amergin." I paused and allowed my words to have their effect. "And I seek the blessing of my chieftain to unveil this way in his hall."

"Why seek the blessing of a chieftain at all if you hold this power on your own?" Alphin asked.

"Because this new way joins Ireland to the Christ way," I said. "And here, in your hall, you are Ireland."

Alphin shone with the compliment. "I will hear what you have to say," he said. Then he clapped his hands twice and called for his servants to bring ale. "A good tale requires a moist throat," he laughed, "and ready ears."

59. Unveiled

I told Alphin three stories. I told the story of how the sky God made the world and was thus Father to the world. To this I added the story of how the child of the sky God, the Son of God, opened the eyes of a blind man. Only a god could do this. When questioned by the religious authority, the child god answered, "I and the Father are one."

"So, you see, the Christ way tells of one God, the same God who shows himself as both Father and Child." Alphin's eyes narrowed as he looked at me and considered this point. Already believing in a triple goddess, a double god was not that big of a hurdle.

I continued with the promise that the Son of God made before he left the world to be with his Father above the skies, a promise to send a third God who would stay with us until the end of the world. Ten days after he disappeared into the skies, the friends and followers of the child god were gathered all together in one house. "A mighty wind filled the whole house," I told the chieftain, "and small tongues of flame rested above the heads of each one there."

"What kind of magic was this?" Alphin asked, leaning forward in his chair.

"It was the third face of god, the breath of God flowing into our world, as tongues of fire" I answered.

"I don't see a flame above your head," were his next words.

"The flame lives now in my heart and the hearts of those who follow the Christ way," I replied. "You cannot see it, it can only be felt and known by those who choose to believe."

"Why would I choose to believe in something I can't see or know?" came back from the chair.

Brigid interrupted our dialogue. "Lord chieftain," she began. "You may choose to believe Easpag Patrick's story or not. It's up to you."

Alphin relaxed back into his seat.

"However, Patrick's story is not so different from what we teach of the Moringa. She is three goddesses worshiped as one. She is the sky, the earth, and the sea. She is the goddess of war, the goddess of ruling, and the goddess who guards the lands of dreams and death. She is mother, sister, and daughter of all. Sometimes she gives comfort. Sometimes she brings joy. Other times, chaos follows in her shadow."

Alphin's face turned serious while Brigid spoke. Her words conveyed her power and confidence in the old ways.

"Druidess, why do you speak on behalf of this new way?" the chieftain asked.

With both her hands, Brigid gathered Amergin's amulet and the chain it hung from around her neck. She drew the talisman over her head. She held the amulet out before her with both hands and took a half step towards the chieftain's chair. "This is the great Amergin's gift to me. Look carefully on both sides," she said, allowing Alphin to hold the charm.

"This is the triple spiral of the Moringa," Alphin declared looking at the upward facing side of the talisman. He then turned the amulet over. "A shamrock?"

"Amergin prophesied that the old ways would soon change," Brigid said. "'Your shepherd lover will return,'" he foretold, "'and bring with him the way of the Romans.' Our ways have grown old. It is time for them to have their winter's sleep. 'Everything changes eventually,' he told me. 'The old ways hold the wisdom of our people.' Amergin said that we'd be able to maintain our wisdom if we remembered what the shamrock told."

"What is that?" asked Alphin.

"Shamrocks are everywhere; they're common clover. They have a medicinal power that almost everyone takes for granted. They also have a secret teaching. Each of them has one stem and three leaves, just like the Moringa is one goddess with three faces, just like this god of Patrick's."

She paused to allow Alphin space to consider her words. After a silence that lasted many, many minutes, Brigid continued. "The father god of the sky and the mother goddess of the world are not at war with each other. They have never been so."

Alphin nodded at this wisdom.

"Sometimes the mother is most in our hearts. Now, winter approaches for the teachings of the mother. It becomes spring for the sky god. How we welcome this change will decide whether our old ways, with their wisdom, are lost or whether they will become seeds, to reawaken in a future spring."

I signaled Cadhla to unveil my new shepherd's crozier. "This staff is an emblem of my power as easpag," I began.

Alphin was captured by the symbol of the shamrock within the cross within the circle of the folded shepherd's crook.

"It is a story within a story within a story," he said with amazement and appreciation in his voice.

"It holds the Moringa secretly within the Christ way," added Brigid.

"It shows how the Christ way may grow here, in your kingdom," I said. "How you may become a follower of the Christ way and honor the memory of the old ways at the same time."

Alphin nodded and signaled for more ale.

60. Comforting the Dead

I talked with Rí Alphin a long time that day. He called for a seat to be brought forward for me. I sat on a bench, slightly below his raised chair, and told him again the story of the birth and death of the Christ. As I began telling the tale once more, Brigid excused herself.

"With your permission, Rí Alphin," she said, "I would leave and seek out Queen Mugain and offer her comfort."

Alphin motioned to one of his servants. "Show our druidess to the queen's rooms," he told her. "Attend to her needs."

As they left the main hall, Brigid asked the serving girl, "What is your name?"

"I am called Mochan," the girl answered.

"Mochan means 'early,'" Brigid said. "It's an unusual name for a servant."

"I am told I arrived before my mother's nine months were full," Mochan supplied. "I've been early ever since." She waited then added somewhat sadly. "Sometimes this pleases my masters, sometimes not."

"I am more sister than master," Brigid said. "I am the child of a slave as well as the daughter of a druid. So, whenever we arrive will be the right time. For now, I have one question."

"Yes," said Mochan.

"Prince Finn died a week before Easpag Patrick came to Rí Alphin's hall. Was Queen Mugain's child's body burned with all the others?"

"No, sister," Mochan offered tentatively. She saw approval in Brigid's eyes for the assumed familiarity. "Prince Finn's body was buried with the bodies of those who died that week." Mochan's words halted. Brigid looked to her in a way that indicated she sought more. "Eleven others died that week," the servant continued. "Three warriors, two of their wives, two men and three women from the village, and one other child."

"Whose was the second child?"

"Do you not know already?" Mochan replied with questioning eyes. "The second child was Deidre, daughter of the man who stands next to your easpag."

"I did not know. Cadhla is a very private man. What of the Lady Etroma? Is she also buried there?"

"Rí Alphin's second wife died at the very beginning of the fever. Her body was buried, on its own, by the king, his guard, and the druid." She waited a bit then added, "No one but they know where the Lady rests. The servants think sometimes it is she that Rí Alphin rides out to see when he tells everyone he has gone hunting. He never takes anyone along on those days other than guards who went with him to bury the lady."

The two women continued to the queen's rooms. One guard stood by the door. He looked to the servant, then the druid. "She comes from Rí Alphin, at his command," Mochan said. The guard allowed them to pass.

Mugain's rooms echoed the earlier gloom of Alphin's hall. Although there were two large windows, heavy curtains closed off almost all the light of the day. One candle burned at a table beside Mugain. A small, simmering pile of coals glowed red in the room's fireplace. Mugain herself sat gathered within a heavy, dark, wintergreen cloak. She had allowed her hair to hang down in tatters around her face and shoulders. Her eyes showed a flat gray.

Brigid took a place at Lady Mugain's feet, just sitting, being still. Mochan withdrew from the room, leaving the two of them alone while she waited past the door with the guard. During the long hours that I told my tale of the Christ way to Rí Alphin, Brigid sat vigil with Mugain. She spoke only once during those hours of vigil. Mugain told that she feared for her life now that her son was dead.

"Before he died, Finn was to be the next chieftain of Dyflinn," Mugain said. "Alphin loved me and loved our son. Etroma was like a sister in our hall. I was the mother of the next chieftain. She was the chieftain's lover. But when Alphin took Aideen for his third wife, everything soured. Alphin withdrew his warmth from Etroma. He sought out advice only from Aideen and gave almost all his father love to her son."

Near the end of my tale, I'm told Brigid said to Mugain, "I'd like to see where your Finn lies."

Startled, Mugain looked at her as if for the first time. "Why?" a coarse whisper escaped her.

"I am Brigid, daughter of Amergin of the North," she answered. "I too follow the old ways; I honor the Mother. I have griefs, almost as large as yours. I would like to pay my respects at Finn's resting spot and send a wishing prayer for him to the Moringa."

"What do you want from me?" sighed Mugain with a guarded voice.

"Nothing," answered Brigid. "Enough has already been asked of you. I only ask to pay my respects where your son lies." When Mugain agreed, Brigid called for Mochan and the guard. "Take us to where Queen Mugain's son rests."

The two women stood by a group of stones arranged just beyond the walls of Dyflinn's inner palisade. Several strong stones the height of a young boy stood around mounded earth. A capstone lay across the standing stones to form a portal. The cauldron of death symbol was carved at the threshold. Small flowers showed their first white buds. The burnt remnants of several homes lingered in piles just beyond the grave site. One or two wattle walls stood here and there; their white coats covered with smoke. Thatch roofs and wood doorways had all burned. The place had a haunted feel.

"Here?" Brigid asked.

"Here," Mugain answered.

"Did Diurmid offer Finn and the others guidance as they died?" Brigid asked the older woman.

"By the time Finn died, Diurmid hardly ever left the hall. He told us that he was praying and chanting to keep the fevers away from Alphin. Finn died without comfort," Mugain said.

"Then it is time to offer him comfort now." She had Mochan fetch a small pot of fresh water and an evergreen sprig for sprinkling the stones. Dipping the evergreen three times into the water, she chanted, "Go with ease to the land of the ancients, let this water carry you across." When the stones had been wet, Brigid turned to Mugain to ask, "Who else rests here?" Mugain offered her no answer beyond flat gray eyes.

That was when Brigid first heard the steps behind her. A plain woman, average in height, weathered with age but otherwise unremarkable, in a simple cloak of two colors had silently joined them. "Thank you for the guiding words for the dead," she said.

Brigid looked at her, dumbstruck. How had she appeared so silently? Was she a ghost come to join them at the grave, one of the mothers buried here?

"I am called Nuala," the woman said. "My daughter lies here alongside Lady Mugain's son."

"You are Cadhla's woman?" Brigid asked.

"I belong to no one," Nuala answered, "Cadhla is . . ." her words ended without finishing the thought.

"And your daughter?"

"Deidre was just 7." Nuala answered. "I come here to speak to her. I find some comfort in it."

Brigid nodded understanding and then looked towards Mugain.

"I see the Queen here almost daily," Nuala offered. "She sees nothing beyond the grave. I worry for her. I've tried to speak with her several times, but it's as if I'm not here."

"A mother's grief is like a dark thicket deep in the forest of loss," Brigid affirmed. "We may light a torch to help her see the way out of the thicket, but each of us must find our own way or stay lost."

Nuala nodded and the three women stood silently by the grave.

After I had finished telling the Christ tale to Alphin, and after Brigid had returned from keeping vigil at the portal grave, she and I spoke. "Were you able to help Mugain?" I asked.

"She is lost, deep within her grief," Brigid answered. "I fear she is mad."

61. Ireland's Champion

"The fever cost me two wives," Alphin said the next day in his hall. He saw the lack of understanding on my face. "Etroma died from the fever and Mugain is gone, far away because of it." Looking towards Brigid, the chieftain asked, "Were you able to comfort her?"

"I went to your son's tomb," Brigid answered. "I offered him, and all the others who lay there with him, the guiding words for the dead." Alphin bent his head forward slightly to listen for more. "And I spent a long time with the Queen before going to the tomb."

"What did you learn?" the chieftain almost begged.

"I learned that her sadness is a well whose bottom I could not find."

Alphin's head drooped with sorrow. "Queen Mugain fears that when you pass from this world, she will also die. She fears that the Lady Aideen's son will be chieftain after you. If needed, the Lady Aideen would serve as his regent until he was old enough to sit in your chair."

Alphin nodded that this was true.

"That will leave Mugain sonless and husbandless, with no future, no past, no place to rest," Brigid pronounced. "She sees no way out from where she is lost in her grief."

"Mugain has my love. I have never withdrawn that from her," Alphin objected.

"Love is not enough," Brigid answered.

"What more can he offer?" I asked.

"I can tell her I love her, reassure her," the chieftain said.

"You could send Nuala to sit vigil with her," Brigid added. "Someone who has felt the same grief and who will know how to sit with Mugain and be a comfort without demanding anything of her."

"You can ask the Lady Aideen to extend her kindness to Mugain," I offered. "That will help her believe her place here is safe if something were to happen to you."

"One more thing," Brigid said. "Arrange for daily offerings of food and drink to be made at Finn's tomb. Have Mugain offer them. I will tell her to continue as long as she feels they are needed."

"Why? The dead have long since gone on to the land of shades," Alphin objected.

"The offerings are not for the dead," Brigid answered. "They are for Mugain. She struggles with her own grief and needs to do something, to make some gesture."

"Yes," answered Alphin.

"And Dyflinn still needs her chieftain," she said.

"Dyflinn needs her chieftain," I agreed, taking advantage of this shift toward Alphin, "and Ireland needs a champion for the Christ way and the draíocht that is stronger than death." Alphin looked at me with a challenge and a question.

"Rí Alphin," I pressed, "will you champion this new way for Dyflinn and for Ireland?"

"Yes," Alphin voiced so softly that the words were almost lost between us.

"Will you become a follower of the Christ way in order to secure for Dyflinn and for Ireland a magic that is stronger than death?"

"Yes," the chieftain said louder than before.

"Will you accept baptism and become a follower of the Christ?"

"Yes," he said with force, looking directly at me. "May the gods help keep safe the old ways. May they heal Mugain's heart and help bring strong draíocht to Dyflinn's arms."

This is how the chieftain of Dyflinn, his household guard, and several of the leading traders and merchants of the town, along with their wives and children, came to the Christ way. Alphin's "yes" led almost 150 new converts to the new religion. When the baptisms were done, we began to plan how to take the new way to Tara.

62. Death Seems the Only Choice

We stayed two and a half months more at Alphin's hall. A message was sent to ard-Rí Leary at Tara, offering to bring tribute to the celebration of the spring fire on Beltane. Alphin promised 20 head of cattle and 1,000 silver coins, more than a king's honor price, as tribute. It was a gift that Leary would not refuse.

It was still the custom that the high king, the ard-Rí, would light Ireland's first fire on Beltane eve. Subject chieftains and allies would come or send delegations to be part of the celebration. Hearth fires were doused throughout Ireland on the last day of April. At sunset, the king's fire would be lit as the first fire of the land. It would burn until after sunset the next day. Offerings of food and drink were made to the fire. Weapons and livestock were blessed with smoke from the fire. Torches were lit and taken to the hearths of chieftains across Ireland, a gesture symbolizing unity.

One fire, one ard-Rí, one people.

Throughout Ireland, similar fires were lit on the far hills and young couples hand-fasted, as Brigid and I had done so long ago atop Slemmish. But to stand at the ard-Rí's Beltane fire, to take part in the ceremonies there, was to declare yourself the ard-Rí's subject-friend.

Ard-Rí Leary replied quickly to Alphin's honor gift and request to be part of the Beltane celebration. "Come," was the answer. "You are welcome as a friend and ally at Tara. Come with your household and your gifts."

It was also the custom of those days that during the three days that preceded Beltane and the three days that followed, all who attended the ard-Rí's festival were under the protection of the king. Safe conduct and truce were the law at Tara for that week. To break the truce was to declare yourself an enemy of the ard-Rí.

Rí Alphin and his household prepared for the two-day journey between Dyflinn and Tara. The hall, indeed all Dyflinn, was busy with preparing. Twenty of the choicest cattle were selected. One hundred and fifty warriors readied themselves to accompany Alphin. A show of force added value to a chieftain's face. Ladies and servants of the chieftain's household prepared to accompany the party. In all, more than 200 souls would depart Dyflinn on April 27th, heading northwest to the ard-Rí's hill. Brigid, Cadhla, Blaise, Niall, and I would travel with them.

One day, shortly before Brigid and I were about to leave for Tara, Nuala approached us with news. "Queen Mugain will not go with the household to Tara," she said.

We both looked saddened. "We hoped she would come," said Brigid.

"Rí Alphin will be disappointed," I added.

"Her mind and heart are still torn with grief," Nuala replied. "Mugain teeters on the edge of darkness. The demands of such a large party will push her over that edge."

"Have you asked her to come?" Brigid inquired.

"I have talked to her for a week or more," Nuala said. "When I speak of going with Rí Alphin to Tara, the Queen tears at her hair and has a haunted look. She will not answer when I ask if she will go."

"Nuala, will you stay here with her," I asked, "to comfort and steady her?"

Nuala dipped her head once in affirmation. "Yes, Easpag Patrick. I will stay with her."

Later, Nuala told me that almost as soon as the chieftain's party left the town, Mugain asked for a sleeping potion from her servants. They assumed that it was so she could find rest and relief in dreams. Mugain poured the potion into a draught she offered Nuala. With her companion lost in sleep, Mugain commanded a guard to find a horse for her. Attended by one guard, she was gone from the hall before Nuala woke.

They searched for Mugain but didn't find her. She and her guard also rode north by west towards Tara. Keeping to wooded paths, the two traveled quicker than Rí Alphin's party with its baggage and cattle offering. Mugain reached the ard-Rí's compound near Tara a full 12 hours before Alphin. She found refuge with Diurmid.

"Queen Mugain," Diurmid greeted her. "You must be weary after the journey from Dyflinn." He signaled one serving girl to bring warm water and towels so

Mugain could refresh herself. Offering his chair to Mugain, he ordered another servant to bring him a stool. He commanded a third servant to find food and drink.

"Now, my Queen," Diurmid said, turning his attention back to the chieftain's wife, "I expected you to arrive with Rí Alphin. What caused you to hasten here without him?"

"The chieftain is in this Roman druid's thrall," she said. "The Christ way now owns Alphin's spirit. You told me that Finn died because of this stranger. Now even more will die."

Diurmid affected compassion for Mugain's suffering while he plotted.

"He must be stopped!" she cried. "He must be stopped!" Before Alphin and the party from Dyflinn arrived, Diurmid turned ard-Rí Leary's heart against me. "He brought a fever to Dyflinn and then pretended to cure it. He has turned Dyflinn's chieftain against the old ways. He keeps company with Brigid of the Sorrows, the druidess your father banished from Tara for spreading false accusations. Patrick brings poison even as Alphin offers cattle."

"They are safe guarded by the Beltane truce," Leary said.

"Ask Rí Alphin as your under-king to leave his druid and the druidess here when he returns to Dyflinn," said Diurmid. "If he objects, tell him that as ard-Rí you are responsible for the peace of Ireland and have heard that they threaten that peace. And that you would like to put them to a trial."

"A trial?" asked the ard-Rí.

"Yes," answered Diurmid. "I have summoned 12 other druids. Word has spread about this Patrick, and they fear that his power undermines the old ways. They will listen to this new way, then condemn this Roman druid and Brigid."

"And their punishment?" Leary asked.

"You are ard-Rí; that is for you to decide," Diurmid said. "I can only tell you that the thrones of Ireland are not safe while Patrick's way contends with our old way. Having banished one Roman druid only to have another stronger one appear, death seems the only choice. But that decision is yours."

63. Avoiding Capture

Alphin's town lay astride the border between Mide and Laigin. Ard-Rí Leary's family lands were in the Kingdom of Mide, five days ride north from Dyflinn. The hill of Tara, with its fort and sacred standing stones, less than three days ride from Dyflinn, was also controlled by Leary. Tara held the mystical heart of Ireland. All the high kings were chosen there, crowned there. When he became high king, the under-kings of Ulaid, Laigin, and Connacht had all paid tribute to Leary there. It was at Tara that Leary chose to light that year's Beltane fire.

Our delegation made good time from Dyflinn to Tara. We could only hurry as fast as Alphin's gift of cattle would walk. Two days after leaving Dyflinn, we reached the boundaries of Tara's fortress almost at noon. A party of 11 soldiers waited just inside the boundary. Their captain wore a coat of three colors and was mounted on an impressive coal-black stallion. The guard all wore the colors of Clan Ui Neill, Leary's family.

"Ard-Rí Leary extends his greetings," called out the captain of the guard as we approached.

Rí Alphin, with his own captain, rode at the head of our line. I rode with Brigid and Niall, slightly behind him. "The High King is quite gracious," answered Alphin, "May peace dwell at his door." Then pointing back along our line to where the cattle were being herded, "And may this gift fatten his herd."

The captain of Leary's guard grinned. "The high king has decreed that Rí Alphin and all his men may keep their weapons when they enter Tara." Looks of appreciation flickered through our party. When high kings feared for their seats, they could ask all guests except under-kings to surrender their weapons. Here was a gesture of confidence on Leary's part. "Ard-Rí Leary only asks one concession," the captain called out.

Rí Alphin had been smiling at his own captain, relaxed and reassured by the initial welcome. His surprised attention snapped forward once more. "What does the ard-Rí ask?" called out the chieftain.

"Leary asks that you surrender custody of the Roman who calls himself a druid and his woman, the druidess Brigid, when they cross into Tara."

"Why?" answered Alphin. "They are under my protection as chieftain of Dyflinn, under protection of the Beltane truce."

"The High King is not in the habit of telling his captain of the guards why," answered the mounted warrior. "I only know his request. The Roman and the druidess are to surrender to the guard when they cross into Tara. You and the rest of your party are to be welcomed and allowed to keep your arms."

"If we surrender," Brigid whispered loud enough for Alphin and me to hear, "we forfeit the protection of the truce. We become Leary's captives."

"I will not enter under these terms," Alphin said to both of us.

"You must enter," Brigid replied. "To withdraw now strongly insults the ard-Rí and challenges him at the borders of Tara. As soon as the truce is over, he will march south with his lords and warriors and attack you."

"But I will not surrender you," Alphin said.

"That makes me very glad," I added. "I had not chosen today to become a captive again." Alphin and Brigid laughed. "If Brigid and I don't cross into Tara," I asked, "what then?"

"Then Rí Alphin is welcomed, and we remain free," answered Brigid.

"Rí Alphin," I asked, "allow a small guard to remain with my party and cross over into Tara without us." The chieftain dipped his eyes with assent and gave the order to his own captain. Thirteen of Rí Alphin's guard, all warriors who had been baptized with Alphin, were given over to my command.

"Easpag Patrick," Alphin said, "I'd like my son, Kevin, to come with me to Tara."

I signaled and the king's 14-year-old son, our first scriptorium student, rode forward. One hundred and eighty-eight members of the chieftain's household, its warriors, ladies, servants, and cattle crossed the boundary into Tara's sacred precincts.

Cold sweat trickled down my back as I watched Alphin ride away. "We are without protection," I said to Brigid.

"Aye, we are," she answered. "Where do we go?"

From the saddle of the horse I sat, I looked around. "We head back to the woods behind us, so we are lost from their eyes. Then we look for another hill."

"Why a hill?" asked Blaise.

"A hill can be defended," answered Niall. "From a hill we can see enemies approaching,"

"From a hill—" Brigid cut her words off before finishing. "Easpag Patrick, I have an idea, but it is for your ears only."

I looked around at my friends, at the guard Alphin had given into my care, and at my followers. "Whatever you have to say, they can all hear," I answered.

"No," she said, "your ears only. I have an idea that will risk your life, risk the future of your work in Ireland. It is for you to first choose the risk. If you choose, then these men and I can choose to follow you or not."

I nodded agreement. "And I know a defendable hill within a hard, half day's walk from here. We can be there before the sun sets."

"Where is this hill?" Niall asked.

"It is called Slane," Brigid answered. "Once we have reached the cover of the woods, we ride around Tara to the north, then east to the hill."

"The safety of Dyflinn lies to the south," interjected the captain of the guard.

"That's why Leary will not expect us to ride north. We ride to Slane," I said, then signaled to Brigid that I was ready to hear her plan.

We rode slightly ahead of the rest of the party, just beyond earshot. Brigid reminded me that the lighting of the Beltane fire symbolized spiritual leadership of all Ireland. Whoever lit Beltane's first fire was the spiritual king of the land. If Leary would take us captive, then certainly he would have us killed as soon as convenience allowed after the Beltane truce. If our lives were already at risk and our necks stretched before the axe, it was time to commit treason.

The druidess' plan was as shocking as it was simple. Find a hill near enough to Tara's heights to be able to be seen from Leary's camp. Just before sunset on April 30, light our fire before the king's druids lit the royal fire. Claim spiritual rulership by right of Beltane's fire. If we could keep our fire lit throughout the next day, we would crack the power of Leary's court druids and become the most important spiritual force in the land. Leary might be ard-Rí, but I would be easpag of Ireland.

64. The Craft of Fire

Twilight skies were clear when we reached the foot of the hill. Slane rose more than 500 feet above the fields where we stopped. The ruins of an old stone fort ringed its crown. "From the top, you should be able to see the hill of Tara," Brigid said.

"If it is true," I said, "I will take this as a sign from the Christ that this is where we make our stand. But surely Leary and his druids will send men. They will want to put out our fire."

"It is good you have a druidess along with you," Brigid laughed, "learned in craft and the lore of fire." She saw that I looked at her, not quite following what she meant. "There are ways to keep a fire burning, even when the heavens flood the earth with water," she said. "There is a craft and knowledge to fires. Amergin taught me. If Leary's soldiers do not find us, we have time to gather the right things before sunset tomorrow."

"Tell my guard what you need," I said. "We will prepare a fire unlike any seen before in Ireland."

We could see Tara's campfires from Slane's crown. The fortified circle at the hill's top was large enough to hold a Beltane fire. Our small party would have to defend the flames. Brigid sent five of the guard foraging for fresh pine and fir wood, rich in resin and sap. Another four guards gathered dry wood from the forest. Brigid knew of a small cave nearby. Three of the guard were sent to the cave and told to bring back the white powdery crystals from within. Brigid told them, "You have to enter the caves on your hands and knees, but once inside, they're large enough to stand. Take as many sacks as your horses can carry and fill them with the powder. Keep it dry when you leave the cave."

"What is this powder?" asked the soldiers.

"Mostly bat dung and decayed moss," answered Brigid. "It smells like death but holds great power."

The guards looked suspicious.

"It becomes a bright-orange flame when thrown into a fire," she told them. "It burns even when wet."

Brigid directed the rest of us to begin to gather any white stones that had lots of small holes or openings in them. We piled them in the center of the old stone fort. As the pile grew, I asked her, "Why just these stones?"

"These are limestone," she answered. "The stone thirsts for water when heated. We will build the fire on top of these stones. When Leary sends his men to put out your fire, they will try to douse the flames with water. Water cracks the stones even as they drink the water. For some reason, the fire burns even brighter for a brief while and the water will disappear into the stones." My face displayed amazement. "And it makes a wonderful noise as the stone breaks." Brigid continued. "You can tell your enemies that it is the voice of your God shouting his challenge back to them."

This is how I remember spending a sleepless night and the next day, preparing to light a fire on Slane. Now that the Christ way has found a home in Ireland, the story is told that I lit the Easter fire that night. Easter comes earlier than the last sunset of April. Our fire was to be the Beltane fire.

65. Laughter

Shortly after we entered the woods beyond Tara, Alphin's party reached the royal enclosure near the top of the hill. A grand tent was set up to shade ard-Rí Leary's throne chair and his court. Alphin rode within 10 paces of the tent, then dismounted. His son Kevin and the captain of his guard got down from their horses and stood alongside their chieftain. Alphin greeted the king,

"Ard-Rí, it gives me great pleasure to join you here for Beltane."

Leary smiled back.

"I'm grateful that you've allowed my men to keep their arms. Your gesture of trust honors me as a friend." The king nodded. "In the spirit of that friendship, I'm pleased to present you with these 20 fine head of cattle," Alphin pointed behind himself to where the cattle were being herded, "and this small token of my esteem." A pair of guards struggled forward with a chest full of silver coins.

Leary strode forward and opened his arms. "My friend," he said and embraced the chieftain, "welcome, welcome! It has been too many years since the Rí of Dyflinn has joined me to celebrate Beltane. Together, we will enrich the land."

Alphin noticed Diurmid standing among Leary's court, just behind the ard-Rí's chair.

"I see my court druid has also found his way here," Alphin observed.

"I hope you will not mind. Diurmid came north just a few months ago. He came to aid my own court druid, who has since," Leary looked for the proper word, "fallen ill." Alphin turned his eyes back to Leary's. "In his absence, your druid has become invaluable. I hope you will allow him to tarry with us a bit longer."

"I am at the ard-Rí's service," Alphin answered. "Now, please allow me to present one of my sons, Kevin." The boy stepped forward and Alphin clapped him on the shoulder. "He's stoutly made and quick of wit," he boasted. "Lucky for him, he has his mother's looks and my arms." Both the chieftain and the king laughed at the joke. Kevin looked embarrassed at the attention.

"The Roman druid and the druidess who were traveling with you?" Leary asked.

"When they heard that they would not be allowed to step within Tara's precincts as free persons, they withdrew," Alphin answered. Leary looked puzzled. Anger flashed across Diurmid's face. The druid left his place behind the high king's chair and came to stand just behind Leary.

"I ordered them taken," the ard-Rí objected.

"Your guard told me that they were to be taken when they had entered Tara," Alphin said.

"They should have been taken at the boundary," Diurmid hissed.

"Old friend," Alphin said and looked with cold eyes at his former druid, "have you no greeting for your chieftain?"

"Rí Alphin," Diurmid answered and offered a slight bow, "my apologies. It gladdens my heart to see you. I forgot myself in my disappointment at the ard-Rí's command not being carried out."

Hearing the druid's response, Leary turned, then tilted his head. It left no doubt whose order it had been to capture and arrest Patrick and Brigid.

"Why did Easpag Patrick need to surrender?" said Kevin. The boy stood forgotten in this gathering of old men. No one expected him to speak. He was there to demonstrate Alphin's wealth in heirs as well as cattle and silver.

"He works evil magic," Diurmid said before he could censor himself.

"What magic is that?" questioned the boy.

"He sent the fever to your town that cost your chieftain a son and a wife and killed many, many others," answered the druid.

"But that fever came weeks, a month or more, before Patrick even landed on our shores. He was in Britain when the fever first started. Are you claiming he is powerful enough to send fever across the ocean?" Kevin pressed.

The ard-Rí took a half step away from his druid and doubt began to creep into his eyes. "That would indeed be fearsome magic," Leary said.

"No, no," answered Diurmid, "only that he made it worse before he came to Dyflinn. He caused your brother's death."

"How could he do that before he even knew I had a brother?" the boy asked.

"He has a magic that freezes words in your throat," Diurmid sputtered, seeking to regain his footing with the high king.

The worst of all possible eventualities happened at that moment for Diurmid. Kevin laughed. He laughed hard and long. Tears ran down his eyes. When he was done laughing and regained his composure, Leary, Alphin, and the druid all stared at him, dumbfounded.

"What are you laughing at?" demanded his father.

"He's talking about writing," Kevin laughed and pointed weakly at the druid. "He has it all wrong. It is magic, good magic. It allows you to keep words forever, fresh on the page, not frozen. It's like he's picked up a dust-covered ruby and thinks it's a turd." Only a 14-year-old with the brazenness and crudity of youth would have said something so direct, so to the point. Diurmid looked horrified. His face turned dark, and his expression froze into a carefully arranged blankness. Leary looked from his druid to the boy to the chieftain and back. Then Alphin punched his boy on the arm,

"Mind your tongue, you rogue," he said. "Respect your elders."

Kevin took the punch and fumed silently. Turning to the ard-Rí, the chieftain continued, "Please accept my apologies, ard-Rí. It is the boy's first time speaking in court. He forgot himself."

Leary nodded as the social waters ebbed back towards more familiar bounds.

"Druid," Alphin said and nodded with a serious look to Diurmid.

"No harm was intended," Diurmid said, not sounding like he meant it.

"It has been a long road, ard-Rí," Alphin said to Leary. "Please allow us to find a place to set our tents. When we are settled, my son and I will rejoin your party."

Leary nodded agreement and the chieftain's party walked away. Five steps away from the ard-Rí and the druid, Alphin put his arm around Kevin's shoulder. "I'm sorry for punching you, my boy. You spoke well. We just needed a bit of time and I needed to allow the druid to save face honor." Kevin beamed simultaneous appreciation and confusion at his father. "In battle," Alphin said, "a key to victory is getting your enemy to believe you are going where you have no intention of being."

"Are we in a battle?" Kevin asked.

"Indeed," answered his father.

"That whelp deserves to be whipped," hissed Diurmid to Leary as soon as the chieftain's party was beyond ear shot.

The ard-Rí turned and considered his druid.

"Perhaps," Leary replied. "It seems there is more than one way to consider this Roman's magic." The ard-Rí returned to his seat and signaled a servant to bring some ale. Diurmid resumed his place, now silent, standing behind the ard-Rí's chair.

66. Lighting the Fire

By midafternoon on April 30th, the limestones were heaped in a circle inside the ring of Slane's old stone fort. Old, dry oak and ash had been cut and split to catch fire quickly and burn hot. A large pile of logs lay to one side. A thatchwork of fir and pine logs formed a cone of wood above the oak and ash. Slane's Beltane fire was ready to light. Four sacks of foul-smelling, white powdery crystal were carefully covered near the stone walls. Having hauled wood and stone and phosphorous powder, Niall kept the warriors busy reinforcing Slane's defenses. Saplings from the forest at the bottom of the hill were cut, sharpened, and driven into the ground outside the stone ring. Horse and man would have a difficult time entering the fortifications except through a single corridor amid the stakes and stone. There, Niall and the warriors would make their stand while Blaise, Brigid, and I tended the fire.

"Everything is ready, or will be," Brigid said as she stepped beside me to look at the stones and wood.

I nodded, distracted by worries about the fire, about my mission to Ireland, about dying that night.

"Patrick," Brigid said with the sound of wanting my attention.

I looked up from the wood and into her eyes. They shone like grass in dawn light. "What is it?" I asked.

"There is one more thing needed," Brigid answered, and desire showed in her eyes.

"Now?" I asked almost incredulous.

"We may die tonight," she answered. "You wish to light the spiritual fire of Ireland. Add the fires of your passion to those of your faith," she continued. "Love is good. Love brings power. Love ignites magic. The external fires are ready. Light the fires within," she breathed.

Taking my hand, she led me to where she had set up a small tent away from where the soldiers gathered. She stooped and held the tent flaps open for me to enter. "Your men will understand," she told me. "We make love for them as well as for ourselves."

Within the tent, mid-afternoon light was rendered gold through canvas. Brigid kneeled on the ground. Unfastening her belt, she drew her tunic over her head and put belt and tunic aside. Then she reached for my belt.

The smell of her stands out in my memory. Her auburn hair smelled of pitch and pine. Her own musky smell of sweat and womanhood was like an animal perfume. My lips found hers. My hands found her breasts, her hips. She took my manhood in her hands and guided me into her. I was in her, on top of her, rising and thrusting and rising again. I felt so alive. Then Brigid shifted. She took her place atop me, riding me, thrusting herself again and again onto me. We flowed back and forth for what felt like an entire afternoon. I attempted to keep myself quiet.

Brigid whispered, "Let your passion flow, let your voice growl and grunt and scream. Let your men hear you as a man."

And so, our throats filled the tent with passion even as we made love. The air within grew heavy with the smell of our sex. Then, as one, our passion crested and broke upon the shores of pleasure.

I held myself full inside her for what felt like a long while. Then, a soft look crossed Brigid's eyes and I let myself lay down beside her. We lay like that, bare-backed and bare-assed within the golden light and funk of that tent for a long time. The light began to change, and Brigid spoke, "Now it is time to light the Beltane fire."

When we emerged from the tent, arranging our tunics and cloaks, Niall and the warriors were all on the far side of the wall, looking towards Tara. I coughed once and they turned to face us. They were smiling.

"The fires are ready," Brigid said and met each of their eyes. "Are you?"

"Aye," they called.

"One more thing is needed," I said. Then I bowed my head and prayed out loud, "I arise today through the mighty strength of the three-fold God. I arise today through the strength of Christ's birth, his baptism, his crucifixion, his overcoming death. I arise today and call upon the strength of cherubim, angels, and archangels, upon the prayers of the patriarchs, the sooth of prophets, and the preaching of the apostles. I arise today with the power of the faith of martyrs, saints, and the Pope. Through the strength of heaven, the light of the sun, the radiance of the moon, the swiftness of wind, the speed of lightning, and the splendor of fire, God grant us victory here this night."

I looked up and into each of my men's eyes, finally into Brigid's eyes and continued. "I call upon the strength of the Almighty to pilot me, uphold me, guide me, look before me, hear me, speak on my behalf, guard me, and protect me from the devil and all who wish us ill. God be our breastplate and armor. Shield us, defend us, be our strength. Grant victory over evil. Bless and keep this fire we pledge to light."

The sun was beginning to set. No smoke or fire was yet visible from Tara's hill. I nodded to Niall who sparked a flame under our fire's tinder. As the first tendrils of smoke rose to the sky, I finished my prayer. "Christ with me, before me, behind me, in me, beneath me, above me, on my right, on my left, when I lie down, when I sit, when I rise, and as I stand by this fire."

Nearby, I heard Blaise offer a loud, "Amen." Several of the newly baptized warriors echoed "Amen." Brigid's eyes burned with the first mirrored flames from Slane's fire.

67. Rebel Fire

Atop the hill of Tara, Kevin's young eyes were the first to catch sight of the smoke from Slane. "Look," he cried and pointed to the north. "There!"

Alphin, Leary, the assembled chieftains, their captains and ladies, and Diurmid—all their heads turned to gaze where Kevin's hand pointed. The upper rim of the sun was still a finger width above the horizon as a pillar of smoke rose from Slane. A pall of silence fell over the hilltop. Leary halted what he was saying mid-sentence. The ladies of the assembled chieftains stopped their small talk. The rustle of clothes and the clinking of sword belts and kit fell quiet. Almost 1,000 heads watched mutely. The first flickering tongues of flame became visible. Kevin voiced the question on each mind: "Isn't the ard-Rí's fire first to be lit?"

Diurmid glowered at the boy and then at the ard-Rí. "Your Highness, it insults your honor. That fire," his arm stretched towards Slane, "takes your place." The druid's voice became a screech. "It must be put out before this night ends."

Leary was confused. This was to be a night of celebration, a night of renewed alliances, a night when hand-fasting between the sons and daughters of chieftains was announced, when marriages were planned, a night to sow peace. The fire on the far hill was a direct challenge to his authority. He had his own guard of over 150 warriors. He could call on them and, if needed, on the guards of Rí Alphin and his other subject chieftains. He would restore his honor and claim primacy for the Beltane fire lit atop Tara.

Turning to his captain, he commanded, "Take 50 of the guard and ride to that hill as fast as your horses will carry you. Put out that fire!"

Then the ard-Rí turned to Diurmid and said, "Don't you think it's time that we light the fire on our hill?" The sun had just inched below the horizon and the first stars were sparkling in the purpled skies.

Leary's captain and 50 of the guard rode like the wind to Slane. It took them almost two hours to get there. The guard cantered their horses when they could, slowing to a walk when the ground was uneven or the woods presented an obstacle. They arrived at the foot of Slane tired, but not winded. The captain of the guard looked up to the crown of the hill, 500 feet above, to see armed men protecting a stone ring reinforced with sharpened stakes.

The hill was steep and not favored for charging up on horseback. "We'll leave the horses here and walk up," he told his men. Then, leaving their horses picketed and watched over by the three youngest guards, the captain and 47 men walked up Slane.

"Hold there," called out Niall when the captain came within 10 paces of the ring of stones.

Slane's fire was now burning brightly behind him. Niall stood blocking the one useable entrance to the stone ring with 17 other well-rested and determined defenders. Although the captain's men outnumbered his more than two to one, they would be fighting in a narrow space between the thicket of sharpened stakes. If the captain's men attacked, they would be fighting uphill, at a disadvantage. The fire at the back of Niall's men loaned them spirit and determination.

I stood, inside the ring of armed men, holding my crozier and repeating my prayer, over and over, "Christ with me, before me, behind me, in me, beneath me, above me, on my right, on my left, when I lie down, when I sit, when I rise, and as I stand by this fire."

Brigid stood beside me, calling upon the Moringa, "By the maiden, mother and crone, take possession of this fire. Protect us in truth and honor. Goddesses who bring all to life, bless this circle and all within it, bless this fire, bless this fire."

Blaise and Cadhla continued to add fir and pine logs. The fire spat with sap and burning resin. I could feel the heat of the flames on my back, see the fire reflected on the cloaks of those who stood between me and ard-Rí Leary's guard.

"By order of the ard-Rí, you are commanded to put out this fire," called out the captain of the guard. I recognized his voice from when he had met Alphin's party at the boundaries of Tara.

"I follow the commands of a higher king than Leary," I shouted back.

My warriors gave out a war cry. I don't know who struck first, but blows were struck. A spear flew past me and added the wood of its shaft to the flames. The clash of steel on steel rang out. Men grunted and cursed as Leary's guard tried to fight its way into the circle. After what seemed like an hour but was more likely less than 10 minutes, the clamor fell away. One of Niall's companions lay bleeding within the circle, a gaping wound in his right shoulder. I saw four bodies from the ard-Rí's guard laying still upon the ground.

Leary's captain called out once more, "This fire must be extinguished, or you will all die."

I heard a mad laugh from Niall and then, "You can try all night, but this fire will burn till Beltane ends." Niall's men cheered and Leary's guard withdrew several more paces.

The captain called out across the widening space between swords, "Are you not the Roman druid who I didn't take captive at Tara's boundary?"

"I am Easpag Patrick," I answered.

"Would you have all your men die to protect this fire?"

"This fire will not die," I called back, "and anyone who dies protecting it is guaranteed life in abundance beyond death." Niall and my men roared once again.

"You can see the king's fire from here," the captain called out, pointing south towards Tara. "Put out these flames and my soldiers and I will leave you in peace."

"This is Ireland's first Beltane fire," called Brigid from beside me. "If the ard-Rí wishes to be at the king's fire, let him come to Slane."

I heard laughter from my men even as I saw disappointment and resolve gather on the captain's face. He withdrew his men 20 paces from the stone ring and set them on guard there. Two warriors were sent downhill to carry a message back to the ard-Rí. "The fire on Slane is a rebel fire, well-defended. Send more warriors so we can defeat the rebels and quell the fire."

68. Greek Fire

"They will send more warriors," Niall worried when the captain's messengers disappeared.

"They will overwhelm us," I said to Brigid.

"We will trick them," she answered and told us the rest of her plan. "The sap in the fir and pine burns very hot," she told us. "When we see more soldiers arriving, pile the fire high with those woods. Until then, keep the fire hot with the harder ash and oak."

Several heads indicated understanding.

"The stones under the fire will absorb water." More nods. "The burning sap will spread when water hits it but not go out." Again, heads bobbed. "And the white powder burns exceptionally hot, even when wet."

I began to understand her stratagem. It was similar to the Greek fire of Archimedes, a fire that would not go out until all the wood was consumed.

"Negotiate a test with Leary's captain when he returns," Brigid said.

"Which test is that?" Niall asked.

"If his men can put out the fire with water, then we will leave," she answered. "Otherwise, they will have to kill us, and many will die making that happen."

"Leary and Diurmid cannot afford to lose this battle," I said.

"They will not be here," the druidess said with confidence. "Leary is slow to adapt to challenges and Diurmid is stubborn and proud." She paused to allow each of us to consider her plan. "They will count on an overwhelming number of their men to die for them and take care of the problem." Again, a brief silence before the next words. "But the captain and his men won't want to die for a fire on a strange hill. There's little honor and no profit in it. They'll take the bargain and try to douse our fire with water."

"And?" I asked.

"They'll fail," Brigid answered, "and that's when Leary will come and the real test will begin."

It took three hours for the next group of soldiers to appear. Leary sent 50 more of his guard and asked four of his subject chieftains to each send 50. In all, 250 additional warriors appeared on Slane. As she predicted, Leary's captain and the chieftains were reluctant to see more warriors die to put out our fire. They accepted the bargain. If they could put out our fire with water, we would with-draw. If they could not extinguish our Beltane flames, they would hold a truce until the ard-Rí came.

Of course, the attackers brought swords, not buckets. It took some time to arrange how they would fetch water up Slane to douse the flames. Eventually they gathered almost 50 large water skins among themselves. They filled their shields with water. They filled every flask, cook pot, and whatever would hold liquid with water. Then they stood beyond the ring of stones and the captain called, "We are ready."

Niall's guard allowed Leary's and the chieftain's men into the ring. By ones, twos, and threes they approached our Beltane fire and tossed water on the flames. They tossed enough water to have doused an ordinary fire. As the water hit the pine and fir, the wood smoked and sputtered. As the water fell to the hot lime-stones under the hardwoods, the stones cracked and popped. Loud whistles and groans emerged from the stones.

"What is that noise?" called out several of Leary's men.

"It is the voice of my god," I answered. "He is angry that you are trying to put out his fire." Then sap and pitch hit the still hot stones and flames flickered up through our fire once again.

"Now," Brigid called out to Cadhla and Blaise, and they threw two of the sacks of dry white powder into the flames. Our fire burned hot orange. In an instant, our Beltane fire was restored, brighter and hotter than when the ard-Rí's men had begun their assault with water.

The captain of Leary's guard looked around at his men. They were exhausted from carrying water uphill. They were amazed at the water not putting out the flames of our fire. They were frightened by the voice of my god from the stones. They withdrew from the renewed heat and flames.

"This is no ordinary fire," Leary's captain called out to me. I saw respect begin-ning to dawn in his eyes. "What now?" he asked.

"Send for the ard-Rí," I answered.

"And for his druid," Brigid added.

Leary's captain and chieftains and their men withdrew once more from Slane's ring. Three hundred tired men waited 20 or more paces beyond the stones.

69. A Conversation Among Chieftains

Alphin and two other chieftains, along with the captain of the guard, rode back from Slane to Tara. When they reached the royal tent, Leary was furious. "What do you mean the fire wouldn't go out?"

"Just that, my Lord," the captain answered.

"This is your doing," Diurmid hissed and looked at Alphin. "If you had surrendered the Roman——"

Leary held up his hand and interrupted the druid there.

"If you had not ordered his arrest," Alphin rejoined, "Easpag Patrick and his fire would be here, not at Slane."

Queen Mugain had been hiding in the druid's tent, not wishing to see or be seen by her husband. Diurmid sheltered her, taking whatever intelligence he could gather from her about Patrick and holding her presence like a secret dagger to use against his former chief. She joined the discussion, unseen until she said, "He is your druid; you brought him here. You didn't fight him when he killed our child."

Rí Alphin and the ard-Rí's heads both turned in surprise.

"What does any of that have to do with this fire?" Leary asked.

"Mugain, you are here?" Alphin said. Then looking at the druid the chieftain continued, "You knew she was here, and you didn't tell me?" Alphin's hand went to his sword, and he made ready to strike Diurmid down. Two other chieftains stopped Alphin before he could strike.

"You knew the Rí of Dyflinn's wife was here, and you hid her?" Leary asked, "Why?"

"It does not matter, ard-Rí," injected the captain of the guard. "The one who calls himself Easpag Patrick is responsible for the fire on Slane. He says he won't put the flames out until you come."

"Then find my horse and gather the rest of my men," Leary called out. "We ride to Slane."

As his groom found the ard-Rí's horse and the warriors readied themselves to leave, the ard-Rí said to the druid, "You are coming with us." Leary commanded his queen, "See that the Lady Mugain is made comfortable in our tent." Then, remembering Mugain was Alphin's wife, he said to the chieftain, "With your permission?"

Alphin nodded, looking stern and sad and full of resolve all at once.

"I am grateful, ard-Rí," Alphin replied.

Once again, it was more than a two hour's ride from Tara to Slane. Not yet dawn, the night had grown long. Darkness hadn't begun to surrender; however, the skies grew subtly less dark to the east as the ard-Rí and the rest reached the foot of Slane.

On horseback, riding from Tara, Alphin had reassured Leary that he had no foreknowledge of Patrick's plans. "I don't know why he lit this fire," the chieftain of Dyflinn confessed. "I thought he planned to tell you of his magic and the Christ way."

"Are you a follower of this new religion?" Leary asked.

"I am," Alphin answered. "Patrick saved Dyflinn, my youngest son, and third wife from the fever. One of Patrick's followers, Otho, went to his own death and took a spear meant for Patrick. He died because he completely believes in the Christ draíocht that is stronger than death."

"And this magic with words?" Leary asked.

"It is amazing," Alphin answered. "Patrick taught my son, Kevin, how to use this magic. Kevin should show you."

Leary held up his hand. "We shall see," he said, "after we have dealt with this fire."

70. Test by Fire

Brigid stood beside me inside the ring of stones as we watched the warriors gather. I saw Ard-Rí Leary arrive at the foot of Slane with almost 200 more warriors. I felt a quiver of fear shake itself through my companions inside the circle. "How do we defeat them?" I asked Brigid.

"I don't know," she answered. "We can't defeat this many. Speak to the ard-Rí. Convince him."

"Why have you stood by me?" I asked her.

"Because we are joined since Slemmish," Brigid answered, and I heard the girl in her voice. "And because the smallness of heart that comes from Diurmid's clinging to power has ruined the old ways. Now kings and chieftains cling to their small powers and the Moringa is forgotten."

She took a few breaths and looked behind us into the fire. "Amergin prophesied that this day would come, and I would help you. He told me that what I did would help keep the old ways safe. I stand by you for all those reasons, but mostly because of my heart."

"Then I will trust in my heart and my wits and in the Christ," I told her.

We waited for the ard-Rí to climb to the top of Slane. The gray twilight of predawn lined the eastern sky when Leary came.

"The ard-Rí wishes to speak to the one called Patrick," called out the captain of the guards from beyond the circle.

"I am here." I answered.

"Come forward," called the captain.

"The ard-Rí is welcome to come within the circle," I answered. "But I shall not leave here until this fire burns out at sunset tonight."

Heads conferred from where the captain called. "Easpag Patrick," called out a familiar voice, "It is I, Rí Alphin. The ard-Rí guarantees your safety if you come out from the circle to talk with him."

"Thank the ard-Rí for me," I called back. "But I stand with this fire for the Christ way until the sun sets tonight."

"Will you allow one old man to join you at the fire?" called out a third voice.

"Who are you?" I answered back.

"I am called Leary," answered the ard-Rí. "I would talk with you by your fire."

"We are honored to welcome you, Your Highness, and guarantee both your safe coming and your safe return." Niall's men stepped aside and made a path through the stakes and stones.

"I would bring one companion with me," Leary called before moving.

"Who would he be?" Brigid called.

"The druid, Diurmid," answered the ard-Rí.

"Done," I called back.

Leary wore his sword belt and a circlet of bronze crowned his head. Diurmid carried his druid's oak staff. After the long night, they were two aging men who looked tired. Leary's eyes showed curiosity and interest. Diurmid's eyes shone flat and dark.

"Easpag," Leary began when we were near enough to speak, "you have caused quite a disturbance tonight."

"That was not my intention, Lord King," I answered.

"Then what was your intention?" the ard-Rí asked.

"To light the fire of the Christ way for Ireland."

"The ard-Rí has the right to light the first fire," jeered Diurmid.

"I lit the fire for the child of the King of the Sky," I answered.

"And this is your Christ?" Leary asked.

"He is, Your Highness. He is the light of the world, and I would share that light with all Ireland."

"Is this," Leary asked gesturing at the fire, "how you claim Ireland's attention?"

"I would rather have met with Your Highness at Tara," I answered and allowed Leary to fill in the details implied by my statement.

"This is an evil fire," Diurmid sputtered.

"The Christ fire is good," I answered. Then I remembered something Cadhla told me about my crozier. "Let's put it to a test," I said, looking at the druid. Diurmid shrank a bit into himself at this unexpected challenge.

"What test?" the druid asked.

"Let us test our staffs in the fire. I'll put my Christ staff into the flames. You put your druid's staff into the flames. The first one that catches fire fails."

Diurmid was confounded by the suggestion of trial by fire. How could he save face if he refused? If he won, then everything would be put back into order as he wished. But if he lost, what then? Could he lose?

"Let it be so," ordered Leary.

I looked at Diurmid and his staff and was confident. "Are you ready?" I asked.

"Get on with it." Diurmid delayed just a bit, allowing me to thrust my shepherd's crook among the flames a few seconds before he joined his staff to the fire. I'm sure he wished that small difference would tell the tale, wished my staff to catch fire first. But Cadhla had made my crozier from yew. The wood of my shepherd's staff had been carved and smoothed by hours of attention at Cadhla's hands. There was no place for the flames to easily take hold.

Diurmid's staff was a noble and aged length of oak. It bore the oil of his hands holding and wielding its length for decades. It was ready for the flames. My crozier darkened but did not burn. Diurmid's staff quickly burst into flame. The druid gasped and dropped the staff.

Leary turned to look at me as I pulled the shepherd's crook from the fire. "You do indeed possess powerful magic, Easpag," he said. "I will hear what you have to say about this Christ way."

71. Lies

Slane's Beltane fire burned on through the morning and into the day while I told Leary about the Christ way. Diurmid fled the circle of stones after his staff burned and made his way down the hill. I'm told the druid made his way back to Tara. There he told the small guard that remained that Leary had sent him to gather the chest of silver coins that Alphin had given him. He pressed two young warriors into helping him carry the chest to a small cart, then into hitching a horse.

"Why does ard-Rí Leary send for silver while he is still fighting at Slane?" asked the guards.

"I am not in the habit of questioning my king or his orders," Diurmid answered back. The threat was clear. To defy the request was to disobey the ard-Rí. The chest of coins dropped onto the back of the two- wheeled dray. Dust flew up from the cart's planking. The cart horse shook itself to adjust to the change in its burden. The two warriors looked to Diurmid for his next order from Leary.

The druid went to Leary's tent to encourage Mugain to join him as he fled south. "We have plenty of money. Alphin has provided for you."

Mugain tilted her chin to the left and considered the druid with narrowing eyes. "Ard-Rí Leary lost to the Roman at the Hill of Slane," Diurmid continued. "All will be lost if Patrick catches us here in Tara."

"And why would the Roman come to Tara when he has defeated the ard-Rí at Slane?" asked Mugain.

"To complete his destruction of your family. To kill you and Kevin."

Doubt clashed with fear across the fields of Mugain's face. *Was Alphin dead? Had Patrick indeed won at Slane? Where was the ard-Rí? Diurmid never said Leary had died. Why had the druid come back alone? Where were the other chieftains, the soldiers, any of them? If Alphin lived, would he forgive her?* These are some of the questions Queen Mugain asked herself. She had no place to go after abandoning the court at Dyflinn and sneaking to Tara. *Where would she find her place of safety? Could she trust Diurmid?* When all these thoughts had chased themselves across Mugain's mind, this is the question she asked, "What happened to Alphin on Slane?"

Without blinking, Diurmid spun a tale. "He died, killed by the Roman. The chieftain was at the edge of the fire, about to douse the flames himself when the Roman stabbed him in the back with a dagger. When Alphin turned around to see who had struck the blow, Patrick pushed him into the fire. Rí Alphin died while crying out your name, 'Mugain, Mugain, Mugain.'"

She knew the druid was lying. Alphin always wore a heavy leather shirt and a vest of forged chain links under his tunic whenever he went to a battle. The shirt and tunic had been a wedding gift from Mugain's father to the young chieftain when he told him that he wanted his daughter's husband to live a long life. Mugain knew that no mere dagger thrust would have penetrated that protection. But even more, she was certain that Alphin, had he died, would have called out for Aideen, not her. Her heart filled with the sadness of knowing how much she had lost. Diurmid lied to her now. He must have been lying to her for a long while.

"I will remain here to await my fate," was the only answer she gave the druid.

Diurmid looked at her, wondering what part in his tale had played false. "You are my chieftain's lady," he tried one last time. "It is my duty to keep you safe."

"If you seek my safety," Mugain turned her sad eyes towards the druid, "then stay here and defend me when I need defense. Don't flee."

"My queen . . . I . . . I . . ." sputtered Diurmid. Then he turned to flee the tent and Tara.

Long months later, I heard that Diurmid had found a court to serve in the Kingdom of Muenster to the South. It all made sense. Muenster was a rival to the Ui Neills and Leary. Muenster was the only Kingdom of Ireland to deny homage to Leary as ard-Rí. Muenster would provide welcoming ears to Diurmid's tales of treachery at the court of the ard-Rí. Until he died a withered old man, Diurmid plotted and planned from Muenster's court to overthrow the Christ way and have his vengeance on me. I am thankful those plans never bore fruit.

72. The Best Ale

In the early morning, maybe an hour and a half after Diurmid had fled Slane, Leary held up his hand for me to pause in telling the Christ story. Brigid, Blaise, Cadhla, and I sat by the fire with the ard-Rí. I was well into the tale, telling of miracles and wonders like walking on the waves or returning sight to the blind.

"All this talk has made me thirsty," the ard-Rí complained. He continued, "I'd like to ask my captain to bring us food and drink, and to have the other chieftains join us by this fire. Do you accept?"

I bowed my head in agreement.

"Captain! Captain!" Leary called out.

I looked to Niall to signal it was all right if the captain entered the circle.

"My King," the captain said as he ran into the circle, his hand on his sword. He relaxed once he saw that no one else had their weapons at the ready and saw that Leary and I were seated on a log by the fire. Kneeling before the ard-Rí, the captain said, "What is it, my King?"

"See to it that we are brought food and drink," the ard-Rí laughed. "I'm perfectly safe here but this Roman," he laughed again, "is telling quite a tale and I'm thirsty. Bring food for both of us, then see to the men."

The captain rose from his knees saying, "As you command."

"One more thing," Leary interrupted the captain's leaving. "Where is Diurmid?"

"He ran from the circle and down the hill," answered the captain. "A short time later one of the soldiers guarding the horses came up to tell that the druid had taken his horse and rode in the direction of Tara." A look of concern crossed Leary's eyes. "Shall I send someone to follow?" asked the captain.

"Yes," answered Leary, "although he is likely long gone by now. But send enough soldiers to make sure that Tara is safe." The captain left the circle of stones to carry out the ard-Rí's orders. The chieftains of Ireland entered the circle to join the ard-Rí in listening to Patrick's tale.

"I was just getting to a marvelous part of the story." I picked up my telling of the Christ way as the chieftains joined us. "The son of the King of the Sky was invited to the wedding feast of a dear friend. He attended the feast with his mother and his other friends." Heads nodded at a familiar beginning. "The guests drank heavily from the beginning of the feast onwards." I knew these chieftains had been at feast after feast. They drank heartily. They drank until either they were sated or fell asleep. They could see themselves in the middle of the celebration at Cana. "The mother of the groom approached the mother of the son of the King of the Sky," I told them. "There was a problem, the guests had drunk almost all the ale." I took the liberty of changing the wine in the Gospel story to ale so my listeners would follow.

"'What shall we do?' asked one mother to another." Heads nodded.

"'I will talk to my son,' said the mother of the son of the King of the Sky.

"Have the servants pour fresh water into the empty ale casks," said her son. His orders were carried out.

"When all the last ale casks were emptied, the servants picked up the refilled casks to serve. Drinking from the new ale, one guest was heard to say, 'This is the best ale yet. Why serve the best ale after an inferior brew?'"

All around that fire, chieftain and king showed agreement with the feast guest's question. Your taste dulls after drinking. They would have served the best ale first, when their guests' tongues were sharpest.

"'That is the way it is in the kingdom of my Father, the Sky God,' answered the son. Even though many years have passed, and the world grows old, the son of the King of the Sky serves the best ale, the ale of truth and a magic stronger than death, now, this night, here on Slane."

"Why now?" asked Leary.

"Because he wishes you and your chieftains to enjoy his feast," I answered.

"Tell us more," called out one chieftain from across the fire. And so, I did. I told them of the Christ draíocht that was stronger than death. I told them how, even after his friends had betrayed him, the King of the Sky helped his son defeat death.

"This draíocht can be yours," I told them.

"How?" rose from several throats together. Alphin smiled and nodded at me from across the fire. Morning had turned into afternoon and then even later as the Beltane flames had burned down to a large campfire within the stones. The remnants of the pile of oak, ash, pine, and fir lay nearby. I walked round the circle to stand beside Alphin.

"To follow the Christ way requires only three things," I told them.

"Are they difficult?" asked Leary.

"My King," I answered acknowledging the ard-Rí, "they are a challenge of the heart." He dropped his chin the slightest bit to listen more intently for what followed. "You must allow yourself to have the obstacles to the Christ way washed away." Leary and the chieftains looked uncertain. Bathing was not common. Allowing someone else to wash you was even more uncommon. I saw a look of hesitation begin to settle in. "Do not fear," I reassured them, clapping Alphin on the back. "Rí Alphin survived and is none the worse for it."

The king and chieftains laughed, relieved. "Second, you must promise to follow the Christ way." I heard several "ayes," before I carried on. "Finally, you must promise to protect this new way even as you safeguard the best of the old ways in Ireland."

"Aye" resounded from around the fire.

"Then as the Beltane sun sets, each of us will add fuel to this fire to strengthen the light of the new way," I told them. So, chieftain and king gathered wood and piled it onto the flame. I felt Brigid tugging at the sleeve of my tunic. She had remained remarkably quiet as I told my tale, as I led the king and chieftains to consider baptism.

"Patrick," she whispered, "the final bags of white powder."

"What of it?"

"Have the chieftains each throw a handful into the fire. Allow the king to be last and to throw all that remains into the fire," she said.

"Why?"

"Because it burns bright and is good magic," Brigid answered. "Because drama helps men remember when their hearts grow weak. Because it is magic from the Moringa and honors the old ways even as the new begins."

"Do we tell them about the Moringa?"

"No," Brigid answered. "Let that remain hidden for the while."

73. Crom Dubh

I talked with Leary and his chieftains until Slane's Beltane fire grew small. The sun of May 1st had set more than an hour ago and a few logs remained simmering among the stones and coals.

The ard-Rí took his leave from the fire saying, "Easpag, I'm glad you lit this fire upon Slane. My eyes have been opened to a new way."

Hearing these words, I allowed relief to flood through me. It all could have turned out so differently. All my friends and companions, Brigid, and I could now lie dead on Slane, with our fire extinguished by sword and water. The fire of my message of the Christ way could lie extinguished, defeated by the resistance of Diurmid and the ard-Rí.

But that hadn't happened. Resistance had been overcome by the courage of our hearts and by Brigid's natural magic. I allowed myself to believe that I would live a while longer to spread the word of the Christ way.

"Come to Tara, when this fire has burned out, when you are ready," said Leary. "I will allow myself to be washed and become a follower of your Christ way, but I will do so on Tara. That is where ard-Rís are crowned. That is where the ard-Rí of Ireland should pledge himself to the son of the King of the Sky."

"I will come as soon as I am able, my Lord King," I answered.

Just then, as Leary turned to leave, I felt Brigid tug once more at my tunic's sleeve. "Yes," I said, turning to look at her. Her irises flashed fire amid their greens and grays. She had a set look about her jaw. Her auburn hair hung down behind one ear and over her shoulder.

"What of me and what of the Moringa?" she challenged. "What plans do you have for us?"

"I have no plans, my lady," I replied.

"That is good, very good, Patrick," Brigid said. "No one hems me in with their plans. I choose my own ways. The same is true, even more so, for the Moringa."

I could only nod, hold my silence, and wait for her to continue.

"I used my draíocht to keep your Beltane fire burning even when it was doused with water," Brigid said.

I acknowledged the truth in her words, my eyes looking into hers.

"I ask that you share your draíocht with words with me."

A little surprised, I asked, "Why?"

"To keep alive the stories of the Moringa, to remember the ways of the goddesses, to keep fresh the craft of the druids." The words rushed out of her. "Soon your Christ way will push aside the old ways. Men have short memories. The old ways will be forgotten. Unless they are served by this word draíocht."

"But how will you learn to write?" I asked.

"As reward for keeping your fire alive, you will give me a teacher of my choosing." I nodded acceptance. "They will go with me to a place that I alone choose."

"You are not staying with me?" I asked.

"We are bound for this life and perhaps beyond," Brigid answered. "But no, I shall not stay with you." She paused. "Your path is this new Christ way. My way is the old one, the way of the Moringa. I may help you; but I fear you serve a jealous god. It will be better if we come together sometimes but live mostly apart."

"But what of our love?" I asked.

"What of it?" she answered. "Is your love for me dependent on seeing me? If so, that's a poor test." I held up my hands, exasperated, knowing that I couldn't argue with her.

"Our love will be strengthened by our time apart," Brigid continued. "When we come together, we will stir the banked fires of passion and share whatever draíocht and wisdom we have found. Agreed?"

"Agreed," I conceded. "Where will you go?"

"To the west, to the Kingdom of Connacht," Brigid replied. "There is a sacred mountain there. Some call it Crom Dubh, Black Bend. Others, because of its height, just call it 'The Stack.'"

"Why there?" I asked.

"It is as far away from your new way as I can walk and still be in Ireland. It is a place where the old ways and old gods are still honored." Then, offering an inviting smile, "And, in a while, when your Christ way has grown stronger, it's not too far for you to come visit me."

"I'm to visit you?" I asked.

"As it should be," was all she would say.

"One last question about this arrangement," I said. Brigid raised one eyebrow in a challenge for me to continue. "Who do you choose as your teacher for the draíocht of writing?"

"Kevin," she answered.

74. Two Truths

The Beltane fire burned itself out a few hours after sunset. Brigid, Niall, Cadhla, Blaise, and I kept watch as the flames collapsed into coals then embers then smoldering charcoal and stones. Nearby, a separate cook fire was lit for the evening's meal and for companionship through the night. Niall set a guard to stand watch at the entrance to the stone circle. There were stars in the sky as a soft breeze touched Slane's crest.

I've often found that life goes this way, intense conflict or change followed by a long period of steadiness. That second night was quiet after the storm on Slane. Only one of our soldiers had died in that first struggle. It saddened me that four of the king's men had also passed. Leary and his chieftains heard the Christ story and were ready to accept baptism. Diurmid had fled, a trouble to be worried over later. These were some of the thoughts that filled my mind as I went to lay with Brigid that night. It surprised me that her tent's flaps were tied from the inside. I softly rapped on the poles that supported her tent. "Who is it?" her voice called out from within.

"Patrick," I breathed back in a whisper.

"Go away," Brigid replied.

"What is it?" I pleaded. "Have I done something to offend you?"

"Not tonight," she answered. I heard the tent flaps being untied from inside. Brigid opened them just enough to be able to look out at me. "It is a night for peace and stillness," she said. "I am conversing with the Moringa." Before I could gather a response, the flaps fell closed and I heard them being tied fast.

I found myself a place to sleep by the cook fire. Blaise and I talked late into the night. We spoke of the journey to Rome, Celestine, and Abbot Germanus. We remembered Otho and all that happened since our boat landed near Dichu's village. We spoke of his progress in training Kevin and the other young students. I shared Brigid's request for Kevin as a teacher with him. Blaise was upset but willing to obey whatever I decided. I reminded myself that even though he was the first priest I had ordained in Ireland, Blaise was still a monk at heart, stubbornly resistant to innovation or change.

"After you baptize Leary and his chieftains, will you become a more normal bishop?" Blaise asked.

"You mean will I become more like Abbot Germanus or Bishop Brannok of London?"

"Yes," answered Blaise. "Of course, Abbot Germanus is a monk and has no wife, but Brannok of London does. They both seem more . . ." he searched for the right word.

"Roman," I supplied.

"Yes, Roman," he answered. "More like the Christianity at Auxerre or even Rome."

"Brother and friend," I began, "our message takes the shape of the culture we pour it into. Rome was orderly, even military in its discipline; all men and rules and conformity."

Blaise bobbed his head up and down in agreement and smiled. "Isn't that the way it's supposed to be?"

"There is no way it is supposed to be beyond carrying the message of God's love," I answered. "When the Gospels made their way to Rome there were tens of millions of slaves and more than a million soldiers within the empire. Soldiers were indentured for more than 25 years of service. If you survived, and not many did, you were free. A message that proclaimed you equally beloved of God as the emperor and promised salvation, even after death, spread like wildfire. The Roman church took the shape of a slave rebellion, eager to impose its rules on their former masters."

"Celestine didn't look like a slave to me," Blaise retorted.

"There's not nearly as much freedom underneath that gold as you might think," I answered. "Our mission to stamp out Pelagius was a mission to defend the idea that every man needs the church?"

"What of it?" asked Blaise.

"It seems to me that Leary and these Irish chieftains have come to the Christ way without needing the authority of Rome. We've started a Celtic Christianity in Ireland."

"Is that any different from Rome or Auxerre?"

"It's different in at least this way. They are warriors and chieftains here. They are proud men and women, not slaves. Women even go to battle. Women can be chieftain in their own right."

Blaise shook his head.

"The way we share the message of the Gospels will need to be poured into this container of courage, bravery, and honor."

Our talk went back and forth through the entire night. One or the other of us would gather the next log to throw onto the coals and our conversation continued. I was convinced of two truths. First, the warrior spirit of the Irish would respond to the bravery, good heartedness, and humor of the Gospels. And second, that the Irish love of a good story would ignite enthusiasm for writing and reading even brighter than our Beltane fire.

Shortly before morning, our talk had run its course. Blaise would help me with teaching writing and training new monks. I would continue to seek out and convert the chieftains and warriors of Ireland. In the hour just before dawn, I lay down by the fire, drew my cloak around me, and closed my eyes.

75. Baptizing a Stone

When our party arrived at Tara's boundaries, the same captain of the guard that had turned me away and attempted to quell the Beltane fire waited for us. This time, not a single hand touched a weapon.

"Easpag Patrick," the captain called out, "Ard-Rí Leary sent me to greet you and welcome you to Tara, to escort you with honor to his tent."

"What is your name?" I asked the captain.

"I am called Brendan," he answered.

"Lead me to your king, Brendan," I said and heeled my mount forward to ride alongside the captain. When we approached Leary's tent, I remained in the saddle. Leary rose from his chair and came out from his tent to stand before me.

"Easpag Patrick," Leary said.

"Ard-Rí," I replied, "are you ready to accept baptism?"

The ard-Rí looked around, at his chieftains and their ladies, at his warriors and servants, and at my party with Brigid, Blaise, Cadhla, and the rest. "I am ready," Leary said. "I have one request." I nodded, willing to hear him. "Before they are crowned, ard-Rís are confirmed when they touch the stone of destiny. If they are the true high king, the stone cries out with power."

I nodded again for him to continue.

"I'd like to be baptized at the foot of that stone. I'd like you to baptize the stone when you baptize me."

Blaise began to object but I held up my hand to silence him. "Why baptize the stone?" I asked.

"The stone of destiny represents the heart of Ireland," Leary answered. "Today, baptize me as Ireland's head and the stone of destiny as her heart."

I couldn't help but smile and agree. That day I baptized an ard-Rí, a stone, and almost 1,000 of Leary's chieftains, soldiers, and their ladies. I baptized servants and slaves. I even baptized the favorite royal cow. That day, in my eyes, Ireland was baptized.

There were those who held back. Not every chieftain or warrior was enthusiastic about being washed with baptism's waters. Many were not ready to promise their allegiance to the Christ way. And some, like Brigid, were immersed within the Moringa. I was exhausted from the day's long rituals when Brigid approached me. A hooded woman I could not identify accompanied her.

"It is almost time I took my leave," Brigid started.

"I had hoped you would stay longer," I replied, "That we . . ." and let my hopes trail unsaid into the air between us.

"I know, Patrick," she replied with love in her eyes. "Thank you for allowing me peace last night."

"Of course, my lady," I answered.

"I am with child."

I know my jaw dropped and I had what some later called my stupid look. "You . . . you . . ." I sputtered.

"From before we left Dyflinn," Brigid said. "I felt her stirring the night before Beltane. She was kicking almost all night during the fire, eager to join our fight."

"She," I finally found my tongue.

"I will call her Brigid," she said and laughed. The sound was like spring's first rain on the thawed waters of a lake, like the calling of small birds, like sunshine. Her laugh held all her power, joy, and passion. I no more wanted to part with her than from my own heart, even though I recognized her wisdom. "How can I help you?" I asked.

"You can allow Kevin to accompany me as teacher and a strong arm when such is needed," Brigid said.

"Done," I answered.

"This lady would be my companion on my journey," she added. "I will need your support to make it happen."

"Why is that?"

It was then that the hood was drawn back to reveal Queen Mugain. "I cannot return to Dyflinn," was all she said.

"Mugain needs a place and I need a helper," Brigid stated. "The Lady Etroma was Kevin's mother. The boy is dear to Mugain. Together, we will be a family and find a safe place to shelter the teachings of the Moringa."

"What of Rí Alphin?" I asked.

"I spoke with him after the ard-Rí's baptism," Brigid answered. "He was in a very forgiving mood."

"He is willing to allow Mugain to leave?" I said, almost incredulous.

"He is," Brigid said. "He loves her and wishes her to be happy and recognizes that she cannot return to Dyflinn."

"Kevin has been baptized a Christian," I resisted.

"That is acceptable," Brigid said. "He can learn the old ways even as he teaches us this magic with words." Her next words waited and then came. "Perhaps he can be one of the first to join both ways in his heart."

I spotted Kevin leading five horses towards us. Three were saddled for riding. Two were packhorses already laden with what was needed for a long road. He had already been recruited. Only my permission was needed to allow him to leave.

"Go with my blessing," I told Kevin. "And with my heart," I said to Brigid.

"This is not the end, Easpag," Brigid told me, "only the next beginning."

76. The Perfection of the Heart

Winter 465 AD

Forty years have passed since that fire on Slane. I am an old man now, dying an old man's death like a candle guttering out at the end of a long night. I lie here, in the bishop's room at Saul, a farm given to my care by the son of my former owner, Muirchil.

After Slane and the baptisms at Tara, I stayed with Leary for almost a year. We built a church where the Beltane fire burned. Blaise trained more young minds to read and write and copy the scriptures. When I left, 10 young men had joined him as brothers.

I went north once again. I was resolved, finally, to pay the ransom price to my former slave master. Muirchil died before I made it back to Slemmish. I'm told that he felt humiliated that his former slave was now the druid to the ard-Rí. In his humiliation, he set his farmhouse on fire and threw himself into the flames crying, "No former slave of mine will have more honor than me." His oldest son, Colum, told me the tale.

"I am so sorry for your loss," I told the young man. "I came to thank your father and to pay him my bond price."

"Why would you thank him?" Colum asked.

"He sent me to Slemmish," I answered. "Without Slemmish, I wouldn't be here today." The young man looked doubtful. "I heard the voice of God on Slemmish. I met the druidess Brigid and the great Amergin on Slemmish. Slemmish was where I took my first steps to true freedom."

Colum was reluctant but finally accepted my payment. As the coins fell into his hands, I felt the last great weight of shame lift from my shoulders.

"My father told me that if you came and if I took the bond price from you, I was to follow him in death," Colum said.

"No!" I exclaimed and reached out to touch his arm. "No. Please let us talk for a while."

And talk we did, about bravery and good heartedness, about his father and mine, about the old ways and the Christ way. We talked a morning and afternoon away. As the day drew near to sunset, Colum asked if I would share the evening meal with him. With the main farmhouse burned, he was staying with Orla, his woman, and three children in one of the farm's smaller huts. Orla made me feel very welcome and the children were a delight. Over dinner and into the darkness, our talk continued. Before that night was over, Colum asked me to baptize him and his family. The next morning, I did.

That is when Colum gifted me with this farm called Saul. A church was built here, then a scriptorium. Twenty years later, when Orla had passed and his children were all grown, Colum came to me at Saul and asked if he could become a brother. It wasn't long before he was the abbot here at Saul, leading a house of 20 brothers. He keeps a room here for me, telling me, "It's your farm." I smile and accept his hospitality. As an old man, what need do I have now for the burdens of property?

Three months ago, I came here to die. I could feel my flame growing dim. I have lived a long and eventful life. Born a child of Rome, enslaved by Irish pirates at 16 years of age, I fell in love with Brigid not a day's walk from this room. The details of my escape to Britain, my journey to Auxerre and onward to Rome, and the return to Ireland, all of them play across my memory again and again. My memory of what happened yesterday is not so sharp, but my focus on the long past is clear.

Amergin's daughter and I had a true meeting of the hearts. She led me from slavery with kindness and passion. Brigid shared the wisdom of the elements with me. She taught me to fill my senses with them and allow the natural world to speak to my deepest self. This was the essence of her magic, what allowed us to carry the night when we lit the fire on Slane.

The shame that came before, my burden at Nevio's death, the stain of slavery, my long indenture as a monk, all of that prepared me for Beltane. That was the night of pushing through uncertainty, of finding my true self. I remember a word for our love, *leannán*, the one with whom you find the perfection of your heart.

I am at peace apart from one question I keep asking myself. Did I choose rightly when I allowed the shamrock, symbol of the healing power of the Moringa, to be identified with the Christ way? Have I spoiled the purity of the Gospel message? Did I debase the wisdom of the old way? Is either way truly served by their union?

There are messages from Rome that ask about this Celtic sprouting of Christianity. Are all the Roman laws being kept? Do new Irish Christians swear fealty to the Church of Rome even as they take on the Christ way?

That has not been my path. I have steadfastly held to the message that divine love is stronger than death and that Jesus is the son of God. I've been willing to allow the Bishop of Rome to fend for himself. I also steadfastly held true to my promise to Brigid at Slane, the promise to help her keep the old way alive within the draíocht of writing.

I visited Brigid several times at her mountain in the west, Black Bend. My brothers and followers think I went there on retreat, to contemplate the voice or the Christ, like Moses going up Mount Sinai. But I went there for love, for the retreat of the companionship of the only one who knew me as a slave and as a young man.

Our last visit was mostly in silence. Brigid's life force was almost gone as she reached for my hand. "When you remember Slane, don't forget the fire of love," were her final words to me.

I also went to Black Bend for the comfort of seeing my daughter. It is in young Brigid that I see most clearly the conflict I feel within my heart. She was fully trained in the old ways by her mother, receiving her mother's cloak, staff, and amulet before my Brigid passed away.

And she was fully trained in the Christ way. She is an abbess now, head of a house of 50 women, all scribes who collect works from the libraries of Europe to copy. They also write down the tales of the old way. When I consecrated her as an abbess, Blaise told me that I made a drastic mistake. I had used the ritual for ordaining a bishop.

"Let it stand," was all I said. In my heart, I know that the wholeness of Ireland depends upon her women as much, if not more, than upon her warriors. I'm told that when the priests visit her abbey, they are shown the copies of the Bible and the Roman books of poetry and science. But no man gets to see the secret library. What will happen to this hidden lore, I do not know. I know that, for now, the Moringa remains alive yet hidden within Abbess Brigid's and Ireland's heart.

The song of the Prophet Simeon from the last prayer of the day dances in my thoughts with those of my lover as I fall asleep: "Now you may dismiss the one who serves you, O God. Only the next beginning."

CPSIA information can be obtained
at www.ICGtesting.com
Printed in the USA
LVHW041355040522
717841LV00048B/1815

9 781039 129276